THE PERFECT KISS

"There's still too much I don't know about you," Jake said. "Too much you don't know about me. We need a crash course. An all-night study session."

"Like in college?"

"Exactly."

"I didn't go to college," Marley confessed.

"See? That's one more thing I didn't know about you."

"But an all-night session sounds good." She trailed her fingers over his shoulder and down his chest, then tugged him closer beside a display of black wool pants. "You, me . . ."

"Together." His voice lowered huskily. *"Yeah."*

Jake thumbed her chin upward. He pressed a kiss to her waiting mouth, one that left her unsteady and yearning. She wanted more of it. More of *him.* More, more, more . . .

* * *

Praise for the novels of Lisa Plumley

"*Perfect Together* is a perfectly spontaneous, perfectly fun, fish-out-of-water splash!" —Stephanie Bond

"Loaded with humor and fun, *Falling for April* is an endearing and light-hearted read. Lisa Plumley has a knack for humor." —*Romantic Times*

"Sparkles with sassy, wise-cracking, off-the-wall fun." —Kasey Michaels, author of *Maggie Needs an Alibi*

Books by Lisa Plumley

MAKING OVER MIKE

FALLING FOR APRIL

RECONSIDERING RILEY

PERFECT TOGETHER

SANTA BABY
(Anthology with Lisa Jackson,
Elaine Coffman, and Kylie Adams)

Published by Zebra Books

PERFECT TOGETHER

Lisa Plumley

ZEBRA BOOKS
KENSINGTON PUBLISHING CORP.
http://www.kensingtonbooks.com

ZEBRA BOOKS are published by

Kensington Publishing Corp.
850 Third Avenue
New York, NY 10022

All Kensington titles, imprints and distributed lines are available at special quantity discounts for bulk purchases for sales promotion, premiums, fund-raising, educational or institutional use.

Special book excerpts or customized printings can also be created to fit specific needs. For details, write or phone the office of the Kensington Special Sales Manager: Kensington Publishing Corp., 850 Third Avenue, New York, NY 10022. Attn. Special Sales Department. Phone: 1-800-221-2647.

Zebra and the Z logo Reg. U.S. Pat. & TM Off.

First Printing: June 2003
10 9 8 7 6 5 4 3 2 1

Printed in the United States of America

Thank you to Daphne Atkeson—
for the laughter, the listening,
and the encouragement.

And thanks to my family,
John, Kyle, and Ian—
for a million reasons, you guys are the best!

One

Sometime between going to sleep on a perfectly ordinary Tuesday night and waking up on Wednesday morning, Jake Jarvis became a bona fide sex symbol.

The news of his official studliness didn't faze him much at first. Possibly because he hadn't had his coffee yet. Or maybe because sex-symbol-dom was a state of mind, and it was hard to slide into it while sprawled in your underwear with Don King hair. Either way, Jake was content to chalk up the revelation to a crazy dream and go back to Snoresville.

That tactic became impossible when someone jumped on his bed, joggling his sleep-deprived brain in the process.

"Didja hear it?" his four-year-old son Noah asked as he jumped. His SpongeBob SquarePants pajamas were a blur of motion. "Didja hear it? Didja hear it?"

"I *mmmph*." Jake's lips were still asleep. He smacked them together. "I heard it."

"You were on TV *again!*" Noah said. "It's not even your reg'lar time."

"I know. Weird, huh?" For the first time since awakening, Jake realized he *hadn't* imagined the six A.M. spot he'd groggily blinked at a few minutes ago. Noah had seen it, too. It had been real.

Tune in to KKZP's Sports at Six *with anchor Jake Jarvis, L.A.'s studliest sportscaster. He'll make you want to get into the game . . . and play!*

Groping for the horn-rims beside his alarm clock, Jake slipped on his eyeglasses and peered through them at his bedroom's TV screen. The logo bobbing in the lower-right-hand corner was for Noah's favorite channel, Nickelodeon.

That wasn't unusual. Noah's typical wake-up routine was to drag his pillow and blanket into Jake's room, then curl up on the floor until cartoon overload jolted Jake awake. Today, since Noah was training for the Flying Wallendas on Jake's bed, he must have decided the usual process was taking too long.

"Did you just change the channel, Noah?"

"Nope."

"I was on Nick?"

"Yup." *Jump, jump.* "Cool, huh?"

"Yeah. Really cool." *Especially with the double-entendre-style delivery of that "get into the game . . . and play" line. Sure. That was going to be a million laughs over goldfish crackers and juice boxes at the day-care center today.* When the other parents of Toddler Time kids caught that commercial, Jake was going to have some major explaining to do.

He blinked again at the TV, nearsightedly trying to focus. Nickelodeon was for kids. Why would anyone buy local advertising space for sports coverage on a kids' channel, especially during the preschool-oriented Nick Jr. time slot?

Then it hit him. *Women.* Mothers, in particular. Women watched Nick Jr. right along with their rugrats, while getting ready for Gymboree and cell-phoning their Mommy & Me group members. Somehow, someone at KKZP had decided women between the ages of eighteen and thirty-five were a target demographic for Jake's sportscast. But why?

Before he could figure it out, Noah jumped hard enough to dislodge the TV remote he'd been holding. It fell from his pudgy hand and landed with a *thwack* on Jake's forehead.

"Bull's-eye, Ace," he said, laughing as he rubbed near his eyebrow. "For that, you win the booby prize."

"Booby prize? What's that?"

"A daddy hug! Rrrrrr!" Jake growled.

He tackled Noah by the ankles and flopped him onto the bed. The sheets and comforter fluffed beneath the impact. Noah giggled, already knowing what was coming. Jake tickled him, captured him in a bear hug, then tickled some more. Finally, when they were laughing too hard to remain coordinated, he rolled them both over and allowed his son to emerge the victor.

"I beat you again!" Noah crowed from his position straddling Jake's middle. A wide smile beamed from his face. Eyes as blue as Jake's own shone from beneath sandy little-boy bangs. He lunged forward, nearly knocking Jake's chin with his head, and locked both chubby arms around his neck. "And I'm never letting you go!"

Affection squeezed Jake's heart. In that moment, he hoped Noah never *would* let him go. Wrapped in his son's clumsy embrace, inhaling the mingled scents of Crayolas and soap on his skin, he felt uniquely happy. He hugged Noah back, doing his best to imprint the memory of this feeling on his mind.

Given the way the boy had come to him, Jake couldn't shake the fear that somehow Noah might vanish just as unexpectedly as he'd arrived. Jake had never planned to become a single father. But now that he had . . . well, Noah was the most important person in his life. He would have done anything for him, and had—including changing diapers, watching *Teletubbies,* and saying "tinkle" *on purpose* to the Toddler Time mothers while discussing potty training. As a father, he was in for the long haul.

As a sex symbol, though . . . well, this was Jake's first official time at it. He had no clue how to proceed. Extra publicity was not what he wanted—not now that he had Noah. Their lives were crazy enough, with the occasional autograph seeker at In-N-Out Burger and the giggling, whispered conversations that followed them through the grocery checkout line at Ralph's. He wanted normalcy for Noah.

Normalcy, ordinariness, and *Leave–it–to–Beaver*-style constancy.

He'll get it, Jake vowed. *No matter what.*

"So, how 'bout we get some breakfast?" he asked Noah. "I think there's still some leftover pizza from last night."

"Yay!" Noah yelled.

He launched himself from the bed, exactly as Jake had known he would, and ran from the bedroom with a whoop. Following slightly less energetically and without the Blue's Clues slippers, Jake pulled on a pair of drawstring-waist cotton pants and made his way to their apartment's kitchen. There, springtime sunlight streamed through the window. Lego Duplo creations littered the countertop. A basketball occupied one of the four chairs in the breakfast nook, and a baseball and mitt served as an impromptu centerpiece at the table.

Dwarfed by the magnet-covered refrigerator door, Noah struggled to remove the cardboard pizza box.

"Let me help." Jake slid it out. Balancing it on his fingertips, he swiveled in his best Harlem Globetrotters–style move to twirl it onto the countertop. While Noah retrieved two paper plates from a drawer, Jake opened the box.

"Mmmm," he and Noah said in unison, gazing at the pizza semicircle.

Jake hefted a chilly slice. He nodded. "Go long."

Noah did, holding up his plate in both hands with practiced expectation. He caught the slice of pepperoni pizza which Jake, after an exaggerated windup, carefully lobbed toward him.

"Six points!" they shouted.

Jake switched on the radio to hear *Sports Talk.* He and Noah settled down at the table, happily munching pizza for breakfast. Such was their life together, and Jake liked it that way.

Sure, this new "studliest sportscaster" ad campaign might put a temporary crimp in things, but he figured he could handle it. He'd explain his position to his managing editor—

maybe even the news director—and they'd rethink the promos. Everything would return to normal. It was only a matter of time.

Time obviously moved differently in the official sex-symbol zone. By the time Jake had showered, shaved, and dressed in a pair of khakis with a crewneck pullover, he'd heard the Nick Jr. "studliest sportscaster" spot twice more. It may have been his imagination, but he'd have sworn the level of suggestiveness in the female voice-over's tone quadrupled each time the words "and *play*" were repeated.

Shaking off the thought, Jake paused at his apartment's front door with the usual armload of travel supplies—books, toys, water bottles, HandiWipes—in a canvas KKZP bag.

"Noah? You ready?"

His son emerged from the hallway with a G.I. Joe action figure in his hands and a frown of concentration on his face. "Uh-huh."

"Is that what you're wearing?"

Noah glanced downward. Shrugged.

"What about the stuff we picked out last night?" The parenting magazines recommended giving your child "easy choices" to build their self-esteem. Jake tried to do that whenever possible. "The little Levi's and the Lakers T-shirt?"

Noah shrugged again. Jake swept his gaze over his son's plaid shorts, cowboy boots, tuxedo-style ruffled shirt, and snorkel mask with hose. "Are you wearing clean underwear?"

Noah bit his lip as he wrenched G.I. Joe's arm in a commando move. "Yeah."

"Fair enough. Let's go."

Leaning forward, Jake wrapped his free arm around Noah's middle. He swept the laughing boy upward and balanced him on his shoulder, then pivoted to leave the apartment. The way he saw it, a dad had to save his energy for the important things: fairness, bedtime, and teaching his kid how to take it like a man when Miss Suzy ran out of his favorite color of Play-Doh at arts-and-crafts time. In the overall scheme of things, wardrobe didn't really matter.

In the car on the way to Toddler Time, Jake heard another "studliest sportscaster" spot on drive-time radio. And then . . .

"Look, Daddy!" Noah said, pointing from his buckled-in booster seat in the Accord's backseat. "You're on the bus!"

"I'm not on the bus. I'm in the car with you."

"You're on the bus! Look!"

Stuck in Santa Monica Freeway traffic, Jake looked. He groaned. There, pasted on the side of the nearest city bus, was his face. His head and torso, too, in a three-quarter shot obviously designed to make the most of his studly sportscaster image. The whole thing loomed at least five feet high, a horror he could barely stand to contemplate. Who wanted to see their own nose in Giganta-Vision? His left nostril was the size of Noah's head.

Below a new tag line—*Jake Jarvis, Sports at Six: Scoring has never been like this!*—Jake's picture grinned at him. In it, he'd rolled up his shirtsleeves and loosened his tie. His hair was suggestively tousled. His horn-rims were not on his face where they could do some good, but were held playfully in one hand while he gazed myopically into the camera. Between the glasses, the partially unbuttoned shirt, and the gaze—which could have passed for smoldering, given its optically challenged lack of focus—he looked like a come-on for the Smarty Pants Dating Service.

It was worse than he'd thought. These KKZP promos might have begun in official sex symbol territory, but now they were veering toward the official sex *object* zone. This must be what the Victoria's Secret models felt like when their pictures wound up on billboards for men the world over to hoot at, slobber over, and talk about. It was almost enough to make him regret the catalog subscription that came to his apartment.

Almost.

Dragging his gaze from the ad, Jake glanced in the supplemental child-view mirror clipped to his rearview. Noah was staring out the window at his father's Godzilla-sized schnozzle. His mouth was agape. He'd even abandoned G.I. Joe. This couldn't be good.

"Noah, let's do the Bananaphone song." Jake dropped in a Raffi CD. Cheerful kids' music filled the car. Usually Noah loved Raffi music, with its silly lyrics and upbeat melodies. Striving to make his deep voice hit the notes, Jake sang, "Bananaphone . . . boo boo be doo be do!"

It didn't work. They inched forward in traffic, Jake singing and Noah staring. In the convertible in front of them, two women pointed at the Jake ad. One blew kisses toward it. The other, the driver, took advantage of the slow traffic to pivot toward the city bus and shimmy at the ad. Her breasts jiggled and the car rocked. Both women giggled.

That was it. Jake scanned the freeway signs, got his bearings, and changed lanes. An exit—and a faster path to Toddler Time via surface streets—loomed ahead, and he meant to take it. He had to get Noah to day care and hurry to the station, where he'd settle this mess once and for all.

At Toddler Time, though, his reception wasn't what he'd expected. Jake had no sooner gotten himself, Noah, and Noah's stuff out of the car than he heard the first wolf whistle.

He wheeled around. No one else was in the parking lot, but the Toddler Time facility's front door was swooshing closed behind a mom and her little girl. Frowning, Jake took Noah's hand and led him inside.

"Mr. Jarvis! So nice to . . . *see* you," the receptionist said. Her up-and-down perusal suggested she'd like to see much more of him. So did her eyebrow waggle. "You're looking terrific today. New workout program?"

"Nah," Jake said, reaching for the sign-in log. "Not unless I'm doing it in bed."

"In bed? Mmmm. You don't say."

"I mean, in my sleep. Working out while I'm sleeping.

Sleepacizing. So I'm not aware of it." Geez, this sex symbol stuff was hard on a guy's equilibrium. Jake finished signing Noah in, then helped him put his things in his assigned cubby. "Between Noah and the usual eleven-to-seven, I don't have time for much more than a daily run and some weight lifting. The gym has a baby-sitting service, though. I think Noah's really found a buddy there who—"

"Short or not, those workouts are working," she purred, eyeballing his biceps and chest. "Keep it up."

Jake blinked, feeling puzzled. He'd been bringing Noah to Toddler Time for over two years now. No one had ever flirted with him before. He'd always figured it was because he and the staff and the mothers had bonded on another level—a Noah level—which precluded anything else. Really, once you'd discussed your child's stranger anxiety, biting issues, and penchant for running through the house naked, flirtation was beside the point.

But as he entered the four-year-olds' room and greeted Miss Suzy, he realized it—apparently—wasn't. Miss Suzy and her assistant both gave him giggly hellos and surreptitiously sneaked glances at Jake while he double-tied Noah's shoes. They exclaimed over his haircut and examined the fit of his khakis. They treated him like . . . like a *piece of meat!*

As he was about to leave, Miss Suzy sidled up. "So I was wondering . . . do you really *need* those glasses?"

"Only if I want to see."

Giggle. "I thought maybe they were just props."

"Nope. With me, what you see is what you get."

"Ooooh!" Both women squealed, blushing. "We wish!"

Jake gave them a stern look. So far, he'd avoided the groupie effect at Toddler Time. But if it started now . . .

"So you've both seen the ad, then?" he asked.

Suzy nodded. " 'If you want more action—' "

" 'Jake Jarvis is your man!' " her assistant added.

" 'KKZP *Sports at Six,*' " they concluded gleefully.

He groaned. Evidently, there was *another* one out there. Who knew what part of him—now that his nose had been bussed all over town—had been glossed and expanded to skyscraper size?

"Okay, okay." He put out his hands, palms down, in an attempt to calm their giggles. "Is this going to be a problem? I'm putting a stop to the promos this morning, but until then—"

"No, sir. Not a problem," Suzy said, sobering immediately. "I'm very sorry. There won't be another word about it."

Somewhat reluctantly—and with a final salacious visual sweep of his torso—her assistant agreed. Jake nodded.

See? he told himself, reassured by their cooperative air. *This whole mess could be handled capably and quickly. By the end of the day, everything would be back to normal.*

He crouched down to hug Noah good-bye. "See you later, buddy."

His son flung his arms wholeheartedly around Jake's neck. He squeezed with all the force a three-foot person could muster, making the enormous sacrifice of ignoring all the Toddler-Time-only toys in the corner.

"Here's a kiss to keep for later." Jake opened Noah's little palm and pressed a kiss in its center. Performing his part in their morning ritual, Noah fisted the kiss as he lowered his hand. Then he shoved his hand into his shorts pocket and opened his fingers, releasing the kiss there for safekeeping.

"Love you, Daddy."

"I love you, too. See you soon."

Jake winked, pushing away the sense of melancholy that always struck him when saying good-bye to Noah. With his back still to the room's doorway, he started to rise.

Another wolf whistle hit the air.

He straightened to confront the culprit, a five-foot-nothing mother of three with a baby on her hip and a defiant expression on her face.

"Hey, my figure might be going downhill," she said, "but my imagination is as limber as ever. Nice tushie."

"Nice tushie! Nice tushie!" the Toddler Time preschoolers echoed, exhibiting their usual fascination with potty humor. "Nice tushie!"

Jake covered his eyes and bolted. This was a nightmare. He had to get to work, and fast.

Los Angeles's KKZP-TV was located in a nondescript two-story building with a security guard in the lobby and no signs whatsoever on the outside of its gated compound. Finding it was easy enough if you knew where to look, but most people didn't. The on-air talent liked it that way. So did the management, producers, and staff. Picketers, crazies, tourists, and desperate aspiring actors looking for any chance to get on TV could make getting to work a real challenge. The station's incognito policy made avoiding those inconveniences possible for everyone.

Having weathered both crosstown traffic and an appalling billboard sighting (Sports at Six *with Jake Jarvis: He knows how the game is played!)* on the way, Jake half-expected to find a clump of screaming, shimmying, kiss-blowing women gathered by the sign designating his reserved parking spot. As he pulled in, though, his erstwhile fan club wasn't there.

Okay, so maybe this problem wasn't as big as he thought it was.

Then he saw the ten-foot banner decorating the lobby. Hanging directly above the security post, it depicted a photographed version of himself lounging poolside. Drops of tanning oil beaded on the bare skin of his tanned torso and legs, and a skimpy Speedo covered the bare . . . essentials of the rest of him. Sliding along his body were the words "Jake Jarvis: the man with the action. For *full* coverage, watch *Sports at Six.*"

Jake saw red. After the bizarre and difficult morning he'd had, this, *this* was the final straw.

It was the Speedo that did it. He'd never in his life worn a banana hammock like that in public. He'd be damned if he ever would. Furious, Jake checked in with security, stalked down the hallway through the newsroom, and approached his managing editor at the end of a row of cubicles.

"Sid!"

Sid Spielman, Jake's long-time boss at KKZP News, jerked at the sound of his name. He glanced sideways. His eyes widened, undoubtedly at the Incredible-Hulk–style fury on Jake's face.

"Jake!" Sid bowed his gray-haired head to dismiss the administrative assistant he'd been talking with. She headed toward the wire service room carrying an armload of papers, leaving the two men alone. "If it isn't the man of the hour. Was that a bellow of delight I heard thirty seconds ago? Or has Skip been editing his fluff piece on mating rhinos again?"

"It was a battle cry. Damn it, Sid! You ambushed me. Do you know what I had to go through just to get to work this morning?"

"Legions of adoring female fans between the ages of twenty-one and forty-five, I hope."

"Wolf whistles! Shimmying! Innuendo." Jake clenched his fists to keep from raking his hands through his hair with frustration. "Thanks to your new ad campaign, I've become a . . . a *boy toy* overnight."

"So?"

"So? So when I was pumping gas this morning, a red-headed jogger swerved from her running path and *pinched* my ass."

"And that's a problem because . . . ?"

"Arrgh!"

Sid moved in with a serious expression. "How old was she? Does she watch TV? Does she watch the news?"

As a managing editor, Sid definitely had a one-track mind. Shaking his head, Jake put both hands on his boss's shoulders. "You're not hearing me. My life is turning upside down, thanks to your ads. I want them stopped."

"You're contractually obligated to perform advertising services."

"Fine. I'll tape a nice series of ads for you. *Without* the Bain de Soleil and the banana hammock."

"Banana hammock?" Sid looked confused, then amused. "Oh, right. The lobby banner. Yeah, it's a miracle what the graphics guys can do with a computer these days. You take a simple picture of a guy at the office pool party last summer—"

"Strip him of his dignity—"

"—swap his trunks for a Speedo—"

"Erase all pretense of professionalism—"

"—add a cabana-boy tan, and voilà!" Sid grinned. "Sex sells, you know. I'm positive you're not naive enough to believe that looks don't matter in broadcast journalism."

"I know that, Sid. I put up with putting mousse in my hair and wearing suits on the air, just like everyone else. But I'll be damned if I'll be made into a laughingstock."

"Those whistling, pinching women weren't laughing, Jake. They were *responding.*" Sid took Jake's arm and led him toward his nearby cubicle, where he leaned against the desk with his arms folded. "The phone's been ringing off the hook. *L.A. Magazine* wants to interview you. The *New Times* is pitching a piece. And that's in addition to the coverage we've got planned on our own *Wake Up, L.A.*"

Amber Nielson, the blonde and freckled host of the lifestyles segment of KKZP's morning show, popped up from a neighboring work area. She nodded. "Yeah. See me when you're done, will you, Jake?"

He groaned. Amber's typical lifestyle segments included features on go-go dancing fish, piercings for your pet, origami as a career choice, and "extreme" knitting. They were, to put it politely, fluffier than cotton candy. Jake didn't want to be cotton candy. He might have fallen into sportscasting as a second career choice, but he took it damned seriously now.

"I. Want. Those. Ads. Stopped," he said.

"Can't. They're critical. The most important demographic today is women aged twenty-one to forty-five. They're the ones making eighty-five percent of the buying decisions.

They're the ones advertisers want to reach. They're the ones *we* need to appeal to if we want to survive."

"Fine. I'll speak to a few garden clubs."

"That's not enough anymore. These women want more. Much more. And that's what you're going to give them."

Uh-oh. "What's what I'm going to give them?"

"More of *you.* That's the number-one request we get in viewer mail, especially from women. They want to see more of L.A.'s studliest sportscaster. More, more, more."

"I'm beginning to feel lucky the graphics guys left me my banana hammock."

Sid grinned. "Ever heard of *Dream Date?"*

Jake nodded warily, willing to see where his managing editor was going with this apparent non sequitur. "I'm familiar with it."

Everyone was familiar with it. It was one of their parent network's hottest prime-time game shows—a cross between *Blind Date* and *The Newlywed Game,* with a little reality TV thrown in.

"Good," Sid said. "Because as part of our new publicity campaign, you're going to be a contestant. Congratulations!"

Two

Some days, it just didn't pay to pull off your leopard-print sleep mask and get out of bed.

For Marley Madison, Wednesday was one of those days. First she awakened to discover that her Yorkie, Gaffer, had chewed up most of the pages of the audition script she'd been studying. Then she met with her personal trainer and slogged through her necessary treadmill-plus-Pilates routine . . . only to step on the scale afterward and discover a disheartening three-pound *gain*. But, determined not to let those little setbacks get her down, Marley got on with the rest of her day anyway.

She dressed in her finest L.A. casual style in a pink designer tee and matching miniskirt, slipped into her cutest pair of Jimmy Choos, and checked her makeup. Forty-five minutes later she swept into her first business meeting of the day, accompanied by her publicist, her manager, and her assistant.

"Go ahead and get some breakfast," Marley told them, gesturing toward the restaurant's famous buffet. "I'm running a little late, so I'd better get started."

She focused all her considerable charisma on the casting director and producer waiting at a corner table, then headed toward them. There was a lot riding on this meeting. A new part, a fresh beginning, a reinvention of sorts. She had to make the most of it . . . starting with her approach.

Fixing a smile on her face, Marley exercised her famous hip shimmy all the way across the room. Tableside, she tossed back her shoulder-length blonde hair. She knew what they wanted: the complete Marley Madison, in all her starlet glory. It was a role she'd been born to play—*had* played, for as long as she could remember.

"Hello, gentlemen. Been waiting long?"

The producer looked up. "Marley! Thanks for dropping by."

The casting director offered her a chair. Marley slid gracefully into it, the way her movement coach had taught her, and arranged her cute, six-inch handbag on the table. She folded her hands in her lap while exchanging general chitchat.

"Have some breakfast." The producer gestured toward the buffet as though he'd conjured it himself—and he might have, given his status in this town. "The almond croissants are terrific."

"Thanks," she demurred. "But I'm on the Zone. My assistant will pick out something wonderful for me, I'm sure."

True to form, she did. A few minutes later, Marley's loyal personal assistant Candace appeared with a veggie omelette, fruit, and a double cappuccino. Marley tucked in. As her entourage settled at a respectful distance at a nearby table, the talk turned to business. They discussed the latest network ratings stunts, ran through the usual "where are they now?" of people they'd worked with in the past, then meandered through an impromptu poll of favorite Emmy parties. Finally, they moved on to the high-profile network drama series pilot Marley had come to the meeting to discuss.

"I read the script last night," she said, cutting to the chase. She wanted this job. *Needed* this job. More, she truly felt passionately about the part. "The character of Elizabeth is beautifully complex. Her motivations, her relationship with her vagabond father, the grittiness she brings to her work as an attorney. It's absolutely galvanizing."

Both men stopped eating to gawk at her.

"As Stanislavski said, to find the truth in a character is of paramount importance. If I delved deeper, uncovered the essence of this part—"

Their mouths dropped open. Literally.

Whoops. Hastily, Marley regrouped. "I mean, I'll bet the character of Elizabeth has a fabulous wardrobe, right? All those Armani suits!"

They visibly relaxed. *This* was the Marley Madison they knew. The style-obsessed, fashionista Pop Tart who'd set trends in hair, makeup, and stilettos during her eight-year run on prime-time TV. That Marley Madison didn't use words like "galvanizing." She certainly didn't think of herself as being capable of portraying grittiness.

The only trouble was, Marley did.

The producer patted her hand. "The wardrobe department is still working on contacting the Armani people."

"That's fine," Marley said. Her passionate, revealing speech about the part of Elizabeth had been risky, but she'd been determined to try. Now she needed to take one last stab at it, before it was too late.

She leaned forward. "In fact, all wardrobe questions aside, I want you both to know that I'd be perfectly willing to audition for this part. To do a cold reading, a test with another actor, whatever you want."

For an actress of her stature, those were humbling concessions. Given all that had happened to her over the past year, Marley was willing to make them.

"Yes, well . . . about the part," the casting director said. "We have a little confession to make. We, er, hope you won't mind."

"Mind? Of course not." Her big opportunity had just taken a wrong turn. She could feel it. She lifted her cappuccino with a shaky hand and took a fortifying sip. "What is it?"

"It's this." The producer reached into his briefcase and

withdrew a glossy magazine. He pushed it across the table to Marley. "Would you mind autographing this? My daughter is a big fan."

She recognized her own smiling face and scantily-clad body on the cover of *Cosmopolitan*. The magazine—and the article inside about Marley's one and only disastrous feature film—was eight months old. At this point, it looked a lot like her last hurrah.

Woodenly, she put on a smile. "Sure. What's your daughter's name?"

He told her. She duly executed an autographed inscription, complete with swirly starlet script and framed with a sketched heart. As she handed the magazine back, Marley's gaze met the sympathetic faces of her assistant, publicist, and manager, looking on from their table. Immediately, they all pretended an urgent need for more coffee. They jumped up and scurried to the buffet.

"This is for me," the casting director said, holding an eight-by-ten glossy that Marley recognized as her own résumé photo. "When this came across my desk, I knew I couldn't just file it. When I was in college, I *loved* your show!"

Determined to soldier on in the face of this unexpected development, she signed an extravagant inscription. There was still a chance this meeting could be salvaged.

"So, about the part," she began as she handed over the photo. "I'm afraid there was an unfortunate accident involving the script"—*Gaffer thought it was delicious*—"but I have most of it memorized. Why don't I do a scene for you right now?"

They both burst out laughing. "Oh, Marley. You *are* a good sport!"

Confused, she examined their faces.

"To come here, to sign autographs, *and* to make a joke about the part." The producer patted her arm again. "You're a hoot."

She didn't want to be a hoot. "I'd rather be an employed actress. In your new drama."

Ha, ha. Ho, ho. "I can't cast you in *Legal Briefs,*" the casting director explained, shaking his head. "Surely you knew that going in?"

"But—but you haven't even heard me audition yet."

"Marley, honey. We know what you can do."

"We've seen you. Hell, Biff here"—the casting director—"practically grew up watching you on *Fantasy Family.* Trust us, the part of Elizabeth isn't for you."

It wasn't? So they'd only brought her here to sign *autographs*?

Her hopes plummeted. There wouldn't be a new part for her, wouldn't even be an opportunity for a new part for her. She couldn't spend the rest of her life with a Sharpie in one hand and a stack of glossies in the other. She had to move on. But how?

"Oh, here comes Talisha now," the producer said, glancing up at the woman lingering near the maître d' station. The casting director nodded, his attention drawn, too.

Marley looked. Talisha was tall, free of makeup, and poor of posture. She schlepped into the restaurant wearing an Army surplus jacket, an artfully embroidered shirt, and a long gauzy skirt. Jeweled thongs adorned her unmanicured feet.

"Now *she's* raw. Real," the casting director whispered confidently to the producer. The producer nodded, his attention fixed on Talisha. "Like a lump of clay. You can mold her."

If Talisha was a lump of clay, what did that make Marley? Immovable marble? A museum piece? A freaking *exhibit?*

"You'll excuse us, won't you?" the producer asked. "We're double booked for breakfast."

"Thanks for stopping by," the casting director said.

Neither one of them looked at her. They were through. *This was so humiliating.* Feeling a lump rise helplessly to her throat, Marley clutched her purse. She left the rest of her veggie omelette uneaten and nodded to both men in an effort to maintain her professional image. They were too busy watching the "raw, real" effect of Talisha chatting up a waiter to notice.

She reached her entourage's table. It was hard to speak. Her throat had tightened up around a big lump of disappointment. "All done," she squeaked.

"Oh, Marley," Candace said. "We're so sorry."

"It's fine." Her supposedly nonchalant wave felt a little animatronic, but it was the best she could do. "My numerologist *said* nine-thirty was a bad time for a meeting today, but did I listen? Obviously there's something else out there for me."

They rallied around. "You bets" were heard. Back patting ensued. All Marley cared about was getting away from the disaster scene before she lost her composure completely.

"Let's go."

Making a determined effort, she breezed out of the restaurant, followed by her staff. She nodded politely as she passed the producer and casting director. She even held it together as she heard one of them tell Talisha, "You're perfect for the part of Elizabeth. We couldn't think of anyone else."

But there was only so much a girl could take. She slid into her BMW's backseat and greeted her driver as her entourage waited for the valet to bring around their separate vehicles. She distracted herself by poring over the appointments in her Palm Pilot and opening a bottle of San Pellegrino.

Then she noticed a chip in her manicure and burst into tears. Sometimes, enough was enough. In this case, it was way, *way* too much.

"I'm a has-been," Marley wailed to her manager, Brian, as they approached the site of her next meeting—another in a long series of attempts at career triage. "Worse, I'm a *typecast* has-been! Nobody wants to see me as anything new."

"Sure they do. They will. Eventually."

She shook her head. "You saw what happened this morning. And it gets worse. You know that date I had last night?"

"The fix-up with the accountant?"

"The very same. He didn't want to date *me*. He wanted to date Tara!"

Tara was her character from *Fantasy Family,* a southern belle with a sassy tongue and a sexy wardrobe.

"Come on. He knew you weren't really Tara."

"I'm not sure *anybody* knows that," Marley said. They strode into the dimness of a West Hollywood restaurant foyer. She slipped off her sunglasses and automatically checked her teeth for lipstick. "He wanted me to whisper sweet nothings in a southern accent. He wondered why my hair was different. He was disappointed—clearly disappointed!—that I couldn't do that knot-a-cherry-stem-with-my-tongue maneuver from the third season."

"You're exaggerating."

"I'm not. I'm washed up, Brian. But I refuse to go down without a fight. That Talisha's got nothing on me. I'm as real as the next girl, damn it!"

"Your cutlets have shifted, real girl," he said, motioning toward her chest. "Better fix 'em before we go in."

Marley frowned and looked downward. Naturally flat-chested, she'd taken to wearing the silicone inserts sometimes referred to as "cutlets" inside her bras. They lifted, they amplified . . . they felt like uncooked chicken piccata against her meager bosom.

Rolling her eyes, Marley leaned forward slightly. Brian, ever a gentleman, turned away as she reached inside her T-shirt to adjust her left insert, then her right. A tug, a wiggle . . . a *flash?*

The unmistakable flare of a camera flash blinded her. She blinked, trying to clear the spots before her eyes. Paparazzi, here?

Apparently so. A man wearing three different cameras slung around his neck grinned triumphantly at the edge of the foyer. "Thanks, Marley. See you in print!"

He dashed away. Undoubtedly, within a week his photo would wind up below a tabloid headline. Something like, "Former sitcom star Marley Madison's secret obsession! Details inside!" Marley groaned.

"I'll go after him," Brian said. "Wait here."

She grabbed him before he could get far. "Don't bother. You don't have to be a white knight for my sake."

"You had your hand inside your bra. It's going to look pretty bad."

She shrugged. "So the world discovers I stuff my A cups. Big deal. I've survived worse."

He frowned. "Are you sure?"

Marley nodded. After spending most of her twenty-seven years in show business, she'd certainly been caught in less flattering poses. At least this one wasn't topless.

They made their way to the restaurant's private back room where, outside its closed doors, she ran through her usual preparations. She drew in a deep breath to calm her nerves, de-lipsticked her teeth again, and ran her hands over her outfit to smooth it. She posed on the threshold. Brian opened the doors.

"She's here!" someone shouted.

The crowd's attention swerved expectantly toward Marley. More cameras flashed. A man to her left raised his camcorder. Voices rose in excited chatter. A few women even pointed in her direction as Marley paused in the doorway, psyching herself up for what was to come.

This was a gathering of avid fans of *Fantasy Family,* Marley's now-cancelled sitcom. It included, she saw as she automatically posed for pictures, sales of the series' episodes on VHS and DVD. Posters of the cast and of Marley alone. Marley Mania T-shirts, fans dressed in character, even a hairstylist in the corner who appeared to be turning out copies of "The Tara," Marley's character's famous hairstyle, for her customers. It was all *Fantasy Family,* all the time.

In short, it was a compendium of everything she'd been working so diligently to leave behind her for the past year.

But *Fantasy Family* had been her bread and butter for a long time now. She couldn't afford to ignore the fans it had gained her . . . which was why she'd come here in the first place.

"Right this way, Marley," a bubbly brunette said, gesturing toward the far corner of the room. "We've arranged a seat of honor for you!"

Smiling and waving, Marley let herself be led past a dozen tablecloth-covered round tables. Their floral centerpieces held cards designating each as a gathering point for discussions relating to particular cast members. There were three "Tara" tables, she noticed. As they passed, someone yelled out, "Marley! Come on, say it! Please!"

Knowing exactly what that request meant, Marley stopped at the table she'd been led to. She smoothed her L.A. pink shirt and miniskirt, then assumed the flirtatious posture she'd become so well known for as the character of Tara. She tossed back her shoulder-length blonde hair and put one hand on her hip. She leaned toward the microphone that had been set up.

"Why, I *do* declare!" she exclaimed in a perfect Southern drawl. "I do declare, indeed!"

At the sound of her signature catchphrase, roars of approval rang out. Applause filled the room, celebrating Marley's portrayal of the spoiled debutante who'd made her famous. Despite her vows to move on with her career and really *prove* her acting abilities, Marley beamed. Ever since her long-running series had ended, this was something she'd been denied.

This enthusiasm. This caring. This *love*.

She basked in it, knowing exactly how short-lived it could be. Her whole life had been spent performing, from kiddie shows to commercials to the eight-year run of *Fantasy Family*. Now, just over a year after her show's demise, Marley paused in her struggles and just *savored*.

This approval, this gathering of people, made her feel good. It made her feel wanted and needed and appreciated, things she desperately yearned to feel after the string of dead ends, false starts, and failed auditions she'd suffered through lately. As the applause and whistles rang out, Marley felt renewed.

Acting was the only thing she'd ever excelled at. Well, aside from shopping, that is. Acting had come as naturally to her as falling in love came to most other women. When she was inside a character, everything else receded. A big piece of herself had gone into portraying Tara. It meant so much, now, that all these people appreciated her work.

A woman stepped up, wearing a "Tara" haircut and cradling a baby. "I named my baby after you. See? Little Marley Madison Polone."

Smiling, Marley leaned forward and cooed at the tiny girl. She took a few moments to chat with the baby's mother.

"I dedicated my Web site to you," a red-haired man said, shoving a *www.MarleyMadisonUniverse.com* bumper sticker into her hand. "I get two million hits per month."

"Good for you!" Marley said, offering him a handshake. She spent a few minutes trying to decipher Internet-speak, then slipped the bumper sticker to Brian, who'd moved to stand beside her. She went on greeting people.

"Please sign this," a woman in dreadlocks pleaded, thrusting a collectible poster toward her. "It's not for me. It's for my mother. She couldn't come here today."

Marley did. Three exhausting hours later, she'd met every conceivable variety of fan. Quiet fans, boisterous fans, fans who were annoyed she was no longer on TV, and fans who wanted to describe their UFO theories to her. She shook hands and signed autographs until her fingers cramped. She smiled until her cheeks felt like she'd forgotten to remove a mud masque at the spa. She grew hoarse from speaking to be heard over the crowd, and toe-pinched from standing in high heels for too long.

Eventually, Brian rescued her. Candace had arrived by then, along with Marley's publicist, Heather. The three of them surrounded her as they made their way to the exit. Marley smiled and waved. Cameras flashed again.

Outside it was quieter and cooler. The air smelled of L.A.'s special mixture—exhaust and sunshine.

"Smaller group this time," Heather observed as they headed for their cars. She frowned. "I'm not sure I can even get a mention of this in the media."

"Events like this are for meeting people, not for generating press," Marley insisted, trying to retain the good feelings being with her fans had given her. "Besides, once I get that fabulous new part I'm chasing, every publicity outlet will be begging for interviews."

Brian paused. "Speaking of that part . . ."

"What about it?" Marley refused to break stride. "Have you heard something from the Warner Brothers people?"

Catching up to her, Brian exchanged a glance with Candace. Warily, Candace unholstered her cell phone from her hip, as though preparing to launch into full damage control mode. If the news was bad, spa visits, manicures, and feel-good shopping therapy wouldn't be far behind.

Uh-oh.

"They went with somebody else for the part," Brian replied with obvious reluctance. He reached for Marley's hand and gave it a friendly squeeze. "I've had my doubts about that role all along, though. It was obviously very brave of you to want to stretch into the part of the criminal profiler, but—"

"But you don't think I can do it. Is that it?"

"No!" all three of them said at once. Brian even held out his hands, palms up in a "stop" gesture. They looked like her own personal backup group. Marley and the Supremes.

"No," Brian repeated. "I believe you can do it. We all do. But playing against type is tough, especially when making the leap from television to film. It'll take something drastic to move your career in the right direction."

He'd been telling her that all along. "How much more drastic does it get?" Marley asked. "I offered to audition. To cold read. Even to screen test. That was humiliating, Brian! And they still turned me down."

They reached Marley's BMW. She leaned against it, arms crossed, and pinned her entourage with a fierce look. In turn, they shuffled their feet. Looked down the street. Examined the sunny California sky for shifting clouds.

As the silence lengthened with no easy assurances, Marley felt more worried than ever. Her bravado seeped away by degrees until she was only a scantily dressed blonde standing beside a car and driver she wouldn't be able to afford much longer. She felt small and alone and insignificant . . . feelings that were as alien to her as unplucked eyebrows.

"What am I going to do?" she asked quietly, desperately. "I can't go on like this. I just can't. I need to work. I need to move on. I need to be *me* again, before it's too late."

Their gazes swerved to hers at last. Sympathetically, they all stepped closer, offering reassurances.

"I do have one new idea," Brian said. "Sondra"—Marley's agent—"and I came up with it. But it's pretty radical, and I don't want to pitch it without her. Meet me in an hour or so at my office?"

"I'll be at the day spa in an hour."

Candace nodded, confirming Marley's standing appointment.

"Can't you skip it today? This is serious."

"So is self-maintenance. I *am* my product, Brian. I have to take my looks seriously."

"Fine. Sondra and I will meet you at the spa."

Feeling immensely reassured now that a plan was under way, Marley smiled at him. It was fortunate she had so many good people to depend upon. "Super! I'll treat you both to the works. And thanks. I really appreciate this. See you then!"

With a wiggle of her fingers and a cheery "bye-eee!" for everyone, she got into her car. Things would work out. She just knew they would. She was willing to work hard, she was talented, and she had a lot of very skilled people on her side.

Brian rapped on the car window. Marley pressed the button to roll it down. She raised her eyebrows in question.

"Oh, and Marley?" he added. "Keep an open mind about this, would you? You can't afford to dismiss any ideas that might help your career, however outrageous they are."

"Outrageous? What do you mean, outrageous?"

Her driver chose that moment to spot his opening in traffic. He put the BMW into motion. Brian obligingly stepped out of the way and waved. So did Candace and Heather.

"Brian? Brian?" Marley hung out the window. "What do you mean, outrageous?" she cried. *"How* outrageous?"

"You'll find out in an hour," he called through cupped hands. Then he smiled and waved and got into his own car, leaving Marley to wonder exactly *how much* outrageousness she really had in her.

Three

"Congratulations?" Jake repeated, stunned. *"Dream Date?"* The reality of the publicity-stunt nightmare he was about to get roped into hit him. He shook his head. "Uh-uh. No way."

He followed Sid, who'd neatly sidestepped him and headed for his own corner cubicle after making his big *Dream Date* announcement.

"No way am I making an appearance on some cheesy game show, Sid!" Jake called, doggedly following him. For a big man, Sid could really move. "I'm not doing it!"

Somehow, Jake realized, this entire day had gotten away from him. No matter what he did, it only got worse. He'd tried to have the ads stopped, and what had he gotten instead? A spot on a game show. What were the odds of that?

By the time Jake caught up with Sid, his boss had slapped on his patented like-it-or-lump-it fake smile.

"It'll be fun," he said. "You'll meet a nice girl, go on a few dates . . . who knows? You might even like the girl enough to marry her—"

"Fat chance. You're talking to a die-hard bachelor."

"—and wind up with a little brother or sister for that kid of yours."

"You leave Noah out of this."

Sid shrugged. "I'm just saying, living like a monk can't be good for you. Look on the bright side."

"The bright side of making an idiot of myself? No thanks." Jake had to make Sid see reason. "Look, I'm willing to do my part. Make publicity appearances, toss baseballs for charity at the Sassy Seniors' Powderpuff League, host parties for Big Brothers Big Sisters. But this? It's ridiculous."

"It's not ridiculous, it's already booked." Richard Holloway, KKZP's news director, came out of his side office. "And it's what our viewers want, Jarvis."

He slapped Jake on the back, demonstrating all the strength that came with his favorite hobby, bodybuilding. With extra-jovial heartiness, he added, "We're going to give our viewers what they want."

Jake shook his head. "I can't do it, Rich."

"Can't?" The news director looked surprised. On the surface. Underneath, a certain steeliness came into his eyes. "Or won't? Because what this station needs is team players. Team players who recognize a terrific opportunity to help KKZP when it's right in front of them."

That sounded ominous. Was Rich actually threatening him?

If he was, Jake wasn't a man who went down without a fight.

"Won't," he said, looking the news director in the eye. "I was hired to cover sports news. I'm good at it. My segment of *Sports at Six* consistently earns higher-than-average ratings. I don't need to morph into some kind of hunk-of-the-month to pull in viewers."

Rich nodded thoughtfully. His silvering hair caught highlights from the office fluorescents and made him look wiser than he deserved. "Yes. Yes, you do."

Stonewalled, Jake stared out over the newsroom. He had a bad feeling about this. His contract was due for renewal next month. Without the insurance and medical benefits

KKZP provided for him and Noah, he'd be no better than an itinerant talking head.

Without references and recommendations from Rich and Sid, it would be tough to score a contract at another station. Broadcast news relied heavily on its anchors for brand identification. Switching stations within the same market didn't tend to work well. In order to find work, Jake would have to approach different markets, in other cities where his face and name weren't associated with KKZP. Going on the road would mean moving Noah from Toddler Time, dragging him from place to place . . . eliminating every hope of normalcy and consistency and ordinariness in their lives.

"It's only for a few weeks," Sid coaxed. "A month at the most. The *Dream Date* people will give you a Q&A interview to start, tape you going on a few dates, then interview you again at the end to find out which couple wins the contest. That's it."

"That's it? A month's worth of blind dates by force, bracketed by two interrogations?"

"Come on," Sid cajoled further. "It won't be that bad. If you make a positive impression with female viewers, it could really boost our profile in the market."

Jake glanced at him. His producer was really sweating this one, he realized. Literally. Sid's job was closely tied to the success or failure of *Sports at Six,* and sportscasters weren't the only ones with contracts up for renewal.

Awww, hell. Jake didn't want to date a stranger for the titillation of a live studio audience. He didn't want to amp up his studly sportcaster image any more than it already had been. He didn't want to take unnecessary time away from Noah, either. But faced with the facts—and confronted with Sid's desperation—Jake knew his wants didn't matter half as much as his obligations did.

He was going to have to get into the game and become a PR player. For Noah's sake, for Sid's sake, and for his own sake.

"All right," he said. "I'll do it."

Rich and Sid both beamed.

"But in return, I want those promos stopped."

Sid nodded with evident relief. "I'll have the graphics guys put your swim trunks back on. We'll print a new banner right away. No more banana hammock. How's that?"

"It's a start." Jake turned to Rich. "When do I make my game-show debut?"

"First thing tomorrow."

"Tomorrow?" Jake boggled. He had stories to work on, on-site footage to shoot . . . hell. He didn't have time for this.

"It shouldn't interfere with your work," Rich said. He added a few more details. "After all, most of your *Dream Date* duties will take place after hours, during your personal time."

Well, that was *much* better, wasn't it?

"Fine," Jake gritted out. "I'll get it done."

After all, he always did. At twenty-eight, he was one of KKZP's youngest on-air personalities, but he made sure his work kept him competitive. He didn't intend to foul up now.

No matter how much he hated being backed into a corner.

"See that you *do* get it done," Rich said. He aimed a pointed glance at Sid. "I'll be deciding whether or not to pick up the options on the talents' contracts all month long. It's always *so* much nicer for me when I can approve them."

"Yeah," Jake shot back. "It's nicer for us when you can approve them, too."

Rich paused in the midst of returning to his office. He looked over his shoulder at Jake. "You're skating on thin ice, Jarvis. I'd watch myself if I were you."

Jake shrugged. "You'll have to be content with watching me on *Dream Date.*" He removed his horn-rims and channeled his frustration into the slow and deliberate motions required to clean the lenses. "I hear viewers are clamoring for the experience."

At Jake's reminder of his popularity with viewers—one

of the tangibles his sportscasting brought to KKZP—Rich offered a thin smile.

"Yes. Well. Good luck," he said as he straightened his tie. "You'll need it."

Jake hoped he wouldn't need luck. The way he saw it, all he needed was to be paired with a *Dream Date* date-ee who wasn't some kind of crazy fan, but who was a reasonable, ordinary, down-to-earth woman. A woman who wouldn't shake up his life, who wouldn't threaten the normalcy he'd built with his son, and who wouldn't be hoping for more than Jake was prepared to give.

Piece of cake, he assured himself as he slipped his glasses back on and watched Rich leave. He said his good-byes to Sid. A few seconds later, he was at his own cubicle, his fated game-show appearance about to be pushed from his thoughts by impending deadlines.

There were millions of practical, sensible women in the world, he told himself as he pulled up his PC's scheduling software and scanned the day's tasks. All Jake needed was one. Surely getting matched up with her wouldn't be that tough.

He hoped.

"Try the green tea and loofa scrub," Marley suggested as she settled back into her favorite massaging recliner at the spa. She lifted a de-puffing cucumber slice from one eye and smiled at Brian and Sondra. "It comes with a *divine* Ayurvedic wrap and heated stone massage afterward."

They looked skeptical. Brian, after all, was something of a germ-a-phobe. He was never wild about being touched by strangers, even for the most delightful of reasons. And Sondra was an eminently businesslike woman, even while clad in a spa robe, as she was now. Marley doubted Sondra unclenched her cell phone and PDA for anything less than full-scale, official relaxation—all ten doctor-ordered minutes per day she accumulated of it. But, being the good sports they were, both Brian and Sondra had settled warily into the recliners flanking Marley.

Directly across from them in their private spa room, Candace and Heather wore terry-cloth robes as they sprawled in identical recliners. Sea mud masques had been professionally smeared on their faces. Pedicure sponges were wedged between their toes. Headphones huddled over their ears, providing the soothing spa sounds of Gregorian chants.

They couldn't hear the conversation Marley was about to have with her manager and agent, but she had a feeling they knew all about it already.

More than likely, her whole team knew everything about her—what she'd done, what she was thinking of doing, what she'd failed at. They shared information about her, Marley was sure. And why not? *She* was what they had in common.

In all, though, her entourage was as much a family to her as her own parents and twin sister were. Her theatrical agent, commercial agent, CPA, publicist, attorney, stylist, manager, personal assistant, housekeeper, personal trainer, facialist, Tarot card reader, driver, chef, and all the others had been with her for years. They knew her inside and out—and they'd stuck by her, too.

Because of that, Marley felt a strong sense of responsibility toward them. In a sense, *their* careers were *her* career. They depended on her for their livelihoods—and, let's face it, for prime gossip. She couldn't let them down any more than she could let herself down. No, she had to do something to get her career back on track, for everyone's sake.

While Brian's assigned technician assured him she had indeed put on sanitary gloves and Sondra's pried the pager from her client's sturdy grip, Marley chose a lovely peach color for her pedicure. She set aside her cucumber slices and allowed the technician to administer a high-tech treatment cream. She ordered papaya-mango smoothies for everyone.

"Be sure to include those little umbrella garnishes, please," she told the girl who'd come to offer refreshments. "They're festive. I could use some festivity today."

The girl nodded and scurried away. Brian chose that moment to scrutinize the toenail clippers his technician was about to wield. Sondra demanded the return of her cell phone.

"This is all about relaxation," Marley reminded them. She glanced at Candace and Heather to make sure they were enjoying themselves, then addressed her manager and agent. "If you two don't pipe down, I'm going to request full-body seaweed wraps and nice long stays in the immersion tank for both of you."

They quieted immediately, as she'd known they would. There was nothing like the threat of forced solitude to subdue the average workaholic showbiz type.

"So, what's this outrageous new plan?" Marley asked. "I'm dying to know what you two have cooked up for me. A stint on the New York stage? A series of overseas commercials? The ones in Japan can be very lucrative, I hear. Or maybe a musical. I've been taking voice lessons since I was five, you know. I had to round out the tap lessons somehow."

"It's not a musical," Brian said.

"Or a play," Sondra added. "Or a commercial."

"It's something even bigger," Brian told her. "Something that will revitalize your entire career."

"Not another makeover." Much as she loved them, Marley knew she had to look deeper to solve this problem. "I went strawberry blonde two months ago and it didn't accomplish a thing."

"No. It's not a makeover," Sondra said. Reluctantly, she closed her eyes to receive her own cucumber slices. "Not the way you mean. What we're trying to get at is . . . Marley, I'm sorry. But you're just not working anymore."

"Well, I know *that.* That's what's been bothering me so much! That's what I've been trying to change all year. Right, Brian? Everything I've done has been an attempt at getting work. At revitalizing—no, *reinventing*—my career."

"What Sondra means to say is, *you're* not working." Brian winced as the technician began buffing the soles of his feet with a pumice stone. His tone remained gentle. "Your image, your approach. *You.*"

Marley blinked, the beginnings of unease making her stomach clench. "Me?"

"You, as a person," Brian said.

Sondra nodded. The technician adorned her face with deep-moisture treatment packs, which made her next words come out muffled. "Brian and I have been over this a thousand times. At this point, we've agreed there's only one thing to do: Change you completely."

"Change me? Me?" Marley repeated in a small voice.

"Yes," they said in unison.

Yikes. She'd been rejected for acting jobs before, of course. But Marley had never been rejected like this. So personally. So persistently. So brutally matter-of-factly.

I thought you were my friends! she wanted to wail, but couldn't. She was too desperate *not* to listen. If what Brian and Sondra had to say could help . . . well, she had to stand tough and take it.

For courage, Marley chose a revved-up red polish for her manicure. For fortification, she took a big glug of the smoothie the refreshments girl delivered. For strength, she drew in a deep breath and visualized a successful outcome, exactly as her therapist had taught her. Then she faced her future dead-on.

"All right, then. Give it to me straight."

First, Brian dismissed the spa technicians so they'd have privacy, a move which definitely made Marley even more nervous. Then he began.

"It's like this," he said. "Industry people are having a hard time taking you seriously. Thanks to your popularity on *Fantasy Family,* you've become the ultimate blonde starlet. You're perceived as glamorous. Sensational. And frivolous, both on-screen and off. It's hard for anyone to imagine you any other way."

Ouch. Marley had known Brian wasn't exactly the type to pull his punches, but sheesh . . .

"This severely limits the roles you can play," Sondra agreed. "Right now, your type isn't what casting directors are looking for. What we need to do is make them see you in a whole new light."

Marley began to understand. "A real, raw light?"

"Exactly," Brian said.

Gulp. Real and raw were uncharted waters for Marley. She specialized in girly-girl. In blonde bombshell. In spoiled debutante. Those were comfortable for her.

"In order to do that," Sondra said, "in order to force the change you need and present you in a fresher, more natural way, we've come up with a plan. It's unorthodox, but—"

"We're sending you undercover," Brian interrupted.

"Undercover?"

"Yes." Sondra sounded assured, as though this whole idea *didn't* seem crazy. "On *Dream Date*. Are you familiar with it?"

"Umm, sure." Everyone was familiar with it. It was prime time's hottest and most-hyped game show since *Who Wants to be a Millionaire*. It was a reality-TV mishmash of *Blind Date* plus *The Newlywed Game*, featuring hot singles looking for love and finding battle-of-the-sexes-style miscommunications instead. "But I still don't see what that has to do with—"

"It's simple," Sondra explained. "You'll audition incognito for *Dream Date*. If you can convince the director and producer that you're an ordinary, un-diva-like girl next door—and they cast you—you'll be on your way."

"We can use your appearance on the show to compile a whole new résumé reel," Brian said, his tone eager. "One that will showcase an undiscovered side of Marley Madison. One that will display the range of your talents like never before. In a real, raw, natural setting."

"Game shows are the most accessible auditions around," Sondra added. "And working on a game show—three times or fewer—is SAG-approved. All you need is a suitable alter ego, then . . . bam! Reinvented, revitalized career."

They fell silent, obviously pleased with their proposition. Marley had to agree that a reinvented, revitalized career did sound good. A second chance at success was what she wanted more than anything.

But this? *An alter ego?* It was kooky. Outrageous. And so . . . gutsy, it just might work. But still . . .

"Wrangling to get cast on *Dream Date* would be a real comedown," she protested. "What if someone found out who I really was? What if my real identity were discovered?"

She shuddered, unable to pursue the awful thought aloud. A two-time People's Choice Award winner, reduced to a bit-part game-show gal? Horrific! Everyone she knew would have a field day. Possibly, the Academy would even revoke her Emmy. She loved her Emmy. It symbolized everything that was special about her luxe life in L.A. It represented her accomplishments and her talent. It had gotten her through some tough, doubt-filled times.

"I want to keep my Emmy!" she blurted, panicked.

To their credit, neither Brian nor Sondra so much as cracked a smile. They were taking this seriously.

"You'll keep your Emmy," Brian said, "and if your alter ego does well on *Dream Date,* you just might find yourself on the path to winning another one. Or even an Oscar. Marley, this can work. You have the talent to pull this off. You can become an ordinary girl next door for the duration of a *Dream Date* taping. Think of it!"

That was the trouble. She *was* thinking of it. Thinking of sacrificing the image she'd painstakingly built, just to morph into Miss Mundane for a questionable game show "opportunity."

"Think of the industry buzz when the show airs and we reveal your image-changing performance as an utterly believable, down-to-earth, blue-collar woman," Sondra urged. "A woman who knows her craft so well, she's been able to fool everyone, including her dream date. Honestly, Marley. This opportunity could very well change your life."

Marley wasn't so sure she wanted her life changed. Not

like this. If she surrendered her special starlet sparkle, who would she *be?* Since childhood, acting had been the only thing that was truly extraordinary about her.

"My celebrity is my greatest selling point," she protested. "If I make up some crazy alter ego, if I audition incognito, I won't be able to rely on it. What if . . ." She hardly dared to voice her next fear aloud, but she had to. "What if I can't even get cast?"

"The Marley Madison we know will rise to this challenge and get cast," Sondra said confidently. Brian agreed.

"But I don't know anything about being an ordinary girl next door!" Marley cried. "I started acting in commercials when I was four. I was cast as a regular on *Playtime* when I was seven. I was in and out of pilots, bit parts, soaps, and second-string roles all through my teens. I know about spotlights, tutors, and learning lines. I know about hitting my mark, walking the red carpet, and smiling for the camera. But when it comes to non-showbiz stuff . . ."

"You'll do fine," Brian assured her. "This ordinary woman thing is a part to be researched, just like any other."

"That's right," Sondra agreed. "So, what do you want to call your alter ego? We should probably decide on that first."

Sondra had already forged ahead to the next step. Brian had, too, as though Marley's participation were a foregone conclusion. Their surety only scared her more.

In the expectant silence that followed, Marley's thoughts ran wild. She imagined trying to create a suitable girl-next-door character—and failing. Imagined the *Dream Date* producers laughing her out of the audition. Imagined her Emmy being toted away and her aura of specialness fading.

Ordinarily, she was reasonably confident. But this . . . this fell outside her realm of expertise. This was too much.

"No. No, I can't do it," Marley told them. "Please, *puh-leeze,* find me something else. Anything else!"

"Well, let's see." Brian tapped his fingers on his spa recliner's padded armrest. "There's always that employee-training video for our Fortune 500 client, remember, Sondra?

They need someone to demonstrate what is and is not sexual harassment. Marley would portray the hapless victim."

"Or that offer from the Tiny Tots Playhouse to portray Miss Minchen in their production of *A Little Princess* on stage. It's a small play, but it would be so satisfying to give back to the community. Especially to the children."

"You two are torturing me!" Marley said. "I'd make a rotten victim, Brian. I'd bust a few TaeBo moves on any bozo who got fresh. Plus I'm clueless about children, Sondra, and you know it."

Brian snapped his fingers. "I've got it! That infomercial you told me about, Sondra. What was the product called?"

"The ZitKit 3000," Sondra replied. "Sure, why not? Marley can become the ZitKit 3000 infomercial spokesperson."

Oh, God. She was trapped between professional victimization, community theater for preschoolers, and—worst of all—infomercial purgatory. It didn't get much more dismal than this.

"Of course, you'd have to share the spotlight with that smart-alecky kid from the Farrelly brothers movies," Sondra remarked thoughtfully. "The one who specializes in mooning people."

Marley covered her eyes and moaned. This just got worse and worse.

"Right," Brian agreed. "The butt guy. In fact, he'd probably get top billing, given the target market."

Marley couldn't believe this. "Exactly *where* are the blemishes the ZitKit 3000 is designed to treat?"

"Well . . ."

"No! Don't tell me." She held her hands in the air, heedless of their moisturizing paraffin-dipped coating. "Uncle! I'll do it!"

"You'll do it?" they chorused.

"I'll do it," Marley said. With a glimmer of hope, she considered the challenge ahead of her. It wasn't going to be easy, and it probably wouldn't be pretty, either. "Hey, no matter what happens from here, it'll probably beat selling my own autographed headshots on eBay, right?"

Marley's first step in researching her new "part"—and compiling her girl-next-door alter ego—was to turn to the only expert in real life she knew: her twin sister, Meredith.

While Marley had spent her childhood studying with her acting coach, memorizing audition monologues, and crying on cue as Bo's long-lost daughter on *Days of our Lives,* Meredith had spent hers being normal. She'd avoided the spotlight. She'd attended public school. She'd experienced first dates (unscripted), first kisses (unfilmed), and first days at USC (unimaginable, for Marley). Expertly and impressively, Meredith had formed a unique bohemian-scholar image that was all her own—and that couldn't have been more opposite than that of her famous sister.

At first, Marley had seen Meredith's vastly different approach to life as a rejection of all things starlet-and-Marley related. Then later . . . she still saw it that way. It was a constant source of friction between them.

She phoned Meredith at the museum where she worked as an advertising historian, then launched right into the explanation behind her need for an alter ego.

Silence fell. Marley didn't worry, though. That was typical Meredith. She liked thinking things through thoroughly before commenting.

"Let me get this straight," Meredith finally said. "You're going to pretend to be a normal, everyday woman. *You.* And you want me to help you do it."

"You don't have to make it sound so mind-boggling," Marley replied, offended. "I'm an actress. I can *act* the part."

"Sure. But you're not a miracle worker."

"Har, har. Can we skip the sarcasm, here? I need help."

As usual, Marley's honest plea brought out her sister's inherent soft-heartedness. "Okay. What can I do?"

"Advise me. I'm pressed for time because the audition is tomorrow. I'm going to have to build this character from the outside in. If I get cast, I'll work on the internals. So I need a few shortcuts to looking real and raw. Down-to-earth."

"Don't shower. Don't comb your hair. Wear Mom's old hippie clothes to the audition. How's that?"

"It's a dating show, Meredith. If I go looking like The Swamp Thing, God knows what kind of Igor I'll get matched up with."

"Good point."

Silence. Marley paced her Hollywood Hills bungalow with her cell phone in hand, waiting. She air-kissed her Emmy. She crouched down to pet Gaffer, who waited for her beside his new Hermès leash. She pictured her mousy, nose-always-in-a-book sister forgetting all about Marley's emergency dilemma and wandering off to work on a scholarly article, or something equally nonsensical.

"Meredith!"

"I'm here." As always, she sounded calm and self-contained.

"Please, help meeee. How can I look ordinary?"

"All right. Let's see." Another pause. "In advertising, wholesomeness is traditionally portrayed using feminine, apple-cheeked brunette models."

Marley touched her expensively blonde-and-highlighted hair. She sighed.

"They wear average clothes. No designer duds."

Marley had this one covered. "I'm wearing a T-shirt and jeans to the audition," she said proudly.

She'd had to improvise. There hadn't been enough time to contact one of her favorite designers and ask him to come up with a few "average" pieces for her. It was too bad, because the *Fantasy Family* wardrobe gal had set Marley up with some amazing style connections.

Her sister scoffed. "Sure, a cashmere Marc Jacobs T-shirt and your Seven jeans, right?"

"What's wrong with that?"

"Nothing. Every 'ordinary woman' wears one-hundred-and-fifty-dollar jeans."

"They do! They must," Marley insisted. Because of the jeans' low rise, she'd even gotten the complete Derrière Décolleté treatment at the spa, including an upper-buttocks wax, a papaya-enzyme peel, and a jojoba-oil massage. She didn't want all that effort to go to waste. "For grittier parts, that's what all the actresses get from the wardrobe people."

"Hmmm. I forgot. We're dealing with TV logic. The same logic that insists a mostly unemployed female chef and a waitress could have really afforded a stylish, twelve-hundred-square-foot New York City apartment on *Friends.*"

"Hey, if you're going to take potshots at my career—"

"I'm not. We've covered that ground. Sorry to get off-track."

Mollified, Marley apologized, too. She needed her sister's help too much to engage in worn-out debates. "Maybe I can comb the thrift stores tonight." She wrote down the types of clothes Meredith suggested. "I might even be able to schedule an emergency dye job with Franco."

"Sounds like a good start," Meredith agreed. "Oh, and whatever you do, don't act too sexy. Girl next door does not equal sleazy. Think Meg Ryan. Think Cameron Diaz."

"They're both blondes," Marley objected.

"You're too literal." Meredith sighed. "Think Sandra Bullock, then. Wholesome, friendly, lovable."

"Wholesome, friendly, lovable. Okay. I can do that."

There was a pause. "You know what? Judging by the determination in your voice, I almost think you can."

Touched, Marley smiled. Sometimes her sister really knew how to cheer up a person. "Thanks."

"Don't thank me yet," Meredith said. "You still have to shed twenty-seven years' worth of glossy superstardom overnight. Good luck!"

Marley hoped, as they said their good-byes and hung up with a promise to talk the next day, that she wouldn't need luck. If she played her cards right, all she would need was skill. That, and a cooperative *Dream Date* partner.

Whatever else happened, she sincerely hoped the man she was matched up with turned out to have both a sense of humor and zero personal magnetism. Because the last thing she—and her about-to-be-launched alter ego—needed was some kind of hunk-of-the-month hottie who'd wreck her concentration and endanger her whole plan.

Then she'd *really* be in trouble.

Four

Jake kicked off his second day as an official sex symbol with an extra-thorough flossing job (so he wouldn't turn up at the *Dream Date* auditions with pepperoni in his teeth) and a set of sixty push-ups. He was sweating through the series of ab crunches that followed when Noah appeared with a Bob the Builder toy in one hand and a quizzical expression on his face.

"Whatcha' doin', Daddy?"

"Exercising." *Seventy-three, seventy-four* . . .

"Because you're a stud muffin?"

Whoa. Jake paused at the top of the move, hands cradling his head. "Where'd you hear that?"

"Natalie's mom told Britney's mom you're a stud muffin. I said that was silly, 'cause people *eat* muffins. You're so big, you'd give somebody a tummyache."

"A tummyache, huh?"

"Yeah!" Noah laughed over his own joke, his little-boy's chortle completely unselfconscious. "A big one!"

"Don't worry." Jake began crunching again, speaking between exhales. "Nobody's mommy is getting a nibble of your dad. So no tummyaches."

Ever since his son had come into his life, Jake had kept

his relationships with women deliberately casual. Raising Noah was challenging enough; he didn't want complications.

"Okay." Noah shrugged and sat down on the carpeted floor beside Jake. He flipped his toy in his hands, talking to himself as he invented a new game.

Jake smiled at him, then got to his feet and headed for the shower. "Better get a move on, champ. I'm taking you to Miss Suzy's early today. I've got a busy day ahead."

Stud muffin's got some surprises in store.

Jake made it to the auditions (a formality, Sid had assured him) which were being held in Studio City. Inside the clean-lined office space, he checked in with the receptionist, then sat down with a clipboard to fill out the personality survey she handed him.

Before starting, Jake took a minute to scope out the competition. Men and women ranging in age from their twenties to their early forties milled about the waiting area. Some did vocal exercises. Some checked their appearances in the room's mirrored walls. Some sat quietly reading scripts, and some watched the door to the inner sanctum with palpable hopefulness.

They came in all types. Good-looking and ordinary. Model-thin and voluptuous. Surly and friendly. One by one they handed in their surveys and were called back to audition.

It seemed like a pretty standard setup to him. Jake would rather have been at KKZP doing real work, preferably dealing with touchdowns, layups, and triple plays. But as long as he had to be here, he was happy to see there were only about a dozen potential dream daters. Maybe this wouldn't take long.

He glanced at his personality survey. The first question read, *If you were an animal, which animal would you be?* The choices, in A-B-C-D order, were: *a kitten, a chicken, a wolf, a shark.* Jake shrugged. No contest. Kittens were too cuddly, chickens got deep-fried after a life of eggy servitude, and sharks had to be in constant motion.

He circled *wolf.* He didn't believe in this kind of mumbo-jumbo in the first place.

"Oh, good! A quiz!" a woman at the receptionist's station exclaimed. She accepted her clipboarded personality survey with undeniable zest. "Just like in *Cosmo.* I love these."

She sashayed—that was the only word for it—to the chair across from Jake and sat down. Her overstuffed purse thunked to the floor beside her. She slipped her sunglasses to the top of her head, revealing a pert face and a sparkly pair of dangling earrings. She crossed her jeans-clad legs and tapped her stiletto-shod foot as she began circling survey responses.

"Done!" she announced four minutes later to the room at large. She delivered her survey to the receptionist with a smile and a pop of her bubblegum, then sashayed—yes, *again*—to the corner coffeemaker. With her hands on her hips, she studied the half-filled carafe, the Styrofoam cups, the plastic stirrers, and the assortment of powdered creamer, sugar, and Sweet'N Low.

Fed up with answering questions about dreams, goals, his childhood, and his favorite make of car, Jake took advantage of the woman's position to study *her.* She had shoulder-length brown hair, a body-hugging pink T-shirt . . . and a way of bending over to retrieve a dropped sugar packet that reminded him of everything he'd ever missed about *real* dating.

The attraction. The thrill of discovery. The moment of connection when a woman spotted him watching her . . . and smiled as though she'd been waiting all day just to see him. Feeling suddenly anticipatory, Jake waited for her to meet his gaze.

To his disappointment, she didn't. Instead, the woman began pouring coffee. The first cup she prepared with one sugar and no creamer. The second she fixed with two sugars and one creamer. The third she doctored with one sugar and two creamers. The fourth she left black. With a slight frown of concentration, she tasted each brew.

On the fourth cup—after sampling and dismissing the first three with various comical expressions—she caught him watching. A guilty expression flashed over her face. She regrouped quickly, though.

"Would you like some coffee?" she asked.

Her voice sounded smooth, vaguely husky. He liked it.

"You seem to have appropriated it all," he said.

"No problem. I'll make more!" she announced. Purposefully, she turned to the coffeemaker. She rummaged through the canisters beside it, probably looking for more coffee and filters.

Jake abandoned his personality survey and joined her. His gaze touched on her four coffees, all neatly arrayed. "Feeling indecisive this morning?"

"No, I'm just getting started on internals. I'm optimistic that way." She saw him looking at her assorted drinks, and smiled. "I'm not sure how my new character—I mean, how *I* like my coffee, though. I didn't have as much time as usual to prepare for all this."

"I didn't know coffee involved such crucial decision making."

"That's where you're wrong. It's very important."

She squinted at the coffeemaker and tried to pry off its plastic top—which, it was easy to see, swung out like most models did. She seemed about as acquainted with the workings of the thing as Jake was with the details of eyebrow plucking.

"How a person takes their coffee says a lot about them," she went on, trying another tactic in her quest to brew a fresh pot. She hit the *on* button and waited expectantly for something to happen, then frowned when it didn't. "A person who likes their coffee black is simple and decisive. A one-sugar person is fancier, but still straightforward."

He nodded. Listening to her coffee theories beat the hell out of exploring his psyche on paper. Besides, she was cute.

"A sugar-plus-cream likes luxury. A two-sugar-no-cream wants things sweet, with an occasional bite. See what I mean?"

"Not really."

"Well, take you, for instance." She picked up the wad of coffee filters she'd discovered and used them to wipe off her hands. She tossed them carelessly into the wastebasket as though they were disposable paper towels, then examined him up and down. "You look like a decaf, extra-hot Italian roast to me. With real cream and no sugar."

Bemused now, Jake quirked a brow. "How do you figure that?"

"It's simple." Wearing a lively expression, she ticked off her points on her fingers. "Decaf, because you seem laid-back. In spite of that suit."

Her roving, speculative gaze didn't exactly disapprove of his audition suit . . . or of the rest of him. "Go on."

"Extra-hot, because I'll bet you like all your experiences to be . . . savored."

This was getting interesting. "Mmm-hmmm."

"Italian roast, because that's the most macho coffee of all," she continued matter-of-factly. "Real cream, because you look lean enough to splurge on something decadent now and then. And no sugar, because if you were *really* sweet, you wouldn't be coming on to a nice girl like me who only wants to do well on this audition. Now would you?"

With an eyebrow quirk of her own, she flashed him a smile. Then she picked up the one-sugar-two-creamers she'd prepared and pressed it into his hand.

"I think the coffeemaker's broken," she confided in a whisper as she leaned forward. "This is the best I can do. Enjoy."

He blinked as she squeezed his shoulder affectionately. The sweet scent of her shampoo still hung in the air as she sauntered away, her remaining three coffee cups in hand.

He'd been had, Jake realized. She'd hooked him, reeled him in like a forty-pounder on *Bassmasters,* and left him flopping in her wake. *Wow.* It was a good thing he wouldn't be dating any of these *Dream Date* women for real. He was seriously out of practice.

Of course, he couldn't just take that kind of treatment lying down. Or standing beside the coffeemaker, either.

Grinning at the sense of challenge unfurling within him, Jake tracked his mystery woman's progress across the room. He'd almost forgotten what it was like to feel this way, to want to flex his more . . . *macho* impulses.

During the past few years, single fatherhood had been his focus. Not flirting. Not connecting with women. Not dragging a brown-haired cutie back to his inner-Neanderthal's metaphorical cave o' love and having his wicked way with her. But something about the quirky coffee woman—with her oddball theories, big brown eyes, and sassy smile—reawakened every masculine instinct for pursuit he'd ever possessed.

Hell, just being here as a potential *Dream Date* contestant gave him license to practice his moves a little, Jake told himself. Didn't it?

Deciding it damn well did, he considered Little Miss Cream-and-Sugar for a pleasurable moment longer. Then he crossed the room, intent on giving just as good as he'd gotten.

Whew, Marley thought as she eased into her reception area chair with all three cups of coffee cradled waitress-style in her hands. *That was close.*

Despite her preparations, she'd walked in here this morning certain she'd be recognized. Certain her last-ditch career-saving maneuver would be finished before it began. But with every moment she'd spent incognito, she'd become increasingly confident in her new alter ego's shoes.

Her revamped hair probably helped distance "Carly"—

the name she'd given her alter ego—from "Marley" the most. Dyed in a caramel brown shade close to her own natural color and styled in a casual, shoulder-skimming 'do, it was to starlet style what culottes were to couture: far, far removed.

Her clothes weren't quite as radical a departure from her ordinary wardrobe, but she still had concerns about going too far. She didn't want to be matched with a mullet-wearing man with missing front teeth, an exclusively-flannel-shirts wardrobe, and a serious attachment to brewskis. It was better, she reminded herself, to play it safe for now.

"You look like you could use some help," someone said.

Marley glanced up. *Uh-oh.* The sandy-haired coffeemaker hunk was headed her way, moving in a loose-hipped stride that was sexy enough to make her blink. He used his body like a well-trained athlete . . . one who'd thoroughly mastered the art of relaxation. Taken as a whole, the effect was quite a contrast to the buttoned-up tailoring of his suit and the intellectual effect of his eyeglasses.

"Let me hold one of those for you." Without waiting for her reply, he positioned his fingers beneath her middle Styrofoam cup. His blue-eyed gaze met hers. He nodded for her to release her grasp, then slid the cup from between the others. "Now you can drink the other two."

"I would have managed."

"Like you did with the coffeemaker?"

"I handled it. You got your coffee, didn't you?"

"Sure did."

He grinned and transferred her cup to join the one he already carried. His hand was big enough to easily hold both drinks, she noticed.

He noticed her noticing. His grin widened.

Oh, brother. What she didn't need today was some kind of man on the make, too full of machismo to realize when a girl just needed to get her alter ego-ing into gear. She couldn't afford distractions. And this man was *very* distracting. Determined to remain focused on the job at hand, Marley ignored the coffeemaker hunk looming over her in favor of assessing the audition competition.

"I never got a chance to thank you for it, either." He picked up the newspaper someone had left on the chair beside Marley. He dropped it onto another seat, rearranging the space to suit him. "The coffee, that is. Thank you."

"You're welcome," she said grudgingly. Meredith's instructions flashed into her mind. *Wholesome, friendly, lovable. Urgh.* Marley sweetened her words with a smile, then gazed around the room in a clear *not now* signal.

Apparently, he wasn't adept at picking up signals. Or at giving a girl her personal space. The hunk lowered himself into the chair he'd cleared, all tall male and easy possessiveness. His nearness made Marley aware of the breadth of his shoulders and the pleasant scent of the soap he'd used.

She inhaled. No-more-tears baby shampoo?

"Your hands are trembling," he said, cocking his head to study her in a friendly way. "Nervous about the audition?"

She glanced down at the liquid vibrations her shaky grasp had caused in her coffee cups. Terrific. He was persistent *and* observant. Just when she most needed to slide by incognito.

"It's my first time auditioning." It was, for Carly.

"You'll do fine. Don't stare into the camera."

"You know about cameras?" she asked, surprised. She'd expected there to be actors at the auditions, since *Dream Date* was a paying gig with national exposure—a gold mine for newbies. The coffeemaker hunk didn't strike her as the desperate out-of-work actor type, though. "Are you . . . in show business?"

Please say no. Please say no. If he was involved in the industry and recognized her, this scheme would be over with before it began. Could he be a grip? An extra? A stuntman? His intelligent demeanor, augmented by the glasses, suggested something more technical, but he definitely had the body for rough-and-tumble stunt work.

Leisurely, he raised the cup she'd given him and drank.

Evidently, he was thinking it over. His expression, when he lowered the coffee again, gave no clue as to his career choices. But it did suggest, incredibly enough, that the coffee was the most delicious brew ever.

Marley knew nothing could have been further from the truth. The stuff was inky and stale. Not even the packets of sugar and powdered creamer had been enough to rescue it. She'd never appreciated her own in-house cappuccino maker, operated daily by her housekeeper, as much as she did today.

"Showbiz? Not really," he replied. "I'm a sports reporter. My news director thinks it would make a great publicity stunt if I appeared on *Dream Date.*"

Reporter leapt into Marley's mind in flashing neon letters. *Publicity* crowded in right behind it. *Uh-oh.*

With a rueful shake of his head, he leaned his forearms on his thighs and blew on his hot coffee. Unable to move, Marley examined him. A reporter. The nemesis of every actress who'd ever donned a baseball cap and sunglasses to catch a flight undetected. The curse of every actor who'd ever punched out a paparazzo for snapping topless shots of his girlfriend-of-the-moment.

The unwitting adversary of every Marley who'd ever pretended to be a Carly in order to save her career.

He was the worst *possible* person for her to be talking to right now.

Sure, this guy's beat was basketball and football and hockey, but sports reporters had friends. Friends, for instance, who were entertainment reporters. Entertainment reporters who'd love to get the scoop on a former sitcom star who'd descended to game-show desperation.

She had to get away from him.

He was watching her. "What, you don't like sports?"

Sports were the least of it. She offered a wan smile, remembering Meredith's *wholesome, friendly, lovable* mantra. She tried to think of an excuse to bolt, one that wouldn't make him suspicious.

He mistook her silence for acquiescence. The edge of his mouth tilted upward in a self-deprecating smile. Marley found it—heaven help her—charming. She must have lost her mind. She downed two of the coffees she'd prepared for "Carly" as though they were tequila shooters, hoping the caffeine would assist in her getaway.

"I'll admit," he said, "running through stats and scores isn't rocket science. But I like it. I can see where a woman like you might not be interested, though."

She paused in the midst of stealthily reaching for her thrift-store purse. "Why not?"

"Well . . ."

His thoughtful perusal touched her from toes to nose. It roved over her in a heated slide much like the one she'd given him earlier by the coffeemaker. The cliché was true, then. Paybacks really *were* hell. Despite everything, Marley couldn't help but feel a teensy quiver of interest stir within her.

More than likely, that was due to the sportscasting thing. Now that she knew what he did for a living, the air of blunt masculinity that clung to him made perfect sense. It was a testosterone teaser, a purely chemical charge. She could resist it, and would.

However, there was one little problem.

She was curious. Too curious to leave before hearing what he had to say about her.

"Because you're obviously a girly-girl."

Marley froze. She was *supposed* to be a girl next door. An ordinary, unnoticeable type. "I am not!"

"Stilettos, ankle bracelet, designer jeans—"

"These came from a thrift shop!"

"—belly chain, tiny T-shirt, big hair, lipstick."

Oh, God. Her cover was unraveling. She should have targeted a brewski man for Carly. Vanity was her biggest weakness—and now it was going to be her downfall, too.

"Hold on a minute," Marley said, soldiering onward anyway. She jabbed her finger at his chest and encountered solid muscle. "Just because a woman likes to look feminine doesn't mean she deserves to be stereotyped. You don't have any idea what my interests are! For all you know, I have front-row seats on the fifty-yard first-base line."

"You've been to a football-baseball game then?"

His easygoing demeanor only aggravated her. She fixed him with a pointed gaze. "I don't see what's so damned funny about gender discrimination."

"Nothing." He spread out his arms, an earnest expression on his square-jawed face. "I just can't picture you cheering on the home team."

"I'd cheer on the visiting team, too," she announced defiantly. *"That's* how much of a sports fan I am!"

"I'm impressed."

He was *amused.* Marley could tell. He was choking on a full-on guffaw. She wasn't used to people laughing at her, especially know-it-all wanna-be jocks with sparkling eyes and an excess of personal magnetism. Usually, men like him were wowed by her.

Or, she should say, men like him were wowed by the *real,* non-alter-ego her. It wasn't easy to find herself on the wrong side of things now. Suddenly, she missed autograph seekers and screaming fans and men who hung her poster in their locker rooms. She wanted to be blonde and bodacious again. Being "Carly" sucked.

But it was her only chance. She had to make the most of it.

"If we get matched up on *Dream Date,"* he was saying, "I'll have to take you to a Dodgers game."

Heaven help her. "Great. I'll take *you* shopping."

"Whoa, no need to make threats." His grin flashed again. "I'm trying to be friendly."

Too friendly. Did he suspect who she really was?

Marley couldn't risk it. She grabbed her purse and stood. "You'll have to excuse me," she said. "I just remembered something I forgot to tell the receptionist."

Okay, as a smooth exit, it lacked finesse. But it worked.

He nodded. "Good luck on your audition."

"You, too."

She bolted to the other side of the room, trying not to wiggle too much. She was certain he was watching her. He was just that kind of guy. All male. Born to appreciate a woman's body, and not the least bit shy about indulging that birthright.

At the receptionist's desk, Marley glanced over her shoulder. He raised his gaze from her derriere, not at all chagrined to have been caught ogling.

She should have been offended. The weird thing was, she wasn't. Instead, Marley felt almost . . . encouraged. As though maybe her extra three pounds weren't that horrific after all, if a regular guy like him still found her desirable.

Despite everything, the notion cheered her. Raising her chin, she decided right then and there that "Carly" didn't practice Pilates. Or jog.

Okay. Back to business.

She turned to the receptionist. "Look, I have to ask you a favor."

"Yes?"

"See that man over there? The one with the suit, the sandy hair, the glasses—"

"—the gorgeous grin, the friendly face, the kick-ass body?"

"Don't point! He'll see you!"

The receptionist nodded. "What about him?"

"Whatever you do, *please* don't pair me up with him."

The receptionist squinted at him. She gave Marley an are-you-crazy? look. When Marley confirmed her request, she nodded. "All right. I'll do my best."

Relieved, Marley thanked her. Then she headed for the last refuge of all women in sticky situations: the ladies' room. If she was lucky, by the time she got back the sportscaster would be auditioning. Their paths would never cross again.

* * *

"Those two," one of the *Dream Date* producers said, pointing through the two-way mirror between the waiting room and the room he'd gathered in with some of the key decision makers on the production team. "Put those two together."

"They haven't even auditioned yet," his assistant protested.

"I don't care. They've got something together." The producer watched as the woman he'd indicated paused at the waiting area's doorway. She snuck a speculative glance at the man he'd chosen, then shook her head and stepped outside. "Something that will make good TV. A sizzle. A spark."

"Yeah. A spark." Murmurs of agreement were heard among everyone gathered there. Everyone except his assistant.

"We're supposed to wait for the results of the personality surveys. Match up like meets like, remember?"

The producer waved away the notion. "I'm willing to take my chances. See that it's done."

Two down, one to go. He went to select the last of their three *Dream Date* contestant couples.

Five

After an audition, a mountain of paperwork, more waiting, and a final callback, Jake made the cut. To his mingled chagrin and relief, he was going to be an official *Dream Date* contestant.

He still didn't know who his partner was going to be. Someone easy to work with, he hoped.

Sid had already called him twice from the station—once to offer encouragement, and once to warn that Rich was already talking about replacing the sports segment with a scores ticker during the weather broadcast. Jake would be damned if he'd let Rich dismiss all his years of work.

More determined than ever, he sat on the soundstage bleachers near the empty game-show set with the contestant finalists. The sports-challenged brunette with the coffee theories was there. So were two other men and two other women. Together they listened to a member of the *Dream Date* staff explain the rules of the game show.

"I'm Doug, your guide to all things *Dream Date!*" the staff member said.

"Hi, Doug!" Everyone applauded.

He held up his palm modestly. "Thank you. Now, before I announce who will be paired with whom, let me give you an overview of the process you'll be going through. You've already completed your paperwork, your personality survey, and your audition. Next will be your dream dates!"

Some of the contestants cheered.

"Each couple will share two dates—one daytime, one evening—per week for a month. At least half of those dates will be filmed for potential airing, with camera and audio crews to be assigned to you."

Several contestants—those who'd never appeared on TV before, Jake guessed—gave excited smiles.

Doug held up his hand in caution. "Just do your best to ignore the cameras. That makes for the most entertaining TV."

He chuckled. A feeling of doom inched over Jake.

"We'll compile those dates," Doug explained further, "along with footage from your initial interviews and month-end debriefing interviews, into five *Dream Date* episodes. As the shows are broadcast, viewers at home will vote via phone or our Web site to rank each couple's *Dream Date-ability*."

Great. Jake was about to be graded on dating. Sort of like taking the getting-to-know-you SATs. *Uggh*.

"But I'm getting ahead of myself." Doug gave a practiced shake of his head. "First, each of you will complete a base-line interview about your life. That's happening today. Then you'll come back for the debriefing interview I mentioned, which will be recorded at month's end. It's really just a follow-up session designed to gather feedback about your partner. You know, what you liked and didn't like about them."

Doug swept them all with a deliberately encouraging look. Disgusted, Jake frowned. He'd seen *Dream Date*. The "debriefing" was usually a televised gripe-fest wherein each date-ee bashed their assigned partner—or, occasionally, raved about them. Given the brutal honesty often involved, Jake didn't doubt that particular episode was must-see TV for the show's fans.

Thank God he worked in sportscasting, where bone-crunching tackles were as brutal as it got.

"As you know," Doug went on, "encouraging communication between the sexes is our primary goal here at *Dream Date*."

Jake scoffed. Encouraging high ratings was the primary goal at *Dream Date,* just like it was at every other show. But unlike at KKZP, at least Jake wouldn't have to wear a banana hammock to encourage those ratings.

"After the debriefing, all three couples will be invited back to the studio to appear before our live audience in the sixth and final episode: the Q&A." Doug paused, doubtlessly ratcheting up the tension. "Where you'll compete for the grand prize!"

Jake directed his gaze toward the coffee girl, several seats away from him. She might have been taking a crucial quiz, so intent was her expression as she listened.

"It won't be easy, though," Doug warned. "Here at *Dream Date,* we pride ourselves on running a top-notch show. To provide maximum challenge between the three pairs of contestants, the final questions will take gender skills into account. Men, you'll be quizzed on your date's feelings, dreams, and shopping habits."

Masculine groans were heard. Jake frowned. What the hell did he care about shopping?

"Women, you'll be tested on your date's opinions, actions, and sports-viewing practices."

The women looked worried. Jake perked up. It wasn't fair that the women got all the easy questions, but he could cope with that. He was relieved to know there'd be sports included.

"Note-taking, sympathetic hinting, and third-base-coach-style signaling will be considered cheating. Is that perfectly clear?"

"Yes," the contestants said.

Jake nodded. This wouldn't be so bad. He felt sure he could wine his date, dine his date, and perform well enough in the final Q&A to have a shot at winning the grand prize.

That would be enough to get Rich off his back—and to ensure the option on his contract was picked up.

Discussion followed about the Bahamas vacation for two that was the ultimate prize, about the prizes for runners-up, and about tax obligations. Jake followed most of it, but he wasn't here for prizes. He wanted to win—even if in this case winning meant achieving temporary coupled bliss with one of the women here—but he didn't care if he got a genuine Jacuzzi brand whirlpool spa for his efforts.

He could do this, though. This *Dream Date* thing wasn't going to affect his life much at all, he realized. He'd take his date to a few ball games, maybe go bowling or throw darts down at Lefty's, share a meal or two. Yeah, this was going to work out just fine. All he needed was a date who enjoyed the simple things in life, the way he did, and he'd be home free.

He glanced at the women. The one to his left sure looked the part in her track pants, sneakers, and plain white T-shirt. He could easily imagine her cheering on the fifty yard line or hurling a twelve-pounder at the pins. The woman beside her might be a good option, too . . . although her obviously amplified breasts might get in the way of a good game of pool.

Briefly, Jake considered the brunette. She was undeniably pretty, but she screamed *high maintenance.* A woman like her would expect much more than he had to give. She'd been fun for a getting-his-feet-wet flirtation in the waiting area, but that was it. There was no way he could see himself with a woman who greeted every home run with a jubilant "touchdown!"

He'd probably be matched with someone else, Jake decided. There was no way he and Miss Cream-and-Sugar had turned up simpatico on that personality test.

Doug explained a few more details about *Dream Date.* Everyone agreed to the process he described.

"Great!" Doug exclaimed, rubbing his hands together. "Glad you're all on board. Because we're starting right now."

Several more employees came from backstage. They carried portable cameras, wireless lavalier mics, and lighting and sound equipment. With well-practiced motions they tromped up the bleachers and waited.

The match-up announcements began. First one couple, who shrieked when their names were called and then high-fived each other. They sat, beaming, as the crew wired them up for remote filming. Then a second couple, who eyed each other warily and grudgingly sidled closer. The two of them watched attentively as the crew prepared them.

"I guess that makes the third couple obvious," Doug announced with a smile. He spread out his arms to indicate Jake and the coffee-theorist brunette. "You're it, you two! Have fun!"

Jake looked at her. She stared at him from the opposite end of the bleachers, dismay plain on her face. She didn't make a move to slide closer, to high-five him, or even to offer a good sport's smile. Instead she crossed her arms, disgruntled.

Offended, Jake crossed his arms, too. Did she think she was the only one who wasn't crazy about this pairing? How about him? It wouldn't be easy dating a woman who thought the Lakers were a resort, and a body check was a kinky version of foreplay.

"Come on, you two!" Doug urged. "It's not all that bad, is it?"

It's worse, suggested the look the brunette sent him.

It's ten-runs-down-in-the-bottom-of-the-ninth bad, added the look Jake offered.

"You should be happy," Doug told the brunette. "You're getting paired up with a local celebrity, Jake Jarvis of KKZP's *Spoooooorts at Six!*"

Jake didn't appreciate his just-joshing delivery of the broadcast's usual intro. He frowned.

"And you," Doug went on, changing gears to address Jake. "You're getting paired up with . . ."

There was a pause as he glanced at the brunette. She tensed. He consulted his clipboard, squinted at her, then shook his head.

"Carly Christmas!" he finished exuberantly.

"Christopher." She cleared her throat, her cheeks flushed inexplicably pink. "It's Carly Christopher, not Christmas."

Doug made a note of it. Jake studied the brunette Carly, who hadn't moved an inch from her unyielding position. She still looked embarrassed. Odd, for a person who'd just auditioned to appear on TV.

Maybe she felt uncomfortable in the limelight, he decided. Maybe she wanted a date, but not publicity. He vowed to make sure no one singled her out for unwanted attention during their time together.

Unless he could change the matchup somehow.

"Listen, there must be some kind of mistake," he said.

"Definitely a mistake!" Carly cried, charging down the bleachers to confront Doug. She tossed Jake a triumphant look as she beat him to it, stilettos and all. "We're not supposed to be matched up together. The two of us are completely wrong for each other."

A shrug. "I just go by what's on the clipboard."

"She doesn't know a fly ball from a fly swatter!"

"Sorry. You two are it. Unless you want to clear out and let the runners-up take your places?"

Jake froze. He looked at Carly. She looked at him. Her big brown eyes turned thoughtful as she bit her lower lip. Was she about to ditch him?

He had to act before she could.

"Hang on a sec," he told Doug. "We'll be right back."

He caught hold of Carly's arm. She tried to wrench from his grasp. He refused to let her. At Doug's words, Jake had realized exactly what might happen if he and Miss Cream-and-Sugar couldn't work together. He couldn't let this job-saving adventure in Date-ville be over before it began.

He towed her to a more secluded spot at the far end of the

bleachers. Studio lights beamed down on them, highlighting the toasty gleam of her hair and the frigid snap of her stubborn expression.

"What do you think you're *doing?*" she asked in a furious whisper. Her gaze darted to the clipboard-wielding staff member and the crew waiting to wire them for filming. "Second thoughts? *Now?* You can't back out on me!"

Relief struck him. She wanted to go through with it, too. Jake smiled.

"You can quit with that panty-peeling grin of yours, too, because it won't change a thing. You heard him. We're stuck together."

"Panty-peeling?" He raised his brow.

"If you were hoping to get hooked up with Miss Hooters over there, well . . . that's just too bad."

She raised her chin. Crossed her arms over her own less-than-spectacular endowments. Glared.

Did she really think he was that shallow? "Look, those two little mosquito bites of yours have got nothing to do with this."

She gasped. "I was talking about *her!*"

Jake nodded. He was sensitive enough to know when there was more to a situation than met the eyes. No pun intended.

"Come on. If I was hung like a hamster, I might feel a little defensive about it, too."

Thunder rolled into Carly's expression. Ah-hah. He was on the right track, then.

"But I'm not." Jake lifted one shoulder in a modest shrug. "I'm actually pretty well en—"

"I don't want to hear it!"

She started to pace. He snatched her before she got far—and before the impatient glances they were earning from the *Dream Date* staff got out of hand. He leaned in.

"I just want you to know," he confessed in a low voice, "that stuff doesn't really matter to me. Physical appearance is not the most important thing in the—"

"Oh, so now you're saying I'm unattractive? Listen, you big dumb jock—"

"No. You're very attractive."

She shushed, apparently mollified.

"I'm really more of a leg man, anyway." Truly, he was an "allover" man when it came to women, but Jake could tell he'd hurt her feelings. He wanted to make her feel better. "I don't care a bit that you have itty-bitty little—"

"Finish that sentence and I swear I'll clobber you with that abandoned boom mic over there."

He glanced at the piece of technical equipment she'd mentioned. Carly was familiar with TV terminology? For the first time, it occurred to him to wonder exactly who she was. Earlier, Jake hadn't asked why *she'd* been interested in dream dating. His motives were plain, but hers?

Whatever they were, they'd have to wait.

"You're cute when you're all fired up," he said.

"You're wasting time. Judging by the way the P.A. keeps checking his watch, we're about to get booted in favor of another insta-couple."

Her accusatory look grated on him. "It's not my fault we're over here. You're the one who started with the eye rolling. And the I'm-having-second-thoughts look. *I'm* managing the problem."

"By practicing breast-size discrimination? Excuse me if I'm not bowled over by your management skills."

"Maybe I need more hands-on experience."

"Ooooh!"

"Look," Jake said, adopting a more conciliatory tone in an effort to calm her down. "Don't blow a gasket on me here. I have no choice but to go through with this. I'm guessing you're in a similar situation—"

"Why? What makes you think that?"

Confused by her sudden alarm, he shrugged. "Just a feeling. Anyway, I'm prepared to make the best of this, but if you're not going to help—"

"If we blow it, it won't be my fault."

"Fine. Let's do this, then."

"Fine."

They tromped back to the other end of the bleachers, where the *Dream Date* crew was waiting.

"Glad to see you two worked things out," Doug said, writing something on his clipboard. At his signal, the crew began wiring them with identical body mics, earpieces, and golf ball–sized "date cams." "I've gotta tell you, though—I wouldn't lay odds on the two of you winning this thing."

Jake figured he had a point. He and Carly, together, were long shots for sure.

One of the crew members scoffed in apparent agreement as he adjusted Jake's mic. "No way," he said, shaking his head. "The sportscaster and the pop tart?"

There were knowing elbow jabs. General chuckles.

"I'll take that bet," Carly announced, holding her chin high. "Fifty bucks says Jake and I win this round of *Dream Date.*"

The crew stopped working. The clipboard guy blinked. Jake cheered up. Maybe little Miss Cream-and-Sugar had more chutzpah than he'd given her credit for. This just might turn out to be interesting after all.

She should have worn her cutlets, Marley thought as she tottered through the muck of the petting zoo the *Dream Date* producers had sent her and Jake to for their first date. Then there wouldn't have been any cracks about her "mosquito bites." Or any need for her to make those very un-girl-next-door-like threats about clobbering Jake with a boom mike.

And that suggestion he'd made about needing more "hands-on experience?" Hah! Jake Jarvis wouldn't be getting close enough to her for that. She wouldn't give him an opportunity to make her feel any more off-balance than she already did.

She'd felt a little wobbly in her "ordinary" persona to begin with. Now, after being briefed on the complete *Dream*

Date process, Marley felt more worried than ever. She'd have to keep up her alter-ego performance twenty-four hours a day!

After all, it wouldn't do for Jake to visit his supposedly ordinary date . . . only to find her wearing a fabulous Gucci gown while polishing her Emmy in her three-thousand-square-foot bungalow. She'd need more clothes, a modest temporary apartment, maybe even a clunker of a car to make her performance ring true.

She'd call her favorite prop guy for the car. He'd know where to find one that looked inconspicuous on the outside but ran well on the inside. She'd call Meredith for advice on her new digs. She'd throw her Jimmy Choos into storage and give her staff some time off. It wouldn't be easy, but Marley figured she could do it for the sake of her career.

When it came to Jake Jarvis, on the other hand, she felt considerably *less* confident. She couldn't quite figure him out. She would eventually, though, she was sure. Men were pretty simple and this one—currently standing near the split-rail fence like the lord of the potbellied-pig pen—couldn't possibly be that hard to handle.

He was easygoing. Earnest. Friendly. Okay, and he was irritatingly free with his opinions, too. His blunt, testosterone-charged assessment of her had stung in places she'd forgotten she had. Enduring her gawky teen years in the glare of appearance-conscious Hollywood should have cured her of caring what other people thought of her, Marley knew. But it hadn't.

Still . . . no one she knew would have offered advice to a supposed newbie on not freezing up in front of the camera. Never mind that Jake's guidance had alerted Marley to the potential dangers of his job as a reporter. That had been a really nice thing for him to do.

She still wasn't sure how they were going to make this *Dream Date* thing work between them, though. The two of them were completely different. He liked sports; she liked shopping. His job involved chronicling feats of sweaty strife and sportsmanship; hers involved making the artificial and preconstructed seem magical. He was the DiMaggio to her Monroe, the Gary Cooper to her Mae West. There was no way they could possibly see eye to eye.

Somehow, they had to try.

"Come on over, princess." Jake beckoned her toward his end of the petting zoo's enclosure. A fat pig rooted there in the mud. "Don't worry about getting your shoes dirty. There's a pump over there to wash them off with."

"Oh, I'm not worried about that!" *Yes, she was.* She searched for a likely alibi. "It's just that this pony over here is so cute."

He looked at the animal approaching her on spindly legs. "That's a goat."

Thank God. She'd thought the poor thing was deformed.

"Of course! That's what I meant."

The black and gray creature stepped closer. Nervously, Marley stepped backward.

Jake gave their little barnyard cha-cha a knowing look. She frowned, not nearly as happy with this petting zoo stunt the *Dream Date* people had pulled as he apparently was.

This wasn't a date. A date involved flowers, candlelight, expensive restaurants, and magnums of champagne. The closest she'd come to those things today were the bougain-villeas at the petting zoo's entrance, the springtime sunshine beating down on her head, the promise of a hot dog from Jake, and a sip of the watery lemonade he'd treated her to.

Naturally enough, he didn't seem to know the difference between this and a proper getting-to-know-you first date. In fact, despite their surroundings, he looked contented. The breeze ruffled his sandy hair. The shadows cast by the nearby trees played tag over his big body, as though they just couldn't stay away. Never had she seen a man more at home in his skin. She should have guessed Jake would make himself completely comfortable anywhere.

The minute they'd arrived at the petting zoo, he'd shed his

suit jacket and rolled up his shirtsleeves. He'd loosened his tie, unbuttoned the top three buttons on his white dress shirt, and hunkered right down in the mud with the rest of the wild, happy beasts.

His ease irritated her. She envied it, even as she puzzled over it. Didn't Jake care that his shoes might never be the same? That these animals might carry fleas or dirt or the barnyard equivalent of a ferocious head cold? He didn't seem to. He petted the pig as though it were his favorite pampered pet. He even murmured words of praise. In response, it rolled in the mud in a fit of porcine delight. Jake glanced up with the expression of a kid who'd found a new pal.

She wanted a little of that. That ease, and that comfortableness. Just to prove him wrong about her, Marley tentatively patted the goat's knobby head. Its fur felt like the coarse false hair of a wig she'd once worn in a production of "Little Orphan Annie" for local children's TV.

"When you're finished, come pet this puppy." Jake scratched between the pig's ears, obviously making a joke at her expense. "Maybe you can teach it to play fetch."

"I—I'm fine over here, thanks." Another goat approached her. Its wiry white hair was longer than the first goat's. "Just a minute," she told it. "I'm busy with this little fella. Er, lady. Umm . . ."

Marley bent at the waist to try to determine the appropriate gender. The gray goat took exception to her nosiness and snorted on the leg of her jeans.

Yuck. Grimacing, she reached for tissues from her purse. The white goat, apparently mistaking her gesture for an offer of food, began rooting at her purse for a snack. Marley twisted sideways, sandwiching her handbag between her arm and side in an attempt to protect it.

She swabbed at the wet spot with a handful of tissues. The goat continued to nose his/her/its way around her purse, but the bag seemed secure for now. Marley was still bent over when she caught Jake watching her. His gaze was pinned to her derriere, and his attention looked gratifyingly rapt.

Hmmm. It occurred to her that there might be at least one way she could hold her own in this *Dream Date* situation with Jake. Even as "Carly"—and even surrounded by goats—Marley figured she still possessed some of her usual sex appeal. It might have been muted by mud-masque-colored hair and a thrift-store wardrobe, but it wasn't completely gone. And every man's weakness was sex, wasn't it?

Throwing Meredith's "don't act too sexy" advice out the window, she shifted to aim her posterior more squarely in Jake's direction. She finished her tissue job, then leisurely bent over to fiddle with her stiletto. Her derriere had been voted "most bootylicious" in *Allure*'s annual "best of" issue two years ago. Marley planned to give Jake a good eyeful—and grab herself the upper hand in her dealings with him at the same time.

Yes! He was looking! For good measure, she gave a subtle wiggle. It was a move straight out of paparazzi heaven. If there'd been reporters here at the petting zoo, they'd have screamed with joy. If Jake could still make fun of her after witnessing *this,* then he was a stronger man than she'd thought he was.

Marley moved to examine her other shoe, using the task as an excuse to smile coquettishly at Jake. The move was wasted. He'd moved and she couldn't see him.

She turned her face this way and that, beginning to feel a little dizzy from hanging her head upside down. She didn't want to bring herself upright again until she knew Jake had been completely snared.

As she pretended to refasten her stiletto's strap, she accidentally dropped the tissues. The gray goat dove at them. Plucked them into its mouth. Began to chew.

"No! Wait!" Marley jerked upright. Tissues weren't edible. For all she knew, they were poisonous to goats.

She didn't want to be responsible for hurting a petting zoo goat. She was a good person. Not somebody who recklessly endangered zoo animals. She reached for the slobbery wad, but couldn't catch hold.

The white goat chose that moment to make its move. It head-butted her in the crotch, bleating insistently. With a yelp, Marley lowered both hands to protect her pelvis. Her purse fell to the mud. The white goat pulled back its lips and grinned—she'd *swear* it did—and began munching on the bamboo handle of her purse.

"Stop, stop!" she cried. Sure, bamboo probably had plenty of fiber, but that didn't mean it was good for goats. "Give that back."

She grabbed the opposite end of her purse. Tugged. The goat tugged back. At the ruckus, some nearby children backed away. A few pointed. "Look at the silly lady wrestling with the goats."

Great. Now she was the official petting zoo crazy lady. Marley stuck her tongue out at the laughing brats. She went on pulling, digging her stiletto toes into the ground for purchase. She would get her purse back, or else.

Suddenly, the gray goat gagged. Coughed. Made all the same sounds Gaffer did when he got ahold of leftover foie gras, which *never* agreed with him. This was serious. More worried now, Marley let go of her purse and took the only action that seemed reasonable. She treated the gray goat like Gaffer.

"Give it over," she demanded sternly, cupping her hand beneath its scraggly-bearded jaw. "Right now."

Obligingly, the goat coughed the gooey wad of tissues into her palm. Marley felt too relieved to be grossed out.

"Good goat." With her unsteady *non*-slimed hand, she patted its head. "Nice goat. *Pretty* goat."

The other goat bleated. It had managed to gnaw open her purse and was pushing it through the mud with its snout. Muzzle. Whatever thing they would have called it on Animal Planet.

Newly courageous, Marley chased it down and snatched up her purse. "No," she scolded. "Bad goat."

It lowered its head and bleated plaintively.

"I mean, naughty goat."

It blinked its big brown eyes at her. Bambi in the barnyard.

"Oh . . . all right. Just don't let it happen again, okay?"

When Jake finally reappeared, Marley was consoling the goats with treats from the emergency stash in her somewhat worse-for-the-wear purse. She glanced up to find him sauntering toward her, a sun-kissed sportsguy wearing a bemused expression.

"Where have you been?" she asked. "Why didn't you help me?"

"Help you?"

"During the goat attack!"

He tilted his head. "Sorry, I was talking hockey with one of the animal handlers. I didn't see any goat attack."

"I could have been gored to death!"

"What I saw was a goat love-fest. You seemed to be handling things all right."

Nonplussed, Marley blinked at him. If any of her staff had been present during the goat fracas, they'd have summoned help immediately.

"I'm glad you're an animal lover," Jake went on. "I like a woman who enjoys simple things. Who isn't afraid to get her hands dirty and her feet wet."

Yeah. Dirty and wet. That was the famous Marley Madison, all right.

"Great. We're a match made in heaven."

"Or made in the petting zoo." He located the camera and audio crew, which had been trailing them since embarking on their date. "We've probably provided enough animal follies for the *Dream Date* people. How about lunch?"

"Sure." *A nice spring greens salad, a piece of seared herb-encrusted ahi, a glass of chardonnay—*

"There's a hot dog stand near the picnic tables."

A diet-wrecking fat bomb on a bun . . .

"Carly" would probably love that, though, so Marley

summoned up some girl-next-door enthusiasm. "Yum. Just let me finish this."

Jake stood patiently nearby as she held out the final handful of treats. The goats nibbled them from her palm, their lips and hairy beards tickling her skin. Once Marley had realized they were just larger versions of Gaffer-like creatures, she'd been fine with them. Now, she was actually quite proud of herself for having survived her goat encounter.

But that didn't mean she was happy with Jake for nonchivalrously abandoning her to the vagaries of the animal kingdom. How had he known she'd be able to cope?

"Hold this, would you?" She slapped the slimy tissue wad into his hand. "That's it, goats. Snack time's over."

They bleated and romped away at top speed. They chased through the pen, kicking up dust. They rose on their hind legs and waved their hooves, jumped onto barrels, and did everything short of the goat mambo in their exuberance.

Jake raised his eyebrows, the tissue wad still in hand. "Hey, what were you feeding them, anyway?"

"Altoids." Marley slapped the dust from her palms. She led the way toward the washbasins beyond the pen's exit gate. "Believe me, they needed them."

Six

When Marley emerged from the zoo ladies' room after freshening up, she found Jake—typically—talking sports with the hot dog vendor. He was laughing as she approached, exclaiming over foul balls and triple plays and buns . . . er, bunts. He had his back to her, so she took the opportunity he'd presented and inspected him from a new angle.

What an angle. His backside looked tight and perfect, even in his dress pants. She would have loved to see him in a pair of well-fitting jeans . . . or even less. Jake appeared to be hiding more than a few perfectly developed muscles beneath his pants and dress shirt. She'd always been a sucker for a fit man.

She'd have bet anything Jake came by his healthy look naturally, via honest work and manly effort. Say, hauling a hundred pounds of baseballs for disadvantaged kids, or building vacation cabins with his bare hands. He was just that kind of guy.

Enjoying the view—hey, there had to be *some* perks to this setup, didn't there?—Marley let her gaze wander up the ever-broadening slope that began at his lean . . . assets and rose all the way to his shoulders. She'd never found a man's back sexy before. On him, she suddenly did. Maybe it was the heat getting to her, maybe it was the fit of his white dress shirt, maybe it was just him. If Jake's back was anything like his front, it would be taut with strength. Slightly tanned. Soap-scented with a fragrance like baby shampoo.

Oh, yeah. She'd meant to ask him about that.

Vowing to do so once he'd finished raving over "Sosa's home run streak," Marley let her gaze linger on the back of his neck. She examined his neatly clipped hair, watched a bead of sweat roll from behind his ear to beneath his collar, savored the allover machismo of a man who actually sweated without calling for a makeup artist to fix the problem. She'd definitely been hanging around actors for too long.

There was something about Jake that called to the non-Stanislavski-ed part of her, that spoke to the most primitive, ravish-me femininity she possessed. Even as she knew their pairing might well be disastrous, Marley couldn't resist wondering about it. Would Jake kiss her good-bye at the end of their date? Would he go home thinking about her, spend his idle moments dreaming of ways to touch her?

She felt positively tingly at the thought. She'd have liked to touch *him*. To approach from behind, slide her fingertips from his shoulders to his broad, blunt-fingered hands, wrap her arms around his middle and give a good squeeze. Her breasts would press against his back muscles. When he shifted position, she would—

"Eat this." Jake held a hot dog beneath her nose. He raised her hand and closed her fingers decisively around its paper holder. "You look faint."

"I'm fine."

"You sound breathless."

"It's . . . the heat." *And the view, the man, the wonderings.*

"You'll feel better after you've had the works."

"Hey, I'm ready when you're ready."

"I've been waiting on you."

Jake grinned and raised his other hand, showing her two more fully loaded hot dogs. They oozed with mustard, ketchup, and relish. They disappointingly put the lie to the ribald thoughts she'd been entertaining about receiving "the works."

It was probably for the best, Marley told herself as she followed him to the nearby picnic tables. She needed to keep her mind on her performance, not on cozying up to a man with whom she had nothing in common. Their time together was a means to an end, nothing more. It was simply a way to show the world exactly how "real and raw" Marley Madison—aka, Carly Christopher—could be. She had to remember that.

The tinny sounds of a sports broadcast coming from the hot dog vendor's radio chased them across the paved area. She glimpsed the *Dream Date* crew at a distant table. Mothers with toddlers and snoozing babies in strollers surrounded them, while a zoo employee moved about beneath the canopied space with a broom and dustpan, scraping the concrete as he cleaned up. The cool breeze carried the scents of smoked sausage and cotton candy.

Jake waited for her to sit first. She glanced up with her hot dog in hand, expecting him to take a seat on the opposite side of their shady concrete table. Instead, he made more trips to the vendor's cart for two lemonades and additional hot dogs. Finally, he straddled the bench right beside her—knees nearly touching her thigh—plunking down paper-wrapped straws and a two-inch stack of napkins as he did.

"Expecting to be messy?" she asked.

With a hot dog halfway to his lips, he gave her a puzzled glance. Marley gestured toward the napkin bonanza.

"Force of habit. Eat. You'll feel better."

She *did* feel better, in an oddly cared-for way. Not in the fussy, spoil-the-starlet, it's-our-job way that her staff cared for her, but honestly watched out for. And she hadn't even taken a bite yet. With a silly grin, Marley raised her hot dog and did just that.

Competing flavors filled her mouth, along with the unfamiliar texture of spicy, fatty meat. She couldn't remember the last time she'd experienced a meal that wasn't designed to keep her in slinky award-show dresses and size I-suffered-for-this wardrobe pieces. Cautiously, Marley chewed.

"What's the matter? You're not a vegetarian, are you?"

"You say that like it might be contagious."

"Oh, Jesus. You are. What are you eating that for, then?" He reached for her hot dog.

Marley held it away. Vigorously, she chewed and swallowed. "I *love* hot dogs." Her stomach roiled.

Jake eyed her suspiciously. "How about hamburgers?"

"Nirvana."

"Pork chops?"

"Heaven."

"Steak?"

"To die for."

A skeptical look. "Chicken and fish?"

She shook her head. "Carly doesn't eat chicken or fish."

Marley had just decided it. Those lean sources of protein had been the staples of her diet for years now. It was time to break free. *Past time* to break free.

"'Carly doesn't eat chicken or fish?'" he repeated. "Why not just use the royal 'we' and get it over with, princess?"

Whoops. She had to remember to stay in character. Being around Jake was completely throwing her off her Method.

"Don't call me that." Blithely, she set down her food long enough to unfold a paper napkin and arrange it on her lap with dainty motions. She brushed a speck of dust from her paper lemonade cup, then took another bite of hot dog. "I'm an everyday, ordinary girl next door."

"Who acts like she's dining with the queen."

She shrugged.

"Well, I'll tell you something, girl next door."

"What's that?"

He leaned nearer. She felt herself being pulled into the warm blue of his eyes. What would Jake look like, Marley wondered all at once, without his Clark Kent–style glasses?

Like Superman, probably.

"Most everyday, ordinary girls next door haven't had vocal coaching," he said. *"You* have."

She gasped, sudden panic turning the bite of hot dog in her mouth to tasteless goo. Marley snatched a napkin to cover her lips and tried to recover.

"I have, too," Jake said casually, using his index finger to spread his hot dog's mustard more evenly. He popped his gloopy finger into his mouth and sucked it clean with unself-conscious motions. "Most sportscasters, most TV journal-ists, have. That's how I recognize the signs."

"Oh."

"La, la, la, la. Oh, oh, oh." He grinned, having executed a perfect example of one of the vocal exercises her coach had used to teach proper projection techniques.

"Oooga, oooga," she said, trying to sound more like a run-of-the-mill good sport and less like a nervous under-cover starlet. In a sense, they were bonding already. Even if it was over a potentially secret-revealing subject. "Gotta love those vocal drills, huh?"

Jake nodded, going on to discuss memories of strength-ening his vocal cords, practicing correct diction, and learn-ing breathing techniques. Marley nodded and listened, occasionally offering a story of her own. Then Jake took a bite large enough to finish his next hot dog. Thoughtfully, he chewed.

Just when she decided he was merely making idle conver-sation, he zeroed in on her face. "Why did you do it?"

She blanched beneath his steady regard. "Do it?"

"Vocal coaching. Are you a journalist, too?"

God forbid. She knew some really nice ones, but mostly journalists were considered part of the enemy camp. A nec-essary evil. Marley shook her head.

"A professional speaker?"

She pantomimed being unable to answer because of an extra-large mouthful of hot dog, realizing in that moment that she hadn't come up with a suitable career for Carly. She had to think fast.

Warming to his guessing game, Jake put down his hot dog and rubbed his palms together. He tilted his head. "You don't sound like voice-over talent, common as that is in this town. You don't *look* like an actress—"

Stung, Marley felt a pang of regret for this stupid scheme. She knew she should have been happy her alter ego was going over so well, but a part of her soundly resented having to force her real identity underground.

"—so what are you?"

What was she? What was *Carly? Arrgh.*

"A self-improvement junkie." The notion occurred to her in a rush of inspiration. She decided to run with it, since it allowed her to sidestep the real question for now. With a shaky laugh, she embellished, "You name it, I've tried it. Voice coaching, therapy, affirmations, hypnosis, motivational speakers . . . if it's supposed to help, I'm game to try it."

"You don't need improving."

Marley was touched. And relieved he'd moved on from the subject of Carly's job. "Thank you. That's sweet."

"Except maybe with your pig handling."

He finished his third hot dog and started in on his fourth. Jake clearly had a voracious appetite. He ate like a man, with big bites and a blatant enjoyment that probably came from being oblivious to calories. Despite that, though, he practiced good manners and had made sure since they sat down that Marley was enjoying her food, too.

"Lester was offended you didn't come over to pet him."

She was scared of Lester. Unlike the goats, he was too muddy to be likened to Gaffer. His hooves looked dangerous, also. "I'm sure he didn't mind. He had mean squinty eyes."

"You would too, if the prettiest lady at the zoo ignored you. He was trying to hide his hurt feelings."

"He was imagining snacking on my shoes."

Jake raised his index finger and thumb, holding them about a half inch apart. "Maybe a little bit. But mostly he felt overlooked."

Quizzically, Marley studied him. Was this about more than a pig's hurt feelings? Was it about *Jake's* hurt feelings? She couldn't imagine a man as self-assured as him ever feeling overlooked, but . . . "For a guy who's crazy for hot dogs, you have a lot of pig empathy."

He looked horrified. "Shhh! Not so loud. Lester thinks *I'm* a vegetarian."

She admired his sparkling eyes and happy-go-lucky expression as he popped the last of his hot dog in his mouth. She'd say one thing for Jake Jarvis—he had good cheer to spare. It seemed sincere, too. After being surrounded by too-sophisticated-to-smile industry types for so long, Marley found his openness as unfamiliar as it was unexpected.

"Besides," Jake said, "Lester's a male and so am I. We have to stick together when confronted with the whims of women."

"Is that so?"

"It is." He wiped his mouth with a napkin, then splayed both hands on his powerful thighs. He leaned slightly forward. "For instance, what would you say if I told you we're going to lie in the grass over there and listen to the rest of the baseball game on the hot dog guy's radio?"

"No!"

"What would you say if I suggested spending the day in the antiquated arcade outside, trying to beat the high score on Galaxian?"

"No!"

"Ripping off our clothes and streaking through the zoo?" *Were these the kinds of things normal people did?* "No!"

"See?" Jake gave a knowing grin and shrugged. "Whims."

Nonplussed, Marley shook her head. She was clearly out of her depth with this stuff. She frowned, trying to figure out whether she was the loopy one or Jake was. She wished she could call Meredith for real-world advice, but slipping away to use her cell phone would look suspicious—not to mention pretentious. Very un-Carly.

She wished she had a script.

"Not wanting to act like a ten-year-old isn't a whim," she said, trying to make light of his theory. "Where would we be if everybody behaved that way?"

"We'd be a lot happier, I'll bet." He watched a nearby brother and sister chase each other beneath the picnic area canopies. A smile tilted his mouth as the little girl made a face at her brother. She ducked beneath a table to elude him in their game of tag. Jake turned back to Marley. "You can learn a lot from kids."

"Sure. Like how to be mean."

He gave her a quizzical look. "Mean?"

She shrugged, not wanting to delve into her own memories for elaboration. "You know. Kids can be cruel sometimes."

"I guess so. But other times . . . they're the best." He hesitated. "You don't want kids of your own?"

Marley couldn't help but laugh. "Me? Heck, no," she said sanguinely. "Me with kids would be like Martha Stewart with ring around the collar. J.Lo with a butt blaster. A Tarantino film with Julie Andrews as its star."

"The hills are alive," Jake sang in his deep voice, "with the sound of gunfire . . ."

"Exactly." She was glad he understood her so thoroughly. "When it comes to me and motherhood, we're completely incompatible. Bordering on impossible."

"Hmmm." Thoughtfully, he studied her. Then he nodded. "Well, we've just about exhausted the *Dream Date* resources for today. If you're going to keep that fifty bucks you bet, we're going to have to stick together longer." He checked his watch. "I have a couple more free hours. How about we blow this Popsicle stand and go shoot some darts at a place I know?"

Before she could answer, the tag-playing boy ran past. He

shrieked, trailing both a zoo balloon and his hapless younger sister in his wake. Both children collided with Carly, looked up at her with Kool-Aid smeared faces, then detoured.

She shuddered. "Sure. Darts. I think I've had about all I can take here in Kid-ville, anyway."

This stupid game show had to be rigged, Jake figured. There was no other explanation for it.

How else to account for the fact that Jake—sportscasting's single dad of the moment, currently wearing mud-smeared shoes—had been stuck with a sports-hating, child-challenged, fussy girly-girl like Carly? Paired with her, it would be next to impossible to win.

He'd been optimistic. Until she'd come out with that crack about kids. Now he knew the path to victory was going to be even tougher than he'd thought. He could already hear Rich canceling *Sports at Six*—and not picking up the option on his contract.

Damn. What the hell were the odds?

Determined not to go down without a fight, Jake decided he'd just have to give Carly a dose of that famous Jake Jarvis, hunk-of-the-billboards charisma. He'd talk with her, have fun with her, and make sure their dates were models of modern magnetism. He could do it. He was a charming guy. He'd make them both winners. Single-handedly, if necessary.

He started while they drove to their next destination in Jake's Accord. Since Carly had mentioned something about having taken a bus to the *Dream Date* auditions, he'd agreed to drive them wherever they went.

"That's nice perfume," he said, sniffing appreciatively at her light fragrance. It enlivened his entire car in a subtle but enjoyable way. "Is it some kind of exclusive designer stuff?"

In his experience, women *liked* exclusive designer stuff. The fancier the better. Jake glanced at her.

She looked back at him as though he'd just suggested she rolled in dog shit on a daily basis.

"No! It's commonplace, ordinary drugstore perfume. *Very* commonplace. *Very* ordinary."

Carly muttered something that sounded like a swearword. She raised her forearm and, while gazing out the window at the busy L.A. streets whizzing by, sniffed her wrist. She shook her head.

Jake didn't get it, but he wasn't done yet. When they reached the sports bar, he hurried around to Carly's side of the car. Chivalrously, he reached to help with her door. At the same moment, she swung it open.

"Ooooof!"

"Oh, Jake! I'm so sorry!"

Which explained why he walked into Champs—a place buzzing with neon, dark woods, and loud music—and placed his weirdest order ever. "A Bud, please. And an ice bag for my nuts."

He looked at Carly and manfully tried not to cry. "What would you like?"

"A vodka martini, very dry. Two olives, please. Oh, and I'd prefer Belvedere or Grey Goose, if you have it."

Jake and the bartender both raised their eyebrows.

"I mean"—she scanned the neon signs covering the walls in all the places not already occupied by sports paraphernalia—"a Budweiser?"

The bartender nodded and served up two longnecks. Jake handed one to Carly, then tossed some money on the bar. He grabbed the ice bag the bartender offered and limped gingerly toward a nearby booth.

Carly slid in across from him. "I'm very sorry about the car door."

He waved off her concern.

"I'm not used to people opening doors for me. Ever. In fact, if I want to go anyplace, I open every single door myself. No special treatment for Carly Christopher. None at all."

She shook her head emphatically. Jake swigged some beer to dull the wallop to his balls. He wondered why she felt the need to protest so strongly.

"I'll be fine," he told her.

"I really am sorry. I just forgot about my open-every-door-myself policy for a second, that's all."

Carly levered upward, bracing herself on the table to peer at his crotch. Of all the ways he might have hoped for this kind of intimate attention from her . . . this sure as hell wasn't one of them.

She winced. "Does it hurt much?"

"Only when I breathe."

Or *you* do.

Her upward-and-forward motion, tentative as it had been, had placed her breasts directly in his line of vision. Only inches from his face, those rounded swells teased him. Her pert nipples distended the fabric of her pink T-shirt.

Sure, her breasts were small. But they were damned cute. Jake imagined himself raising his hand to touch her, encountering the softness of her skin beneath his palm, feeling her suck in a breath as he stroked her.

Nice fantasy. He suffered the inevitable consequences of it a nanosecond later. A tingle shot to his groin, his cock valiantly tried to respond as usual . . . his balls throbbed. *Ouch.*

He swigged more Bud and made himself think about the starting rotation for the 1969 Mets.

"Only when you breathe? That's worse than I thought." Carly bit her lip, looking remorseful. Concerned. Then, she brightened. "But I'll bet I can help."

She formed a circle with her manicured thumb and middle finger, then brought her hand to her lips. A moment later, the rumble of nearby conversations, the ever-present jabbering of ESPN on the wall-mounted TVs, and the music from the jukebox were all dwarfed by a piercing whistle.

Carly beamed. "Neat, huh? I learned to do that for a movie."

Jake nodded gamely. She'd whistled so loudly, he'd temporarily lost hearing in his left ear. He wasn't sure what she'd said, but she looked so happy about it he couldn't bear to disappoint her.

She waved for the bartender. He stared blandly back at her.

"I know he can see me!" Carly groused, obviously perplexed. "He knows I'm trying to get his attention. There aren't any other customers getting drinks right now. What's his problem?"

Jake was about to tell her that Champs was a small place, where customers ordered for themselves at the bar. The owner didn't have the money for cocktail waitresses and bartenders who came at a whistle. He'd spent it all on satellite access and Pay-Per-View sports coverage, the real draws in this place. Before he could speak, though, Carly hustled to the bar.

"This man"—she gestured dramatically back toward Jake— "has a serious, *serious* groin injury!"

Jake sank lower in his booth.

"He's in a lot of pain," she went on. Jesus, but her voice carried. "Probably more pain than he'll admit to me."

At this, she threw a proud look over her shoulder. Did she expect Jake to applaud her insight? She was making him look like a damned crybaby. He cleared his throat and endeavored to look macho.

"He'll need more ice. A clean towel. Maybe a free beer, too!"

Some of the customers—regulars whom Jake all recognized—nudged each other and hooted. Some merely grinned. All watched avidly as Carly somehow secured everything she'd asked for, plus a bowl of pretzels, from the chagrined bartender. She sashayed across the sports bar, her trek an unexpectedly sexy display that didn't do anything to remove her from the guys' radar. She plunked everything down on the table.

At the sight of the second ice bag she held toward him, Jake shook his head. "My boys need numbness, not freezer burn."

Her forehead wrinkled in confusion. She waggled the bag.

"I don't need it. Thanks, anyway."

Her pleased, hopeful expression began to fade. Jake couldn't stand it. He accepted the second ice bag and carefully arranged it in his lap. His nuts already felt like the equivalent of two Ping-Pong balls in a deep freeze. What were a few more degrees of frostbite?

"Is that better?" she asked hopefully.

He grunted "yes" and wished for amnesia. No, he wished for amnesia for their amused spectators.

"Good. It's the least I could do to help."

She patted his hand, looking relieved. Obviously, she felt better now about whacking him with the car door. Carly had serious misperceptions about the healing powers of ice and Budweiser when it came to a man's prize package. Jake forgave her anyway. What else could he do?

They ignored their bonus pretzels. Jake was still too full from lunch, and Carly claimed she avoided anything that was fat-free. She assured him the pretzels might well be.

"The fattier, the better, that's my motto!" she told him as she pushed the bowl away. He didn't have the heart to reveal that the beer she'd been daintily sipping was completely fat-free—a fact he'd gleaned from Skip at KKZP. Skip was Jake's sometime running buddy, and was always on some crazy fitness plan or other. His Beer Bong Blast had only been the latest in a long—and failed—line of diet regimens.

Jake and Carly talked for the next half hour. During that time, the *Dream Date* crew caught up with them. Stealthily they filmed from a corner of the sports bar. Until the crew appeared, Jake almost forgot what he was supposed to be doing there. The reminder of their arrival kicked his original plan back into gear.

He was due to pick up Noah from day care in about an hour. Not much time left, but probably long enough to do what he had to do: charm Carly. No matter what.

"You know what?" she mused suddenly, resting her elbow on the table and plunking her chin in her hand. "We've been having such a good time talking, I forgot all about playing darts. That's what we came here for."

He took in her casual posture, the easiest she'd sported all day, and felt himself drawn toward her. Toward her princess-y appeal, her prettiness, her quirky sense of nut-crunch healing. It was almost as though . . . hey. Was he planning to grab the upper hand here, or what?

"Don't worry, we'll get to the darts," Jake said. "Hear that song?" He tilted his head toward the corner jukebox, from which a ballad had just started playing. "Let's dance first."

Before she could say no, Jake abandoned his spent ice bags. He stood, intending to whisk her away to the three-by-four dance floor. All women were ridiculously impressed by a man who danced in public. Voluntarily. Especially to Michael Bolton–style crap like they were playing right now. If he moved quickly, he could still keep up with his initial game plan.

The minute his feet hit the floor, Jake realized his mistake. His ice-benumbed groin was connected to his ice-benumbed hip flexors and all the other muscles that helped operate his legs. At sub-zero temperatures, none of them worked properly. His knees buckled. He pushed one arm onto the table for support and held the other out to Carly. He could do this.

No pain, no gain.

She looked oblivious to his tottering state. Also flattered, he noticed with relief. She gazed up at him with sparkling eyes and a semi-smile on her lips, then put her hand in his. They whooshed toward the dance floor—okay, *staggered* toward the dance floor. Gritting his teeth, Jake drew her into his arms.

"Are you sure you're up for this?" she asked.

She looked dubiously at him, as though he were a ninth-round draft pick. Her skepticism only made him twice as determined. He wasn't some kind of wuss. After all, he'd been whacked in the nuts with the door to an Accord, not a Buick.

"I'm fine." He tightened his arm around her slender waist, drawing her a little closer. "Better than fine."

It was true. As they danced, his body thawed . . . all over. Jake forgot about everything except Carly. She was a good dancer: graceful and steady, with an excellent sense of rhythm. He kept a respectful amount of distance between their bodies, but even so he felt in sync with her. They swayed together. They dipped and twirled. They laughed. Once, he swore he heard Carly sigh happily.

"This is nice." She tilted her face upward, giving him an appreciative look. A slight smile touched her lips. "I feel so anonymous."

Huh? That didn't make sense. "Anonymous?"

Her eyes widened. Her body tensed in his grasp. Carly sprang away, coming to a standstill about a foot away. "I mean, um, I feel so . . . like I might miss-the-bus. Missthe-bus." She mashed the words together. "You know, to get home."

Jake frowned. "But you said—"

"Miss-the-bus. Yup, that was it. Ha, ha. Sometimes those voice lessons really fall down on the job, don't they?"

She bolted for their table and grabbed her purse. Jake watched in confusion as she hastily crossed the room to stand in front of him again. She rose on tiptoes. She lifted her mouth as though she meant to kiss him on the cheek, then apparently thought better of it and stuck out her hand instead.

Automatically, he shook it. Then *he* thought better of it— what was he, a man or a mouse?—and lowered his head to kiss her good-bye.

Carly ducked. He'd swear she did. *That* was going to look super on their *Dream Date* compilation tape. He could hear the smarmy host narrating it already: "Whoa! Just grazed that one, buddy. A sa-wing and a miss!"

"Sorry to dance and run," she said, shrugging prettily.

"Wait. I'll drive you home."

"Thanks, but I'm really more of a bus girl."

He considered the logic of a stiletto-wearing Carly on the city bus. What was she, crazy?

She'd get her flimsy high heel stuck in a wad of gum, flail her purse to break her fall, wallop some unsuspecting criminal type with the twenty pounds of girl stuff she probably carried, and wind up inciting a cross-town brawl. Half the bus would take her side—Carly was just that kind of woman— the other half would take exception, and she'd have to escape from the brouhaha with a broken ankle and a sticky shoe. Knowing her, she'd announce the condition of the bus driver's nuts as she made her getaway. She'd indirectly cause the first embarrassment-related mass-transit fender bender ever.

He had to stop her.

Jake turned. Too late. She'd already gone.

Seven

Okay, so those "scrubbing bubbles" on the bathroom cleaner were a sucker's bet, Marley realized. Despite what the ads claimed, they really *didn't* "do the work . . . so you don't have tooooo!"

Perspiring and grungy, she swiped her forearm over her forehead. Wearily, she sat back on her heels. She glared at the bright-eyed cartoon scrubbing bubble on the spray bottle of cleaner, remembered all the commercials she'd seen as a kid touting this product, then glared at the bathtub in her new, *modest* apartment.

Okay, so it was really Meredith's apartment. After much coaxing, Marley had convinced her sister to temporarily swap living spaces with her—clearly, the most elegant solution to the problem. Marley had needed an everyday, ordinary apartment for Carly, and Meredith lived in one. Voilà! They'd switched lives for a while. Sort of.

Until now, Marley hadn't quite regretted her decision. But at this moment, she did. Because while lucky Meredith was probably lounging beside *her* swimming pool, enjoying *her* fruity drinks with tiny umbrellas as dispensed by *her* staff, Marley was stuck attempting to clean. It was like some freakish revenge for all the chores she'd skipped as a kid. It just wasn't fair.

No, hang on. It got even worse, she realized. Knowing Meredith, she was probably *reading* beside the pool. Reading not something entertaining (like a paperback novel) but something (ugh) enriching (like a study of advertising through the ages).

Thinking of it, Marley couldn't help but shake her head. Some people just didn't know how to enjoy life. And here *she* was, a person who *definitely* knew how to enjoy life . . . trapped in Blahville.

She glared at the scummy bathtub again. Like everything else here in Meredith's place, it required a ton of work to look respectable. The apartment was old, circa 1988 or so, and although it had come furnished with all of her sister's things, it wouldn't quite come clean.

Marley couldn't believe she was living in a place built before *Fantasy Family* had gone on the air. What was the matter with her sister? Didn't Meredith aspire to better things? The two of them had been buying training bras and worrying about getting braces when this one-bedroom-plus-bath was new.

Nestled in a quiet neighborhood filled with retirees and young families, Marley had to admit it was perfect for her purposes, though. Perfect for Carly, too. It was humble, unremarkable, and completely forgettable.

Her first nights here had been awful. Lonely and silent, they'd stretched through the darkness in a way that had thoroughly unnerved Marley. She'd never been alone before. Growing up, she'd lived with her family, of course. Later in her teen years, she'd had the company of Meredith and her friends and her co-stars on whatever soap or sitcom she was currently cast in. Once in her twenties, she'd been part of *Fantasy Family,* and had been able to afford round-the-clock companionship. She'd never expected doing without it to be so hard.

All during those first nights, Marley had clutched Gaffer to her in Meredith's creaky double bed. She'd whispered in the dark to her dog, knowing by his snuggles and occasional whimpers that he could sense her unease, and wanting to help him feel better. Now, after having weathered three such nights, she'd emerged stronger than ever.

Not strong enough, however, to battle soap scum.

Marley had begun the skirmish with lots of energy and positive vibes. She'd even dressed for success, in blue jeans rolled at the ankles, a red gingham shirt tied above her navel, a kerchief for her hair, and Keds. She looked like a housewife straight out a fifties Spic and Span commercial, and she'd thought she'd be able to scour like one, too. Apparently not.

The bathtub resisted her efforts the same way everything else did. The dishwasher burped soapsuds all over the earthtoned kitchen linoleum. The "free cable" constantly went on the fritz. The air conditioner blew burnt-smelling breezes, and the wall-to-wall sculptured carpeting soaked up stains like it had thirsted for spilled store-brand diet soda all its half-inch-high life. Existing here in the land of ordinary, everyday girls next door was no cakewalk, she'd discovered. But Marley was nonetheless determined to make a go of it.

As her acting teacher had once told her, it was impossible to truly build a character without having walked a mile in her shoes. (The character's shoes, not the acting teacher's. The acting teacher generally wore Birkenstocks, which were comfortable but limiting as far as characterization went.) So Marley was doing exactly that.

As far as was possible, she was getting by only on the resources Carly would have had. She'd turned over her bungalow and staff to Meredith, surrendered her BMW and driver, and relinquished all her starlet perks. For the time being, those things were her sister's to enjoy. From here on out, Marley intended to be as real and raw as they came.

Of course, it had all begun with that crash course on the city bus. After having blurted that ridiculously revealing "I feel so anonymous" to Jake, she'd skedaddled out of Champs in a blind panic . . . and found herself confronted with the necessity of doing something she'd never done before.

Taking public transit.

Two minutes after hesitantly sidling up to the bus shelter to peer at the schedule posted there, Marley chickened out. Other people were waiting, people who looked confident about the idea of abandoning taxis and limos and private, chauffer-driven cars. People who belonged. She grabbed her cell phone and called her sister.

"Meredith, you've got to help me!"

"What's wrong?"

"I'm about to ride the city bus!"

Silence. ". . . And?"

"That's it." Marley hugged herself. A car whizzed past on the street just inches from her feet, sending a blast of hot air toward her. She shrank back. "Help, please! What do I do?"

A woman sitting in the bus shelter gave Marley a shove on the backside. "Hey, watch it. You're standing on my foot."

Glancing over her shoulder, Marley mouthed an apology. Then she huddled into herself and whispered into the cell phone, "The other bus riders are hostile. It's like the fifth-grade cafeteria all over again."

"Everyone loved you in fifth grade," Meredith said, sounding distracted.

What was she doing? Working? During her twin sister's moment of distress? "Meredith!" Marley pleaded. "You're not that far away. Come pick me up, please?"

"What, is your driver off having a cosmetic butt lift or something?"

That wasn't a bad idea, Marley mused. Hugh had been complaining lately about the broadening effects of his long hours in the car. Maybe when this was over, she'd . . . nah.

"I gave him the rest of the day off."

Quickly, Marley filled in her sister with a shorthand version of all that had transpired since Hugh had dropped her off at the *Dream Date* auditions that morning. Jake. The coffee philosophy. Jake. The goat attack. Jake. The delights of fatty food, and the horrors of rowdy kids high on Kool-Aid. Jake, and his sexy version of slow dancing—which had mostly involved lots of touching, easy movements, and staring soulfully into each other's eyes.

She left out the part where she'd nearly maimed the man. It was too devastating to reveal, and she already felt bad enough. Jake had been forgiving, though.

Somehow, Marley already felt a little closer to him. Close enough to feel warm where he touched her, tingly elsewhere, and a teensy bit breathless. Close enough to relax in his arms, to savor the novelty of being noticed for *herself* instead of her role as that bubble-headed Tara . . . to blurt out things both truthful and better left unsaid.

"Besides, even if I hadn't given Hugh the day off, I can't let Jake see me jumping into my BMW," she explained to Meredith desperately. "I told him I was taking the bus."

"So take the bus."

"I . . ." Wow, was this embarrassing. "I don't know how."

More silence. "Sometimes I forget exactly how sheltered you really are."

Marley knew her sister was shaking her head. She pictured Meredith behind a pile of the research books she loved so much, with her hair in that unflattering scraggly ponytail of hers and her face devoid of makeup. Both non-style choices were further rejections of all things starlet-and-Marley related. Marley tried not to let that fact hurt her feelings.

As always, it did. A little.

"Please, Meredith. Please, please, please. I see the bus headed this way." Marley leaned sideways to track the progress of the huge vehicle. Out of the corner of her eye, she glimpsed Jake as he emerged from Champs and headed in her direction. "Jake's coming, too! I see him."

He would insist on driving her home. He was just that kind of guy. But she couldn't let him. Home was a decidedly non-Carly Hollywood Hills bungalow worth a cool few mil.

Meredith sighed. The sound of a book thumping closed

came through the receiver. "First you'll need correct change. Bus drivers accept exact fares only."

Marley searched her purse. "I have two twenties, five tens"—tip money for messengers and maître d's—"my American Express card, and a Platinum Visa."

"The fare is a dollar thirty-five."

"I'll tip the driver eight-sixty-five. He'll be happy."

"He'll be shutting the doors in your face."

"Because I offered him a tip? That's crazy!"

"Welcome to the real world, sis."

Shaking her head, Marley examined her resources again. Nothing in her "Carly" life functioned the way she expected it to. She spotted Jake waving to catch her attention. The bus lumbered ever closer, spewing exhaust fumes.

"After you get on," Meredith went on instructing, "you'll have to watch for your stop."

"Can't I just give the driver my address?"

"Tell me you're not serious."

She had been. Sort of. After years of being driven places, Marley wasn't comfortable with fending for herself. How would she even know if this bus went to her neighborhood? She'd certainly never noticed it, if it did.

Biting her lip, she tried squinting at the schedule again. At the same moment, Jake saw the bus approach and hurried up.

"Carly!" he yelled. "Wait!"

His pursuit gave her the nerve she needed. Marley turned to the "you're standing on my foot" woman and traded a ten-dollar bill for several ones and some coins. In the process, she made a friend for the day. The woman smiled and let Marley move to the front of the small waiting group, just as the bus squealed to a stop. Hot air and street dust billowed from beneath its tires.

Yuck. But Marley didn't have time to be particular. Portraying Carly had pushed her to the limit of her improvisation skills. Another one of Jake's smiles might coax the whole truth out of her. That would jeopardize everything.

She teetered onto the bus in her heels, frowned as she tried to get her bearings on the crowded vehicle, and then deposited her money in the fare box the driver wearily indicated.

Twenty minutes later, having made a clean getaway, she looked through the window and recognized the distinctive script letters of the Beverly Center sign. Although she wasn't home yet, Marley decided it was better to get off the bus someplace familiar.

She excused herself from her companions, offered the driver a grateful smile, and stepped onto the sidewalk. As the bus pulled into traffic again, she watched it go with a sense of accomplishment . . . and confusion. Was that really *Jake's* picture on the side of the bus?

It was. And it was Jake's picture on the ad banner at the top of the taxi she hailed, too. Curiously, Marley peered at it as she opened the rear door. *Get your motor revved,* it read. *Jake Jarvis, Sports at Six. For complete NASCAR coverage.*

She wasn't sure what NASCAR was, but judging by the seductive look on Jake's face—and his state of partial undress in a mostly unbuttoned shirt—its coverage was delectable. Hmmm . . . maybe sports were worth watching after all.

Marley's mass-transit adventures had come to a happy ending when the taxi deposited her in front of her bungalow. She'd strode through the security gate, successfully fought an urge to kiss her BMW parked outside, and then immediately launched into full-scale alter-ego mode . . . beginning with moving to Meredith's ordinary-girl apartment.

Which was what had brought her to this point. Scrubbing soap scum.

The stuff was like radioactive waste. It wasn't budging. Probably, Marley had introduced some unusual dirt molecules when giving Gaffer a bath last night (even her dog had been denied his usual pet pampering). Either that, or she was just clueless when it came to cleaning.

Okay, clueless won. Hands down. She'd never had chores as a child, because she'd been too busy going to auditions, lessons of every variety, or tutors to help make up school-work. Her parents had cut her a certain amount of slack due to her career. Later, she'd employed household help. Now, Marley realized, she'd grown into a stunted person, incapable of more than rudimentary tidying.

She braced herself on the tub and examined the scum at close range. From here, she could see that the tile grout needed spiffing up, too. *Ugh*. She'd have to call in professionals. Experts with knowledge and equipment . . . and heavy-duty super tools.

Sure, that's what she'd do. Call in a cleaning service. She owed it to her sister, didn't she? In thanks for all her help?

She reached for her cell phone. At her side, Gaffer watched her. His fur still gleamed from the silicone styling gloss she'd sprayed onto it. It occurred to Marley that maybe he didn't need the three-hundred-dollar "pampered pooch" treatment he usually received from her private grooming service. He looked pretty darn good.

She looked up the number of her cleaning service and dialed. As she waited for an answer, she gave Gaffer a pat. He looked balefully back at her, his big brown eyes filled with the knowledge that she was cheating. *Cheating*.

You made me endure a homemade bath just so you could call in the cavalry when the going got tough? his doggie gaze seemed to say. *I endured amateur blow-drying, for this?*

Guilt-stricken, Marley hung up the phone. "You're right, boy. There must be another way."

Four days of living as Carly had taught her a thing or two. One of the most significant of those things was the importance of creativity. Biting her lip, Marley gave the situation some thought. Then she picked up an exfoliating facial puff from the vanity and went to work.

Voilà! Perfection. Proudly, she gazed at the results her ingenuity had wrought. The bathtub gleamed a decidedly glorious white, and the grout looked better, too. The facial puff had really done the job.

Marley lifted the puff and looked at it. She was considering what the heck it had been doing to her *skin* all these years when the doorbell rang. Company!

Smoothing her gingham shirt and jeans, she hurried to the door.

"In the good old days, news viewers were predominately white, middle-aged males," Rich said. He leaned back in his upholstered desk chair at KKZP and fixed Jake and Sid with a serious expression. "They watched broadcasts in taverns on dinky black-and-white TVs, and were damned grateful to do it. But these days, more than half of our viewers are female."

Sid shifted uneasily.

"Women care about who's on *Oprah*. About what happened on their soaps. About human-interest stories and sentimental real-life bullshit. They don't care about sports."

"Tell that to the women of the WNBA," Jake said. "They're probably too busy scoring three-pointers to worry about who married whose long-lost ex-husband on *All my Children*."

Rich ignored that. "We're going to make them care about sports. Sports as human drama. Sports as inspiration. Sports as entertainment. That's the reason for the media tie-ins—"

Jake thought of the lobby banner, only subtly toned down by the addition of banana-print swim trunks. He frowned.

"—and that's the reason for using you, Jake, as a draw. For some damned reason, your appeal skews high among female viewers. Our mail and our call-ins show it. So we're going to make the most of it. We're going to focus on you harder than ever—"

"I'm a serious journalist." Jake didn't want management to forget that in this idiotic chase for ratings. "That's what *I'm* going to focus on. This *Dream Date* thing won't last forever."

"Neither will you, with an attitude like that." Rich glanced at the stack of contract renewals waiting for his approval, then folded his arms. "Remember, sports is an entertainment product that just happens to be aired on my newscast. It's expendable."

So are you. It didn't take a genius to read the subtext here.

Reluctantly, Jake settled in. "Why the chase for female viewers, anyway?"

"Advertising." Rich rubbed his fingers together as though handling money. "Women make most of the purchasing decisions in households today."

Advertisers wanted to buy spots during the programming that hauled in their target audience. Even as a former jock, Jake knew that much.

"We should program *to* them, then," Sid suggested. "Load up on talk shows and infomercials and soaps—"

Rich shook his head. "Opposite other news broadcasts? We'd be cutting our throats. As a local affiliate, news—especially weather and local crime—is still our bread and butter. If we can lure female viewers from other stations' news to ours, though—"

"Our bread is buttered on both sides," Jake finished. "Fine. I've got it." He stood. "And I've got an interview with Robert Horry in half an hour, plus a voice-over/sound on tape to get ready for tonight's package. Thanks for the pep talk, Rich."

"Not so fast, Jarvis. I'm not finished yet."

Hell. There was more. Jake waited.

The news director steepled his fingers and remained silent until Jake took a seat again. Then he said, "I'm cutting your duties. Temporarily. You need time to spend on the *Dream Date* project. Until it's finished, you're off reporting. Skip will pick up the slack."

"I can do both."

"You don't have to. For the next few weeks, it's anchor only. Now scram, and go buy that *Dream Date* lady of yours some flowers or something. Make a good impression. That's an order."

Jake frowned, pissed that he was being denied the part of his job he loved most. Anchoring was all right, but the real challenge was in reporting. Talking with players, managers, and coaches; covering games; interviewing fans; putting together video plus voice-over packages for the nightly broadcast. He loved the real work involved.

He glanced at Sid. The poor guy shifted in his seat, nervously waiting to see if Jake would agree. For his sake, Jake nodded. "Fine."

Rich must have seen the muscle twitching in Jake's jaw, because he spread his arms in a conciliatory gesture. "You won't be docked those hours, of course. Consider it a paid hiatus for the guy who's about to hook the minnows that will draw in the bigger fish."

"They're women, not bait."

"Whatever. Beat it. Go be charming."

Jake turned to leave.

"Oh, and Jarvis?" Rich added. "There's a lot riding on this. You'd better not lose that game show."

When Marley opened her sister's modest front door, Meredith was standing on the concrete second-floor stairway that served as a stoop. She held a bundle of something in her arms. Before Marley could so much as greet her, her sister's gaze shot to the facial puff in Marley's hand.

She rolled her eyes. "What, you knew I was coming and decided to ambush me into a facial? Please, Marley. Give me a little credit."

"Would you prefer a makeover?" Marley shot back, arching her brows innocently. "A new haircut, some lipstick—"

"Bite me."

"Charming. Really." She opened the door wider.

Meredith made a face and entered. Apparently, sibling rivalry never died. It only curled up and hibernated occasionally.

But honestly . . . seeing Meredith schlump into her apartment's humble living-room-slash-dining-area in a mismatched set of khaki pants and a droopy black T-shirt just about broke Marley's heart. Didn't she have any pride in her appearance? Didn't she care if her ponytail made her look like a reject from a sock hop, her lack of makeup made her look like a low-rent Camille (not the Garbo version), and her posture stole three inches from her height?

"Let's not start that makeover business again," Meredith said, scraping something unidentifiable and brown from the sole of her combat boot. "I'm on my lunch break. I just stopped by to drop these off."

She held out her armload. Marley gingerly accepted and examined it.

"A pink polyester uniform? This looks like something Helga would wear."

"Your housekeeper should be so lucky. It's for you. I got you that job you asked me about."

"I'm a professional fashion victim?"

"Har, har. You're a waitress."

A waitress? Nervousness clutched at Marley's heart. It was true that she needed a part-time job for Carly, but she'd hoped for something a little more . . . *glamorously* girl-next-door-ish.

"Don't panic, it's only temporary. Just like you requested," Meredith said.

She made her way around the apartment, probably checking to make sure Marley hadn't destroyed it somehow. She was such a skeptic.

"One of the ladies in the museum coffee shop is going on vacation to Niagara Falls," Meredith went on, "and they needed somebody to fill in. I suggested you."

In dismay, Marley raised the uniform to her body, assessing the effect. It was an above-the-knee zippered dress with a white collar and cuffs. *French-maid style, in Pepto Bismol pink.* Its fabric was thin, with permanent darts stitched at the bustline.

She'd never fill it out. Not in a million years. She'd have

to wear her cutlets just to garner any tips. After all, she wanted Carly to do well.

"It's Fifties Month at the museum," Meredith went on to say. She worked as a researcher, historian, and all-around gal Friday at a local popular-culture museum. "That's why the uniform looks like that, to complement the collections. Last month, all the waitresses wore togas."

"It's . . . polyester," Marley said.

Meredith rolled her eyes. "It's yours." She explained the details of where and when "Carly" was expected to report for duty. "Don't make me regret doing you this favor."

Marley was hurt she could even think that. "I swear, I'm dead serious about doing a good job with this."

"That's what you said about Sparky."

"Our goldfish died twenty years ago!"

Meredith sighed. "Look, just don't fluff this off, okay? Please. My reputation is on the line."

Her reputation as a scholarly, slobby, stick-in-the-mud, Marley thought, still miffed over the Sparky accusation. She didn't voice those thoughts, though. Instead, she nodded solemnly.

"I'll do my best," she said . . . and hoped like heck her best would be good enough.

After receiving a few more words of advice from Meredith—and after giving her sister a grateful hug for her help—Marley said good-bye to Meredith at the door. She watched Meredith navigate along the sidewalks of Carly's apartment complex, her stride schlumpy but her gaze fixed on her destination.

Marley envied her that. Meredith had a purpose in life, an interesting job she loved, and the respect of her colleagues. Marley's Hollywood colleagues had already forgotten her, she suspected. Stardom didn't have a long life span, but it was all she knew. She needed it.

She closed the door and picked up her temporary waitress

uniform. Thoughtfully, she stroked her thumb over the awful, scratchy pink fabric. The woman who usually wore this uniform lived an ordinary life, a life Marley was only imitating. Was she happy with it? Or did she yearn for something more, the way Marley did?

Sighing, she set the uniform aside. It was time to meet her favorite prop guy, Archie, to pick up the atmospheric clunker of a car he'd promised her. Marley could hardly wait to find out what he'd turned up.

Eight

Saturday was a sacred time at the Jarvis house.

It was sports time.

Jake selected a game on TV; as a professional necessity, he subscribed to every Pay-Per-View sports channel. Noah selected a variety of snacks. Then they snuggled up together on the sofa to watch grown men wallop the hell out of each other in contests of skill, brawn, and bravery.

Today, the game du jour was football. A classic 1998 matchup between the Philadelphia Eagles and the New York Giants, rebroadcast on ESPN Classic.

"Yay!" Noah yelled as the tailback broke away and completed a fifty-yard running play to tie the game. "Touch-down!"

He leaped from the sofa with his Nerf football tucked under his arm. Still in his pajamas, Noah ran circles around the coffee table, whooping and hollering. He stopped to exchange a high five with his dad, then ran across their apartment to the kitchen doorway.

"Daddy! Daddy!"

Jake looked up to see the Nerf ball sailing a wobbly trajectory toward his head. He caught it easily, then tossed it back to Noah. Grinning, the boy scampered back to the sofa. He grabbed two Chee-tos from the open bag and munched, adding to the fluorescent orange mustache already on his upper lip.

Jake leaned forward to wipe it away. "Be sure to brush your teeth extra thoroughly today. You know how it is on Saturdays."

"No Miss Suzy for me," Noah recited, hugging his football in the crook of one arm. "No work for you. All junk food, all day. Yahoo!"

He started running again. He paused to watch the Eagles' kicker go for the extra point, then whooped when it was good. He came back to the sofa and fidgeted beside Jake, then selected a Twinkie and settled down to eat it as the game continued.

Contented, Jake glanced down at Noah's happy face and sticky little fingers. He stroked a hand over his son's hair, considering how lucky he really was. Noah was his. All that little-boy love was Jake's to savor and to return. He didn't have to share Noah with anyone else.

Even more importantly, Noah didn't have to share his dad. Jake's attention wasn't divided between several children, the way his father's had been. Everything he had went to Noah, and that was the way Jake liked it.

Some would have said Noah needed a mother. Hell, some had. Jake didn't agree. They were doing fine as they were. Adding a woman to the mix would only divide Jake's attention and steal time from his son. He could count on himself, Jake knew; he wasn't so sure about anyone else.

Besides, this way no one could complain their weekly junk-food fest was giving the kid a food complex, food allergies, or high cholesterol. No one could argue with Jake's methods of ensuring cooperation (baseball-card rewards), doling out punishment (a stern look usually did the trick), or regulating proper little-boy attire (the pajamas at ten-thirty were a case in point).

He and Noah were a perfect team. They didn't need anybody else.

The game continued. During halftime, Jake and Noah grabbed baseballs and mitts, then went outside to their apart-

ment complex's grassy play area. A few grounders later—
their games of catch were more like lawn bowling, but that
was the way Noah liked it—they were back on the sofa for
the second half.

"Hey, what's that sound?" Noah asked, cocking his head.

"I dunno." Jake listened.

Tap, tap, tap.

"Somebody at the door?" Noah wondered.

"It doesn't sound like knocking. It sounds like—"

Before he could guess, somebody *did* knock. Jake
brushed the Chee-tos crumbs from his T-shirt, stretched out
his legs in his worn Levi's, and went to answer it.

"Surprise!" Carly said when he opened the door. "I figured it was my turn to organize a date for us, and we did exchange addresses at *Dream Date,* so here I am! I've come to
kidnap you for a picnic."

She hefted a wicker hamper, looking bright-eyed and
beautiful. She'd done something to make her dark hair wavy.
It was different. Nice. A quick glance downward told Jake
that either she'd dressed in a white lacy shirt and shorts
which weren't visible behind her picnic basket, or she was
naked from the waist down.

He hoped for the latter.

"Aren't you going to invite me in?" she asked.

"Uh, sure." He held the door open.

Carly sashayed in. He realized the *tap, tap, tap* he'd heard
earlier had been the sound of her high-heeled shoes clicking
against the sidewalk. When he saw her from behind, he also
realized she was *not* naked from the waist down. As consolation, though, what she had on was the next best thing: a pair
of denim cutoffs that made the most of her long, long legs.

She caught him looking. Seemed flustered. "I know these
shoes aren't exactly Saturday casual."

"I wasn't looking at your shoes."

Even more flustered. "But this *is* a date, right? And
they're thongs. And the heels are only an inch and a half
high. I figure that's close enough to appropriate."

In that getup, Jake didn't want her anywhere near "appropriate." He wanted her wild and willing and headed in his direction. Carly looked riotously fresh, from the froufrou fabric daisies on her shoes to the cotton-candy pink on her fingernails. She also looked sexy as hell. Sure, she was wearing enough jewelry to rival a major league player's collection, but jewelry could be removed, piece by piece . . . just like everything else she had on.

"You look good," he said.

This "sportscaster and the Pop Tart" match up of theirs might actually work, he decided in that moment. At this rate, Jake felt ready to send the *Dream Date* viewer vote tallies into overdrive.

Sexual attractiveness? A billion points, Doug!

In the background, the TV pumped out the sounds of the game and Dick Enberg blathered on about a penalty. The natural noise—crowd sounds—increased. Jake realized dimly that the Giants must be going for that game-saving fourth down they needed.

Carly frowned slightly, seeming unsure as to where to put her picnic hamper. "I hope you don't mind that I stopped by. It looks like you're in the middle of a—oh!"

Suddenly, Jake felt two small arms clamp around his thighs from behind. Next came the telltale sensation of a face being buried in the back of his jeans as Noah hid behind his dad. His son had a death grip on his quadriceps, and didn't appear to be planning to let go anytime soon.

"My son, Noah," Jake said by way of introduction—and explanation. "He takes a little while to warm up to new people. Just don't make any sudden moves, and he'll be fine."

"Your . . . your son?"

"Yeah. He turned four last month."

Eyes widening, she looked around the small apartment. If she was looking for Noah's mother, she wouldn't get far.

"Tell me you're divorced," Carly said, backing up.

He shook his head. "I'm not divorced."

She gawked, then swiveled on her heel. "The *Dream Date*

people really should have screened for this type of thing," she said as she strode back to the door. "Married men should *not* be trolling for dream dates!"

He smiled. "I didn't exactly have to troll. You picked *me* up at the coffeemaker, remember?"

"Arrgh!" Carly marched back and jabbed her finger at his chest. "I was just being *nice!* Besides, *you* picked me up."

Noah angled his head sideways. "She looks too big to pick up," he whispered.

"Shhh," Jake told him. "Every lady is light as a feather. Remember that, son. Your life will go lots more smoothly."

Carly glared at him. She tossed her head. "I," she announced, *"am* light as a feather."

"See?" Jake told Noah. The boy nodded wisely.

"And I *don't* need to be picked up." She strode to the doorway again, then paused for a dramatic moment. "Not that I'd allow *you* to do it, anyway."

Noah tugged on his dad's sleeve. "She goes back and forth a lot."

"Kind of like one of your remote-control cars, huh, buddy?"

Carly huffed and opened the door. Jake realized he'd misled her. He unpeeled Noah from his legs to hurry after her.

"Don't do that." He met her in the doorway. Gazed down at her seriously. "Stay. I'll call my sister to hang out with Noah, and we can go on your picnic. I'll explain everything."

Suspiciously, she examined him. "I don't date married men. *Or* men who are involved with other women."

"You say that like it's some kind of loophole you're dragging closed."

She arched a brow.

He was offended she thought so little of him. "I generally stick to one woman at a time. It's better for my sanity."

"Fine." Carly adjusted the picnic basket in her arms. She glanced over Jake's shoulder at Noah, who'd plunked himself on his knees on the sofa and was watching them over the back of it. "But I can't let you call a baby-sitter."

"It's no trouble. My sister lives pretty close by, and—"

"And if I'm going to learn all about you, I'll have to learn about your whole life," Carly pointed out. She seemed gamely ready to accept this new development and run with it. "Including your son. Noah will come with us, of course."

When she'd concocted this picnic scheme, Marley had planned to launch a wonderfully romantic rendezvous on the grounds of the Griffith Observatory. Ever since seeing the place in *Rebel Without a Cause,* she'd decided it was the perfect spot for couples. Because honestly . . . if it was good enough for Natalie Wood and James Dean, it was good enough for anybody, right?

But Marley and Jake and Noah were a threesome. Not a couple. Plus, it seemed possible that seeing his father get romantic with an unknown woman might scar little Noah for life. So Marley switched plans. She piled everyone into her battered-looking car, and they headed for the kid-friendly La Brea Tar Pits instead.

"This is a *great* car," Jake said as Marley navigated through the endless L.A. traffic. "A real classic."

"It is?" It had four wheels and it ran. It looked decrepit enough for Carly to afford. That was all that had mattered to Marley when Archie had dropped it off. "What's so classic about it?"

"Are you kidding me? Everything. This car"—he paused for dramatic effect—"is the 1977 Super Bowl of cars. I mean, look at it. It's totally classic."

"Oh, I get it." Marley gripped the steering wheel harder. "That's just a nice euphemism for 'hunk of junk,' isn't it?" She felt wounded on Carly's behalf. "Well, maybe this is all I can afford. Have you thought of that? Huh?"

For a moment, Jake looked discomfited. Obviously, he was considering exactly how ordinary, how real and raw, Carly really was. He ran his hand over the vinyl dashboard soberly, as though realizing how common all of it truly was.

"Are you kidding me?" he asked. "This is a '69 Mustang

Coupe with a 302 V-8 engine, fastback body, and all the goodies. This is not a hunk of junk."

Uh-oh. Had she inadvertently bagged the car equivalent of an original Chanel suit, designed by Coco herself?

She remembered Archie saying something when he'd dropped off the car. Something like, "You're not exactly the '89 Yugo type, Marley." She hadn't had a clue what he'd meant.

"Well . . . it's pretty loud," she said skeptically.

"It's supposed to be loud. *Vroom, vroom.*"

Noah joined in from his buckled-in booster in the backseat. *Vroom, vroom* competed with the rumble of the engine. Men and their cars. Glancing sideways, Marley caught the look of admiration on Jake's face as they continued to their destination, and wondered if she and Archie had blown it. This car was impressing Jake way too much to help establish Carly's ordinariness.

"It doesn't even have a CD player," she pointed out.

"That's what radios are for."

"An automatic transmission would really be nicer."

He scoffed. "Where's the adventure in that?"

"I'm pretty sure it's an official antique."

"Like I said, a classic." He gave her a boyish grin. "But if it's that tough on you, let me drive."

Marley couldn't help but grin back. "No way. I have a feeling I'd have to crowbar you out of the driver's seat afterward."

"Maybe." Jake watched her drive for a moment. "It's still a pretty great car for a bus girl."

She felt his gaze sweep over her, beginning at her white eyelet peasant-style shirt and moving downward to her legs. She wished Carly had been able to afford a self-tanner application session at the spa. As it was, Marley had been forced to make do with a tube of drugstore InstaTan, and the resulting color had been neither golden enough nor dark enough to truly . . . Hey, it wasn't the state of her fake tan Jake was checking out, Marley realized. It was *her.*

Instantly, she felt warmer. Sexier. More feminine. She glanced sideways again, and found him still looking. His gaze lifted from her legs to her breasts, and her nipples tightened in response. She was braless. Surely he could see the effect he was having on her. After a few moments, though, Jake only released a pent-up breath and examined her profile.

"Where have you been all my life?" he asked.

Marley sighed. He really was too sweet. Dreamily, she braked for a stoplight. "Say that again," she begged.

"I said, where was your car earlier this week? When you rode the bus?"

Screech. The pleasant fantasy she'd been building in her head clanged to a stop. She must have imagined his first question in her eagerness to spin a gooey, hearts-and-flowers fantasy around poor Jake—the original sports-and-sportscars type. Now, she had to address the real issue.

What was that line Archie had told her to use? Oh, yeah.

"My car's been in the shop," she said, being sure to employ the long-suffering delivery Archie had specified. "You know. Marigold problems."

Jake squinted. "Manifold problems?"

"Those, too." Marley spotted the modern gray architecture of the Page Museum at the La Brea Tar Pits and swung the car into a parking space. Hurriedly, she switched off the ignition. "We're here! Who's ready for a picnic?"

"Me!" Jake and Noah yelled. Noah waved his stuffed armadillo toy. Gleefully, he hurled it toward Marley.

It pelted her in the head.

"Sorry!" he shouted. He chuckled.

"That's okay," she said, trying not to grit her teeth. She could be a good sport about this, and she would. She handed back the armadillo.

Jake had already gotten out of the car. He was headed for the rear door to unbuckle Noah from his booster seat. Marley followed suit and opened the driver's side rear door to retrieve the picnic basket.

She leaned in. Jake did, too. Their eyes met, and Marley's hand stilled on the picnic basket handle. Jake really was the most wonderful-looking man. His square jaw was shadowed with stubble—it was a Saturday, after all, and she *had* caught him unaware—lending him a rugged, macho look. His jeans and T-shirt showed off his fit physique and highlighted the sturdy ease with which he carried himself. His horn-rims added just the right touch of practicality. They transformed Jake from untouchable hunk to very approachable everyday guy. The combination was powerfully appealing.

He smiled, and she was sunk. Just like that, she knew she had to have him. Here, there, on the car's marigold—she didn't care where.

A horn honked. An electronic news gathering van pulled into the parking space behind them, then their assigned *Dream Date* camera and audio teams piled out.

"I've gotta pee!" Noah hollered at the same moment. "Right now!"

The intimacy between Jake and Marley vanished. A short distance away, the TV crew began setting up.

"Great." Jake gave her an accusing look as he finished unbuckling a squirming Noah. "We're on *Candid Camera* again."

"It's part of the gig," she reminded him.

He stepped back to allow Noah room to get out. Marley wrestled her picnic basket free. They stared at each other over the top of the car.

"I didn't want my son on TV."

"Well, I didn't want you to have a son at all!"

That did it. Jake's mouth flattened into a straight, stubborn line. He stooped to capture Noah's hand in his. "We'll be right back."

"Jake, I'm sorry!" Marley said, hurrying around the car to stop him. "That came out all wrong. I didn't mean—"

He held up his palm, his back already to her. "Save it."

"I was just surprised, that's all," she told him earnestly. "You can't blame me for that."

But he did. Clearly. And words to the contrary were useless. Spine rigid, Jake led Noah up the grassy slope outside the museum . . . farther and farther away from her.

"I'm no good with kids, that's all," Marley murmured, bleakly watching as the two of them crested the rear stairs and headed toward the entrance to the building. Noah did a little gotta-pee jig, then trundled down the steps out of sight. "Never having had a chance at being a real kid myself, that is."

Marley sighed. She'd made a mess of this all right, and she had no idea how to fix it. Children were at least as foreign to her as the goats at the petting zoo had been—probably more so. She doubted she could placate Noah with a handful of Altoids and a pat on his tummy.

A member of the *Dream Date* crew approached her. Mutely, she put down her picnic basket and stood as he outfitted her with a wireless lavalier mic and Minicam.

"Good thing we followed you in order to get some establishing shots of you driving to pick up Jake," the crew member said. "Otherwise, we'd never have tracked you here. You're supposed to call in if your date plans change."

"I know. Sorry," she mumbled. "I'll do better next time."

She had to do better, Marley knew. And she swore she would. She'd do better at everything. Just as soon as Jake and Noah returned.

When Jake exited the rest rooms with Noah, the *Dream Date* crew was waiting to wire him with the usual reality-TV accoutrements. After they'd finished and returned to their filming spot, Jake continued down the hill. The first person he saw was Carly.

"Thank God! You came back!" she cried.

She hustled up the grassy slope outside the museum, her face alight with relief and her hands filled with what looked like little blue pillowcases. Napkins, Jake realized. Cloth napkins, each one probably bigger than that itty-bitty sleeveless shirt she had on. Formal linens, for a picnic?

With those napkins fluttering, Carly closed the distance between them. Clearly, she meant to continue their conversation. Given what she'd said about his having a son, Jake knew he wouldn't want Noah around for this.

He released Noah's hand. "Go on and run around a little," he suggested. "Stay on the grass. The I-Zone. I don't want to have to give you ary penalty warnings."

"Okay. The I-Zone," Noah agreed, confirming their usual game plan. Noah would play only in the places where Jake could see him—the I-can-see-you Zone. "Yippee!"

He scampered off, jumping up and down with an excess of little-boy energy. Now all that remained was telling Carly exactly what she could do with her damned "I didn't want you to have a son!" remarks. Jake frowned, started forward . . . and was instantly flattened by a surprise tackle.

"Ooof!"

The breath squeezed from his midsection as Carly barreled straight into him. She flung her arms around him, too. Okay, so it wasn't technically a full-on tackle, and he wasn't technically flattened by the wee hundred-odd pounds of feminine impact she mustered, but Carly did have a killer hug.

Jake resisted it. He was pissed, dammit. He had a right to be. It didn't matter how good Carly felt. The wonderful curviness of her body slapped up against his would not change his mind.

"You took so long," she mumbled against his chest. "I was worried you wouldn't come back."

She sounded so pitiful, he had to withstand an urge to comfort her. "You've obviously never taken a four-year-old to the bathroom," he said grudgingly. "Washing hands takes days. Playing with the dryers takes weeks. Glaciers move faster."

She squeezed harder, pinning his arms against his sides. "I'm just glad you're not mad."

"Oh, I'm mad."

Carly leaned backward. She examined his face. For a moment, he thought she might panic and run. But she only drew in a deep breath and appeared to gather her courage.

"I'm so sorry. I didn't mean that the way it came out." She grabbed his hand in an iron grip and dragged him across the grass. "Let me make it up to you. How about some water?"

Hastily, she knelt at their picnic spot. She'd covered the grass with a blanket—a five-by-five square of fabric that co-ordinated with the froufrou napkins—and she'd spread out an array of dishes, too. Real dishes, not paper plates. Jake also spotted cutlery, stemware, and a bouquet of flowers propped in a jar of water.

Carly had really gone all out, as though she truly wanted this picnic to be a nice one. And she was moving as though she feared he'd bail out on their alfresco date at any moment. He watched her frown of concentration as she hurriedly retrieved a few more things, and felt himself waver still further.

Then Jake spotted Noah creeping up on a sparrow pecking at the grass, his little boy's concentration fierce. Love for his son welled up. It easily outweighed the appeal of Carly's good intentions and bodacious body. Jake might be a *Dream Date* contestant for the next few weeks . . . but he was a father for life.

He folded his arms over his chest. "You were out of line with that crack about Noah."

"I know. I was surprised." Her voice sounded muffled as she fished something out of the picnic hamper. He couldn't see her face. "You never mentioned having a son."

"I try to keep him out of the limelight."

"Understandable." Nodding, she uncapped a bottle of Evian and poured some into a glass. From a compartment in the picnic basket, Carly retrieved ice and a lime wedge. She added those to the glass, too, arranging the garnish just so. "Being in the public eye can be tough on kids."

"You're right. It can be."

"I know. I once had . . . a friend who did some acting as a child. The kids in our school never let her live it down. If they weren't making fun of some part she'd played, they were accusing her of being snobby. Or laughing when she fell behind in schoolwork after being away on location."

She handed him the water, nestling the delicate stemware in Jake's big palm. Icy condensation chilled his fingers. He felt ridiculous holding it—Carly's idea of a simple glass of water was one umbrella short of being a sissy blender drink. But he cradled it, all the same.

"Her mom always said those kids were just jealous," Carly went on. "But I had my doubts. There were so many of them, and only one of my friend. Majority rules."

"Not necessarily." Jake drank. He could recognize a peace offering as well as the next guy. This wasn't just sissified water. It was an apology in a glass. "Where's your friend now?"

"Still acting. At least as much as she can." Carly poured another glass of water, no ice. She fiddled with arranging three lime wedges in it. "Only now she can pay for friends. An entire entourage of them."

Pay for friends? Jesus, that was a sad idea. Only in the screwed up world of Tinseltown, Jake guessed. "Except you."

"Me?"

"You're her friend without being paid for it."

"Sure. Of course." Brightly, Carly glanced up at him and changed the subject. "So, what's the deal with you and Noah? Where's his mom?"

Jake hesitated, studying his glass of water. He considered the fact that Carly liked her water specially bottled in France, served up in a fancy goblet, and enhanced with a garnish . . . while he occasionally liked his straight from the garden hose while washing his car.

Maybe, as a woman who'd never experienced parenthood, Carly really didn't understand how thoughtless her words had been. Maybe Jake needed to cut her some slack. Maybe he *did* owe her an explanation.

"Noah's mom?" Carly prompted.

"Upstate. She lives in the Bay Area," he said. He lowered

himself to the blanket beside Carly, resting his arm on his upraised knee. He swirled his water, still gazing into it. "The short version is, the two of us had a fling after college, she got pregnant, and wasn't ready for a baby. I offered to raise Noah, and here we are."

Jake glanced over the museum's landscaped grounds. Several yards away, Noah lay belly-first on the grass, chattering to himself as he played. The sunlight sparked from his hair and highlighted the babyish curve of his cheeks. He still looked much the same as he had when Jake had first seen him screaming with indignation in a hospital nursery.

"And the long version?" Carly asked.

"The long version is, I wanted him. It surprised the hell out of me, but once I knew Noah was on the way, I couldn't wait. The way I wanted him was bigger than anything."

He sensed Carly's gaze on him, and felt suddenly self-conscious. He'd never revealed that much to anyone. Jake cleared his throat.

"Not very macho, huh?" he muttered, gulping more water.

"Hugely macho," Carly said. Her honest nod confirmed it. "Are you kidding me? Men don't realize what an amazing turn-on it is when they take on responsibility."

"Right."

"Really! Women love responsible men. Especially when they volunteer to be responsible for the dishes, the laundry, the groceries—"

Jake laughed. Carly's answering grin lightened him, and encouraged him to go on. Feeling unexpectedly free, he did.

"I come from a big family—five kids, including me," he explained. "My mom is crazy for babies. My dad is too, even though he'd never admit to those goo-goo faces he makes. I had plenty of help when Noah came."

"What happened to his mother?"

Jake shrugged. "She's happy in San Francisco, working as a broker. I've always encouraged her to visit. To spend time with Noah. She's never had much interest."

"Oh, Jake." Carly reached for him.

Her hand on his shoulder felt surprisingly welcome. Jake relaxed beneath it.

"Don't get me wrong. She's not a bad person. It was just a case of bad timing. We keep in touch, but mostly it comes down to cards and gifts at Christmas and birthdays. Noah doesn't seem to mind."

"He knows about her?"

"I'm not going to lie to him." Jake glanced at her surprised face. "Don't worry. I'm not the brothers Grimm. I don't fill his head with evil-birth-mother stories. I tell him as much as he can understand."

Together, they gazed across the grass at Noah. There was no denying that he seemed like a very well-adjusted child. Chee-tos mustache aside.

"The rest of the time," Jake said simply, "I love him."

"Oh, Jake." Carly sniffled. Actually *sniffled*. "That's just about the sweetest thing I've ever heard."

Uh-oh. He'd said too much. Dammit, what the hell had gotten into him? He'd been acting like one of those share-your-feelings blubberers on *Oprah*. Christ.

Carly gazed at him through watery, emotion-filled eyes. She looked ready to slap a wedding ring on him, chain him to a dishwasher, and make him wear pink golf shirts.

Jake tossed her one of those froufrou napkins and stood. "Dry your eyes and blow your nose, princess. I'm not a man to spin fairy tales around, remember?"

He waited above her, arms crossed, as she dabbed at her eyes with the napkin. Eventually, Jake glared her into nodding.

Satisfied, he strode across the grass to get Noah. "Let's eat!" he bellowed in his deepest voice—mostly for the benefit of Carly, who claimed to love those let's-be-responsible wussy men so much. "I'm so hungry I could eat a woolly mammoth!"

Nine

They did not eat woolly mammoth.

They did, in fact, feast on ham and Brie sandwiches on pumpernickel bread. On salad of roasted red new potatoes with spring peas and tarragon vinaigrette. And on fresh fruit tarts filled with pastry cream and jewel-like slices of berries, kiwi, and tiny sweet oranges—all courtesy of a local gourmet deli.

Marley, having only planned a meal for two, shared all of hers with Noah. She led off with the goblet of Evian she'd poured, carefully pressing it into his hands as the boy approached their picnic spot with Jake at his side. Noah glanced into the glass, frowned as he rotated it, then broke into a grin.

"There's a smiley face in my water!" he cried.

Marley hid a grin as Jake put a hand on Noah's shoulder and peered along with him into the glass. "So that's what you were doing with those lime slices."

With a shrug, Marley nodded. She'd learned the trick on set, at the craft-services table, where a bored caterer had taken pity on her jittery, six-year-old actress self and rigged up a surprise to make her smile. It was only fair now that she pass on the tradition.

Carefully, Noah raised the goblet in both hands and drank. She watched his little grass-stained fingers flex as he tilted it upward to drain the last drops, heard his satisfied exhalation of breath as he finished. He handed back the glass, the lime slices spent at the bottom.

"Delicious!" He beamed.

Her heart gave a little flutter. This boy was a charmer like his father. No doubt about it.

Then Noah hopped away. Literally. "Like a bunny!" he cried as he bounced a path along the perimeter of the picnic blanket. He wrinkled his nose, his face glowing with exertion and pleasure.

Okay, so he had a few rough edges. Like his father. Marley could live with that.

"Does he ever wear down?" she asked as she offered the food to Jake. "Or is he always like that?"

"Like what?"

"Like a schnauzer on speed."

Jake gave her a wary look. She made a face to show him she was only kidding.

He smiled. "He's always like that."

"You must have a lot of stamina."

"I've got plenty of stamina." He winked at her, clearly not referring to his parenting skills. "Remind me to demonstrate it for you sometime."

Zing. Warmth raced through her, reminding Marley this was a date—a date with a man who, so far, seemed very interested in her. In *her,* not Tara. She couldn't help but feel drawn into the illusion of their couplehood. After all, Jake had just shared some very personal details about his life with her. She'd shared some things about her childhood. There was a new intimacy between them . . . an intimacy that tempted Marley almost as much as fresh new scripts tempted Gaffer.

Too bad she couldn't nibble a tiny sample of Jake.

Marley sighed. With all that was at stake, she was forced to walk a tightrope between cozying up to Jake so they'd do well in the *Dream Date* competition and keeping her alter-ego performance at the forefront of her mind.

Being with him wrecked her concentration, though. When confronted with his wide shoulders, ribald jokes, and perfect forearms, all she wanted to do was enjoy him. More and more, being "Carly" felt like an imposition, an imposition that interfered with all the things Marley really wanted to do—most of which involved her, Jake, and a long stint in some romantic, deserted place.

She experienced a sudden impulse to tackle him. In an entirely different way than she had before. She'd push him onto their blanket, straddle him in her girl-next-door ensemble, and run her hands all over the hard planes of his chest. His T-shirt would feel soft beneath her palms, but his body wouldn't. His body would feel strong and masculine and oh, so good.

Jake would tuck his hand at the nape of her neck and pull her down for a hot, leisurely kiss, murmuring how he'd been waiting so long to taste her. She'd succumb like the heroine in a romantic movie, the whole world going soft-focused and candy colored as they . . . *ahem.*

"Oh, my God. You're a winker," she said, giving a struggling little laugh. "I'm not sure I can date you anymore."

"Why not?"

"Uncle Mortys wink. Dirty old men wink. Midlife crisis victims wearing gold chains and leisure suits wink. Superhot superstuds definitely don't—"

Jake edged closer. He winked. Her knees wobbled and her collarbone got hot. Marley was forced to reconsider her objections.

"—wink," she concluded emphatically, all the same. "They don't."

"You know a lot about superhot superstuds?"

"I've worked the red carpet with the best of them. Brad, Tom, George, Hugh."

He raised his eyebrows.

"Grant. Hugh Grant. Devastating, I assure you."

"That's good to know, but it's not what I meant." His eyes teased her into coming nearer. "You've worked the red carpet?"

Whoops. Ordinarily, she possessed a laser-sharp focus when it came to acting. Studio audiences, guest stars, temperamental directors—none of them got to her. None of them distracted her. So what was the matter with her now? When it, um, *mattered?*

"No, of course not!" Marley fluttered a hand carelessly. She began piling salad of roasted new potatoes with spring peas and tarragon vinaigrette onto Jake's plate. "I meant working the red carpet as in *watching* award shows. The Oscars, the Grammys, the People's Choice Awards. I'm a major award-show junkie."

"A self-improvement junkie *and* an award-show junkie?"

Confused, she cocked her head to the side.

"You said you were a self-improvement junkie. Voice coaching, affirmations, therapy—"

"Oh, right! Sure. I'm wearing motivational underwear right now."

Marley bit into half of her ham-and-Brie-on-pumpernickel and chewed rapidly. She busied herself with cutting the other half-sandwich into perfect mini triangles for Noah, then arranged them on a plate with a scoop of salad. When everything was just so, she glanced up to call Noah . . . and encountered Jake's avid, curious gaze instead.

He cleared his throat. "What, *exactly,* does your underwear motivate you to do?"

Umm, jump your bones? If there'd been so much as a shred of truth to the outrageous statement she'd just made, that would have been it. But since Marley could hardly admit *that,* she settled for forcing her fingers to carefully set down Noah's plate.

"I really want to know," Jake went on, earnestly. He touched her chin with his fingertips, turning her face to his. "I feel a sudden interest in exploring the possibilities of self-improvement."

So did she. She couldn't help it. His voice was like a rough caress, reaching inside to all the closed-off places Marley hadn't visited for years. The vulnerable, hopeful places she'd tried to forget.

For a heartbeat, she allowed herself to remember.

"I just want you to know," she said, "this has nothing to do with my underwear."

Then she leaned across the few inches still separating them, sucked in a crazy breath, and kissed him.

The world narrowed to the meeting of their mouths, to the feel of Jake's lips hot against hers. It was a small kiss, a gentle, how-are-you-doing kind of kiss, but it shook Marley all the way through, just the same. Kissing Jake was like standing on the edge of a precipice and leaping into the sky. In a single moment she fell into something completely new.

It felt like love, but she assured herself it was lust. It felt like exploration, but she needed it to be satisfaction. That way, she wouldn't be lured into trying it again.

No sooner had Marley realized this strategy would never help her concentrate on the job at hand, than Jake recovered from his initial surprise . . . and took control of the kiss altogether.

His version was hotter. Harder. More deliberate and yet still amazingly tender. His hands rose to cradle her cheeks, and his thumbs stroked sensitizing little circles over her skin. He tasted of certainty and demand, smelled of green grass and clean shirt. He felt like heaven, wrapped up in equal measures of playfulness, stubbornness, and machismo, and Marley greedily demanded more.

He delivered everything she wanted, along with something she didn't: a sense of honor. Of honesty. Of genuine connectedness. Here was a good man, Marley realized hazily, and she was misleading him. How could she let Jake get closer when he didn't know the truth about her? It wouldn't be fair, it wouldn't be right, and it wouldn't be . . . honorable. Suddenly, Marley wanted to be that. Honorable. For him.

She ended their kiss and lurched backward. "Whew!" she cried, fanning herself. "I guess the powers of suggestion are stronger than I'd thought. I'd better not trot out these underwear in public again."

A giggle came from beside her.

Noah.

And here she'd thought this situation couldn't get any more awkward.

"He thinks 'underwear' is one of the most hilarious words in the universe," Jake explained. Now he seemed completely—and disappointingly—unaffected by the momentous kiss he and Marley had just shared. He pulled a laughing Noah onto the picnic blanket and handed him his plate of food. "Other laugh riots include under*pants,* booger, and butt."

Noah covered his mouth with his hand and chortled. "Booty!" he cried.

"Elbow," Jake offered. He shrugged at Marley. "You've got to admit, it's a funny name for a body part."

"Foot!" Noah yelled, then dissolved into giggles. He'd taken a bite of potato salad, and his exclamation delivered a marvelous view of its half-mashed state amid his teeth.

Jake matter-of-factly flicked a tarragon fragment from his shoulder and got back into the game. "Fanny," he said.

"Pooper-scooper!"

"Butt, butt, butt."

At that, they both guffawed. Jake even wiped a tear of laughter from his eye.

"Do you two do this often?" Marley asked, eyebrows raised.

"Hey, don't knock it till you've tried it. This is the height of humor at Toddler Time."

Noah agreed with a nod, his baby-fine hair flopping into his eyes. He swiped it away. "You do one, Carly."

"Oh, I couldn't," she demurred.

"Come on!" they urged.

"I wouldn't know where to start."

Jake shook his head. "We gave you plenty of examples. You're just chicken."

"Bawk! Bawk!" Noah chimed.

Exasperated, Marley eyeballed them both. "You can't be serious."

They silently waited. Noah flapped imaginary chicken wings.

"Fine." She searched for something appropriate, drawing herself up to her most dignified, Pilates-assured seated posture. Finally, a suitable phrase occurred to her.

"Ummm . . . ear wax!" she declared triumphantly.

They both stared at her blankly.

"Ear wax?" Jake echoed.

"Yeah. Get it? It's gross, it's funny—"

Noah shook his head. "She doesn't get it," he told his dad.

"It's okay, son. Women usually don't." With a disappointed air, Jake went back to his lunch. He urged Noah to do the same.

Nonplussed, Marley watched them. "What's wrong with ear wax?" she demanded.

They shrugged. "It's not funny."

"Sure it is!"

But they only went on eating their food, clearly unconvinced. Marley felt on the outside, all of a sudden. Left out. She wanted in.

"Toe jam!" she yelled.

Jake glanced up. "We're trying to eat, here."

"Not me." Noah opened his mouth and let a bite of ham-and-Brie-on-pumpernickel fall onto his plate. *Blah.* "This cheese tastes squishy. And there's something wrong with my bread."

He examined everyone else's plates with obvious little-boy suspicion. Marley wanted to respond with something encouraging, something along the lines of, "It's from France! It's gourmet!" But she was too busy realizing she could never, ever become a mother—not if it involved butt talk, bunny hopping, and this weird variety of reverse eating.

"Eat it," Jake instructed his son. "Or no dessert."

In an effort to be helpful, Marley used her best game-show-hostess routine to display the miniature glazed-fruit tarts.

"Ugh, fruit." Noah wrinkled his nose. "Okay. No dessert."

He abandoned his lunch and immediately launched into a game of "be a snake." At least that's what Marley assumed it was, given the way he wriggled belly-first through the grass.

"His clothes are going to get completely ruined," she said.

Jake gave her a carefree look. "He's the one who's got to wear them." He glanced downward at his son's plate. "Say, do you want the rest of that sandwich?"

As if. That thing had spent way too much time being "evaluated" by Noah. He was like a pint-sized culinary version of a wine taster. Sip, swish, spit . . . bite, taste, blaaarch.

"Go ahead," she said.

Unbelievably, he did—ignoring the spit-out portions, of course. Both sandwich triangles disappeared within three minutes. "That cheese *is* pretty squishy," Jake commented.

Marley shook her head. Obviously, these Jarvis men needed the civilizing touch of a woman in their lives. They ate like linebackers, talked like sailors, and—ohmigod, now Jake was belly wriggling through the grass, too!—gave no thought at all to decorum.

In small doses, it was kind of fun. But on a larger, more permanent scale? Well, Marley was just glad *she* wouldn't be called upon to tame their wilder impulses. She was definitely not the domesticating type.

It was a good thing, she assured herself, that this *Dream Date* arrangement was only temporary. Because the "be a snake" routine or the "butt-butt-butt" game definitely wouldn't play long term during her own paparazzi-filled personal appearances.

"Come on, Daddy!" Noah cried, scrambling eagerly to his feet. "Let's go see the woolly mammoths! And the saber-toothed tigers, and sloths, and wolves, too." He hurried to Marley's side and pointed to the museum. "They've got all that stuff inside. My daddy said so."

"Sounds like fun," she said.

Jake came to stand nearby, his shadow falling over the remains of their picnic. "I know you probably didn't plan to visit the museum. It's pretty geeky. But we've got time for a visit if you do. What do you say?"

"Yeah, what do you say?" Noah crouched down. He angled his head until his face was on a level with Marley's. His impish blue eyes urged her to join them. "You come too, okay?"

Marley wasn't sure she should. Being here with Jake and Noah felt suspiciously like being welcomed into their family. Being welcomed into their family made her feel like even more of a fraud than she already was. That was bad.

On the other hand, Noah's presence might enable her to keep a lid on her more alter ego–scrambling impulses—like kissing Jake again. If she were smart, Marley realized, she'd arrange to have their three-foot chaperone present at every date, just to avoid further "work the red carpet"-style blunders. Avoiding future slipups would be good.

Noah grabbed her hand and tried to tug her to her feet. Despite the butt jokes, he really was very sweet. Marley laughed and levered upward as though the boy really had lifted her on his own.

"Okay, let's go," Marley said.

Happily, Noah danced a gonna-see-woolly-mammoths jig, making up a song to go along with it.

She knelt and began gathering their picnic gear. Jake joined her, taking on the more mechanically inclined job of assessing the dimensions of her basket and packing the items neatly. By the time he was finished, her hamper looked like the inside of one of those pocket tool kits Marley's dad owned. Compact. Efficient. Not an inch of wasted space.

She waited while Jake chivalrously stowed the basket in her Chanel-worthy vintage car, then enjoyed the view as he moved to meet her with that athlete's stride of his.

"Let's go, Carly!" Noah yelled, gesturing toward the tar pits and museum.

Jake caught up. He gave her an assessing glance. "Noah likes you," he said. "I guess you're in."

She was in. Imagine that.

"I've never been given the seal of approval by a four-year-old before," she said. "It's nice."

Jake only *hmmphed.* He offered his son a speculative look as the three of them headed up the hill. Then he shook his head and took Marley's hand. Not even the unexpected bonus of his touch could turn her thoughts completely from the course they'd rambled onto, though. Studying his stony expression, she couldn't help but wonder . . . exactly how did Jake feel about her being "in" with Noah?

"I didn't know they'd all be *dead!"* Noah sobbed, collapsing on a bench inside the Page Museum. "They're nothin' but bones!"

Marley knelt beside him. Tentatively, she patted his back. They hadn't ventured far inside the museum—having spent a lot of time choosing a cuddly plush woolly mammoth for Noah in the gift shop—but it was obvious this visit had already gone south.

"But they can't feel a thing," she explained gently. "They've been dead a long time now."

"How long?"

"Oh . . ." She squinted at the nearest plaque. "Thirty thousand years or so."

"Thirty thousand? That's even worse!" He clutched his toy mammoth, sobbing harder.

"It's, umm, the circle of life, Noah." *Pat, pat.* "Animals are born, they live and have babies, they die. The lucky ones get to become famous museum exhibits!"

He rubbed his blotchy face on his forearm, then raised his teary-eyed gaze to hers. "Being famous must be awful."

Boy, he'd nailed that one. "Sometimes it is," Marley agreed.

"Look, Noah! Over here." Jake waited until he had the boy's

attention. "I'm a caveman, conquering the mammoth that scared you."

He raised his arms and pretended to clobber the nearest exhibit—which actually necessitated jumping up and down, because the thing was so big. Each of the mammoth skeleton's curvy tusks were as tall as Jake. Nevertheless, he pretended victory.

"See?" He spread his feet and planted both hands on his thighs in a victorious-warrior's pose. "It's safe now. I won."

Slowly, Noah lifted his head. He blinked. "You beat up that mammoth! Waaah!"

"But it was already dead, slugger," Jake explained, abandoning his pose. Clearly, he'd expected his Cro-Magnon routine to help. "It got caught in the tar pits a long time ago."

That engendered more sobs. Marley shook her head and went on patting Noah's back. Jake joined them. He stood awkwardly nearby, obviously hating his helplessness in this situation.

"Let's go outside and look at the tar pits," he said.

Four minutes later, the three of them stood at the chain-link fence which enclosed a pool of thick black tar. To Marley, it looked like swampy mud, although she knew from reading the museum signs that it was technically asphalt. In the center and at the edge, displays had been erected to depict a mammoth family—daddy mammoth, mommy mammoth, and baby mammoth—being sucked down into the goo. She had to admit, it was fairly horrific. This was educational?

Suddenly, she was glad she'd usually missed school field trips, those longed-for adventures of fun and frolic Marley had so pined for while stuck on a TV show set someplace. Her school friends, and even Meredith, had made them sound terrific. Now she knew the truth.

Noah hooked his fingers in the chain links. He peeked through them. "Aaaah!"

He averted his head and closed his eyes. Jake stared down at him in puzzlement. "What's the matter? Those mammoths aren't skeletons and they aren't real. They're just statues."

"They *look* real," Noah said accusingly.

"Be tough. Shake it off," Jake advised.

"*Really* real."

"They do." Sympathetically, Marley again hunkered down beside him.

They looked real to her, too. She could just imagine the poor mama mammoth's fear when she realized her baby would be trapped in the oozing asphalt right along with her. She'd flail around trying to help, probably get stuck deeper, and trumpet a mammoth 911. That, of course, would lure the daddy mammoth to his doom, and the whole family would be . . .

Marley averted her head, too. Sometimes it was a curse to possess an actor's imagination. Here she was, all but practicing The Method on a museum display.

Noah must have that same kind of imagination, she realized. It was all too much for him.

"You know what?" she asked him briskly. "I'll bet those scientists have it all wrong. I'll bet the mammoths and all those other animals came here on purpose."

The boy sniffled. He opened one eye. "On purpose?"

"Sure! I'll bet this wasn't a dreaded tar pit at all. Heck, no. I'll bet it was an Ice Age version of a day spa."

Noah hugged his toy mammoth. He bravely opened both eyes.

"The animals probably came from miles around," Marley said, really getting into it now that her story seemed to be helping Noah. She spread her arms wide, as though offering the place's Pleistocene pampering to one and all. "They enjoyed mud masques, herb baths . . . maybe even steam treatments. I'll bet they had a waiting list."

Jake rolled his eyes. "And a maître d', right?"

"Don't be silly. It wasn't a restaurant."

Jake scoffed. He hunkered down, too, and clapped his hand on his son's shoulder. "Look, Noah. Sometimes nature is cruel—"

"And sometimes it isn't," Marley interrupted, glaring.

"You just have to accept it."

"Or, you can choose not to."

Noah turned around. He looked at them both, his little face scrunched as he considered things. Then he smiled at Marley. "Do you s'pose they had TVs?" he asked. "I wish I had a TV while I take my baths."

"I'll bet they did," she announced. Pride surged inside her, making her wonderfully glad. She'd actually helped Noah feel better. It was, quite possibly, the best thing she'd accomplished in years. "Cable, too."

"And snacks?"

"I don't see why not."

"But not gooshy cheese sandwiches with black bread."

"Oh, no," Marley agreed seriously. Hey, she was on a roll.

"Yippee!"

Plainly relieved, Noah skipped a short distance ahead of them. He jumped over cracks in the sidewalk, making up a mammoth snack song as he did.

Jake shook his head. "In the long run, pretending won't help him," he told Marley.

"I know that," she replied. "In the long run, pretending doesn't help anybody. But it's fine for now."

At her breezy statement, a part of her squirmed. She hoped the universe wouldn't punish her for tempting fate.

It did. An instant later, she and Jake rounded the corner to return to the car and Marley's words were proven prophetic. Coming straight toward them were her personal manager, Brian, and her agent, Sondra, apparently out for a weekend stroll.

"Marley!" they cried, and rushed to greet her.

Ten

He could have handled that, Jake groused as he and Carly and Noah prepared to leave the tar pits and museum behind. He didn't need anybody else to help out with his own son, dammit.

Carly had stuck her adorable button nose where it didn't belong. If she hadn't been there, Jake would have cheered up Noah on his own. No doubt about it.

He sure as hell wouldn't have conjured up an Ice Age day spa to accomplish it, either. Imagine—an animal as fierce as a saber-toothed tiger, submitting to a mud masque? Ridiculous. That would be about as likely as Mike Tyson having a pedicure. Randy Johnson getting a bikini wax. Dennis Rodman shooting baskets without eyeliner on.

Carly was obviously one of those buttinsky types. Women who couldn't leave well enough alone, especially when it came to kids. Didn't she know how dangerous crying was for a little boy? The misery of confronting mastodon bones was nothing compared with the anguish of having six other boys pointing, laughing, and labeling you a crybaby for the whole of first grade.

Jake needed to protect Noah. He needed to toughen him up a little, before the cruel kiddie world did it for him. Carly had no business undermining his efforts. What did she want to do, turn Noah into some kind of Poindexter?

Protectively, he watched the boy as he skipped along just ahead of them. If Jake were smart, he'd try to keep Noah and his dream dates with Carly separate from here on out. There was no reason why he should treat her any differently than any other woman he'd dated.

Except he already had, and Jake knew it.

He'd never allowed the women he'd been casually involved with to spend much time with Noah. Somehow, Carly had made an end run around his defenses. Now he was dealing with the consequences.

Not that all of those consequences were bad, exactly. He remembered the kiss they'd shared, recalled the moment between his realization that she was about to kiss him and the first touch of her lips against his. Jake had felt his whole body tense. His breath had shortened and his thoughts had stopped. Once their kiss had begun, his entire awareness had been centered on the wonderful softness of Carly's mouth, on the sweet taste of her and the heat that gathered when they came together.

Kissing Carly had opened a door to something Jake hadn't let himself feel for a very long time. Something that had slipped inside to leave him both warmer and brighter for the experience.

No matter how he tried to pile up new barriers now, the simple truth remained. He'd felt something special when that door had opened. Now it was too late to pretend he hadn't.

Too late.

Jake considered that. He squeezed Carly's hand and, given the distance of a good hour between mind-blowing kiss and simple hand holding, decided he was wrong. Hell, yeah. He could pretend he hadn't felt anything remarkable, and he would. Probably, he'd just gotten a little too rambunctious because of his need to perform well on *Dream Date*.

Sure. That was it.

Reminded of their ever-present entourage, he scanned

their surroundings. Yup, the TV crew still followed them. Kids and tour groups milled about the Page Museum grounds. Just in front of them, a yuppified pair of business types headed directly toward him and Noah and Carly.

"Marley!" the woman cried, looking surprised. She urged her partner, a stuffy-looking man, to hurry closer. "Marley! Fancy meeting you here."

Beside him, Carly froze. Her face paled. She looked left and right, as though searching for this "Marley" person.

"It's *Carly,* dear," Stuffy said. "Remember?"

"Oh, that's right. Carly!"

Tittering, the woman thrust out a handshake. She appeared to think better of the gesture, and tentatively enveloped Carly in an awkward, shoulders-first hug instead.

The yuppie woman seemed a complete stranger to spontaneous shows of affection, possibly because her entire body was accessorized with electronic gadgets. A pager hung from her hip. A PDA sat in a holster slung over her shoulder. Not one, not two, but three cell phones competed for space elsewhere, and she wore a hands-free headset around her neck.

A slobbery kiss could have seriously short-circuited her.

"I see you're not spending *your* weekend alone," Yuppie Electro-Woman said, nudging Stuffy. She waggled her eyebrows toward Jake, then wiggled her fingers in a wave to Noah. "So, who are your friends?"

Carly introduced them. She held out her hands to indicate Stuffy and Yuppie. "This is Brian and Sondra. They're, ummm . . . members of my Beef Jerky Addicts support group."

Jake raised his eyebrows. A self-improvement junkie, an awards-show junkie, and a *beef jerky* junkie?

Sondra laughed, ignoring the flashing light summoning her to one of her cell phones. She nudged Carly in the ribs. "You silly. We're not in her Beef Jerky Addicts group. We're her—"

"Cousins!" Brian interrupted. He rocked upward on the balls of his feet, looking absurdly pleased with his announcement. "We're Carly's cousins."

"Both of you?" Jake asked. He'd been sure he'd noticed a

romantic vibe between them when they'd approached. "But you looked like you were—"

"Sondra's my cousin," Carly said. She hugged her closer. "But Brian isn't. They're just in town for a visit."

"From Appalachia," Brian explained, bright-eyed.

Carly stared, openmouthed.

"Yup. I'm just here with my hillbilly husband-to-be," Sondra agreed. "We're gonna get ourselves hitched."

The two of them beamed. Jake frowned, trying to take it all in. Carly had hillbilly beef-jerky-addict relatives? Relatives who hadn't even remembered her name?

Sondra peered at him, as though picking up on his confusion. "I can see we're losing you, Jake," she said. "It all makes perfect sense in Appalachia, I promise. Say, we were just about to head out to go, umm—"

"Bowling," Brian said. A look passed between them.

"Good one!" Sondra told him, nodding. She turned to Jake again. "Bowling. And you know bowling is always more fun with a crowd, right?"

"Well," Jake began, "the last time I bowled with a crowd, I—"

"You three come along with us!" Brian said before Jake could refuse. He issued his invitation in a hearty voice. "There's nothing, uh, *Carly* likes more than a good round of bowling. Is there?"

"Uhhh . . ."

"Why, you wouldn't believe the bowling cups she's got."

Carly glanced at her breasts, looking confused.

"Trophies?" Jake asked.

"Yes!" Sondra and Brian said in unison. "Trophies."

"I wanna go bowling, Daddy!" Noah said.

"It'll be a hoot, honest," Sondra urged. By now, her various devices all flashed, making her look a little like a walking Lite Brite. "Wait'll you see Carly bowl a hole in one."

"Now *that* I've got to see," Jake said, smiling at a clearly uncomfortable Carly. He wanted to see her "bowling cups," too. But that would have to wait. "Let's go."

*   *   *

At the bowling alley—a stinky, fluorescent-lit cave last decorated during the Rat Pack era—Marley cornered Sondra the minute Jake went to the opposite side of their assigned lane to help Noah put on his rented—*yes, rented! And used!*—shoes.

"What are you doing?" she cried in a muffled voice. She fixed Sondra with an urgent look, keenly aware of the *Dream Date* crew diligently setting up at a nearby lane. "*Hillbilly cousins?* The closest you and Brian come to being hillbillies is attending a revival showing of *The Grapes of Wrath.*"

Sondra looked defensive. "I think Brian and I are very convincing country folk."

"Convincing? The closest you've been to the country is Napa Valley. Your idea of the simple life is going to New York and not staying at the Plaza. Oh, and by the way—I seriously doubt your pappy really made corncob pipes for a living."

"That was Brian's pappy." Sondra folded her arms.

"I mean it, Sondra. You should have pretended not to know me. When you saw me at the museum, you and Brian should have walked on by. Just walked"—she gestured eloquently with both arms—"on by."

"Not a chance! We care about you. We want to help you."

Marley sighed. "So far, all you've 'helped' me do is discover a serious phobia of pre-worn shoes." She eyed her assigned pair of garish saddle shoes with distaste. They didn't even have a paltry half-inch heel to enhance her legs. "I swear, after this I'm going to dunk my feet in a whole vat of Purell."

"Oh, check with Brian," Sondra advised readily. "He's got gallons of sanitizers at his place. He's probably packing Lysol, Handiwipes, and a bar of Safeguard right now."

"Maybe I should," Marley said. "I feel sort of itchy already."

Ugh. And if *she* felt that way, how did her personal manager feel? Aware of his germ-a-phobe tendencies, Marley frowned with worry. Why had Brian suggested coming here, to the nearly deserted bowling alley? The one place most teeming with microbial mayhem, short of a producer's hot tub?

As though sensing her question, Brian joined them. He leaned down, keeping their conversation private. "Isn't this terrific? This bowling thing will completely cement your alter ego," he said urgently. "When Sondra and I saw you at the museum, the first thing we thought was, what would be best for Marley in this situation?"

"And what you came up with," Marley asked, "was hillbilly cousins with a beef-jerky fixation?"

He tilted his head censoriously. "*You* came up with the beef-jerky thing."

"Oh, yeah." Marley frowned. A few feet away, near the bowling ball, um, regurgitating thingie, Jake finished tying Noah's shoes and stood. "Well, just don't get me into any more trouble, okay? I need to lead this thing. Let me handle the cover stories from here on out."

"Fine," they murmured.

Marley felt somewhat reassured.

Sondra glanced toward the *Dream Date* crew. "Does my hair look okay?" she asked. "I probably need a blowout."

Brian showed her his teeth. "I had spinach for lunch. It would look bad on TV. Do you see any?"

Marley groaned. Just what she needed. Her personal manager and her agent, both usually so sensible, even straight-laced, had been suddenly stricken camera crazy. She rolled her eyes.

"You both look great," she said. On top of this, she was supposed to actually *bowl?*

Well, she wasn't enduring the agony alone. Getting to her feet, Marley left her plastic molded chair behind and went to join Jake. He'd finished outfitting both himself and Noah with bowling balls. He offered to help Marley choose one, too.

"Sure," she agreed. "Thanks." They headed for the long

racks of black and multicolored balls. "Say, did I ever tell you what Sondra and Brian do for a living?"

Four frames in, Jake leaned back in his seat at the little scorekeeper's desk. He watched Carly take her turn, her gaze focused on the lane arrows. She hefted her ball (a pearly pink child's version), took careful aim, lined up her shot . . . then realized her shirt had come partway untucked. She plunked her ball at her feet, tucked in her shirt, straightened her shorts, fluffed up her hair, then gave him an over-the-shoulder smile before resuming her turn.

He grinned. Bowling with Carly was unlike bowling with anyone else.

Beside Jake, Noah fidgeted, doodling with crayons on a menu from the bowling alley's snack bar. To his right, Sondra primped and made eyes with a *Dream Date* cameraman. To his left, Brian swiveled his tongue around his teeth. Jake wondered if the man had a dental disorder to go with his beef-jerky fixation.

"So, Carly tells me you're in the sanitation business." Brian started. "The what?"

"Oh, right. You guys in the field probably think those euphemisms are pretentious," Jake said. "Sorry. How's life as a garbage man treating you?"

Brian emitted a strangled sound. He glanced at Carly, then back at Jake. He straightened the lapels of his very tidy dress shirt. "Fine. It's fine."

"It must pay pretty well, if you can afford Armani."

Now Sondra and Brian both boggled at him.

"I'm a sportscaster for KKZP," he explained. "You should see the getups some of the players can afford. Designer clothes, amped-up sports cars, gold rings as big as your knuckle." He shrugged. "After doing interviews for a while, you get so you recognize the fancy stuff."

Sondra gulped. "We may have underestimated you, Jake."

"Hey, that's all right. I underestimated you, too, Sondra.

If Carly hadn't clued me in, I'd never have pegged you as a stripper."

Sondra choked.

"Oh, sorry." Apparently, Sondra *liked* euphemisms. "Exotic dancer."

She mustered a wan smile as her various gadgets continued to blink. Jake supposed she used them to keep up with work issues—pole-dancing lessons, G-string shortages, pasties problems.

"I can't believe Carly told you that about me," Sondra said, shooting a nervous glance toward the camera guy.

The man nodded, having obviously overheard. He waggled his eyebrows lasciviously.

Jake smiled. "Hey, don't worry about it. Your job is probably a lot like mine."

"You perform for sweaty, drooling men?" Brian asked innocently. "Wearing not much more than a smile?"

Sondra glared. "Butt out, garbage man."

Noah giggled. "She said 'butt.' "

Jake ruffled his son's hair. "No, I mean people tend to think sportscasting—especially working as an anchor—is an easy job. To the rest of the world, it looks like I just sit there reading scores off a TelePrompTer. A monkey could do that."

Noah circled the score table, making monkey sounds.

"Nobody sees the field reporting," Jake went on, "the long hours of research, the time spent at batting practices, scrimmages, and shootarounds, the hours of watching game tapes. The writing, the rewriting, the editing—"

"The dance lessons, the practicing, the choreographing," Sondra chimed in. She flung a hand dramatically over her brow. "You're right, Jake. We're kindred spirits."

A *klunk* reverberated through the mostly empty bowling alley. Carly had just thrown her second ball . . . straight into the gutter.

Shoulders slumped, she watched it wobble toward the pins. It disappeared without touching a single one of them. The lane machinery swallowed up its jolly pinkness.

"Hey, garbage man," Sondra nudged. "Get busy. We need somebody to clean up Carly's game."

"Har, har," Brian said. He got up to take his turn.

Carly took his seat.

"You really bowl with gusto," Jake told her.

"Is that a nice way of saying my bowling stinks?"

"Nah. But I'll admit, I've never seen anyone plant a big lipstick kiss on their ball before every throw."

"It's for good luck," Carly explained.

"Carly's very superstitious," Sondra said. "Lots of actors are."

"Not that I want to be like an actor!" Carly laughed, waving her hand. She shot her cousin a disapproving look. "I mean, who would? Those kooky Hollywood types are into some pretty weird stuff."

"That's for sure." Jake made a note of the two-ten split Brian's first throw had earned him. "I try to avoid the industry types in this town. Noah and I like to keep it real."

Sondra seized on his statement instantly.

"Your son's adorable," she said, as though eager to change the subject. Probably she considered herself "in the industry" because of her exotic dancing. "Isn't he, Carly?"

"Very adorable." Carly lifted her gaze to Noah. She smiled slightly as the boy tilted his head upside down and looked at her from between his knees. "I like him a lot."

She sounded a little surprised at that, and very sincere. Thoughtfully, Jake studied her. Carly had come a long way in a few hours.

"Hey, Carly." Noah clambered over the welded-together plastic chairs to sit beside her. "Will you teach me how to bowl better?"

At that moment, Brian returned. "Yes, do it, Carly," he urged. "Do it for all of us down at the Garbage Men's Local 624."

He offered Carly a toothy grin, then sat down to clean his hands with the wipes from his pocket dispenser.

"You have a union in Appalachia?" Jake asked.

Before Brian could answer, Carly did. "Sure! In fact, there's nothing Brian doesn't know about Appalachia," she said, her sweet tone at odds with the inexplicable glare she offered her cousin's fiancé. "You should quiz him."

She turned to Noah. "Sure, I'll teach you how to bowl better. As long as your dad doesn't mind."

"Yippee!"

Jake stopped her part way to the ball return. "Thanks. But are you sure you ought to?"

"Why? Because my bowling is so terrible?" Looking hurt, she put her hand on her hip. "Look, I'm just warming up, here. I'm perfectly capable of instructing a four-year-old."

"I'm just saying—"

"I might even be better than *you*."

That stopped him. Shaking his head, Jake eyeballed her. She dared to challenge him, after all the gutter balls she'd thrown today? Carly was gutsy, he'd give her that. Deluded, but gutsy.

"I'll prove it on the next game," she bragged.

He scoffed.

She sashayed away to help Noah retrieve his ball. "I will. Care to make it interesting?"

Sondra and Brian both perked up, listening.

Jake spread out his arms. He'd tried to take it easy on her, but . . . "I couldn't take advantage of you like that."

"Oh, yeah? Well, twenty bucks says you can."

He looked her over. First her bet with the *Dream Date* guys, now this. "I think you have a problem. Have you considered that you might be a gambling junkie, too?"

With a shrug, Carly shook her head. "Okay, never mind. I guess you're just a big old . . ." Grinning, she crooked her arms, flapping them in a dead-on imitation of Noah's "chicken" routine from their picnic.

Noah chuckled. He started flapping, too. "Toe jam!" he cried gleefully.

Okay, this was too much. *Toe jam?* Even his son had gone

over to the other side. Jake bolted from his chair and offered a handshake.

"You're on."

Carly grinned and prepared to bowl.

An hour later, Marley held out her hand toward Jake and wiggled her fingers. "Pay up, hotshot."

"One more game," Jake protested. "Double or nothing."

"You're already into me for sixty bucks. Don't you think you ought to quit while you're ahead?"

He scanned the bowling alley, looking adorably disgruntled. "We should try another lane. This one's lost its polish."

"So? I don't mind a less-than-spiffy lane if you don't." As it turned out, even on a dull lane, "Carly" was an excellent bowler—or at least she'd become one, just as soon as Marley had remembered her lessons from the movie *Gutterballs Wild* she'd made as a teenager. "Does anyone else mind this lane?"

Garbage man Brian and stripper Sondra both shrugged. Noah lay down on the connected plastic chairs and sang the "Itsy-Bitsy Spider" song, complete with hand movements.

"The slickness of the lane affects the spin of the ball," Jake told her seriously. "When the glossiness is gone, so is some of the surface tension. Losing that is enough to throw off a man's entire game."

He obviously wasn't accustomed to losing. Especially to a woman. Marley considered taking pity on him.

Nah. She wiggled her fingers again.

Jake glanced at Sondra and Brian, then ducked his head. He rubbed the back of his neck. His direct, beautifully blue gaze met Marley's.

"I don't have that much cash with me," he admitted.

Instantly, she felt contrite. How could she have been so thoughtless? Jake was a sportscaster—basically, a reporter. He probably didn't rake in bundles of money, especially with a son to support.

"Fine," she said lightly. "You cook dinner for me tomorrow night at your place, and we'll call it even."

"I, uh—" His gaze shifted to Noah. Returned to her. "Okay."

Triumphantly, Marley allowed herself to savor her victory.

"But no TV cameras," Jake specified. "No *Dream Date* crew and no microphones."

Marley nodded. He probably didn't want Noah taped for TV any more than necessary. She understood that. "All right."

But that wasn't all. Jake leaned a little nearer, so Sondra and Brian wouldn't overhear. They helpfully took the hint and picked up their balls to return them.

"We don't have that much time to get to know each other," he said. "I think we could use a crash course in togetherness. Off the record. I don't know about you, but I plan to ace this show."

"M-me, too." *Gulp.* Spending time with Jake off-camera wouldn't help show off her acting abilities. It wouldn't augment her résumé reel or garner publicity later. It would only tempt her to buy into the whole we're-a-couple illusion they'd spun together.

He had her trapped, though. Backing out now would be cowardly, and reneging on her offer to change their bet would be stingy. Not to mention ungracious. Marley looked into Jake's rugged, ridiculously handsome face, and found herself unable to disappoint him.

"If we're going to nail those *Dream Date* voter tallies," she said with forced brightness, "we'll have to work together."

"Yeah." Jake moved closer. "We will."

"That's right." She nodded vigorously.

Me, deceiving you, a part of her jibed. *You, being the wonderful, honest, upstanding, aw-shucks kind of guy you are.* Criminy. She was lower than pond scum.

She'd have to be careful. It would be all too easy to really fall for him . . . and too distracting by far. There was no way Marley could pull off a good "Carly Christopher" while she was falling in love for real.

"I'm glad you agree," he said. He raised his hand to her face, briefly cupped her cheek. Jake's earnest gaze met hers. "I'm glad you're a good person, Carly."

Hearing her phony name spoken so tenderly made Marley feel even worse than before. Now she was really low. Unimaginably low. Lower than low.

"A lot of people wouldn't have changed that bet," Jake went on. "But you did. Thanks."

His caressing palm casually touched her hair. She felt the wavy strands slide through his fingers, and struggled against an urge to reciprocate. Jake's hair looked thick and smooth. It also looked exactly the color of the expensive, buttery Scottish shortbread that had always tempted her . . . and that her diet had always denied her.

Until now. Heck, now she was Carly, wasn't she? Marley thought defiantly. Carly could have whatever she wanted . . . the more tempting, the better. Nothing could have been more tempting than Jake. He was still talking, his voice rumbling and affectionate. It lulled her, drew her a little closer.

"You're a more caring person than your cousin and her fiancé realize," he said.

He lowered his hand. Marley blinked. "Huh?"

Jake lifted a shoulder, indicating Brian and Sondra as they trotted across the bowling alley to return their rented shoes. "Let's just say I don't believe everything I hear from those two."

Uh-oh. "What did they say?"

"It's not important." Jake hefted his bowling ball in one hand and Marley's in the other. She followed as he strode to the ball racks, trailed by Noah. "Given the jobs they have, I think they resent your ordinary work as a waitress."

Hah. "What did they say?"

"Especially Sondra. I don't think she likes being a stripper much."

"Jake." She grabbed his arm. She resisted an impulse to squeeze the muscular bulge of his biceps. Geez, was he ever strong. "What did they say?"

"They said you're not really the sweet, gentle bowling champion you seem to be." Jake grinned. "They said you're secretly an actress."

Eleven

The following Sunday afternoon, Marley slumped in her chair and leaned her head back, giving herself up to the ministrations of her new pedicurist. Given the way this day had gone already, she desperately needed a little pampering.

The pedicurist offered her a choice of coconut lotion or peppermint spray. Wearily, Marley indicated both. Soon, the pedicurist's soothing strokes as she buffed calluses, applied lotion, tended to overgrown cuticles, and performed the other miracles of her art lulled Marley into relaxation. *Ahhh*.

"Christopher!" someone barked nearby. "Break's over!"

Marley's lazy oasis dissolved. Her surroundings jolted back into focus, hurling her into full awareness. All around her, grungy fellow employees rushed through the noisy, steam-filled kitchen in the coffee shop of Meredith's museum. Waitresses rushed through the swinging doors in search of ice or towels or trays. Busboys hustled past bearing tubs of filthy plates, and other crew members accepted their disgusting burdens, matter-of-factly shoving them onto the racks of the gigantic steel dishwasher.

The smells of burnt coffee, grease, and fried meat hung

in the air, sharpened by the ever-present tang of bleach. Sock-hop music played on the old-fashioned jukebox out front. Everything passed by in a pink polyester–tinged blur.

Against all reason, this had become Marley's life.

Resignedly, she scraped fifteen one-dollar bills from the meager pile of tips in her uniform pocket. She handed them to her pedicurist—one of her customers who'd happened to mention her expertise at the exact moment Marley and her aching feet had been granted a break.

"Thanks a million, Rowena." Marley thrust her tootsies into a pair of flip-flops and stood. "Do you want that piece of apple pie you ordered now?"

"Sounds great."

They navigated to the front of the museum coffee shop, Rowena reclaiming her place at the restaurant's long counter. Marley flopped her way to the pie case and slid out the last uncut whole pie in its aluminum foil tin. She surveyed it.

Serving pie was new to her. So far she'd handled one patty melt, several cheeseburgers, a chili, and any number of milkshakes, with only a few mishaps—and her dented pride—to show for it. Since this was Carly's first day on the job, Marley wanted to do well. She bit her lip, glancing at the jumble of serving items beside the enormous coffee urn. Decisively, she grabbed a thick white serving plate and knife and began to carefully cut a slice of pie.

"Not like that," another waitress interrupted, her orthopedic shoes squeaking as she hurried past.

She gave Marley an impatient over-the-shoulder look and set down her stack of vinyl-bound menus, then grabbed an implement from nearby. It looked a little like a miniature version of her accidental-Chanel car's hubcabs—round with spokes radiating from the center. One side of the spokes had serrated edges.

Marley thought it looked a lot like something she'd once seen on a Style Channel documentary on Max Factor, the king of Hollywood makeup. He'd been known for his scientific methods, for his carefully calibrated approach to beauty, and for his torturous-looking glamour "measurement" machines made of metal and pins and—

The waitress slammed the thing onto the pie. One thud later, she lifted it to reveal eight slightly smashed slices.

"Wow, that's really handy," Marley said, impressed. "You know, if that thing cut smaller pieces, it would be terrific for serving pâté de foie gras at parties."

She nodded, happily looking to the other waitress for confirmation. The woman raised her eyebrows.

"Whatever you say, your majesty." The waitress offered a mocking curtsy. "While you're crooking your pinkie over your tea and pâté, the rest of us will be over here, working our asses off."

She snatched up her menus and clipped an order ticket to the cook's rotating steel wheel, then bustled away. Marley watched her go, feeling inexplicably beaten.

This was exactly like being in school. Once again, Marley didn't fit in. Everyone knew it, and used that fact to make fun of her. Even as Carly, somehow people could see right through her—and then dismiss her.

She'd only ever been good at one thing: acting. Real life failed her. Dammit! What did she have to *do?*

Just serve the pie, she told herself. *And keep going.* So she did. She arranged a slice on a plate, nearly blinded a fellow waitress while squirting on whipped cream from the E-Z spray canister, then finally slid the dessert in front of Rowena. Triumph!

The pedicurist picked up her fork. "Wow, tough day?"

Her innocent sympathy was Marley's undoing. Tears rushed to her eyes and her throat closed up. Being a waitress was horrible. It was hard, hurried, unforgiving work, performed in an atmosphere of expectancy for people who didn't even have the decency to acknowledge her as a human being. The surroundings were stinky. The wardrobe was like something Joan and Melissa would savage on the red carpet. Being a waitress, Marley decided as she blinked back her tears, was the polar opposite of being a star actress.

She *needed* to be a star actress. This proved, once and for all, that she wasn't cut out for anything else.

"It's been a little tough," she forced past her tight throat.

"Hang in there," Rowena said. "Whenever you get down, just look at your toes."

Marley did. At first, the view was hazy with unshed tears. But gradually those tears cleared. Her new pedicure came into view, complete with the diminutive white daisies with yellow centers Rowena had expertly painted on the pink background of each big toe.

At the whimsical sight, a smile wobbled onto Marley's face. It became a full-blown grin.

"You're a genius," she told Rowena, feeling better already. Encouraged, she sniffed away her tears. "You ought to be on some big star's payroll as her personal pedicurist."

Rowena made a face. "Yeah, right. I'll do that. Just as soon as I magically make the rent on my hole-in-the-wall salon in West Hollywood."

"You've got your own salon?"

"Not for much longer." Rowena fished a foot-shaped business card from her purse and handed it over. "My partner and I can barely keep it afloat. When the economy goes south, nobody can afford extras like manicures and pedicures."

"Extras? Those are essentials!"

"I know!"

Both women smiled at each other. Marley examined the card. "Can I keep this? I know somebody who knows somebody who knows somebody. There might be a chance I can hook you up with one of those spoiled starlet types. A major trendsetter. If you started doing her nails, you'd be set."

"Like with a feature in *InStyle*." Rowena gave her a dreamy look. "Hey, whatever you can do, honey," she said gratefully. "I need all the help I can get."

Thoughtfully, Marley pocketed the card. She had a feeling Rowena's shop was about to get all the publicity it could handle.

By the time her shift was half an hour from being complete, Marley had started getting the hang of things. Sure, she still hadn't mastered the complexities of the coffee-maker, and the cook had looked like he'd wanted to strangle her a few times for messing up her order tickets, but she'd managed to persevere.

She approached her next table in the busy restaurant, efficiently handing out menus.

"Hello, I'm Carly and I'll be your waitress today. Our specials are the Reuben plate with onion rings, or the club sandwich, and the soup of the day is—" She took out her order pad and glanced up. "You! I can't believe you have the nerve to show up here."

Sondra and Brian grinned back at her. Beside Brian, Meredith sat with her nose in a book. It was thick and oversized, like a glossy coffee-table collectible. Knowing her twin sister, though, Marley figured the volume was more likely one of those dreary old historical texts.

"I'll have the club sandwich," Brian said.

"The Reuben," Sondra told her, "with a salad instead of the onion rings, dressing on the side. Not too much cheese on the sandwich." One of her cell phones rang. She flipped it open, holding her palm over the mouthpiece as she finished ordering. "A Diet Coke, extra ice. Oh, and tell the chef not to use too much butter when grilling that Reuben, would you? I don't—"

Marley seized their menus. She snapped the vinyl-covered stack fiercely onto the table. "Have you lost your minds?"

Sondra paused in mid-cell-conversation. "Oh, sorry. *Please* bring me a Reuben, would you? With a salad instead of the onion rings, dressing on the—"

"Stop." Marley slid into the booth beside Sondra, nudging her sideways with her hip. Unsurprisingly, her agent didn't complain. "I have a bone to pick with you two, and I'm not waiting an instant longer. You snuck out together yesterday before I had a chance to corner you."

Warily, Sondra hung up her phone. Brian paused in the act of polishing his fork with a napkin. They both looked sheepish.

They ought to look sheepish, Marley told herself. *After what they'd told Jake about her, they ought to look for new jobs.*

They said you're secretly an actress.

Sheesh. She could still feel the panic that had whooshed through her in that awful moment at the bowling alley. She'd never in a million years expected that statement to come from Jake's lips.

"Are you both insane?" Marley demanded. Her authority felt lessened by her hideous Pepto Bismol polyester uniform, but she tried to muster her usual clout, all the same. "You told Jake *the truth* about me! You told him I'm an actress!"

They nodded, obviously and outrageously pleased.

"That's right," Sondra said.

"Hiding in plain sight," Brian agreed. "It's brilliant."

"Brilliant? It's suicidal!"

They looked wounded.

"It's the oldest trick in the book," Sondra explained. "Dazzle 'em with the truth. If Jake thinks you're an amateur thespian, he won't think twice whenever you slip up—"

"Great. You *assume* I'm going to slip up?"

"—he'll just think you're making an 'I'm an actress' joke."

Marley put her head in her hands, groaning. "It wasn't enough that you ambushed me into your wigged-out ideas of lowbrow entertainment, hillbilly relatives, and beef-jerky addiction—"

"Hey. For the last time, the beef-jerky thing was your—"

She glared at Brian and he snapped his mouth shut. "Now you've turned me into a double liar, too! I hate lying to Jake. Really, I do. He's a nice guy. He doesn't deserve this."

"Don't worry," Sondra told her, patting her hand. "You'll get better with practice."

"I don't want to get better with practice! I want none of this to be necessary."

"Don't worry. You're doing great," Brian reassured her.

"Yes. You're fabulous," Sondra agreed.

"No help from the two of you." Marley turned to Meredith. "Did you know they actually took me *bowling* yesterday?"

"They told me that," her sister said, blithely turning the page in her book. "I didn't believe it."

"Bowling was fun," Sondra said brightly. "That Jake's a real hottie. You could do worse." She gazed longingly at the plate of food another waitress carried past their table. "So what happened when he pulled out that 'you're an actress' line?"

"I told him you were both mental patients."

Brian and Sondra laughed. "No, what did you really tell him?"

Marley arched a brow.

"Ha! Good one, sis," Meredith said.

Marley relented. "I told him that my mother had always wanted me to become an actress—"

"That much is true, at least," Meredith muttered.

"—and that because of her, I'd dabbled in some community playhouse work. I think he bought it."

But she still felt terrible about it. Playing the role of Carly was one thing—actively denying her real career was something else again. Somehow, it seemed doubly deceptive.

"Good thing," Sondra said, nodding. "Because Brian and I have news."

"Yes." He abandoned his efforts to buff-clean his coffee cup. "We've seen a tape of the *Dream Date* footage they've shot so far—"

"What? How did you—"

"They smuggled it out," Meredith interrupted, still reading. "Payola among the crew."

"—and it's remarkable. A real hoot," Brian continued eagerly. "I'm telling you, Marley, you have incredible comedic flair."

"With the material on that tape," Sondra said, picking up the gauntlet, "we could successfully market you to Woody Allen, the Farrelly brothers, even Nora Ephron or Garry Marshall. They've done wonders for Meg Ryan and Julia Roberts, you know."

"But, but—" Stricken, Marley gaped at them. "But I want to be a serious actress. That's the whole point of this *Dream Date* thing. To show I can play against type. Against Tara. To show how real and raw I can be."

They shrugged. "All we're saying," Sondra explained with a nonchalant wave, "is that we could not stop laughing while watching the footage of your dates. The goats, the hot dogs, the slapstick! Brian practically howled when you whacked Jake with that car door."

"That whole 'I'm a bus girl' thing you improvised was genius," Brian said. "As *if!*"

Marley sunk lower in the booth. This was terrible. All her efforts . . . just for laughs. Was she doomed to be a sitcom has-been forever?

"It'll be different when Jake and I are more comfortable together," she said defiantly. *Comfortable—as in, kissing?* her conscience taunted. She gave it a mental dropkick and went on. "There won't be so many awkward moments. In fact, I'm meeting him for dinner tonight. We'll start morphing into the perfect couple in approximately"—she checked the wall clock—"two hours. So there."

"Good luck," Meredith muttered. "You'll need it."

Marley turned to her. "What are you doing here, anyway? Don't you have some kind of boooooring advertising historian work to do? Or did leaving your office just to pester me take priority?"

"As a matter of fact." Her sister looked up from her book.

"It did. I had to come down here and make sure you hadn't (a) burned the place down with your curling iron, (b) forgotten to come to work at all, or (c) caused a mass revolt among the coffee shop staff by suggesting they all get highlights and wear lipstick."

"Very funny," Marley said. Although the waitress who'd helped her with the pie-cutting *could* have used a mustache-bleaching kit. "Besides, I'll have you know I use a straightening iron these days."

"Oooh. I stand corrected."

"You stand slumped over. Your posture defies Darwinism."

"Darwinism?" Meredith snorted. "To you, Darwinisms are the sweet nothings you whisper in your latest Hollywood stud muffin's ear. 'Oh, Darwin, you cuddly-wuddly hunk of he-man-ness,' " she mocked. " 'Come on over and help polish my Emmy.' "

Marley seethed. "You take that back! Nobody makes fun of my Emmy! I treasure that Emmy!"

"Girls, girls," Brian interrupted mildly. "Let's not cause a scene."

They both glanced at him. Marley realized where she was and what was at stake. So, apparently, did Meredith. With a final glare at each other, they crossed their arms and looked away.

"You know," Sondra remarked, "now that your hair is closer to its natural color, Marley, the resemblance between you and Meredith is astonishing."

"It's true," Brian agreed, nodding as he examined both sisters. "Meredith could be your stand-in. Your body double. Your stunt person."

"My biggest headache."

Beset by worries about her supposed laugh-riot performance as Carly, Marley didn't have time to babble on about the similarities between her and her sister. She and Meredith were identical twins, after all. It didn't take a rocket scientist to recognize they'd look alike.

She slid from the booth and stood. "If you'll all excuse me," she said with dignity, "I have butter pats to stock."

They nodded. Nearly respectfully.

How about that? Marley thought. Maybe, after seven-and-a-half hours of serving food, shuffling plates, and reciting specials, she'd been blessed with an aura of practical, blue-collar confidence. Go figure.

Emboldened by their response to her, Marley paused. She fixed them with a no-nonsense look. "And, for the love of Jennifer Aniston's latest hairdo, please—*please*—stop interfering with this. I've got it all under control."

"Your cutlet slipped again, Control Girl," Brian said, nodding toward her chest.

What was it with him and the cutlet watch? Marley slapped her hand over the breast augmentation device currently sneaking toward her armpit. She wrenched it into place, then resumed her decorous pose.

"You've seen the last of the slapstick," she promised them. "By this time tomorrow, Jake will be completely under the spell of Carly, girl-next-door extraordinaire. *And* there'll be some very memorable moments on upcoming *Dream Date* tapes to prove it."

Congratulating herself on her steely resolve, Marley flounced toward the waitress's station. She only hoped she could resist succumbing to those memorable moments herself. After all, it wouldn't do for Carly to fall in love with her co-star . . . especially not when that co-star was completely unaware of the script.

In the tiny kitchen of Jake and Noah's apartment, Noah scrambled onto one of the two stools fronting the Formica island. He put his chin in his hands. "Whatcha gonna cook for dinner?"

"I dunno, sport." Jake ran his hands through his hair, then squinted through his glasses at the possibilities arrayed on the countertop in front of him. "Carly's a pretty fancy lady. She deserves something really special."

Again, he surveyed his choices. Frozen chicken pot pies? Take-out pizza? Hot dogs? Nah, they'd already done hot dogs at the petting zoo. Hungry Man dinners? Hormel chili? Canned beef stew?

"Macaroni and cheese?" Noah suggested. "That's special."

Jake considered the box. It was their family favorite, especially with cut-up hot dogs in it. But that brought them right back around to the hot dog issue. He shook his head. "I'm thinking . . . something different."

"Cheerios for dinner! Yay!"

Noah got down and whooped through the kitchen.

Jake nabbed him as he ran past. "Not Cheerios. I think . . . I might have to cook something."

His son's eyes widened. "Cook it?"

"Yes," Jake agreed gravely. "Possibly"—he lowered his voice—"from scratch."

"Yuck. I don't like scratch."

"It's not a kind of food. It's a way of making food."

"Yuck. I don't like scratch," Noah repeated.

"You'll eat it and like it," Jake commanded.

"You sound like Grandpa."

"When I was your age, Grandpa would have sent me to bed without supper for saying something like that."

Noah only laughed. He could recognize a bluff when he heard one. "Make some waffles for Carly. That would be good."

Dubiously, Jake picked up the box of Eggos. If he stashed the package someplace, she might never know they weren't homemade. All waffles looked . . . waffley, didn't they?

Nah. The fake blueberry bits would give him away. Nobody kept fake blueberry bits on hand, unless they lived in an industrial kitchen. Jake and Noah lived in a mostly un-used kitchen. Although the path to the phone (used for speed-dialing pizza delivery) was well grooved into the linoleum.

"If I want to do this right for Carly," Jake said, "I'm afraid I have no choice. I'm going to have to call in an expert."

"Yay! Pizza guy!" Noah jumped up and down.

"Nope." Gently, Jake put a hand to his son's head to make him quit hopping. He stroked the hair away from his face, then chucked him on the chin. "An even better expert."

Noah wrinkled his forehead. "The Hamburger Helper?"

Jake shook his head and reached for the phone. "Grandma."

Twelve

Stephanie Jarvis was the ultimate California girl turned mother. She kept her blonde hair highlighted, her tan perfectly golden, and her smile sunnily bright. At the age of fifty-six, she dressed like a woman half her age—and pulled it off. Where other mothers yearned occasionally for moments to themselves, Stephanie embraced every instant with her family. She didn't like to be alone . . . so consequently, she never was. Stephanie always got what she wanted.

Today, Jake realized, what his mother wanted was to help him with making dinner. She arrived at his apartment bearing grocery bags, pink tulips, and a bottle of chardonnay, and immediately proceeded to take over.

"I'm so glad you called me," she said as she breezed inside. She kissed Noah hello. "I've been waiting years."

"Come on, Mom." Jake stepped aside as four more people followed Stephanie inside—his father, his two brothers, and an unknown twenty-something man. "I call you once a month, at least."

She tsk-tsked. "I've been waiting for *this* call. About a woman."

Trailed by her entourage, Stephanie bustled into the kitchen. Her yellow blouse and tropical-print Capri pants were brighter than anything else in his apartment—louder, too. Her platform wedgies lifted her nearly to her son's shoulder level as she began unpacking groceries.

"It's just a dinner," Jake said.

"It's a dinner you're prepared to cook. That makes all the difference in the world."

He leaned against the counter. Everyone else took seats, either at the island or at the kitchen table. Noah stood beside his grandmother, gazing up at her with obvious devotion.

"I told you about this whole *Dream Date* thing," Jake said. Although this particular date with Carly wouldn't be on camera, he remembered. This date was private, and all the more anticipated because of it. "That's all this is. It's practically a business dinner, to help me keep my contract with KKZP."

His mother only smiled—a knowing, delighted smile. "I thought we'd make one of your grandmother's old recipes. One she handed down to me."

Jake braced himself. Other families shared recipes for treasured old-style favorites like four-cheese lasagna, pierogies, Swedish meatballs, tamales, or corned beef brisket. *His* family's idea of timeless traditionalism was—

"A nice poached chicken breast with steamed asparagus and mango coulis. How does that sound?"

"Like spa cuisine from the sixties."

"Stop that. It'll be lovely." Stephanie reached up and attempted to brush a wrinkle from Jake's shirt. "Don't argue with your mother."

Beneath her clear-eyed gaze, Jake softened. Just for a moment, he felt like an eight-year-old boy again, yearning for a piece of his mother's time all for himself. Now, his wish would be granted. They were both adults, but that didn't mean they couldn't spend some quality time together. Jake felt glad he'd called her.

Stephanie smiled fondly at him. She shook her head as though marveling at the fact that she was actually looking *up* at her own son. Then she turned briskly to the counter.

"Of course, we'll need some appetizers to start with. James, you start peeling this shrimp"—she handed a two-pound bag of jumbos to Jake's older brother—"and Nate, you find a plate or something to serve it on. You'll need ice, too. Chop, chop!"

She clapped her hands like the seasoned household general she was. At her command, Jake's other older brother got up from the kitchen table and began rummaging through Jake's cupboards. His father left the table, too.

"I'll turn the TV this way," Henry Jarvis said. "There's a Braves game being broadcast on TBS." Sounds of grunting and swearing were heard as he wrestled the living-room TV and its stand sideways so the unit faced the kitchen doorway. He turned it on, then flipped through the channels.

James stationed himself at the sink to start on the shrimp. Jake received four mangos to peel and slice—his assignment—along with a cutting board and knife to use in fulfilling his culinary mission.

Soon, his tiny kitchen teemed with activity—and people. His brothers, both solid six-footers like Jake, dodged Jake and Stephanie and Noah as they went about their assigned tasks. Dishes clattered. Water ran. Everyone began talking.

So much for a private, shared mother-and-son moment. Jake should have known better than to hope for such a thing.

"Henry, you help, too." Stephanie shoved a bowl and a bottle of cocktail sauce toward Jake's dad. "You know I can't open these bottles all by myself."

Like hell she couldn't, Jake thought, suppressing a grin. His mother had been taking aerobics classes and Nautilus training for as long as he could remember. Working out was like a religion to her—the fit-into-my-Capri-pants religion. She probably could have bench-pressed a Frigidaire and not broken a sweat.

But his dad bought into the ruse every time. Looking grumpy—and flattered—he accepted the bowl and bottle.

"Ulrich, you help, too," Stephanie said, gesturing toward the lone man remaining at the table. As he unfolded his tall frame from the chair, she turned to Jake. "You haven't met Ulrich yet. He's visiting California as part of a German cultural program. A month from now, he'll be back in Göttingen, but until then, we're happy to have him staying with us."

Ahh. Jake had forgotten his mother's propensity for taking in strays. As a kid, he'd always come home to a house filled with half the neighborhood—his brothers' friends, his sisters' giggling cheerleader pals, his mother's fellow Mary Kay Cosmetics representatives in the days before she'd defected to Avon. There had never been a dull moment in the Jarvis household—and there'd never been a peaceful, intimately shared one, either.

Stephanie unpacked an enormous bundle of asparagus from her grocery bags and turned to Ulrich. "Do you know how to clean asparagus? Just wash it under some running water, then hold each piece like this"—Stephanie demonstrated—"and snap it."

"Ja." Ulrich nodded. "Der Spargel."

"Excellent!" Stephanie beamed. "Now, Jake. About the poached chicken breast . . ."

Jake listened intently as she instructed him in seasoning, then poaching, the chicken. A few minutes later, Noah edged in beside him and tugged on his grandmother's blouse.

"Grandma, can I help?"

"Oh, sweetie." Stephanie paused in the midst of searching for a flower vase, the tulips cradled in her arm like a particularly froufrou football. "You can just go right into the other room and play. That's how you can help."

Noah's mouth turned downward. "I wanna *really* help."

Jake's heart ached for his son. He remembered the feeling of being put aside—however gently—all too well.

"Why don't you help Uncle James with the shrimp?" he suggested, glancing to the counter space near the stove where his brother had set up a shrimp-on-ice assembly line. "He could probably use your artistic eye to make a nice display."

"Sure, sport!" James urged. "Come on over."

Happily, Noah skipped to his uncle's side. "I'll make it look great!" he crowed.

Stephanie watched. "Honestly, Jake. He's not a little caterer-in-training. I'd think he'd have more fun playing with his toys. Why should he want to be cooped up in the kitchen with the grown-ups?"

"Because G.I. Joe's no substitute for *that*." Jake nodded toward the other side of the cramped kitchen, where his brother and his son were laughing as they pretended to make two peeled shrimp do the mambo. "That's why."

His mother looked. Frowned. "I don't know where Noah gets that from. *You* certainly preferred your toys."

"Sure. At least, that's what I wanted you to think."

"What?"

"Nothing, Mom."

Still, she gazed at Noah, then back at her son, perplexed. "Why, your father couldn't have paid you to help him work on chores in the garage with him."

"He paid me *not* to help him," Jake told her.

Stephanie locked eyes with Henry. He shrugged. "By the time Jake came along, I'd realized it was easier just to do the damn chores myself."

"You're lucky, Jake," Nate remarked, glancing up as he got out a blender for the coulis. "Dad almost sawed off my thumb with a circular saw once."

"Yeah," James chimed in. "He beat me over the head with a length of PVC pipe. And almost superglued my hand to an electrical cord while repairing a lamp."

"Almost, almost, almost," Henry mimicked. "Those were accidents." He waved his hand as he turned back to the base-ball game. "You're all a bunch of crybabies."

Stephanie grinned. "See? You didn't miss much, son."

But Jake, gazing at his family as they worked together, still believed he had. Hell, he didn't hold any grudges. He'd let bygones be bygones a long time ago. Still, being with his folks again only reminded him how different he wanted his life with Noah to be. He wanted Noah to feel all the love, all the singular attention and care, he could possibly muster.

His mother found a vase, then carried it to the stool where her husband sat watching the Braves. She sorted the tulips, snipped their stems, and arranged them in water, all while chattering to Henry about the game. As Jake looked on, his father silently put his arm around Stephanie's waist.

She smiled at him, still saying something nonsensical about the color scheme of the Braves' uniforms. Henry smiled back. The intimacy between them was plain to see, and a little bit remarkable, after all these years, too. No matter how crazy things had gotten in their household, Jake recalled, his parents had always been rock solid. Preoccupied, busy, and occasionally embarrassing, but always rock solid.

He looked at Nate and James. His brothers still worked diligently at their stations, occasionally sneaking glances at the baseball game and frequently cracking jokes with Noah. Ulrich cleaned and snapped asparagus with good-natured Teutonic industriousness, the pile of green veggies beside him growing with every passing minute.

Jake shook his head. He'd forgotten that his mother only understood how to cook for an army of seven people, three of them ravenous teenage boys. No matter how old he and his brothers got, Stephanie still prepared enough food for a pillaging horde.

"Grandma, Grandma! Come look at this!" Noah called. He ran over to Stephanie and grabbed her hand. "Come look at what me and Uncle James did."

Carrying her finished flower arrangement, Stephanie went to the counter. There, James displayed the shrimp he and Noah had laid out circularly on ice.

First course: the ShrimpCapades.

"Does it look pretty?" Noah asked his grandmother, looking up at her with an eager expression. His hair stuck up in a cowlick. His clothes—a T-shirt, swimming trunks, and one of Jake's old neckties—didn't match, as usual. But he clearly wanted Stephanie's approval. "Do you think a lady would like it?"

She studied the shrimp. "Yes, Noah. Yes, I do. It's lovely."

"Yippee!" Noah hooted, running around the room. He high-fived his uncle on his second pass, then ran some more. "Carly's gonna like it, Carly's gonna like it," he sang.

Uh-oh. Instantly, Jake lowered his gaze. He went back to work on the chicken, frowning as though sprinkling on salt and pepper required every ounce of concentration he possessed.

"She's going to love it," his mother told Noah, her voice laden with significance.

Jake cringed, hearing the well-meant lecture lurking behind her words. But she was talking to Noah, he assured himself. It would be safe to glance up long enough to get the chicken in the pan.

Thinking exactly that, Jake lifted his gaze. His mother was staring straight at him, with a look he, unfortunately, recognized all too well. It was the Noah-deserves-a-mother-you-stubborn-idiot look.

Stephanie raised her eyebrows and nodded toward her grandson. Defiantly, Jake met her meaningful gaze with one of his own.

"We're fine, Mom," he said. "You can quit campaigning, already. Noah and I don't need anybody or anything."

Naturally enough, an instant later Carly arrived . . . and proved him completely wrong.

The first thing Marley noticed when she arrived—uncharacteristically early, and with Gaffer in tow—at Jake's place for dinner was that he wasn't alone. The second thing she noticed was that the people surrounding him looked more like a fantasy family than the cast of *Fantasy Family* had.

They were all tall, blond, and beautiful, with Pepsodent smiles and casually coiffed hair. Jake's dad—introduced to her as Henry—looked hearty and vaguely golden, in a pro-golfer sort of way. His mother, Stephanie, could easily have been an ex-Bond girl . . . if 007 had ever boffed beach bunnies. His two brothers were like something straight out of *Hunky All-American Monthly*. And their friend with the dark, curly hair, Ulrich, somehow brought a European flair to everything he did.

"Ein reizender Hund," he said, nodding toward Gaffer. "Wie heisst er?"

"He says that's a lovely dog," Stephanie translated while Marley bent to pick up her Yorkie. "What's his name?"

"Gaffer," Marley told them, unsnapping his favorite rhinestone-studded leash. "His name's Gaffer."

They gave her clueless looks.

"You know, like the chief lighting technician on a TV or movie set?"

"Oh. So *that's* what that means," Jake's brother Nate said.

Marley nodded in confirmation.

At the same moment, so did Jake. Also in confirmation. She tilted her head in surprise.

That's when it struck her, oddly enough for the first time: their worlds were alike. If she were herself instead of Carly, she and Jake could have shared funny we-work-on-TV stories about technical crew members and other below-the-line types. About craft services and the ultra-caloric feasts they provided. About honeywagons and their script-memorizing inhabitants.

Or maybe sportscasters didn't get star trailers, she realized. That was a shame. While on the set, hers had been Marley's home away from home—and Gaffer's, too.

"Hello, Gaffer!" Stephanie exclaimed. "You're sooo cute!" She scratched the dog between his perked-up ears, cooing baby talk at him.

Marley liked her already.

She caught Jake giving her a funny look, and stepped closer to him, still cradling her dog. "I hope you don't mind that I brought him," she said earnestly. "It was an emergency."

"An emergency?"

She nodded. "A doggie psyche emergency. Since I started *Dream Date* and my new waitressing job, poor Gaffer's been left home alone so often. He's really getting lonely. He used to spend every day with me on the—"

Set. On the set. Marley stopped herself just in time.

"—job hunt. You know, pounding the old pavement? Hitting the want ads?" She forced a laugh. "Since I started working at the coffee shop, he can't come with me anymore."

"Of course," Stephanie said. "They don't allow dogs."

"Actually, he can't handle all the caffeine. He gets a doggie buzz going, runs around, tries to get lucky with the other waitresses . . ." Marley shrugged as if to say *what can a dog owner do?* "He made us both look bad."

"You could never look bad." Jake stepped nearer, oblivious to the meaningful glances his family shared at the movement.

He stroked a tendril of hair away from her cheek with his fingertip, his gesture both tender and uniquely welcome. "Not even as the owner of a waitress-humping, caffeine-addicted, troublemaking bundle of fur."

"Jake!" his mother objected.

But everyone else laughed. Everyone, that is, except Marley. Because even though Jake's dazzling smile and his joke both demanded an answering grin—for politeness' sake, at least—she found herself completely unable to comply.

At the first brush of Jake's fingertips against her skin, Marley was suddenly immobilized by the fluttering of her heart, by the overwhelming sense that he'd touched her not because her hair had been too messy to bear . . . but simply because he hadn't been able to help himself.

Simply because he wanted, *needed,* to make contact with her, just that much.

She wanted him, too. Now. All at once, Marley realized it. Her pulse tripped into overdrive and her mouth went dry. That was real desire she saw in his eyes, real interest and real affection. More than likely, his feelings were mirrored in her eyes, too. She couldn't help it. How had this happened so hard, so fast, so *now?*

Sure, Jake was gorgeous. Sure, he was smart and funny, and he had a way of looking at her that made her feel as though she were the only woman in the universe. But did that mean she had to fall for him—*wham!*—just like that?

Yes. Yes, it did, she discovered next.

"I love dogs," he said, reaching to pet hers.

He loved dogs! Even more of her resistance crumbled.

His big hand nearly covered Gaffer's skinny, shaggy body as he gently pet the dog. Gaffer thumped his tail in canine ecstasy.

Incredulously, Marley watched the two of them together as Jake muttered sweet nothings and went on petting. Gaffer was a girly dog, a gawky, skinny, rhinestone-collar-wearing fur bag, and she knew it. He went to a dog spa every month for a massage, haircut, and pedicure. He ate custom-blended dog food and snacked on imported vitamin chews. He slept on a tiny featherbed and owned several sweaters. He was exactly the kind of spoiled sissy dog most men—especially macho men—hated.

But Jake liked him. She could tell. It endeared Jake to her all the more.

"I never expected this," he said, giving her a delighted look. "I can't believe you're a dog person."

"What else would I be?"

"A"—he made a face—"cat person."

"Now, why would I want a pet who had no interest in me, thought it was better than me, and couldn't be bothered to snuggle?"

"Exactly!" Jake said. His grin widened. "Look, Noah. Carly has a dog."

The boy had already edged closer, beside his grandma. He tentatively pet Gaffer, looking to his dad for reassurance. Jake nodded to let him know he was doing fine. Emboldened, Noah cooed to Gaffer in an exact imitation of Stephanie's baby talk.

Everyone smiled. Marley felt welcomed into their family . . . *again,* she realized. A panicky feeling edged over her, ruining the mushy, I'm-falling-for-you sensation she'd been enjoying. The whole world got dark. Movie-dark, like when the camera men on old black-and-white classics used to put filters on their lenses to simulate nighttime. The shadows and brightness were all still there, only they were muted.

Falsely muted.

Just like her.

Marley glanced down at her inexpensive discount-store ensemble. She fingered her—*Carly's*—plain brown hair, and considered the discount-store, wooden-heeled Candies slides she'd shoved her aching faux-waitress's feet into. None of this was *her.* None of it was real. She was deceiving everyone—and worse, they all appeared to love her for it.

On cue, Noah grabbed her free hand. "Come on, Carly. Let's go play."

His sweet little face begged her to agree. His eyes were blue and bright beneath his sandy bangs, and his cheeks bore faint freckles that made him look adorable. He tugged at her hand insistently. Just like that, Marley felt something inside her give way. It was warm and cozy and wonderful.

She didn't like kids, she reminded herself. They were noisy. Jumpy. Irritating. But looking down into Noah's hopeful expression, she had trouble remembering exactly how she'd formed such an opinion. She had even more trouble remembering how to stick to it.

It's business. This is a business dinner, Marley told herself. But if that had been strictly true, she'd have insisted on having cameras here tonight. She'd have demanded that Jake agree to be filmed for *Dream Date* for the résumé reel he'd unknowingly been helping her make. She hadn't done any of that.

She was falling, falling . . . and the worse part was, even if Jake returned her feelings, it would be Carly he wanted. Wouldn't it?

"I'll take Gaffer," Stephanie offered. She scooped the

eager dog into her arms and nodded toward her grandson. "You go on."

Marley glanced at Jake. He looked troubled, too, as though he'd just realized where all this might lead.

"Come on, Carly," Noah urged.

So, she did. She trouped into Noah's bedroom, where everything was scaled smaller, like in a playhouse production. She patiently ooh-ed and ahh-ed over the Lego Duplo creations Noah showed her, exclaimed over the crayoned scribbles he variously described as "Daddy," "a football game," and "me." She sat down on the floor—after Noah cleared a space amid the action figures and building blocks—to begin a game of Candy Land . . . and found herself actually enjoying it.

"Oh, no!" Marley cried, staring in horror at the fat green cartoon monster on the card she'd just drawn. "It's Plumpy!"

Noah chortled. "That means you've gotta go back to the start."

She knew that. She'd already done it twice. Resignedly, Marley moved her red gingerbread man plastic marker to the other side of the board. Next she'd be stuck in the Molasses Swamp for sure.

This game never ended. If she'd ever engaged her agent and the *Fantasy Family* execs in contract negotiations over a round of Candy Land, they'd have given her anything she wanted, just to make it to King Kandy at the end.

It was fun, though. As a child, Marley hadn't played games. She hadn't had time, between lessons, auditions, and acting jobs. On set she'd usually had a tutor—as mandated by law—but her tutors hadn't been Mary Poppins types who'd offered up sugarplums and board games and singalongs. They'd been no-nonsense women, paid to ensure their charges could read, write, and compute back-end percentages.

This was different. Sitting cross-legged with Noah, Marley discovered fun for its own sake was perfectly worthwhile—especially when it was shared. She could happily have stayed there all day amid the Bob the Builder posters, Play-Doh, and Hot Wheels cars.

Being with Noah was like having a second shot at childhood. All at once, Marley wondered if that was one of parenthood's big secrets—mothers and fathers everywhere were enjoying all the things they'd missed in their own childhoods by experiencing them through their children's eyes.

But there was Noah, too, with his inquisitive nature, gift for funny voices, and boundless imagination. Undoubtedly, *he* was the most wondrous part of parenting for Jake. For an instant, Marley envied him. He had so much. And she . . . well, she had even less than she'd realized, as it turned out.

For now, though, she had this moment. Marley drew another card and successfully navigated over Gumdrop Pass. She smiled as Noah took his turn, exaggeratedly swooping his plastic gingerbread man marker four spaces to a purple square. He was about to win. She didn't mind a bit.

She only wished the game didn't have to end so soon.

Thirteen

His family had settled in for the duration.

Jake realized it about the time his two sisters arrived, bearing fruit salad, two loaves of French bread, and more chardonnay. Rebecca and Bethany were younger than he was, but they were both Stephanie Jarvis's daughters—and as such, they were drawn to family gatherings like NBA players to souped-up SUVs. They fluttered into his apartment all chatter and curiosity, and immediately sat down with his mother to get the scoop on Jake's new girlfriend.

"She's not my 'girlfriend,'" he explained before they could get carried away. "She's just my assigned partner for *Dream Date.*"

"Oh, yeah?" Rebecca looked him over with classic little-sister nosiness. "Then how come you're cradling her dog?"

"You look," Bethany added, "like one of those hapless husbands waiting outside the dressing rooms at Macy's, holding a purse at arm's length and trying to ignore the girdles to your left."

He did not. "This dog is perfectly respectable. Macho, even."

"He's wearing a pink rhinestone-studded collar."

"That's how secure he is in his doggie masculinity."

"His toenails are painted Passion Purple."

Jake held Gaffer at arm's length. He looked. *Gah.* Somebody needed to stop Carly before she emasculated this poor mutt altogether.

"So what?" he asked, hugging him close again. "He's the Dennis Rodman of dogs."

"That's hardly a recommendation," Stephanie said, then went back to dishing gossip with her daughters.

Jake listened, carrying Gaffer in a football hold. He used his free hand to lift the lid on the pan of chicken, nodding contentedly at the rich aroma that wafted out. Sure, he'd rather have had a nice beefy T-bone—and he'd bet Gaffer would have, too—but the traditional Jarvis family spa cuisine would have to do. It probably would impress Carly a lot more than Day-Glo mac 'n' cheese would have.

Reminded of her, he cocked his head, listening for sounds of the usual mayhem coming from Noah's room. He didn't hear a thing. That was strange. Typically, Noah didn't do anything quietly—not even sleeping. He tossed, flailed, and talked his way through every night, making a twisty mess of his SpongeBob SquarePants bedding by morning.

Jake moved on, checking Nate's progress on the mango coulis. He watched James and Ulrich set out plates and cutlery, buffet style, on the kitchen island. He caught a double play on the Braves game, high-fived his dad, then shared a bite of shrimp with Gaffer.

All the while, his mother and sisters went on gabbing. Within minutes, the women had dubbed Jake and Carly "soul mates." They gushed about how lucky he'd been to find a nice girl in the midst of La-La Land. They tossed out theories on subjects ranging from Jake and Carly's next date to the best caterer for their inevitable engagement party.

They progressed all the way to suggesting potential housing bargains in the San Fernando Valley and issuing advisories about using enough sunscreen while on honeymoon in the Bahamas before Jake had had enough.

"Look, cut it out. Carly and I don't have a future together."

"Well, not with that attitude, you don't."

"Yeah, Mr. Commitment-phobe."

"Wake up and smell the Ben-Gay, Jake," Bethany said. "You're not getting any younger."

"What the hell does that mean?" *No. He wouldn't be baited, dammit.* "Carly and I don't have a future beyond the final *Dream Date* taping, and that's the way I like it."

"Who're you trying to convince, son?" Henry asked, one eye still on the TV. "Us? Or yourself?"

Jake looked at his dad. *All of us,* he thought.

That gave him pause. The minute he'd realized Carly was caring enough to love a shaggy mutt like Gaffer, though, a part of him had begun to think she might be willing to put up with a couple of sloppy, football-watching, uncoordinated-wardrobe-wearing knuckleheads like him and Noah. He'd begun to envision the three of them together. He'd begun to think he wanted that . . . or at least wasn't ruling it out altogether.

Hell. "Carly doesn't even like kids." Jake cut his family's instant protests short with a look. "She's clueless about them. At the petting zoo, she couldn't get away from the rugrats fast enough."

"Those kids weren't Noah," Stephanie said blithely.

"Yeah," Bethany put in. "Nobody can resist my nephew."

Jake wasn't so sure. Everything about Carly screamed not-child-friendly. She wore high heels. Lipstick. Dangling jewelry that begged to be grabbed and pulled. She was squeamish and girly, and couldn't even play the funny-body-parts game properly.

Although she *had* tried . . .

Nah. If and when he ever did choose a mother for Jake, it wouldn't be someone like Carly. The last thing Noah needed was constant exposure to an award-show-loving self-improvement junkie with a beef-jerky fixation.

Although he and Noah *did* both enjoy the occasional Slim Jim beef snack. . . .

Nah. Noah didn't need a mother. He didn't need anything that Jake couldn't provide. That was that.

When dinner was almost ready, Jake headed down the hallway to find Noah and Carly. Their voices reached him as he neared his son's room. He slowed to listen.

"Get him in here. Stat!" Carly said.

"He needs help," Noah agreed.

Rustling sounds could be heard. Toys clanked. Jake edged closer, his curiosity piqued. He'd expected to find Carly sitting bored on Noah's twin bed, eyes glazed over with apathy while she pretended to be interested in Lego Duplos or Noah's stuffed animal collection. One of Jake's dates, Natasha, had reacted in just that way when she'd offered to play with Noah while Jake dealt with the baby-sitter.

It had been their last date.

Of course, Natasha had volunteered to play with Noah— even though the boy hadn't exactly been chomping at the bit. Today, however, Noah had all but handcuffed Carly to his wrist and dragged her into his room, so eager had he been to play with her. *That* was new. . . .

"This is going to be a tough case." Carly's voice was exaggeratedly dramatic. "He'll need expert assistance."

"I'll put him on the table," Noah said, sounding equally serious. "You go to work."

Slowly, Jake edged nearer. Silently, he peeked around the corner into his son's room.

At first, he thought they were playacting a medical drama, with heroic doctors and expert nurses. Noah's Hot Wheels cars were lined up all in a row, as though they were emergency vehicles. Stuffed animals of all shapes and sizes waited on the sidelines, apparent witnesses to the pretend tragedy. Action figures posed in the midst of a plastic Hot Wheels track, like superheroes waiting their turn in the action.

He spied G.I. Joe laying on what must be the "operating table"—four wooden blocks arranged end-to-end and topped with a "Go Fish" playing card. Carly bent over Joe, rapidly unfastening his tiny fatigues. Nearby, Noah scanned his assembled Crayolas and Magic Markers—medical instruments, Jake assumed. Seriously, he chose a brown marker. At Carly's signal, he handed it to her.

Their fingers touched. Carly glanced up, her profile toward Jake's still-undetected position. She smiled at Noah. He smiled back. At their affectionate exchange, Jake felt something inside him loosen. As though he'd been holding his breath, a part of him eased in that moment.

Had he *wanted* the two of them to get along? Or had he secretly been hoping for another Natasha-style incident?

He didn't know. But he frowned slightly as he continued to look on. The funny glow in his chest, near his heart, was seriously at odds with the unsettled sensation he was experiencing elsewhere.

Jake hadn't felt this mixed up since his first day in the broadcasting booth, at a high-school football matchup. Then, he'd been discombobulated by carrying on sports commentary while simultaneously listening to the director's voice on his earpiece. It had taken a while to get used to being instructed—"ease up on the statistics" or "let it go, Jarvis"— while appearing to spontaneously do his job. Now, he suspected it would be just as hard to appear unaffected by this new closeness between Carly and Noah.

Carly held up G.I. Joe—who was now, Jake saw, clad in a pair of surfer-style board shorts, a tank top, and his dog tags. In her opposite hand, she raised the Magic Marker Noah had given her.

"Are you sure this marker is washable?" she asked Noah. "We don't want to tattoo G.I. Joe permanently."

Noah nodded.

"Okay. Hmmm. I think . . ." She bit her lip, studying the macho military action figure. "A goatee. For that poet-on-the-beach look."

Huh? What kind of heroic, Hasbro-loving doctor dealt with facial hair before injuries? What about the tough case? What about needing expert assistance?

"These sideburns are *so* 2001," Carly announced. "Skin color, please."

"Skin color," Noah mimicked, handing over a Crayola.

Earnestly, Carly scrubbed the crayon over G.I. Joe's rugged sideburns. Gradually, they disappeared.

"There!" she announced. "He's ready."

Noah grabbed G.I. Joe. He posed him at the end of the Hot Wheels track, near the hairpin curve. Then, with practiced motions, he began walking him along the track.

"Your limo is waitin'," he said in a fancy voice, sounding as though he'd memorized the phrase just today. In fact, he probably had. Jake sure as hell hadn't ever had the budget to take Noah for a limo ride.

After a Noah-guided jaunt atop a black Hot Wheels Corvette, G.I. Joe arrived at the middle of the track. As he did, Carly crouched behind the stuffed animal spectators. She made the elephant wave his trunk and the teddy bear clap his paws. She roared out crowd sounds, really getting into the game now.

Jake couldn't help but grin. Whatever this game was, it was ridiculous. But Carly's enthusiasm was as charming as it was unexpected.

"Thank you, thank you." Noah made G.I. Joe wave a muscular plastic arm in acknowledgement of the applause. "Thank you very much."

Smiling, Jake leaned one shoulder against the door frame. "I guess he's all cured, huh?"

"Cured?" Noah and Carly both frowned in puzzlement.

"Of whatever serious malady you two needed the expert for."

"He needed an expert *stylist,*" Carly said, looking happy to see Jake. "Those fatigues were *so* not working for the red carpet."

"The red—" Jake paused. "Exactly what game are you two playing?"

"Movie premiere!" Noah announced. He scrambled to his feet and grabbed his dad's hand, pulling him all the way into the room. "Carly taught it to me. This is the red carpet"—the Hot Wheels track—"these are the limos"—the Hot Wheels cars themselves—"and these are the fans."

The stuffed animals near Carly seemed to droop beneath Jake's gaze. She straightened from her hunched-over position, her cheeks pinkened by a blush. She eyed him defensively.

"It's fun," she said.

It occurred to him what they'd been doing when he arrived. "It's . . . a makeover! You were turning G.I. Joe into some kind of goatee-wearing pantywaist."

"We were playing," Carly said, lifting her chin. "There's nothing wrong with that."

Jake grabbed poor Joe. "G.I. Joe," he told her seriously, "is a *commando*. He fights bad guys. Belly-crawls through bushes. Disarms grenades. He's not a fashion victim—he's an action figure."

"He's a doll," she said blandly.

"A doll?" He felt his eyes widen in horror. "G.I. Joe is *not* 'a doll!'"

Carly shrugged. "He's eleven-and-a-half inches tall, with a changeable wardrobe and lots of accessories—"

"His 'accessories' are little plastic M1 rifles, combat helmets, dog tags—"

"I left those on, see?" Carly interrupted. Noah helpfully held up the revamped G.I. Joe for her. "They lend a nice hip-hop flair to his ensemble."

"He doesn't have an 'ensemble!'" Jake couldn't believe she could be this dense. "He has a SCR-625 mine detector. A Halo Jumper parachute. A twin-mount anti-aircraft gun and a flak vest."

"So, basically . . ." Carly appeared to think about all he'd said. "G.I. Joe is Barbie, with more hardware."

"*Barbie?* No, G.I. Joe isn't Barbie." Jake scoffed. The whole idea was ridiculous. "He's an American hero."

"He's a doll," Carly said.

Noah nodded. "I like playing with dolls."

Okay. Jake figured he was an enlightened father. He could handle his son's more sensitive instincts. He didn't mind if Noah dragged his stuffed armadillo everywhere, slept with a soccer-ball-shaped night light, and sang along to the TeleTubbies. But maligning the greatest toy action figure of all time . . . well, that went too far.

All he needed to do, Jake figured, was show them exactly how heroic G.I. Joe could be. Because they weren't handling this right at all. He hunkered down with the action figure still in hand, then posed him atop the Hot Wheels track.

"Look out!" he yelled in his best commando-style voice. "A runaway train! I, G.I. Joe, will stop it, before those innocent bystanders"—he gestured toward the stuffed animal brigade—"get hurt."

Ignoring Carly's look of amusement, Jake stomped G.I. Joe toward Noah's model of Thomas the Tank Engine. He put out Joe's arms and made him push the train.

Noah rolled his eyes. "He's not Superman, Daddy."

"And that's not a train," Carly pointed out. "It's a bus filled with paparazzi."

"It's a runaway train." Jake set his jaw. "We're going to save the day."

"You're going to ruin G.I. Joe's shoes."

"Yeah, Daddy."

He looked. Then recoiled in horror. In place of Joe's usual combat boots, Carly had drawn on a pair of Magic Marker lace-up gladiator sandals. Between the goatee, the surfer clothes, and the lack of sideburns, G.I. Joe already looked like a complete sissy. With these shoes, he'd get his ass kicked for sure.

"Oh, come on," Jake said, muffling an obscenity. "Next you'll have him wearing one of those stupid toga skirts."

A beat passed.

Carly and Noah exchanged an inspired look. "Gladiator!" Carly cried. "We can play gladiator."

That wasn't quite what he'd meant. But still . . . gladiator was a macho game. It would teach Noah the value of being strong and brave. It would show him what it felt like to be a victorious hero. Warily, Jake relinquished G.I. Joe.

"Of course," Carly announced, "it'll have to be a cruelty-free version."

Noah nodded seriously.

"We don't want any of the animals getting hurt."

"No way."

"Gladiator G.I. Joe can just tame the wild beasts in the arena, instead of fighting them."

"Oh, for Chrissake," Jake mumbled. "Girls play *weird*."

Defiantly, Carly dragged over a green vinyl play mat striped with football field markings. She designated it as the gladiator arena. Noah assembled wild animals from his jungle play set. Moments later, the gladiator challenges began.

Carly portrayed all the animals. Noah, as G.I. Joe, represented the gladiator. In a voice-over, Carly announced that Gladiator Joe had been tossed into the arena as punishment for staying up past his bedtime . . . then the games got under way.

Jake cringed. He covered his eyes and turned away. Carly and Noah chattered and played, and made some truly ridiculous sound effects.

Finally, curiosity got the better of him.

He peeked.

Carly and Noah sat across from each other with the football-mat arena between them. They played unselfconsciously together, with Noah making Gladiator Joe hug all the animals and Carly making all the animals nuzzle him back.

It was ridiculous. Sappy and silly, like watching *Touched by an Angel* meets *America's Funniest Animals*. Jake wanted to hate the whole Doctor Doolittle–style production . . . but with one look at Noah's shining face, he couldn't. This girly game was making his son happy. *Carly* was making his son happy. How could he stand in the way of that?

Feeling suddenly decisive, Jake looked around. He grabbed a Star Wars Jango Fett action figure (complete with missile-firing jet pack and two blasters), then walked him into the arena.

"I'm the vet," he announced. This was stupid as hell. He was making an idiot of himself. "I'm here to make sure all the animals are healthy."

"And happy," Noah insisted.

"Yeah." Jake cleared his throat. He caught the grateful look Carly sent his way. He scowled to let her know this touchy-feely stuff wasn't affecting his masculinity in any way. "Happy, too."

You're playing with dolls, Carly mouthed playfully.

His scowl deepened.

She raised her chin, her eyes sparkling with good humor. "Good thing you're here," she teased. "Because this monkey just got his feelings hurt."

Meaningfully, she thrust the plastic chimp toward Jango Fett. Jake stared at it. Her challenge was plain.

Hurt feelings, his ass. She wanted him to go all the way to Wuss-ville, with his son as a witness. But Jango Fett was an intergalactic bounty hunter, he protested silently and indignantly. Not some kind of animal shrink who . . . awww, hell.

"Poor monkey," Noah said. "He needs a hug, I guess."

Jake drew in a deep breath. There was nothing he wouldn't do for his son. He was about to prove it.

He shuffled the Jango *Vet* action figure closer. Feeling rigid with resistance but unwilling to wimp out in front of Carly and his son, Jake made it hug the monkey. For good measure, he even made it murmur some encouraging simian psychology about bananas and trees.

There. He'd done it.

Noah and Carly practically applauded. Jake glanced up to meet Carly's radiant expression . . . and knew he would have gone even further, just to glimpse the admiration in her eyes.

When had her opinion become so important to him? Why had it become so important to him? Sure, he needed to impress the woman with whom he'd be rated on the *Dream Date* audience tally consoles. Otherwise, he couldn't win the competition and couldn't ensure his contract renewal. But this . . . this felt like more. Being with Carly suddenly felt as necessary to Jake as thirty-four inches of flame-treated Northern white ash felt to Mark McGwire when he stepped up to the plate.

He needed her. There were no two ways about it.

The realization scared the hell out of him. He didn't want to need anybody. He *refused* to need anybody. Needing someone was like handing them a pair of boxing gloves and inviting them to beat the crap out of you, just for fun.

Somehow, Jake had to get the upper hand here. He had to regain control of the situation.

"That was really sweet of you," Carly said.

She reached over, still beaming, and squeezed his fingers with hers. The gesture was innocent, a mere way-to-go between friends, but the instant Jake felt her touch him, the answer he'd been searching for struck him. There was one arena in which he was sure to reign supreme.

Sex.

No woman he'd ever pursued had turned him down. No woman had ever been struck by the Jake Jarvis charm and successfully resisted it. All he had to do, Jake realized with a burble of relief, was take charge of the attraction simmering between them . . . and show Carly exactly who'd be calling the shots between them from here on out. That was a man's natural role. He'd just overlooked it, in his quest to keep things professional for the sake of *Dream Date*.

Besides, moving on to the next, more intimate (and, let's face it, inevitable) level would probably cure him of this stupid neediness, Jake told himself. More than likely, unsatisfied sexual curiosity had made him view Carly as more than an everyday, ordinary date—the kind of date he typically kept at arm's length without breaking a sweat.

Sure, that was it.

Whew. Feeling immensely better, Jake twined his fingers with Carly's and offered her an anticipatory smile. Things were about to get interesting between them.

Really interesting.

Fourteen

Jake's family stayed for dinner.

It was obvious to Marley that they'd intended to stay all along—given the quantity of food they'd helped prepare—but Jake seemed to have been under the impression their visit would be a short-lived one. He'd actually tried to bustle them out the door just before they all sat down to eat.

"Well," he said, "you all must have things to do . . ."

"Not really."

"Not until the nine o'clock movie starts."

"On a Sunday? Heck, no."

"Nein."

Despite their protests, Jake herded everyone toward the door. "Seriously, this has been fun. Thanks for the help making this nice, *romantic* dinner for Carly and me."

Everyone stopped. Stephanie put her hands on her hips. Pointedly, she directed her gaze to her grandson.

Marley did, too. With relief. Given the schmaltzy ideas that had been running through her head all night, she was glad to have Noah there as a buffer between her and Jake. She needed her Candy Land partner to keep her honest. To keep her from ruining everything.

She'd been battling a crazy impulse to abandon her plan.

To reveal her alter ego and find out if Jake could possibly want her for herself. She'd been tempted, time and again, to tell the truth, no matter the consequences. Every time Jake looked at her, smiled at her—or, worse yet, *touched* her—Marley forgot the importance of being Carly. All that seemed to matter was Jake and her . . . together.

"We made enough food for an army," Stephanie protested, reaching out to ruffle Noah's hair. She smiled at her son. "Did you seriously think we'd expect the two of you eat all of it by yourselves?"

"We couldn't do that to you," Bethany told her brother.

"Of course not!" James and Nate added.

"Your mom's right," Marley agreed quickly, visions flitting through her head of a night wherein Noah went to bed early and left her defenselessly alone with Jake. "We can't eat all that, with just you and me and Noah."

At her agreement, the Jarvises trooped cheerfully back inside, chattering as they headed for the kitchen.

Whew. Crisis averted. Not only did she have Noah for a buffer, now she had six Jarvises and an Ulrich, too. That ought to keep her on the straight and narrow, Marley figured. On the path toward her goals, where she belonged.

After all, she couldn't disappoint Sondra and Brian. Or Candace and Heather. Or any of the rest of her entourage, staff members, and hangers-on. They all relied on Marley Madison, TV starlet, for their livelihoods. If she couldn't kick-start her new career with a real, raw Carly résumé reel, all of them were sunk. For the sake of everyone depending on her, Marley had to keep her mind on business.

Not on how much she wanted Jake.

Faint conversation drifted from the kitchen, along with the sounds of clanking cutlery. Marley realized she was still standing near the apartment doorway with Jake. Alone. Defenselessly alone. With his teasing smiles, his sexy voice, his big, deft hands. He'd been reaching for her all night with those hands . . . reaching for her, and touching her in more ways than one.

Ulp. Even with buffers, this was going to be more difficult than she'd thought.

"Guess it's time to eat!" Marley chirped. She headed toward the kitchen, which lay just out of sight around the corner.

Jake's hand closed over her upper arm before she could get far. With inexorable patience, he hauled her back to face him.

Cautiously, she lifted her gaze. There was something new in his demeanor all of a sudden. Something dangerous and tantalizing. Something she hadn't seen in him until now.

Jake's face was still his face—square-jawed, sinfully handsome, and bespectacled. His hair was still his hair, his body—*mmm, his body*—was still his body, all six-feet-whatever of taut muscle and disciplined strength. But the energy that passed from him to her was different. It felt . . . purposeful, for lack of a better word. Intent.

And the way Jake leisurely scanned her body before melding her gaze with his? Well, that was just plain *hot*.

"Afraid to be alone with me?" he asked.

She scoffed. "Of course not."

Liar, liar, pants on fire.

"Because you seem a little jittery."

"I'm not."

"Hmmm. Maybe I'm wrong."

Experimentally, he raised his hand to cup her face, then stroked his thumb over her jaw. The contact jolted her. His callused palm tenderly abraded her skin, and warmth spread from the place where he touched her. Marley wanted to close her eyes, to tilt her cheek into his cradling hand, to strip off both their clothes and find out if the sizzle between them could ignite more than kisses and the occasional, unstoppable caress.

"But I'm not wrong."

At the deep rumble of Jake's voice, she fluttered her eyelids open again. Damn! She'd gone and closed her eyes to savor his touch in spite of herself. Didn't she have any self-control around him? Defiantly, Marley bugged her eyes as wide as they'd go.

His smile seemed knowing.

"I'm not afraid of you," she said with a toss of her head. *I'm afraid of me. Of the way I want you, and how it jeopardizes my future.* "But I *am* starving," she said for diversion's sake.

"Starving?"

"Yup." She wheeled sideways, just as though it *didn't* cost her a mile of regret to cut short their contact. "I'm so hungry I could eat a woolly mammoth. Ha, ha."

"Look, with my family here, we might not be alone again for a while." His gaze touched her lips, lingered. "I have to tell you—"

"What?"

"That I can't wait another minute to taste you again."

Given the husky note in his voice, she should have known what was coming next. But Marley only knew she couldn't move . . . not until she learned what he intended for certain.

Curiosity had always been one of her weaknesses.

She hesitated. That was all the opportunity Jake needed. In one swift movement, he captured the back of her head in his hand, backed her into the door behind her, and brought his mouth down on hers. She went willingly, dimly mindful of the thump their bodies made as they collided against the door, thrillingly aware of exactly how illicit this whole position felt. Jake's need for her must be immense, she realized in a flash. At the realization, her need for him doubled.

His fingers spread to cup her nape, holding her steady as he tasted, and tasted, and *tasted*. Pleasure, hot and instant, whooshed through her. Marley clung to his shoulders, feeling the muscles there bunch and flex beneath her fingertips as Jake crowded closer, held her tighter, continued to make her mindless with his kiss.

Her knees wobbled. She wavered, only to find herself pinned fully between his body and the door a moment later. His knee thrust between her thighs; his lean hips and pelvis held her in place for the next long, sensuous meeting of their mouths, their tongues, their breath.

His hands roved everywhere, touching her all over. Marley felt her skin tingle, felt her nipples tighten with anticipation. Giddiness filled her—that, and a certain knowledge that Jake knew exactly what he was doing to her . . . and he intended to do much, much more of it.

"Again," he murmured as the far-off sounds of the family feast in the next room retreated a little further.

"More," she begged, arching against him.

"Again," he repeated as he dragged his mouth from her lips to the side of her neck. He plied her with teasing nips and knowing kisses. "Again, again, again."

"Please." She shivered, only wanted more.

"You feel so good." He framed her face in his hands and brushed his mouth against her lower lip, gliding back and forth. His gaze, dark and intense and affectionate, met hers. A slow smile curved his mouth. "So good."

Another kiss, deeper this time. Feeling frenzied, Marley forgot everything except the man in her arms. She let her hands rove across his shoulders and down his broad chest, fanned her fingers over the flat expanse of his abdomen, held him to her with both arms around his middle.

Emboldened by his moan of pleasure, she dared to meander lower, to cup his tight backside in her hands. As a reward, Jake ground against her, letting her feel the hard length of him nestled in the vee of her legs. This was as good as it got while clothed and vertical, and the passion of it all swept Marley away.

"You should have let my family leave," Jake said hoarsely. He closed his eyes, briefly, swallowing hard. She watched his throat work with the effort, watched his beautiful eyes open again and focus on her face, as though nothing else were quite as mesmerizing. "You should have let them leave, and we'd be alone right now."

"What about Noah?"

He grinned. "Early bedtimes have their uses."

Marley faltered. She cut short the kiss he delivered to her earlobe, then tugged his hair to make him meet her gaze. "Do you often send Noah to bed early so you can get lucky with your dates?"

"Never," he swore. "Most women don't come here."

She believed him.

"For the record, I've never lost all self-control with a woman while my family was in the next room, either," Jake said. He smiled, looking rueful. "At least not since the Harvest Dance in tenth grade, when Amber Mattucci corralled me in the kitchen between Yoo-Hoo nightcaps while waiting for her mother to pick her up, and let me stick my hand down her dress."

"Lucky Amber," Marley teased.

"Lucky me, right now." He settled his hands on her hips, watching as his fingers flexed against her curves. He let his attention wander upward from there, lingering on her breasts. Hunger darkened his expression, made him twice as sexy . . . twice as irresistible.

"I'll find a way to get us alone," he announced.

Before she could blink, Jake had released her. With a purposeful stride, he headed for the kitchen. Marley flew after him. What was he, nuts? If he marched into the kitchen looking the way he did, all rumpled and hot and, well, *rigid,* every last one of the Jarvises would know exactly why Jake and Marley hadn't managed to arrive for the appetizer course yet.

They already knew. By the time Marley caught up with Jake, he was confronting his family's indulgent grins and perceptive elbow jabs. Incredibly, he didn't seem to care. He propped two fists on his lean hips and surveyed the whole group like a favored prince addressing the rest of the royalty.

"I hope you're all enjoying dinner," he said.

They gave murmurs of agreement. Polite avowals of satisfaction.

"The ambiance leaves a little something to be desired," Bethany said with an arch of her eyebrows. "I could have sworn I heard a thump of some sort a few minutes ago."

Jake smiled. Marley wanted to sink into the floor and become one with the Mop 'N Glo, a product she'd gotten acquainted with for the first time just a few days ago.

"Very funny," Jake said. "Eat hearty, but don't dawdle. I'll need the private use of my apartment as soon as everyone's done."

He waggled his eyebrows at her. Mortified, Marley covered her face with her hands.

"Of course, son," Henry said. "We won't be long."

"We were just talking with Noah about having him over to our place to spend the night," Stephanie added serenely. "Wouldn't that be fun, Noah?"

The boy cheered. Marley felt her plan unraveling all around her. Her buffers were disappearing. With embarrassing avidity.

It was almost as though Jake's family wanted her to be with him.

This wasn't going to work. Coming here without the *Dream Date* camera and audio crews had been a mistake. She needed their presence to keep a lid on her feelings—to keep her mind on her gritty alter-ego performance. Without them, Marley was just a girl . . . a girl who was crazy about a boy she'd just met.

A girl who'd rather be with him than do the job she'd set out to do.

"I really have to go." She shouldered her purse, then knelt to scoop up Gaffer from his snug spot beside Noah's chair. "I just remembered something urgent." *Namely, self-preservation.* "Thanks for a lovely evening, Jake. See ya."

" 'See ya'?"

"It's been nice meeting you all."

" 'See ya'?"

"Bye." Cradling Gaffer, Marley bolted for the door.

Jake was right behind her. He slapped his hand over the glossy wood just as she made a break for it. The door thunked shut again.

"Don't leave," he said.

She closed her eyes against the candor in his voice. No one she knew had ever begged her to stay. They all understood. Fashionably late arrivals ruled in her crowd, as did fashionably early departures.

"You haven't even had dinner yet."

Marley faced him. Valiantly, she managed not to crumble at Jake's earnest expression. She knew what he was really asking: *stay with me.* She understood the path they'd set out upon, right against this very door. Remembering that, it was hard not to do as he suggested and stay—stay for the togetherness, the unexpected joviality, the sizzling make-out sessions.

"Let's get together in a few days, okay?" she asked instead, shoving the latter from her mind. "We're still required to have a nighttime date this week."

She set Gaffer down to dig out Carly's day planner, a paperbound giveaway from the Hallmark store. She flipped open the pages. "What time works best for you?"

Silence. She peeked upward, trying to look businesslike.

"Tuesday," Jake said, crossing his arms over his chest with clear sarcasm. "I think I can fit you in between my dentist's appointment and a tire rotation."

Whatever *that* was. "Great! See you then."

"Hold it."

She put away the day planner. "Sorry, gotta run."

"Kiss me good-bye."

How she wanted to. "Let's save it for the *Dream Date* cameras, shall we?" Marley asked.

Jake didn't speak. A heartbeat later, she'd grabbed Gaffer again and obtained her freedom. Unfortunately, it tasted bitter. The knowledge that she was doing the right thing—the only thing that might ensure a successful conclusion to Operation Carly Christopher—didn't sweeten things, either.

Suddenly, all Marley could remember was the shock on Jake's face as she'd blurted out her "save it for the *Dream Date* cameras" comment . . . and the loneliness of walking away from the coziest family get-together she'd ever experienced.

She hadn't even gotten to say good-bye to Noah.

Swallowing past a sudden lump in her throat, Marley hugged Gaffer closer. She slid behind the wheel of her Chanel car, then looked up at the bright lights streaming from Jake's second-floor apartment.

Marley Madison didn't belong there, she reminded herself. Only Carly Christopher did. It was better she limit things now, before she entangled herself too deeply.

She was fine. She was giving the performance of a lifetime. She'd simply gotten caught up in the moment, the way an actor sometimes did. Her feelings for Jake seemed real because she was a talented actress, and because Jake's aw-shucks charm masterfully complemented her portrayal of Carly.

Sure, that was it.

Even so, the drive across town to her stark new home felt twice as long as usual. And Meredith's apartment, when Marley threw the keys onto the prefab side table and stepped inside, felt twice as lonely. But hey, that was the price of success. Marley had been paying it for a lifetime now. There was no reason tonight should be any different.

Except that tonight, Marley had fallen in love.

Late on the evening of the romantic-dinner-that-wasn't, Jake sat on his sofa with the remote in hand, bathed in the glow of *Sports Center*. The apartment was quiet. Noah was tucked in bed, having decided not to sleep over at Grandma and Grandpa's. Dinner had come and gone, and so had Carly. Jake had tried drawing her near with his best, sexiest, most from-the-heart moves . . . and had only succeeded in enchanting himself.

Damn it.

After Carly's departure, his family had been sympathetic. Optimistic. Understanding. But the fact remained that Jake had struck out with the only woman who'd really mattered to him in a long time. She'd bolted like a jittery long-shot mare in the Preakness, leaving him looking like a fool for having bet on her at all.

Sighing, Jake scanned the score ticker on TV. Usually, ESPN comforted him. Its broadcasts had followed him from grade school—when he'd first discovered sports beside his dad—through college all-nighters. They'd been there on the harrowing and joyful afternoon of Noah's birth, and during the long nights of midnight feedings and colicky two A.M. wakefulness afterward.

Since its inception in 1979, ESPN had offered Jake instant absorption in a world that wasn't his own. But right now, it was failing him. ESPN wasn't enough.

Tonight, something was different. *He* was different. At this moment, he didn't care about hockey scores and NBA drafts. He only cared about Carly, and wondered what he'd done to make her leave.

Disgusted with himself, Jake switched off the TV. He wandered through the shadowy apartment, mindlessly toeing aside plastic magnetic letters and scattered crayons. Beneath his feet, he felt the carpet, gritty in spots with sandbox sand spilled from Noah's shoes, and vowed to vacuum tomorrow. He listened to the hum of the refrigerator as it broke the silence, ran his fingertips over the front door where he'd lingered with Carly.

Why had she left? She'd returned his kiss eagerly enough, with enthusiasm and ardor to spare. She'd felt perfect in his arms, all warm and caring and graceful—even in those ridiculous skyscraper shoes, which had raised her nearly to nose-height with him. There'd been no mistaking Carly's interest in him during that kiss, Jake recalled . . . and at the remembrance, was struck with an inspiration.

It hadn't been until after she'd had a chance to think about things, until after they'd broken apart long enough to confront his family, that Carly had gotten skittish. Clearly, while not in his arms she'd had time to have second thoughts.

The solution to that particular glitch was clear, Jake decided. He'd simply have to keep Carly engrossed so thoroughly that she wouldn't have a chance to second-guess things. He'd have to exercise all the charm, all the charisma, all the sex appeal that had landed him so infamously on buses and billboards and lobby banners, and aim every bit of it at her.

For as long as it took to win her heart.

Jake stopped, frozen by the thought.

Win her heart? He scoffed, bending in the hallway to pick up a cast-off T-shirt and a pair of mini scrungy socks. In the feeble glow of Noah's night-light from the bedroom down the hall, Jake shook his head. He'd meant *win her body.* He'd meant *woo her into bed.* He'd meant, *counter her undeniable effect on him with an offensive game plan guaranteed to regain him the upper hand.*

Sure, that was it.

Winning Carly's heart had nothing to do with it. Jake wasn't in the market for true love—wasn't even sure he believed in it. This thing between them, this Dream Date-sanctioned series of encounters, was nothing more than a game. It was a sport. A contest of wills, of minds, of strength, and of heart.

Arrgh! There he went again, with the heart stuff. Eating spa cuisine must have scrambled his brain, Jake decided as he dropped Noah's dirty clothes into the hamper and then stripped off his own shirt and drawstring-waist pants. Naked, he strode through his moonlit bedroom. Jake Jarvis wasn't the kind of guy who nattered on about sappy bullshit like hearts and flowers and relationships with a capital R. He was fine on his own. Better than fine.

And if, on this night, his big double bed felt twice as lonely as he slid between the sheets? Hell, that was just his libido talking. He was a man, with a man's needs.

Those needs included *love* like G.I. Joe's footlocker included a coat of pink glitter paint and a two-month supply of Tampax.

Satisfied with his resolve to pursue the woman he wanted, Jake exhaled. He dragged the blankets over his body.

He dreamt of Carly, even before his eyes closed.

Fifteen

For the next three weeks, Jake saw Carly every couple of days. They went the traditional date route—dinners, movies, strolls on the waterline near the Santa Monica pier. They went the nontraditional date route—a rodeo upstate, a musical performance of "Spring Fling" at Toddler Time (in which Noah was brilliant), a Dodgers game during which Carly insisted the umpire's public calling of fouls and strikes was inhumane and cruel to the struggling ballplayers. They hiked to the "Hollywood" sign like tourists and taught Gaffer to catch a Frisbee in the park.

The *Dream Date* crew followed them everywhere, of course. The camera and audio people captured every smile and wave, every teasing word and gesture. They shot miles of footage. Later, Jake knew, they'd edit it into a perfect game-show montage, and the studio audience would vote on Jake and Marley's compatibility at the final taping at the end of the month.

But Jake didn't care about any of that. Because all the while, he was busy keeping up his campaign to make Carly see how perfect they'd be together.

He touched her at the least provocation, warming to the lightness that filled him whenever she lost her head and squeezed his hand or pressed a kiss to his cheek. He let himself forget the unlikeliness of his pairing with Carly and simply savored the time they spent together.

In response, Jake's need for her grew.

At first, that worried him. Then he realized such a thing was completely natural. It was only because his wooing was so convincing that he'd begun to feel something more for Carly. Obviously, he was just that good. Even better than he'd thought.

As talented as he considered himself at seduction, though, Jake quickly realized that Carly was equally skilled at resistance. She melted toward him, then pulled away. She smiled affectionately, then frowned with clear—and puzzling—dismay. She talked freely about a million subjects—and just as it began to dawn on Jake that they were sharing and relating and communicating with a capital C, she withdrew.

As hard as it was for Jake to believe, he came to understand that Carly was *purposely* evading him. Her reticence was maddening. It rocketed her beyond appealing, all the way to irresistible. He'd never encountered its like in all his years of dating.

"If we don't look like a convincing couple," he'd told her one day while they watched Noah and Gaffer scamper in the surf at the beach, "we won't win *Dream Date.*"

"If by 'convincing couple' you mean groping couple who should get a room, then I guess we won't win," she'd replied, her face fine-boned and beautiful in the sunlight. "Because I can't concentrate when you touch me."

Good. His touch made her as scattered as her smile made him. "This is a date. What's there to concentrate about?"

"It's a public date." She nodded toward the ever-present camera and audio crews. "There's everything to concentrate about. Besides, aren't you afraid of looking bad on TV?"

"Hell, no." He grinned. "That's a nightly hazard. I'm immune to it by now. But maybe you're camera-shy?"

She'd only given him a rueful shake of her head, then changed the subject by challenging him to a sandcastle-building contest. As a man, of course, he couldn't possibly refuse a challenge.

Jake's castle had looked like a fortress, all battlements and moat. Carly's had looked like a Malibu estate or maybe a shopping mall—sweeping lines, too much square footage, and decorator details like seashells pressed into the walls. He should have known their visions would be completely different.

Carly was different, too. She was a waitress who couldn't brew coffee, a blue-collar girl who sported a perfect pedicure. She claimed to be a TV soap-opera fanatic, yet had never seen Jake's sportscast, or any promos for it on KKZP. She drove a perfect classic car but was oblivious to its specifics. She was a brunette who disliked dumb-blonde jokes, a beautiful woman who insisted she was plain, a smart-mouthed talker who censored herself at the oddest moments.

The dichotomies in her were puzzling. There was definitely something . . . off-kilter about Carly. Something that just didn't fit. But then, for Jake, there were lots of things about her that *did* fit.

She was impossibly quick to laugh and endearingly dedicated to playing the funny-body-parts game, no matter how terrible she was at it ("Nostril!" had been her latest entry). She took in everything they did together with absolute openness and a fresh perspective. It was as though the whole world was a new experience for her.

She was unimpressed with his sex-symbol-sportscaster image, and instead admired Jake for himself, not his semifamous on-air persona. Carly didn't pester him for intros to Sid, like an aspiring actress he'd disastrously dated had. She was unfazed by the occasional autograph seekers they encountered while they were out together. She stood by peacefully, an enigmatic smile on her face, and patiently waited for him to finish with his fans. His fears about becoming involved with a publicity-hungry, sports-hunk-dating, wannabe actress who would mix up his and Noah's lives gradually fell away.

More and more, he began to feel Carly was the perfect woman for him—and her effect on Noah wasn't half-bad, either. Jake watched the two of them together, lying in the grass at his apartment complex to watch the clouds, or sharing a cupcake with icing-smeared fingers, and understood the value of Carly's unique perspective. She calmed Noah. She cared for him. And even if her idea of "playing" involved things like bathing and brushing Noah's stuffed animals, hosting a pink-lemonade-and-petit-fours stand, and dancing to Beach Boys tunes, she was good for him.

So what was the problem?

Convincing Carly to make their dream dates real, and to take them to the next step. That was the problem. But Jake wasn't giving up yet. . . .

Sixteen

For Imogene Madison, having a child actor in the family had been a full-time job. She'd been the one to drive Marley to auditions, to entertain her while waiting, and to comfort her during the inevitable disappointments that sometimes followed. She'd been the one to help Marley learn lines. The one to wait patiently on the set or on location while her daughter worked. The one to arrange for headshots and wardrobe, and lessons of every kind. The one to keep up with those lessons, and make sure Marley kept up with them, too.

Of course, in most instances, the parents of child actors stepped out of the picture once that child was of age. They happily relinquished their various roles to agents and managers and experts of every kind, and went on with their lives.

Marley only wished her mother had been so inclined. Instead, while scouting out lessons for her daughter, Imogene had discovered a passion for learning in herself.

Sure, she'd started innocently enough, with a beginner ballet class meant to improve her posture. But before long, Imogene had moved on to harder stuff. Russian, French, and Italian lessons. Karate, Tae Kwon-Do, Krav Maga. Piano, harp, steel guitar. Before Marley had realized the truth, Imogene had become deeply enmeshed in studying esoteric histories, art, and new forms of dance. There'd been no stopping her.

In fact, Marley was ashamed to admit, she had actually enabled her. She'd networked to find instructors, paid tens of thousands for lessons . . . and now, influenced by the knowledge that this habit had given her mother so much joy, Marley had gone all the way. She'd actually joined her.

Which was how she came to be strapped into a safety harness at her mother's trendy new gym, staring up at a wall of faux mountainside meant for pretend rock climbing.

She wondered if anyone had ever devised a more heinous method of showing the whole world your backside. For the entire ascent and descent, Marley's recently un-Pilates-ed booty would be on display, bobbing up and down, crisscrossed with those hideous harness straps. In those straps, even Calista Flockhart's butt would have looked lumpy.

Butt. She suppressed a smile. Noah would have laughed over that. Funny how often he—and especially his father—were on her mind these days.

"So are you coming up, or what?" Imogene asked.

She'd already assessed the wall and had chosen appropriate hand and footholds. Clad in bright Spandex with her dark hair in a pixie cut and her requisite gold jewelry still on, she clung expertly to the "mountain" about eighteen inches off the ground. Imogene was round, especially in the middle, and not particularly rugged looking. But what she lacked in strength she made up for in will.

How else could she have helped turn her daughter into a sitcom star by the age of twenty-one?

"Mom, I really need to talk to you. Can we do this another time?"

"Talk to me up here!" Imogene scrambled a few inches higher. "Climbing the rock wall clears your mind like nothing else."

"I'm . . . not sure I can."

"Don't be a baby. Do it!"

"Is there an escalator to the top? I'll meet you there."

"You're the one with the fancy trainer, missy. Don't tell me you can't handle thirty-five feet of fake rock climbing. Or does Gunther do all his *real* training in your bedroom?"

That did it. Anger propelled Marley off the ground. She scrambled to a position on a level with her mother. "I *told* you. Gunther is my Pilates instructor. He helps me strengthen my core—"

"Is that what they're calling it these days? Kinky."

"—and then he does cardio with me on alternate days. That's all."

"For this you pay him three hundred dollars a visit?" Imogene snorted, then climbed higher. "In my day, a woman would have gotten her money's worth out of a fella like that."

"He's not my gigolo."

"Whose fault is that? Hmmm?"

How could parents be so maddening? Had Imogene taken classes in that, too?

"You're right, Mom. It's just that I've been so busy seducing the pool boy." Despite her years on the periphery of show business, Marley's mother was still frighteningly susceptible to every Hollywood cliché. "I haven't had time to tackle my trainer yet."

"Don't be fresh." With her mouth pursed disapprovingly, Imogene climbed higher. "I didn't fight traffic taking you to voice lessons every week just so you could backtalk your mother."

"Sorry, Mom."

"Besides, I'd rather talk about the new man in your life."

Jake. Marley clung to the simulated rocks, feeling a silly grin cross her lips. He'd been wonderful for the past three weeks. So thoughtful and funny and sexy. Trying to resist him had been killing her.

"The *Enquirer* ran a story about you and some man vacationing together in Bermuda," Imogene went on, huffing a little. "Have you seen it? There were even a couple of topless photos of you."

Exasperation filled Marley. Those photos had been taken

a long time ago. And the man with her wasn't Jake. Nevertheless, thinking of the *Enquirer* story embarrassed her. Those photos had been grainy black and white shots depicting nothing racier than her naked shoulder blades, but still . . . frolicking in public while nude was not exactly a dutiful daughter's best icebreaker.

She lifted her gaze to meet her mother's censorious one. "I can explain."

"You'd better. Do you know what kind of damage the sun does to your skin? SPF forty-five! I swear by it. Wrinkles and skin cancer will not help your career."

"Gee, for a second there, I thought you were worried about my reputation."

"Ha. Topless starlets are a dime a dozen in this town. I'd be worried if you didn't show a little skin."

"Show a little skin? You should know all about that, after that belly-dancing-for-charity stunt you pulled."

"It freed my inner femininity." Imogene sniffed. "And raised a bundle for charity. Besides, I'm good at belly dancing."

Marley was still getting over the trauma of witnessing her own mother *gyrating*. On purpose. While wearing *I Dream of Jeannie*-style veils and bells. She shuddered, then searched for a new handhold.

"Anyway, those photos are at least a year old," she said as she climbed. Her arm muscles quivered, more accustomed to toting Neiman Marcus shopping bags than hauling her entire body weight against gravity. Why had she let Jake talk her into eating those onion rings last night? They'd probably added at least half a pound to her thighs. "And it wasn't Bermuda, it was Malibu. Some creep with a telephoto lens snapped me at my manager's pool party."

"Naked?"

She'd been changing into her swimsuit. So technically, yes. "Well . . ."

"It's good to see you networking, dear."

Marley rolled her eyes. She loved her mom, but she never knew what to expect from her.

All around them, other climbers tackled the fake mountainside. Muscle-bound men grunted beside silent, wiry women and chatty couples. Harness ropes hung slack, or zinged with tension as climbers gave up and let the harness support them. The tang of sweat and the musty aroma peculiar to all gyms rose to greet each of Marley's gulping breaths. Geez, this stuff was hard work.

Effortlessly, her mother continued to climb. She'd already neared the halfway point. Marley vowed to speak with Gunther about a cross-training regime—as soon as she became herself again, that is—and followed.

"I need your advice about something, Mom."

"Yes, that brown hair color looks dowdy on you."

"No, that's not it."

"No, I don't think you should get your nose pierced."

"Mom—"

"Fine. Drag it out of me." Imogene paused in her ascent and squinted over her shoulder at her daughter. "Maybe you *have* put on a few pounds lately."

"It's not about how I look!" Marley cried. Her voice reverberated through the gym. She tossed her head, daring anyone to decry her right to stop the motherly auto-criticism routine that had kicked in. "It's about . . . how I feel."

Thoughtfully, Imogene continued to gaze at her. "I see. Well, with that plain-Jane hair, that aberrant piercing idea, and those childbearing hips you're sporting, I can see where you might be feeling a little down lately. You need a new acting job to motivate you into pulling yourself together."

Oddly enough, Marley did feel "together." Even in her ordinary, everyday Carly persona . . . some of the time. And of course, her stint on *Dream Date* was all about garnering new acting jobs. But she didn't want to talk about work.

"I think I'm falling in love, Mom."

Imogene was silent.

"He's warm-hearted and generous," Marley continued, clinging to the rocks. She wasn't sure how much further she dared go. "Honest and thoughtful."

"Not an actor, then."

"He makes me laugh, and he's so cute. Smart, too."

"Ah-hah. Smart. Not in showbiz at all."

"He accepts me just as I am." Well, just as Carly was. But the few "real-Marley" tidbits she'd delivered while undercover had been greeted positively. "He's strong and helpful, and no matter how terrible I try to look"—as Carly, of course—"he always seems to think I'm beautiful."

Imogene wrinkled her brow. "Is he employed? Or is this sweet talker after your money?"

"Yes, he's employed. And no, he's not exactly a sweet talker. Not unless you consider, 'I'd like you better naked,' an acceptable answer to 'how do you like this outfit?'"

"Hmmm. A few rough edges, then."

"A few." Marley smiled, remembering Jake's audacious comment. "And no, he's not after my money. He thinks I'm broke. Last week, he even forced twenty bucks on me for gas money because he thought I didn't have any."

"You? Broke? I thought you said he was smart."

"He is."

Marley had lost a great deal of money when her former (shyster) agent had skipped town with some residuals checks. His thievery hadn't done her finances, or her sense of trust, any favors. Between him and all the relatives and friends she'd given money to over the years, her financial situation wasn't nearly as remarkable as it might have been. All the more reason why she desperately needed the new résumé reel *Dream Date* would garner her.

"He's my *Dream Date* partner," she told Imogene. Her mother knew the basics of her plan to revitalize her career, although she hadn't been entirely convinced of the need for a "dreary alter ego" in order to demonstrate Marley's acting versatility. "He thinks I'm just an ordinary girl."

Imogene scoffed. "You are anything but ordinary. You're special. You always have been. I knew it from the moment you were born."

Not for the first time, Marley wondered why she—and

not Meredith—had been the chosen one. The "special" one. After all, they'd been born only minutes apart. Did she owe her entire career to having entered the world six minutes ahead of her twin sister?

Still, Imogene's staunch loyalty touched her. If Marley hadn't been wavering against the stupid fake rocks, she'd have enveloped her mom's squat body in a big, grateful hug.

Marley figured she had outgrown most of her childish needs. She no longer wished for a mother who played with Barbie with her daughter, rather than one who looked to Barbie for audition wardrobe ideas. She no longer hoped her mother would applaud her performances, rather than critique them. But she did still yearn for her mother's approval, however elusive it might be.

"That special quality you have is why you owe it to yourself not to leap into anything rashly," her mother went on. "This *Dream Date* thing is only temporary, honey. Don't let it confuse you."

"Too late." Miserably, Marley hung on the rocks, suddenly feeling jittery. Had the handholds gotten scarcer, the footholds more treacherous? Or was it just her? "That's why I'm here. That's why I need advice. Because I think . . . he's falling in love with me, too."

Imogene frowned, ostensibly searching for a new handhold. Her expression looked skeptical—and not about the likelihood of finding a ledge upon which to wedge her chalked fingers, either.

Marley forged ahead anyway. She had proof to back up her feelings.

Starting with the big guns, she announced, "Lately, he turns off the TV whenever I arrive at his apartment."

Her mother stilled, hand outstretched. "Even during a football game? Your father doesn't even do that."

Marley nodded. "It's baseball season right now, but yes."

She couldn't believe she actually knew about sports seasons. Being with Jake was changing her so much. Just a few days ago, she'd donned sunglasses and a baseball cap and ducked into Barnes & Noble to buy a copy not of the latest *Vogue,* but of a *Baseball for Dummies* book. Just to impress Jake.

Okay, so she'd bought *Vogue,* too. But still.

"He turns off whatever sports he's watching," she said, "just to be with me. Unless we're watching them together. Last night was my first double play."

"I don't want to know about your sex life!"

"It's a baseball thing." She and Jake hadn't slept together yet, despite the immense temptation to do so. "Not only do those guys look hot in their color-coordinated uniforms, but they're talented, too."

Warily, Marley examined the next position. The top of the rock wall loomed in her vision, but she wasn't sure she could make it that far.

A part of her really wanted to, though.

"If you hadn't mentioned the ballplayers' coordinated uniforms, I'd have been worried about you," Imogene said. She'd reached the wall summit and was now climbing down. She paused on a level with her daughter. "I don't want my little girl turning into someone I don't know."

"I'm not sure you ever knew me, Mom."

"What?" Imogene hesitated mid-descent.

"Nothing. It's just . . . *what do I do?*"

"About falling in love?"

Marley nodded.

Her mother pursed her lips. Urgently, Marley awaited whatever pearls of wisdom would be forthcoming. She needed help, and she knew it. This situation with Jake—unlike Stanislavski's Method, the Zone diet, and everything to do with sitcom hairstyles—was completely unfamiliar to her. She felt vulnerable. Needy. So crazy with loving feelings that she'd actually agreed to try a game of touch football with Noah, Jake, and Noah's Nerf football—just to make Jake smile.

He had smiled, too. Right before informing her that in football—especially kiddie football—dissing the players' choice of ensembles did *not* qualify as bona fide trash talking.

Marley had been so sure she'd been getting the hang of it.

Her mother's voice brought her back to their conversation.

"Nothing," Imogene said at last. She found her next climbing position with assurance and powered her way downward. "For now, you shouldn't do a thing. Just remember Bobby Christopher. That's all I can say."

Marley froze. Of all the things to remind her of—the Bobby Christopher incident. *Ugh.* With one last despondent look at the pinnacle she'd never reach, Marley abandoned her efforts altogether. She barely had time to regret her decision before harness and rope carried her back to the ground.

"Bobby Christopher?" Meredith asked, wrinkling her nose in confusion. "What makes you think of *him?*"

"Nostalgia, I guess." Marley shrugged, unwilling to reveal to her sister the true source of her blast-from-the-past questions. "Just thinking about old times."

They'd gone to the farmers' market at Fairfax and Third, and now were meandering among the vendors with vanilla iced blendeds in hand. Every imaginable foodstuff was being sold all around them, from fruits and vegetables and fresh herbs to oven-baked bread, homemade salsa, gourmet cheese, and candy. Gaudy Los Angeles souvenirs flourished everywhere. Restaurants serving everything from sushi to crepes competed for the attention of the throngs of visitors crowding the market.

Meredith shouldered her macramé bag and stopped to examine a display of mangoes.

"Do you remember him?" Marley asked her again.

"Bobby? Sure."

She squeezed a mango, then moved on. As an advertising historian, Meredith was usually more interested in examining the vendors' signs and handbills than sampling their goods. Shopping with her was like watching movies with a director. Like eating hamburgers with a butcher. A person tended to find out more about the *process* of it all than she wanted to know.

"I remember you breaking his heart," Meredith added.

Ugh. There it was. Marley had hoped she'd remembered the situation wrong. "We were only seventeen. He couldn't have cared about me that much."

"Have you forgotten what it's like to be seventeen? When you're seventeen, you care about *everything* that much."

Morosely, Marley had to agree. She walked beside her twin sister to the next vendor, sniffing as the sweet scent of English toffee filled the air.

"You weren't there," Meredith continued. "Bobby cared about you enough to sit in our living room wearing a tuxedo. He clutched the corsage he brought until the plastic box cracked."

Marley had never gotten the details. Or she'd chosen to forget them. Now, she imagined poor Bobby waiting for her in vain and felt fresh regret knife through her.

"Mom agreed with me," she protested, somewhat half-heartedly. She turned away, sorting through a display of colorful kites without really seeing them. "We both knew what I had to do."

"You only ever have to do what you choose to do."

"That's easy for you to say," Marley shot back, in no mood for empty platitudes. "You were never pulled in two directions at once."

Meredith stilled. "No, I wasn't," she agreed. She ran her fingertips over a kite's sheer nylon wings, gazing at it instead of at her sister. "I was never pulled in any direction at all."

"That's right! You weren't." Marley turned her triumphant gaze on Meredith, ready to continue making her case ... only to feel every bit of righteousness drain from her at a single glance.

Her sister looked sad. She wistfully traced the kite's wings, as though yearning to experience the soaring heights they would achieve someday when guided by a skilled enough hand. Had Meredith wanted the demands Marley had sometimes resented? Had she longed for a spotlight of her own?

"Shoddy merchandise," Meredith remarked, frowning as she moved on from the kites. "They'll need lower prices if they want to move those suckers."

Relieved, Marley followed. Her sister wasn't unhappy. She was only being analytical, as usual.

They reached an ice cream stand and perused the flavors without really intending to make a choice. Their frosty coffee drinks had filled them up. They passed by a flower stall and a newsstand.

"Are you sorry about Bobby?" Meredith asked.

The casual tone of her voice told Marley she meant for the question to sound idle. Unfortunately, Marley couldn't respond in kind.

"I'm sorry I hurt him," she said seriously. "I'm sorry I didn't remember to call him."

"But you'd do it all over again, wouldn't you?"

Marley hesitated. "Well . . . that last-minute audition I missed the prom for was what landed me my part on *Days of our Lives*. It launched my career in earnest. I had a choice to make. I can't honestly say I wouldn't—"

"Save it," Meredith interrupted with a wave of her hand. "For a minute there, I thought you'd developed an actual conscience."

"Hey, I named my *Dream Date* alter ego in tribute to Bobby," Marley offered quietly. "Bobby Christopher, Carly Christopher. Get it?"

"I can't believe you think that means anything."

"Well . . . at the time I did."

Her sister shook her head.

Marley frowned, biting her lip. Meredith was right. Naming her alter ego after the boy she'd left waiting for her all those years ago was a paltry effort. On prom night, all Bobby had wanted was to be with her—and Marley had hurt him. Now she'd probably do the same thing all over again, with Jake. They'd gotten closer and closer over the past few weeks, but it was all a lie. No matter how much of herself she shared while pretending to be Carly, the intimacy she and Jake achieved could never be complete without the truth.

She had to tell him.

She couldn't tell him.

He'd hate her for deceiving him. He wouldn't understand that her feelings were real, even if the name she'd given him wasn't. He wouldn't understand how much their togetherness meant to her now. Between the two of them, she and Jake had created a perfect shiny bubble of happiness. Was it so wrong to want it to last as long as possible?

As Carly, she'd discovered true love. As Marley, all that awaited her were heartbreak and a ZitKit3000 infomercial.

Gee, put that way, the decision didn't seem so tough after all. She had to savor her time with Jake as much as possible, Marley decided. The future—and the final *Dream Date* taping—would drop-kick her back into reality soon enough.

She and Meredith neared an instant-photo booth at the center of the market.

"Come on, let's take our pictures together," Marley cried, grabbing her sister's hand. She tugged her toward the booth. "It'll be fun."

Meredith resisted. "I hate having my picture taken."

Surprised, Marley paused. "Since when? When we were kids, we used to cram into these booths all the time. We had so many of those photo strips, you used them as bookmarks."

A sudden rush of affection filled her. Meredith was the only person who always stuck by her, no matter what. The only person who truly played it straight with her. She wanted to recapture a little of the camaraderie they'd shared as little girls, before the quest for showbiz success had gotten in the way.

"Let's do it."

Meredith shook her head. "Times have changed."

"Why?"

"Oh, I dunno. Maybe because you're a TV starlet and I'm not?"

"What difference does that make?" Marley smiled, trying to coax her nearer. "It's a photo booth, not a screen test."

Her sister shrugged. "You'll use the pictures as makeover ammunition. You'll send them to *Allure* for one of those SWAT-style styling fests they do."

"I promise not to." She crossed her heart. "Okay?"

"You'll show them to Mom. She'll lecture me about wearing stripes with plaids again."

"Somebody ought to," Marley joked.

At Meredith's pained look, she sobered. Was Meredith serious? Did those things really bother her? Marley had taken her mother's criticisms—and the showbiz-related need for frequent makeovers—so much to heart. They were part of her job, part of her mind-set. It hadn't occurred to her Meredith might take any of it personally.

"I'm sorry." She gave her unyielding sister a hug. "I was only kidding. Honest."

"Whatever."

"I only want you to be happy. Really."

A big sigh shuddered through Meredith. "Me, too. For you."

Marley smiled widely. Relieved, she leaned back to examine her sister's face. Meredith offered a wan grin in return, and Marley knew everything was okay again.

"So, what do you say? Pictures for old times' sake?"

"Sure. Why not?" Meredith relented. "The worst that can happen is I break the camera."

Marley rolled her eyes. "Don't be silly. You look fine. Besides, appearances aren't everything."

"Hmmph. They are in your world."

"So? That doesn't mean I hold you to the same ridiculous, liposuction-and-Botox standards that have been forced on me all these years."

Meredith looked skeptical. Marley began to protest . . . and in that moment, realized the truth. Oftentimes, she *had* viewed her sister through the warped lens of Hollywood perfection. She'd spent so much time caught up in that funhouse view herself, she hadn't realized it.

"Oh, Meredith. I *have* done that, haven't I? I'm so sorry!"

Her sister waved away her apology.

"I wasn't fair to you. I didn't mean it, but I wasn't fair to you. Can you ever forgive me?"

Meredith looked uncomfortable.

"I only wanted you to be happy. It just didn't occur to me you could be fully content *without* a good blowout and some lipstick." Repentantly, she shook her head. "I've been so shallow. Please, *please* forgive me."

A moment passed.

"I mean, really," Marley begged. *"Fantasy Family* once shut down production because I had a zit! That would give any girl a disturbed worldview. Please, please forgive me."

A small smile lifted Meredith's mouth. She gave Marley a thoughtful look. "Okay. On one condition."

"Anything. I'll do anything you want."

Meredith's smile widened. "Anything?"

A quaver of unease squeezed the remaining vanilla iced blended in Marley's stomach. But she was committed now. She wouldn't back down.

"Anything," she confirmed. When she'd finished making amends to her sister, she'd do her best to make up for other, more long-standing hurts she'd caused, too. "Anything you want."

"Okay. Here's the deal. . . ."

Seventeen

On Jake's next day off, his sisters Rebecca and Bethany volunteered—as they often did—to spend the day with Noah.

Jake suspected they did it partly because they loved their nephew (who wouldn't?), and partly because they wanted to make sure Noah had steady feminine influences in his life. Either way, it was fine by him. As reluctant as he was to miss a day with his son, Jake knew that realistically, a single dad needed a break now and then. Although he took his responsibilities as a father seriously, sometimes a guy just wanted to kick back and *not* be a positive role model for a while.

Besides, with Noah in capable hands, Jake was free to spend some quality adult time with Carly. He planned to surprise her, sweep her off her feet, and then finish what they'd started up against his front door—once and for all.

Pleasurably contemplating everything this day might hold, he showered, shaved, and dressed. Then, on the verge of leaving, he debated over the bottle of Old Spice Noah had given him last Christmas. Aside from an obligatory splash beneath the flashing lights and homemade paper chains on the tree, he hadn't used it. He wasn't a cologne kind of guy. But for the sake of impressing Carly, who was always so perfectly groomed . . .

Jake dabbed some on his neck. He scrutinized his appearance in the bathroom mirror, inhaled deeply, then frowned. To him, the stuff smelled like fruitcake crossed with tobacco. Carly might not find the combination entirely appealing. If she was a hungry chain-smoker, sure. But she wasn't.

He perused the row of cologne bottles remaining in his medicine cabinet. Dead soldiers all, they'd been given to him by his mother, his aunts, his ex-girlfriends. Each had been opened, used once, and then stashed here in the aftershave graveyard. Jake had always thought his natural qualities had been enough. He hadn't needed help with women, in an olfactory sense or otherwise.

But that had been before Carly. Carly, who resisted giving in to the attraction between them. Carly, who bewitched him but kept herself at a definite distance. Carly, who needed to be completely bowled over by Jake before he went completely crazy.

Decisively, he grabbed a bottle of Obsession for Men. Then a bottle of Allure Por Homme by Chanel. Next, a bottle of Aramis. Soon, he'd dabbed on a little of everything.

Try and resist *that!* he thought as he grabbed his car keys. The motion made fumes waft upward. His eyes watered a little.

No problem. So what? Obviously, women liked a fine-smelling man, Jake told himself as he headed out the door. Otherwise, so many different colognes wouldn't exist. Between the many he'd sampled, Carly was bound to find one that sent her over the moon.

Then, once he'd hooked her for sure, he'd send them *both* over the moon. Together. He could hardly wait.

His knock at Carly's apartment door took a long time to be answered. Jake had almost decided she must be out when he heard the chain rattle inside. An instant later, the brown-painted wood inched inward.

Carly's face peeked out. Sort of. She appeared to be shrouded in a blanket.

"Jake! What are you doing here?"

"Surprising you." His smile faltered as he caught a better glimpse of her. Between the folds of the blanket atop her head, her cheeks were pale. "Is this a bad time?"

"Ummm. Well . . ."

"You're sick, aren't you? Oh, Carly."

"Sort of," she agreed. She gave a feeble cough, nudging an interested Gaffer away from the door with her toe. "Let's do this another time, okay? Sorry."

"Sure." He paused, hoping she'd change her mind. Disappointment pushed through him when she didn't. "All right."

It was the least he could do.

With a rueful shrug and another apology, Carly quietly closed the door. Jake stared at it. Poor Carly. He understood her need to be by herself. Whenever he wasn't feeling well, all he wanted was to be left alone in his misery, too. He headed downstairs again.

Hang on a sec.

Something wasn't right here.

He was halfway across the parking lot to his car before he realized the truth. He couldn't leave Carly alone! She was a woman. Women *never* wanted to be left alone when they weren't feeling well. Growing up with two sisters and a high-maintenance mother had taught him that much. They wanted talking. Commiserating. Hot soup and trash TV. They wanted *caring.*

Jake could deliver caring.

A half-hour later, he bounded back up the stairs to Carly's second-floor apartment. Cradling the things he'd brought, he knocked on the door again. This time when Carly opened it, Jake refused to take no for an answer.

"I'm here to take care of you," he announced, shouldering the door open still farther. He strode past her, dodging Gaffer's scampering doggie welcome, and put everything on the round table near the kitchen. "I've got chicken soup from the deli, two quarts of Gatorade, Kleenex, cereal, a stack of magazines"—he fanned out a selection from the Borders nearby—"three videotapes, and a deck of cards."

"Oh, Jake!" She shut the door. "How did you . . . ? Why did you . . . ?"

"I've got to warn you. I play a mean game of Go Fish."

She looked nonplussed. "But all this? You shouldn't have."

"There's no use arguing." Jake looked up from the welcoming pat he'd been giving Gaffer. He delivered her a stern look. "You're letting me stay until you're better."

Slowly, Carly made her way to the table. Her blanket trailed behind her. *"Allure, InStyle, Cosmo.* All my favorites. How did you know?" she exclaimed, reaching out a hand to touch the magazines. She shifted the topmost issue aside. Paused for a beat. *"Sports Illustrated?"*

He shrugged. "You might fall asleep."

"You'd stay by my side if I did? Reading *Sports Illustrated?"*

Or watching you dream. Jake grunted an affirmative and turned away, undone by the unexpected urge he felt to make sure she was cared for. With businesslike gestures, he went to the living room sofa—ground zero for all his childhood illnesses—and fluffed the pillows.

"No water? You need a glass of water over here." Rolling his eyes at her in a *sheesh, amateurs* way, he strode into the kitchen and filled a glass. When she didn't even ask for ice, he grew concerned. "When you feel up to it, I'll make you a bowl of Cap'N Crunch. Peanut Butter Crunch. The best kind. My mom only let us have it when we were recovering from the chicken pox or something."

He glanced at her. She still hadn't moved, wasn't even swayed by the promise of the ultimate sugary breakfast cereal. Probably, she didn't have the strength. His worry grew. Propelled by it, he went to her.

Gently, Jake wrapped his arm around her waist. He felt the soft waffle weave of Carly's blanket against his skin, sensed the heat pouring from her body. "You feel feverish. Let's get you over to the sofa."

He led her there. A third of the way across the room, he lost patience and scooped her up in his arms instead.

"Jake! Put me down. You'll hurt yourself."

What was she trying to do? Offend him? He was strong enough to carry her measly weight. All day, if necessary. For demonstration's sake, he circled back for the water glass she'd abandoned on the table and made her pick it up. Then he went to the window, ignoring her protests, and checked the weather. Then finally, carefully, he lowered her to the sofa.

He gazed at her tenderly.

She wrinkled her nose. "What did you do, bathe in a tub of Aqua Velva? Get caught in the cross fire between rival perfume spritzers at Macy's?"

"You noticed!" Grinning, Jake sat on the coffee table opposite the sofa. "My neck is Old Spice"—he leaned nearer, so she could sample it—"this arm is Aramis, this arm is Allure Pour Homme, and my chest is Obsession for Men."

He fluffed up his shirt, the better for Carly to catch a swoon-worthy whiff. "Oh, and my leg is some green stuff. The label had worn off the bottle, so I don't know what it's called."

Eagerly, Jake propped his leg on the sofa. He yanked up his jeans. After a moment, her bemused gaze lifted from his hairy, fragranced calf.

"All this? For me?"

He shrugged with deliberate carelessness. "I'm just trying out the contents of my medicine cabinet. But if you like one . . ."

"Let me sample."

She thrust a hand between the folds of her blanket. Her fingers clamped onto his shirt. She dragged him nearer, so his body hovered only a few inches from hers.

"This feels nice," she remarked breathily, temporarily diverted from her cologne-sampling mission by her fistful of shirt. "A little silky. Freshly ironed, too."

He grunted. "You can get that at the dry cleaner."

Not for anything was Jake revealing the hour he'd spent hunched over with a borrowed iron, trying to smooth out the wrinkles in his shirt. He tucked his hand beneath the edge of her blanket to hide the singed spots on his knuckles.

"You look very nice," Carly said. She pulled him nearer and sniffed his neck. "Mmmm. My dad wears Old Spice."

Hell! He wanted to scour his skin clean. Reminding her of dear old dad was not his prime objective.

An arm. "Hmmm."

Hmmm? What did that mean? Was it good or bad?

Another arm. "Interesting."

This just got worse and worse. *Interesting* was code for *weird,* Jake was sure.

His chest. "Nice."

Okay, that was encouraging.

"I'd better try your leg."

He levered backward and sideways a bit, so she could sample the mystery fragrance without exerting herself too much.

"I don't like that one. Sorry."

"Hey, honesty is the best policy, right?" But secretly, he felt crushed. There weren't many more options in the cologne boneyard. If one of these didn't turn her crank, then Jake didn't know what to do.

"C'mere and let me have another go at it," Carly coaxed.

Her blanket rustled as she beckoned him nearer. Jake wished she felt well enough to do without it. With ten yards of pastel waffle weave over her head and body, he couldn't get a clear look at her. It had him worried.

Some of his worry evaporated as Carly all but dragged him on top of her. She wiggled around to make room for them both on the sofa, then made a contented little sound.

He wanted to do the same thing. She felt wonderful beneath him. Her nearness sparked up ideas . . . ideas of what Jake had originally come here to accomplish. He still wanted her. Only now, his desire was mixed with a tenderness he hadn't expected. He felt a little like kissing her, a little like making her smile, and completely undone by his mixed emotions.

Carly brought him back around to the task at hand.

"This is better. Okay. Here goes." She nuzzled his skin, sliding her cheek against his. "Just hold still while I reconsider this cologne idea."

A nibble on his earlobe made him jerk in pleasurable surprise. If he hadn't known damn well that Carly was too sick to be laying moves on him, he'd have thought . . .

"Mmmm. Easy there. Just testing," she murmured.

Jake steeled himself. She was sick. Maybe a little delirious. He had to be a gentleman.

A teensy lick. Another nibble. A tentative inhalation.

"Did you just blow in my ear?" he asked.

She ignored the question. "I like the way you smell right here." A kiss behind his ear demonstrated the spot she meant. "What's this one called?"

He tried not to sound disgruntled. "Safeguard, maybe. Shampoo. I dunno. My natural smell."

"It's my favorite."

"You're crazy."

"About you. Yeah."

Jake stilled. For a wild instant, he actually believed she meant it. *Crazy about him.* But then he reached for her, touched her damned blanket, and realized the truth.

"You *are* delirious." He bolted upward. "I'll get you a cool cloth for your forehead."

He returned a few minutes later with a wrung-out cold washcloth in hand. Determination dogged his every step. If Carly could say she was crazy about him while she was sick, then there must be some accuracy in the statement, right? Probably, her inhibitions had kept her from revealing her true feelings.

And had kept her pushing him away. Until now.

"Here. Hold this on your forehead. Do you have a thermometer? You probably need some Tylenol to bring down your fever, too."

"I don't have a fever."

"You're too delirious to realize it." Jake put one hand on her shoulder to ease her down onto the sofa, then laid the cloth in place himself. Damned stubborn woman. Didn't she know she needed care right now, just like every other female on the planet? "Just hold still and try to rest. I'll be right here."

"Jake, I can't let you do this."

"Sure, you can."

Blindly, she grabbed his hand and tried to yank it away from the cloth. He'd held it in place purposely, guessing she might fight it. He tightened his grasp and used his other hand to catch hold of her flailing hand. He kissed it.

She relaxed. "Oh, Jake."

"Shhh. I'm here for you."

Jesus, that sounded wussy.

He cleared his throat. "You take a nap. I'll, uh, go change the oil in your car." Sure. That sounded suitably macho. "Your spark plugs probably need testing. Your timing might need adjusting, too. Those classic cars need maintenance, you know." Soothingly, he stroked her hair through the blanket.

She moaned. "I can't do this to you."

"It's not as though you meant for me to come work on your car."

"You're being too sweet! I thought I could go through with this, but now—"

"It's okay," he interrupted before she could upset herself further. Gruffly, he softened his voice. "Do you want some soup before I haul out my tool kit?"

He actually did keep a rudimentary mechanic's kit in the trunk of his Accord, thank God. He could make good on his offer.

"No," Carly said. "I don't deserve soup. I don't deserve you!"

"Hey, I'm not doing anything I don't want to do."

"Yes, you are! You just don't know it."

He waited patiently.

"Jake, I've misled you."

"Misled me?"

Her blanket shifted as she retreated into it. She nodded.

Slowly, he sat up. He considered things. "You hate *all* the colognes!"

"No. No, that's not it." Urgently, Carly grabbed his hands. "Jake, I'm sorry. I didn't know how to tell you the truth. *Again.*" She muttered this last. "I just . . . I didn't want you to see me like this, that's all."

"Like what?"

"This!" she cried miserably. She released his hands and flung her arms wide. Her blanket flopped with the force of her gestures, as though she were Casper the Pastel Ghost. "This!"

Confused, he leaned nearer. "You're sick. It happens. Do you want some Kleenex? A sip of Gatorade?" Inspiration struck. "Tell you what. I'll make you a bowl of Peanut Butter Crunch right now."

He got up to do just that. Carly grabbed his wrist before he could.

"Okay. I'll come clean," she said. "But if you don't want to come back here after this, I'll understand."

Jake frowned. "You're not making sense."

She sniffled, sounding more upset. "Just remember what I said, okay? And try not to scream."

"Scream?" He scoffed. "Why would I scream?"

Carly inhaled. With a sudden gesture, she flung off her blanket. Without it, she blinked like a couch potato at the beach in July. Slowly, she raised her face to his.

"See?" she asked, voice quavering.

He blinked. "What?"

"Me! *I'm* what I've been hiding."

He squinted. Okay, so her hair was a little messy. It stuck up on top where the blanket's rubbing against her head had generated static electricity. And she still looked pale. But that wasn't a crime. Jake didn't understand.

Apparently, Carly sensed his confusion.

"My sister did my hair and makeup today," she confessed.

Her voice shook, suggesting this truth was almost too horrible to reveal. She bit her lip, watching for his reaction.

"But . . ." He sensed he should tread carefully here. "It looks like you're not wearing any makeup."

"That's Meredith's idea of cosmetic perfection. It's her idea of penance, too." She touched her hair self-consciously. "I volunteered for this, to make up for something I did. To learn a lesson."

He made a noncommittal sound, still unsure what was so heinous about the situation.

"I have to spend two whole days this way," Carly continued. "Even on *Dream Date!* I mean, in a way it'll probably improve my image. But then there's you . . ." Her voice trailed off. She gave him a plaintive look, then brightened inexplicably. "I have to say, you're doing an excellent job of not staring, though. That's really thoughtful."

"Let me get this straight. You're *not* sick?"

"I feel fine. I just don't look that way."

Relief filled him. She felt fine! He grinned.

"Technically, you're *supposed* to rebut that part," she groused. "About me not looking fine."

"You look incredible to me," he assured her.

"Well, don't go crazy."

"I mean it." Jake came nearer, sat on the coffee table again. He tilted her face toward him with his hand. "I don't care if you have lipstick on. It's just one more thing for me to kiss away. I don't care if you're wearing eye makeup or hair spray or that gooey stuff on your cheeks."

"Blush?"

"Whatever. I only care if you're *you.*"

"Right now, I don't *feel* like me. I feel naked."

"Say—there's an idea I can get behind." He waggled his eyebrows teasingly. "You, naked. Me, joining you."

Carly smiled faintly, her first semi-cheerful expression since her big revelation. "This is a big deal! I haven't appeared in public without makeup since I was thirteen, you know."

"Hey, I'm not the public." He spread his arms. "I'm just me."

"Yeah," she agreed. Her wistful gaze raised to his. "You're more important than any public could ever be. I don't know what I'd do if you . . . well, never mind that. So far you're handling all this really well. I'm impressed."

"I'm tougher than you think."

"I guess you are. That's encouraging."

Looking slightly relieved, Carly blew air-kisses to Gaffer. The dog tromped merrily across the blanket, crawled onto her chest, and lolled as she snuggled with him. "I'm braver than *I* think. I can't believe I showed you . . . this."

Her waving hand indicated her natural-looking face and hair. Her giggle sounded a little hysterical.

Jake shook his head. "There's nothing about you that could ever disappoint me. Don't you know that?"

She turned her face to his. Eyed him contemplatively. "Do you mean that?"

He nodded. "I wouldn't say it if I didn't."

Hopefulness glowed in her expression, brightening her eyes.

"You don't know how much that means to me, Jake. Someday . . . well, someday I just might call you on that."

Carly urged Gaffer down from the sofa. With new energy, she lurched upward and got to her feet. She padded over to the kitchen table and surveyed the items on it.

"You know, if we added a pint of Phish Food and some Chunky Monkey to this, we'd have the makings of a perfect romantic afternoon at home. What do you say? We could close the blinds, crank up the VCR, cozy up in front of a movie . . ."

"Uh-uh," Jake disagreed with a flash of inspiration. "I have other plans for you. *Dream Date* plans. All this time, we've been doing things I like. Baseball games. Touch football. Shooting pool. If we're going to win that game show, we're going to have to get serious. We're going to have to start paying attention to the other half of things."

"The feminine half of things?"

"Right." He braced himself. "And that means"—he couldn't believe he was about to say this—*"shopping."*

Eighteen

Marley still couldn't believe Jake had talked her into this. She was barefaced in public, without so much as an all-in-one stick to lend her some color. Her hair was fluffy, bereft of the necessary styling products to achieve glossy smoothness. And her clothes . . . well, her clothes were hand picked by Meredith, straight from "Carly's" closet of thrift-shop and discount wear. They were schlumpy, uncoordinated, and indisputably designed to teach Marley a lesson about fashion tolerance.

Today, *she* was wearing stripes with plaid.

It was nothing worse than she deserved, though. Her revelation at the farmers' market had driven home some important points to Marley. Talking with her sister had made her realize certain things about herself and her luxe life. Looking good wasn't as important as *being* good. Generosity couldn't replace thoughtfulness. Excuses didn't matter when feelings were at stake.

Which brought her right back around to Bobby Christopher, and the terrible way she'd treated him.

Needing to make amends, Marley had started by tracking down Bobby via her high school's alumni coordinator. She'd proceeded through apartment changes, job switches, and more than a couple of false leads before finally locating her former prom date on a construction site in the Valley.

She'd never forget the look on Bobby's face when he'd spotted her picking her stiletto-heeled way through the dirt, a bright hard hat contrasting with her low-cut, va-va-voom wrap dress. Marley had decided to morph into her usual starlet self for the occasion, and (with Meredith's blessing) she'd pulled out all the stops. Lipstick. Cutlet-boosted cleavage. Sex-kitten hair and her wildest shoes. The whole combination was designed to be as man-friendly as possible, and Marley figured poor Bobby was entitled to the full treatment.

"Bobby!" she called. "There you are! I've been looking everywhere for you."

He gawked. Blinked. Shoved back his hard hat and scratched his head. "Marley? Marley Madison?"

She nodded, working her patented hip wiggle all the way to the block wall in progress where he sat with his buddies having lunch. The men boggled. Their jaws dropped. They stared at Marley, then at Bobby, then back at Marley.

"Holy shit, Bobster! You really *do* know her!"

"Uh, yeah." Bobby still looked confused.

Obviously, Marley needed to take control. She slipped her hand into his and gently urged him to his feet. "Come on over here and talk to me for a while. Please, Bobby."

Silently, he came.

The years hadn't changed him much, she saw as they stopped a few feet away and faced each other in the relative privacy of a girder's shadow. He still had the football player's beefy build he'd possessed in high school, still wore his class ring, still rubbed his eyebrow with the heel of his hand when he was unsure about something.

Marley tugged his wrist downward. "You're probably wondering what I'm doing here. The truth is, I owe you something. Something I should have given you a long time ago."

He glanced over his shoulder. His pals were all watching. One of them gave him a thumbs-up sign. A crooked grin emerged from the uncertainty on Bobby's face. He turned back to her.

"I never thought I'd see you again," he said. "You look good. Real good. Your hair's different—"

"It's for a part," she told him, touching her darkened tresses. "Hair color."

"—but you look really amazing."

His up-and-down perusal gave proof to his words. Marley was glad she'd abandoned her alter ego for the occasion. Real and raw Carly would not have been enough for this. Luckily, Meredith had agreed she could make an exception in her makeup-free, uncoordinated, bad-hair days—for Bobby's sake.

"So do you." She squeezed his biceps for good measure. "You look great."

His coworkers hooted when she touched him. They cat-called. One even beckoned over a few extra construction workers to watch the spectacle.

Bobby flushed. He scooted himself and Marley a few feet farther into the shadows. He hooked a thumb over his shoulder. "Gino over there has seen every episode of *Fantasy Family*. Twice. He's gotta be thrilled to be seein' you like this."

Naively, she'd hoped *Bobby* might be "thrilled" to see her like this. She searched his face. In it, she saw the same seventeen-year-old boy who'd asked her, the school curiosity, to the prom. Gratitude swamped her. So did sorrow.

"And you? Are you glad to see me?"

He lifted his dirt-smudged shoulder in a shrug.

"Because it took a lot of effort to find you." Marley gathered her courage—not an easy task in the face of his apparent indifference. "This was really important to me. Seeing you, I mean."

"Seeing me? Heck, there were hundreds of people in our graduating class. You coulda seen all of us next year at the reunion."

"That wouldn't have been the same. I needed to talk to you now. Alone."

"Me?" Bafflement creased his brow. His gaze swept over her again, taking in all the starlet accoutrements she'd decked herself out in. She was a walking pinup. His expression suggested that seeing her in the flesh was good enough for him. Not to mention his pals.

Then . . . he remembered. Marley saw the recollection flash across his face, saw his fingers flex as though he still held a crushed corsage box in his hand, and knew Bobby understood what she'd come there to talk about.

His expression turned mulish. "Yeah. I guess you never did get a good laugh over what happened, did you?"

"Oh, Bobby! I never laughed! I wouldn't have done that." Marley clung to his arm, pleading silently with him to listen. "I never meant to hurt you. I was young and stupid and thoughtless. I had an audition that day, and the producer invited me to a cast party later that night to meet with some of the bigwigs on-set. It was a good sign! A really big deal. I'd been trying to break into soaps for months—"

"I'd been thinking about the prom for months," he interrupted. "I could've asked lots of girls. Lots of them! But I didn't."

"I know," Marley said quietly. "You asked me."

Why, she didn't know. In high school, she'd either been ridiculed for her acting pretensions or snubbed altogether. Presumably, her classmates had decided that she, as a working teen actress, would be a snob. They'd fired their preemptive shots before she'd had a chance to prove otherwise.

"I'm grateful for that," she went on. "Honest, Bobby. To tell you the truth, I wasn't even sure you'd show up that night."

He gave her a suspicious look. "Why not?"

This time, it was her turn to shrug. "Sometimes . . . people let me down. That's all."

She refused to tell him about the party invitations that were promised her—but never came. About the giggling and whispering in the girls' bathroom. About Leah Webster and Brenda Basson, who'd pretended to be her friends just long enough to score autographed photos of a sitcom hottie who worked at the soundstage next to hers. Bobby didn't need to know any of that. He only needed to know one thing.

"I'm sorry," Marley said truthfully. She squeezed his hand. "I'm sorry I wasn't there, and I'm sorry I didn't call you afterward. It was inexcusable. I can only say that you deserved better. Much better."

A moment passed. The only sounds were the traffic on the street nearby, the distant chugging of heavy construction equipment, and the scuffling of Bobby's boots in the dirt.

"Well . . . that's what I came here to say." He wasn't going to forgive her. He wasn't. She'd hurt him too much for that. At the thought, Marley felt her lower lip wobble. She caught it between her teeth, hoping to keep her dismay to herself. "I guess I'll . . . be leaving now. Thanks for listening."

Resignedly, she headed back the way she'd come.

"Wait."

Marley did. Holding her breath, she turned.

Bobby shoved his hands in his pockets. He squinted up at the building he'd been laboring on. "Awww, it wasn't that bad," he finally said, kicking his work boot in the dust. "You did what you had to do, Marley."

That was what her mother had said. She didn't dare reveal as much aloud. Having Imogene Madison's blessing hadn't changed things.

"We were just kids," Bobby went on. "No permanent harm done. Hey, I'm fine. I've *been* fine, all these years."

Marley nearly sagged with relief. A part of her had imagined poor Bobby scarred for life, unable to trust that the women he cared for wouldn't let him down. A smile burbled up from someplace inside her. She couldn't help but let it show.

"Thanks," she said as she hurried back. Impulsively, she hugged him. "You're the best."

More hooting and catcalling reminded her they weren't alone. Embarrassed, Marley stepped back.

Bobby hauled her close again. "Hang on," he whispered in her ear. "I forgive you, Marley. But I've got an idea."

Ten minutes later, Marley had given the virtuoso performance of her career—in a stormy "breakup" scene direct from her supposedly clandestine relationship with Bobby. She wailed when he hardheartedly announced they were through. Begged when he shrugged off another hug. Tearfully nodded when Bobby explained that she would simply have to find a way to move on with her life without him.

His coworkers, edging closer with every dramatic word and gesture, listened in. Their mouths gaped. Their eyes bugged. By the time Marley and Bobby were finished, they stared at their buddy with newfound interest.

"Whoa," Marley heard one of them say as she walked away, a secret smile on her face. "Don't you think you were a little harsh on her?"

"Yeah," another said. "You made her cry!"

"Hey, I did all I could," Bobby explained. "Is it my fault she's having trouble getting over the Bobster?"

With that pronouncement, Bobby had glanced over his shoulder toward a retreating Marley. Her former prom date had winked at her then, and ten years of worry and guilt had fallen away. Marley had known all was forgiven.

In a way, seeing Bobby had given her the courage to go on being Carly, Marley mused now. It had given her the hope that Jake might eventually forgive her this deception. Maybe they'd be able to be together, even after *Dream Date* was finished.

With that reminder of the purpose of her on-camera afternoon with Jake in mind, Marley smiled. Working together, they would win the game show. Their futures would be assured. The gritty new roles and revitalized career she craved would be within reach, and everything would be wonderful.

All that remained now was the final preparatory push.

Ready to get down to work, Marley tugged Jake by the hand until they'd stepped from the shadows of the parking garage onto the open-air shopping and entertainment complex that was the Third Street Promenade in Santa Monica.

The faint brininess of sea air mingled with the California

sunshine. All around them, people strolled along the promenade. The street had been closed permanently to traffic, making the various shops, restaurants, movie theaters and clubs easily accessible to visitors. Tourists meandered among the locals, café owners dressed outdoor tables in preparation for the lunch crowd, and street performers set up impromptu shows along the way.

Walking past a saxophone-playing man and his dog, Marley eagerly scoped out the stores. Ordinarily, she shopped at exclusive boutiques with private locations or in the famous Golden Triangle, at the center of which Rodeo Drive offered just about every luxury imaginable. But Carly couldn't afford any of those places, and Jake had seemed determined to take her shopping. So they'd settled here.

Now, if she could only avoid her favorite splurge spot—Fred Segal. She'd never maintain her cover if she ventured in there.

Jake scanned the street and storefronts. "Where to first?"

"You sound like you're being dragged to the guillotine."

"Ha. I sound like *you* did, when I suggested hitting a few rounds at the driving range."

She wrinkled her nose. "I just didn't see the point. If the ball isn't *going* anywhere except onto the green with the other balls, how is that supposed to improve a person's game?"

"It's called practice."

"It's called boooring." Marley spotted an adorable shoe display at a nearby shop and scurried toward it. For Jake's sake, she refrained from pressing her nose against the glass. "Stilettos! My favorite. Those baby blue ones are really cute, aren't they?"

Jake shaded his eyes and peered at the shoes. "For the price of those shoes, I could make a car payment."

He looked shocked. Poor baby. Maybe they *were* a little pricey. She moved on.

Almost an hour later, they'd meandered through nearly every clothing store east of Wilshire Boulevard. As Marley shopped, Jake watched her carefully, noting which racks she gravitated to first, which stores she skipped, which items deserved the full fitting-room treatment and which items were off-the-rack purchases. He stood stoically nearby ("I draw the line at holding your purse"). He fortified her with refreshments and conversation. He even, on more than one occasion, offered an opinion on the things she considered buying.

Of course, those opinions were more along the lines of, "Yes, a shorter skirt would be great," and "How about that lingerie section over there?", but Marley valued them all the same. Jake's comments meant he was participating. His participation made her feel closer to him.

As they entered A/X Armani Exchange, he went straight to the same display of charcoal-gray sweaters that Marley made a beeline for. She beamed at him.

"You're amazing!" she cried. "A-plus. My mother still hasn't mastered that trick. Of course, when we shop together, Mom doesn't take notes."

Jake *hmmphed.* "I didn't take notes."

"You might as well have, you were concentrating so hard." She smiled affectionately as she smoothed her hand over the sweaters, then moved on to a rack of crisp white shirts. "I'd say you're a shoo-in to ace the final *Dream Date* quiz."

He disagreed. "There's still too much I don't know about you. Too much you don't know about me. We need a crash course. An all-night study session."

"Like in college?"

"Exactly."

"I didn't go to college," Marley confessed.

"See? That's one more thing I didn't know about you."

"But an all-night session sounds good." She trailed her fingers over his shoulder and down his chest, then tugged him closer beside a display of black wool pants. "You, me . . ."

"Together." His voice lowered huskily. *"Yeah."*

Jake thumbed her chin upward. He pressed a kiss to her

waiting mouth, one that left her unsteady and yearning. She wanted more of it. More of *him*. More, more, more.

Something about his touch felt different today . . . or maybe it was she who had changed. Marley wasn't sure. Suddenly she felt awhirl in mixed emotions. She didn't know if she wanted to hug Jake or drag him into the fitting room for a stand-up quickie. She couldn't decide if merely talking to him would satisfy her, or if she needed to feel his body next to hers—all over. She wanted to see him smile and hear him laugh, to know all there was to know about him and to keep him with her forever. This went so far beyond anything she'd experienced.

"But first," he said, "why didn't you go to college?"

Marley gulped, stirred from her reverie. His question hauled her unwillingly into the make-believe world of Carly Christopher—where she belonged, if she was going to win the game show. She had to remember that.

"I was busy with other things," she said, glancing around to locate the remote TV crew still following them. Their presence was a powerful reminder of what she needed to focus on. "Remember how I told you my mother always wanted me to become an actress? Well, I spent my college years in pursuit of that dream."

"Drama school?"

"Some studying, sure. I worked with an acting coach, did exercises, dabbled in Stanislavski's Method and other techniques. I auditioned a lot. I even did a little regional work."

On the set of Fantasy Family, *that is.* Geez, she was lower than low to deceive him like this. But most of what she'd revealed was true—about Marley, if not Carly.

"How about you?" she asked, wanting to change the subject. "College? Journalism school?"

Jake considered her question as they left the domain of Armani's secondary retail line behind. His fingers clasped with hers while they walked. She savored the sensation of his strength within her grasp.

"I went to college on a baseball scholarship," he said.

"Ah-hah. Your studly athlete's bod makes sense now."

He grinned, pleased. "Glad to know I haven't lost my edge."

No, but she'd lost her heart.

Arrgh. She had to quit thinking this way. It was almost a relief when Jake went on with the pre-quiz prep they'd agreed upon.

"Anyway, I was recruited out of high school with a .455 batting average. I thought I had it made. I was going to be the next Mark Grace, for sure."

"You were a first baseman, then?"

He blinked in surprise. Nodded. "Yeah. Cocky as hell to boot, but determined to make a name for myself."

They entered a bookstore. The low murmur of patrons selecting hot hardcovers, serious nonfiction, and best-selling paperbacks surrounded them. Automatically, Marley headed for her favorite haunt, the romance novel section.

"What happened?" she asked, picking up a book and pretending to read the back cover. "Weren't you any good?"

"Wasn't I any—hey!"

Jake frowned, saw she was teasing, then broke off to pull her nearer. He offered another kiss, this time a soul-deep melding of lips that made her forget their surroundings altogether. It made her drop her book, too.

"I was very good."

"Mmmm. I believe it." Dreamily, she smiled as she retrieved her fallen book. "You seem very talented to me."

"You don't know the half of it."

"But I want to."

"That could be arranged."

Smiling too, he slid his palm up her arm. She shivered beneath his touch, gazing up into his eyes to find the same kind of hunger there that she sensed in herself. How much longer, Marley wondered, would they be able to keep things casual between them?

How much longer, she wondered, would she be able to keep her mind on the job at hand, in the face of so much temptation?

Jake recovered first. "I played in college," he went on, clearing his throat. Another patron passed by, chose a paperback, then left. He leaned against the span of bookshelves beside Marley. "I resisted the majors as long as I could, got drafted as a senior when I couldn't hold out against the lure of the big-league ballpark any longer, played in a few games."

"You were a major-league player? So why isn't some sportscaster reporting about *you*, instead of the other way around? What happened?"

"Noah happened," he said simply. He tickled the books' spines with his fingers, stared at the colorful bindings, offered her a shrug. "I quit to be with him. Spending two-thirds of the year on the road is no way to raise a child."

"But your dream—"

"Didn't seem so important anymore."

Marley stared at him. He'd sacrificed everything he wanted for the sake of a son he'd never expected. She didn't know what to say.

"I needed a more regular income," Jake added. "Making a living off something as uncertain as the human body, athletes can't count on anything. A single injury could have ended my career. Even if I'd wanted to leave Noah with someone while I went on the road—my parents offered—"

Wow. Goodness permeated the whole family.

"—I couldn't take the chance. Luckily, I'd studied journalism in college as a fallback, with an emphasis on broadcasting. I'd done a couple of stints on college radio. It was pretty easy to segue from playing sports to reporting on them."

Marley squeezed his hand, awestruck by his generosity. By his easy acceptance of fate, and the way he'd manfully shouldered so much responsibility.

"You're remarkable," she said.

"Tell that to my first director on a big game." Jake rubbed his jaw, making a rueful face. " 'Keep talking, Jarvis,' he'd say over the earpiece, whenever I got engrossed in the game and shut up for too long. 'Tell 'em why that play worked.' "

She smiled too, imagining the scene in the booth.

" 'Okay,' I'd answer," Jake said. "And you know what he'd tell me? 'Your mic's on. You just said okay to six million people, bonehead.' "

Marley laughed. He grinned good-naturedly.

"It was a humbling experience, let me tell you."

She grabbed his arm and gave a reassuring squeeze. "Well, that's all behind you now. These days, you're a star."

"Right. Or at least a pinup."

"Either way, it's not so bad, is it?"

"Not since I found you."

Awww. Feeling even more lovestruck than before, Marley followed as Jake detoured into the children's section. He chose a copy of *Harold and the Purple Crayon* for Noah. They got in line to pay for it, along with the paperbacks Marley had picked up.

"But if I don't ace *Dream Date,*" Jake said, resuming their conversation easily, "then my news director won't pick up the option on my contract. He's obsessed with snaring the female demographic. He's convinced the game show is key."

He shot an irritated look at the TV crew tailing them from a distance. The audio operator waved back cheerfully.

"So you know what that means. More prep work for us."

"One of those all-nighter thingies?" Marley asked hopefully.

"Absolutely," Jake said, pocketing his change.

He slipped his arm around her waist as they left the bookstore, Jake carrying all the packages and Marley doing all the wondering. Something electric quivered in the air between them. She could feel it. She'd bet Jake could, too.

If she wasn't mistaken, there was a certain anticipatory gleam in his eye that had nothing to do with studying each other . . . and everything to do with getting close to each other. All at once, excelling on *Dream Date* didn't seem all that important—but finding out exactly what Jake had in mind most definitely did.

Nineteen

The next stop in Jake and Carly's getting-to-know-you pre-quiz prep work was Carly's apartment. She'd insisted on offering him a tour, claiming there was no better way to get to know someone than to explore their home environment.

"You make us sound like wildebeests," Jake told her. He held up a pretend microphone and gestured toward the living room, mimicking a Crocodile Hunter–style naturalist. "Here, in their natural habitat, the wily wildebeests test their mettle against predators of all kinds."

"They elude the fierce camera people," Carly said, getting into the spirit, "ripping off their body mics in the chase."

"They leave a trail of disappointed TV crew people in their wake. Now that they've achieved freedom, these beasts—also known as gnus—will never look back."

"Gnus?" She looked puzzled.

"They're a kind of African antelope. With a head like an ox, a long tail, and horns. A wildebeest and a gnu are the same thing."

Carly only stared at him.

Jake shrugged. "The things you learn when you have a kid. Next to Nick Jr., Animal Planet is Noah's favorite network."

"Noah! That reminds me." She snapped her fingers, then disappeared down the hallway. A moment later she re-emerged with a shopping bag in hand. "I got this for him a few days ago. I even wrapped it myself."

He peered into the bag as she set it on the kitchen table. Inside was a package, haphazardly wrapped in polka-dotted paper, studded with a bright blue bow, and secured with about ten pounds of cellophane tape.

"It looks . . . sturdy."

She beamed. "I haven't hand-wrapped anything myself for a long time. I wanted to make sure it held together."

"You didn't have to do this."

"I wanted to! I just hope he likes it." Carly gazed at the gift, fondness lighting her expression. "I was window shopping after work one day, trying to air out the French-fries-and-cheeseburgers smell from my waitress's uniform, when I saw it. I thought of Noah first thing."

Jake was touched that she'd remembered his son that way. Although the three of them hadn't quite spent a month together yet, it had been a very intense three-and-a-half weeks. A lightweight woman like the disastrous Natalie or the wannabe actresses he'd dated would never have survived them. With her easygoing ways and unpretentious demeanor, Carly had proved to him more each day that he'd been right to want an everyday, ordinary woman in his life.

Now, looking at Noah's gift with its discount-store wrapping and heartfelt exuberance, Jake knew he would never have come this far with someone less down-to-earth than Carly. Trailing around her apartment as she (and Gaffer) offered him a tour only strengthened his convictions. Here was a woman both kindhearted and honest. Her character was plain in everything she showed him.

There were no designer details in Carly's place. No gold-plated bathroom faucets. No "important artwork" on the walls. No glossy coffee-table books designed more for displaying than for reading.

Instead, there were ordinary fixtures in the cosmetics- and

hair-spray-strewn bathroom. There were poster-size prints of vintage Ivory soap and Holeproof hosiery ads on the walls—reproductions, Jake figured, that Carly had found beside the ready-to-hang artwork at Target. There were pillows on the plain brown sofa and chair, paperbacks on the chipped coffee table, and his own get-well-soon supplies on the standard-issue kitchen dinette set.

There were homey touches, too. Potpourri scented the rooms with spicy fragrance. Kicked-off shoes decorated the floors, and cast-off sweaters draped the chairs. Framed photographs cluttered the top of Carly's bedroom bureau. In the kitchen, a collection of clocks ticked off the time from their shelves, making Jake smile at their assorted shapes and sizes.

"You seem very interested in clocks," he said, giving her a kiss beneath them. "Worried about running out of time?"

She jerked in his arms. Blinked up at the collection. A shadow crossed over her face.

"Ummm . . ."

"Or are you one of those people who needs to be told the party starts a half-hour earlier than it really does in order to get there ten minutes late?"

"Ha! You caught me." Unsteadily, Carly stepped from his embrace. "I'm a habitual late arriver. I'm seriously time-challenged. Heck, if I were one of Santa's elves, Christmas would come in July every year."

"Okay, elf." He skimmed her shoulder, reluctant to let her go. "Just don't be late for the *Dream Date* taping."

Two days from now, they were both due to arrive separately at the studio for their follow-up interviews. Those interviews, combined with the initial compatibility quizzes and the opening interviews, would be the basis for the final Q&A session.

"I wouldn't dream of it," Carly assured him.

Biting her lip, she stepped briskly past him with the air of someone determined to finish her tour. She paused at the refrigerator and whisked open the top door to reveal the freezer compartment, stacked high with Lean Cuisine packages and two pints of ice cream.

"Hey! Did you know you don't have to buy ice?" Carly pulled out one of the ice trays in demonstration, clearly inspired by its ingeniousness. "These little gadgets let you make your own. At home!"

Was she serious? "Sure, I'm familiar with them."

"Very handy for mixing up cosmopolitans on the weekend." Enthusiastically she pantomimed, using a cocktail shaker. "And the stove!" She twirled to give the appliance a pat. "Sure, it looks intimidating. But once you've given it a few trial runs, this baby really cooks!"

"I use mine for boiling water. Noah likes instant cocoa." So did he, truth be told. With mini marshmallows.

"See? We're just a couple of culinary geniuses."

Still chattering, Carly led the way down the hall again. She paused long enough to slide open the louvered doors hiding the compact washer and dryer ("If you measure the detergent, these things do *not* belch soapsuds at you!"), then entered the bedroom.

"I forgot to show you. This is my finest accomplishment," she said, gesturing proudly.

"Creating a Rorschach test with cast-off clothes?"

"No, silly. The bed."

Jake looked past her skirt-and-lingerie-strewn carpet, ridiculously reassured by her messiness. A woman like Carly would be comfortable to live with, he thought. She wouldn't insist on having everything rigidly in its place, with knick-knacks littering every surface and color-coordinated toilet paper in the bathroom. She would make things cozy. She would be able to deal with the overflow of Noah's toys without freaking out, and she would—

Hang on just a damned minute. What was he doing thinking about living with Carly?

Severely, Jake eyeballed the simple wood-framed queen-size bed, with its multitude of throw pillows and its innocent pastel quilt. It looked pretty good to him—but only because he'd automatically imagined Carly curled up on top of it, giving him a come-hither look and a beckoning smile.

What would she do, he wondered, if he took her in his arms? If he backed them both a little closer to the froufrou dust ruffle? If he made them forget about everything except heat, touching, kissing, needing . . .

"I made it!" she cried excitedly, obviously too thrilled by this declaration to wait for him to guess. "I made the bed!"

He forced himself back from the fantasy zone. "Funny. You don't look like a furniture builder." Jake crooked her arm, giving her girly biceps a squeeze. "I'd never have guessed."

"No, I made it," she explained, lowering her arm and seeming inexplicably satisfied. "I tucked in the sheet corners, arranged the pillows, even smoothed the quilt perfectly over the top so the overhang was even. Doesn't it look great?"

Confused, he blinked at her. "Didn't you have to make beds all your life? Didn't your mom make you clean your room as part of your chores?"

"Chores?" She seemed mystified for a moment. Then inspired. "Oh, sure. Of course. But who cares about chores, anyway? The best part of making the bed has always been in the reward, you know."

"The reward?"

"Mmm-hmm. Messing up the bed afterward."

Before Jake could so much as figure out what the hell she meant, Carly lunged toward him. He felt their bodies collide, felt himself falling . . . felt the cottony cloud of her quilt and pillows embrace him as they landed together on the mattress.

"See? Isn't this fun?" she asked.

Then she kissed him.

Their mouths came together, the joining as natural as the laughter that always came to Jake when he was with her. They shared breath and heat, desire and eagerness, and even though Jake had never believed in anything as hokey as fate, somehow he knew then that he and Carly were meant to be together. Close together, like this.

He twined his fingers in her hair and held her to him. She moaned sweetly and deepened the kiss, her feminine aggression an unbelievable turn-on. Carly made his heart beat faster with every slide of her tongue against his, with every wriggle of her body as she straddled him.

Her knees pressed against his hips, pinning him sideways in place on the bed, but Jake was a willing prisoner. He wanted this. *Needed it.* There was no loving gesture from her he wouldn't welcome, no tender touch he didn't crave. Sappy as it sounded, he yearned for *all* of Carly, in a way he'd never yearned for any woman before.

As though sensing his urgency, she paused in their joining just long enough to make him crazy.

"I love the way you kiss me," she said, her voice low. Her mouth hovered only inches from his, tempting him. "So masterfully. So hungrily. So—"

"So much for the play-by-play," he interrupted, and shut her up with a demonstration. In this, talking was overrated. "I like the instant replay better. Don't you?"

"Ahhh. Mmm-hmmm. I do."

Carly nodded with exaggerated seriousness, then abandoned all pretense of conversation to nuzzle his neck. She was forceful, teasing, and wonderfully womanly, all at once. Helplessly, Jake arched beneath the nibbling bites she delivered, then decided enough was enough. It was time to show her exactly who would lead things from here on out.

He grasped her neck in his hand. It fit in his spread palm easily, lending him the control he needed. He angled her just enough to offer the access he wanted, then pressed his lips to her skin.

"You taste sweet," he said, flexing his wrist to hold her steady. He nipped gently, then blew on her neck, delighting in her responsive shiver. "So hot. So good."

"Then taste more. *Please.*"

Blindly, Carly sought his mouth again. Their tongues met; the bed creaked beneath their undulating weight. She rubbed her palms over his chest, her movements creating a pleasurable friction between his shirt and skin. She rocked her hips against him, the motion seeming as uncontrollable as his answering upward thrusts.

They broke apart and kissed again, breathily whispered and groaned aloud. They gently placed their foreheads together, their gazes melding into one. Being with Carly felt new to Jake, new and amazing . . . and he wanted it to go on forever.

He groaned and closed his eyes, then immediately opened them. He didn't want to miss a thing. As a reward, Carly levered upward atop him, her soft smile nearly as erotic as her touch. She trailed her fingertips over his shirt. Like magic, the buttons parted beneath her hands, leaving him exposed to her. He gaped hazily, impressed by her dexterity—but even more eager to discover what she planned to do next.

If this was what ironing a shirt could encourage, Jake figured he could manage at least, oh, six or seven ironing sessions a day. Why not?

"Mmmm. Perfect," she murmured, gazing down at him. "You look absolutely amazing."

Her provocative smile gave proof to her words. So did her actions. For long moments she explored him, running her hands over his bared chest and delving beneath his shirt to caress his shoulders. Pleasure rolled through him. Then her palms skimmed eagerly downward, moving past his chest to his abdomen, and Jake's muscles clenched on a stifled gasp.

Thank God for those crunches, he thought crazily. But in the next instant, he forgot to think altogether. Carly seized the waistband of his jeans, thumbed the metal stud past its buttonhole . . . and then meandered lower.

Yes, *yes.* Fresh air cooled that small triangle of newly-exposed skin near his pelvis, and his whole body tautened with expectation. Leisurely, Carly neared that part of him which needed her touch the most. He jerked beneath her gliding fingers, felt his stiffened cock leap to meet her touch.

His damned jeans didn't allow the contact he needed. All

Carly could manage was to trace him teasingly, to palm him indirectly, to make him harder than ever before. Dimly, he knew he should shuck his jeans and take things further between them, but for now, lust held him captive. He didn't want to move and risk losing the pleasure she was giving him.

Just so long as Carly continued stroking him, Jake could be content with that. Just so long as she continued to love him. However slowly. However torturously.

More, he begged silently—or maybe, inadvertently, aloud. Because in the next instant, she offered a wicked smile and whisked her hand to his chest again.

Jake groaned. "Awww, Carly. You're killing me."

"Sure. But what a way to go, right?" She paused, giving him a mock-pensive look. "Or maybe you'd rather I stopped?"

"No!"

"I didn't think so. Now be quiet, and let me finish taking advantage of you."

"Is that what this is?"

"Either that, or love," she said lightly. With her fingertip, she traced a heart on his chest, then kissed its center. "What do you think?"

I think it's love, Jake confessed.

Silently.

He couldn't say as much aloud. Not yet. Not while Carly would believe he was only gibbering with passion. So he settled for offering her a devilish grin as he remarked, "I think there's too much talking going on here. I'm going to have to take over this seduction myself. Show you how it's done."

"Oh, you think so, do you?" She arched a brow. "Ha! Guess again, mister."

" 'Mister' ?"

"Yeah."

Carly kissed him, proving herself the ultimate victor. There was no way he could resist her. Apparently, she knew it.

While that should have scared the hell out of him, Jake

was enjoying himself way too much to be concerned right now. In this moment, whatever the future held didn't matter. He didn't care about tomorrow, or about keeping a part of himself distant from her. Somehow, that no longer seemed important. He wanted to give her everything.

However, he was still a man. With a man's pride and a man's need to take control—most of the time. Jake put on a thoughtful frown and gazed at the path his fingers made on her plaid-covered thighs as he caressed her.

Why was it they were both still partly dressed, again?

He pretended to consider her last kiss.

"Yup. I'm definitely taking over," he threatened.

"Hmmph," she bluffed. "I'd like to see you try."

Carly's playful smile was Jake's undoing. Warm and affectionate and filled with challenge, it reminded him of all the reasons he'd stuck by this woman . . . no matter how unlikely their pairing had seemed at first. For her, he could withstand agonizingly slow lovemaking. For her, he could withstand teasing and needing and a pleasure that made him shake without reason or control.

For her, he could withstand anything.

Except maybe what came next.

He boggled as Carly reached for her rumpled shirt, then lifted it over her head. She tossed it away. Her soft dark hair swung in the sunlight, hiding her expression. She deftly unfastened her bra and flung it over her shoulder to join with her cast-off stripes. Then, bared to him from the waist up, Carly gazed directly into his eyes.

The intimacy in her gesture, the trust inherent in it, humbled him. Jake looked at her in awe, hardly able to believe that she'd revealed herself to him. A fleeting vulnerability flashed over her face—a vulnerability he found almost as endearing as the woman who claimed it—then melted away.

He couldn't imagine what Carly had to feel unsure about, though. Her shoulders, her arms, her torso—okay, her breasts—were perfect. Just as incredible as he'd imagined and exactly as cute as the rest of her.

Which was pretty damned cute.

Okay, Uncle. I give up, he thought wildly. If Jake had held a white flag of surrender, he knew he would have waved it.

"Awww, Carly. You're beautiful," he said, reaching for her.

Rapidly, she caught his outstretched hands and clamped her fingers over his wrists. Then, before he guessed what she intended, Carly pushed his arms over his head and held them there, pinioned in her grasp. Her sense of triumph was plain.

Illusory, but plain.

"Who's doing the seducing *now?*" she asked saucily.

He planned to protest. To argue his case and his innate seductive superiority . . . but he couldn't find the words. Because next Carly began to move, sensuously dragging her naked breasts across his chest. Every rational thought Jake might have entertained was buried beneath intense pleasure. As her movements continued, becoming slow figure eights and invisible patterns of desire, Jake groaned aloud. He surged upward, desperate to feel her soft curves and taut nipples more fully against his skin.

Carly kept him in place with whispered words and a stronger grasp on his wrists, her negligible strength less a deterrent to him than her obvious wish to guide things between them. If the woman he cared for wanted to drive him crazy with this diabolical teasing, then Jake figured he could handle it.

Hell, yes. He could handle it, and then some.

She rotated above him, letting her breasts trace a lethal, heated slide from his collarbone to his abdomen. She kissed him, briefly offering her incredible softness in a closer embrace. She licked his earlobe to alert him, then whispered, "Doesn't this feel great? I can't wait to feel your hands on me. You know that, don't you? I can't wait to feel you—"

The sizzling suggestions Carly offered next made Jake wild with need. He listened to her husky words, imagined himself fulfilling the desires she voiced . . . and finally lost control altogether. Carly might not have known the kind of passion she'd rouse with naughty talk like that—but she was damned sure about to find out.

With a mighty roar, Jake broke free from her puny grasp. He surged upward, catching a surprised Carly easily in his arms, then twirled her around until he straddled her.

"That's it," he rumbled fiercely. "It's my turn."

Twenty

This was what she got, Marley figured, for coming up with diversionary tactics on the fly. She'd never been very good at thinking on her feet.

She was even worse, it turned out, at thinking in her bed. There, her body took over and her mind checked out altogether.

This encounter with Jake had only begun because she'd been desperate to deflect his attention from her obvious unfamiliarity with childhood chores. And now look what had happened.

She'd gotten herself into an even more dangerous situation.

Jake loomed over her, all hard male and seductive eyes. She lay beneath him, all foolhardy nakedness and desperate expectation. Between the two of them, they were living, speaking, raggedly breathing examples of impulsive-and-probably-unwise behavior, but as the mattress gave beneath her weight and the quilt soothed her bare skin and Jake's body straddled hers, Marley didn't much care.

She wanted this. However crazy it was.

Since Jake had first met her gaze over a quartet of variously prepared coffees, she'd wanted this. Since Jake had first smiled at her, touched her, made her laugh . . . she'd wanted this. Since Jake had first opened his heart to her—showing her his son, his dreams, his family—she'd wanted this.

Resisting him had taken every bit of strength Marley had had. Trying *not* to fall for him had been tougher than auditioning, tougher than facing Bobby, tougher than sitting by her phone the morning the Emmy calls went out. Every day, she'd needed him. The more she knew him, the worse her need became.

Now, Jake examined her. He steadied himself with one splayed hand atop the mattress and just . . . looked at her. A faint smile curved his lips, a tender expression passed over the hard angles of his face, and he shook his head.

"You asked for this, you know," he told her.

The deep rumble of his voice, so masculine and so sure, sent a tremble through her. Marley loved to hear him speak, loved to discover the wry opinions and occasionally off-color jokes he offered. Most of all, she found, she loved to hear him promise to make love to her . . . and make no mistake, that was exactly what he'd just done.

"I don't know what you mean," she bluffed.

"Ahh. Innocent, huh?" His gaze swept her again, dark and meaningful. His anticipatory smile deepened. "We'll see about that."

She loved that he could tease about this, even while giving her a look hot enough to make her nipples pucker and her skin tingle. Not many men had the knack for making a woman feel at ease, both with herself and with him. Jake, as it turned out, possessed that talent in spades. She was glad.

"Promises, promises," Marley goaded, because she knew he wanted her to. "That sounds like lots of talk, with no act—"

His kiss cut off her words and stole her breath. Hot, demanding, and expert, it made her quiver beneath him. Jake

kissed exactly the way he lived—full out, no holds barred—
and the result was a union that both thrilled and excited
Marley beyond belief. In his arms, she felt deeply desired.
Wantonly sensual. Giddily carefree. Those were things she'd
dreamed of experiencing, but had never truly hoped to find.

Today, this moment, she had. Jake kissed her and held her
close, and she surrendered to the pleasure of it all. From
here on, she wouldn't think of tomorrow. Wouldn't question
the joining she'd craved. Wouldn't worry about the wisdom
of giving herself to Jake. She would only savor whatever togetherness they found, and hold it in her heart to keep for
later.

In case tomorrow never came.

Closing her eyes, Marley reveled in the brush of Jake's
mouth against hers, in the gentle nip of his teeth against her
lower lip and the gliding sweep of his tongue in her mouth.
She panted beneath his touch and delved her fingers into the
sleek fullness of his hair, holding him to her. She begged
without words for him to continue. Jake complied.

"Open your eyes," he commanded.

She did. In return, Jake delivered her a devilish smile and
grasped his shirt. He dropped it from his wide shoulders in a
single sweep.

"Oh my God," she said.

Marley had touched him. She'd glimpsed his naked torso
as she'd unbuttoned his shirt. She'd even imagined, countless
times, what he'd look like undressed. But nothing, *nothing*
had prepared her for the reality of Jake, naked from the waist
up.

His jeans hung low, revealing sculpted abdominal muscles and two intriguing indentations near his hips that were
uniquely male. His sides were lean, his chest strong and
broad, his shoulders ample enough to cradle her or to flip her
upside down and carry her away.

His arms broadened at well-defined biceps, looking
sturdy, useful, and surprisingly graceful. His forearms were

rugged, his wrists well-made, his hands competent and endowed with long, blunt-tipped fingers. She yearned to feel those hands on her body, to sample the rhythms of those fingers and lose herself in those arms. She hungered to rub herself against him again, skin on skin, to make Jake feel as wild as she did.

She decided to indulge, reaching for him.

"Not so fast." He captured her seeking hands in his. "It's my turn, remember?"

"But I—but you," she protested. "But you look so—"

"You've had your fun. Next *I'll* be tormenting *you.*"

His meaningful look promised he meant it. Marley quivered and felt herself grow even hotter. Why hadn't she touched him more when she'd had the chance? Why hadn't she spent at least an hour or two running her palms over that brawny chest, those well-defined abs, those overly generous shoulders?

Her ruminations ended on a startled gasp as Jake trailed his fingertips over her collarbones and lower. His hands were warm and gentle and strong, and they possessed a surety that made her sizzle. He kissed her, all the while tracing circles around her breasts, sensitizing her skin. He thumbed her areolas, making her pant with the need for more contact, more heat, more of *him.* He covered her breasts completely in his big hands, leaving her fully aware of his dominance.

In this, he could have whatever he wanted, Marley knew. Just so long as he went on touching her. Just so long as he gazed at her so intently while he did, giving her the delicious feeling they were the only two people in a world gone hot and heady and brilliant.

"You feel wonderful," he murmured. "I've dreamed of touching you like this."

"I think we must both be dreaming," she managed. He'd cupped her breasts and had begun teasing her erect nipples, making rational thought next to impossible. She gasped again. "Nothing real could ever feel this good."

"It could . . . between us. Ahhh, you're beautiful."

She *felt* beautiful. Also sexy and free, feminine and beloved. But his words were welcome, all the same. They fixed the loving feelings Marley had so staunchly tried to refuse even more firmly in her heart. Now there was no denying them.

This man was the one for her. Jake, forever. His touch confirmed it, and her response assured it. If she could have, Marley would have hugged him to her, just for the pleasure of embracing the man she cared so deeply for. But in the next instant, Jake kissed his way from her neck to her meager cleavage, and she lost the will to move at all.

Only arching upward seemed possible—and that, because it offered the reward of a deeper suction between his mouth and her breast. Only moaning seemed meaningful, because it encouraged Jake to lavish his attention on both her breasts with seductive thoroughness. Only clenching his head seemed sensible, because it kept him with her. But then Marley became aware of a deeper, more insistent need. Her awareness grew divided between the lovely licking, sucking, kissing attention being paid her top half . . . and the throbbing, needful *urgency* growing ever more steadily within the rest of her.

Jake wedged his knee between her thighs. Unable to help herself, she ground her pelvis upward, delighting in the solid contact of flesh against flesh. Desire lurched in her belly. Hearing only his whispered, loving words, feeling only his hard strength above her, Marley abandoned herself to the mindless pursuit of pleasure.

She clutched at Jake's smooth, powerful back, seeking steadiness in a world gone topsy-turvy. She moaned and flung herself against him, crying out when he leisurely slid his hand to her hip . . . then to that part of her which throbbed for his touch. After long minutes of teasing, he finally slid away her horrible plaid pants. He rapidly discarded her panties, Marley lifting her hips eagerly to help him. He gazed at her nudity with wonder and something close to awe . . . and then, at the juncture of her thighs, his fingers worked their magic.

Intense pleasure surged through her, wrought by Jake's eagerness and the expertise of his touch. His fingertips glided against her slippery heat, drawing forth new quivers and a stream of nearly incoherent encouragement. Shuddering, Marley clutched his shoulder, unable to resist praising him. Occasionally, she guided him. More often, she simply burned.

When she did speak, Jake listened intently to every word. He listened, heard, kissed away her doubts and offered more, more, *more* of all the things she loved best.

"Oh, Jake. That feels so good. Please, please don't stop."

"Never. Everything I have is yours."

"And I'm yours. Mmmm. More than ever."

His gratified look stole her heart. This was a man who knew how to lead . . . but who would never forge ahead without bringing her along. A man who would respect her and care for her. For that, Marley felt overwhelmingly grateful.

Inherently, he understood the lovemaking time she needed. He accepted—even reveled in—the journey they took together. With patience and pleasure, Jake learned her body one gasp at a time . . . one moment after the next. Quaking in his arms, Marley found herself unable to hide, unwilling to pretend, utterly vulnerable and completely giving. Without knowing why, she let herself be herself, with no pretensions and no secrets.

In this, she was Marley. She was Carly. She was both parts of her, combined. In her soul, she believed Jake knew it.

How else could he have loved her so well? So tenderly?

Her need built, made even greater by the love in Jake's eyes, by the enchantment of his hands and the intoxicating thrill of his erection against her thigh. The control he displayed awed her; the unbelievably rigid size of him aroused her curiosity almost beyond enduring. That he desired her was obvious. Marley couldn't resist the urge to palm him as she had before. Even as Jake drove her wild with his hands, even as her climax drew nearer, she blindly groped for him.

"Make love to me, Jake," she begged. There was something wonderfully erotic in the sensation of her naked body snugged up against his denim-clad one, as though they simply hadn't been able to wait for full nudity before coming together. But Marley needed more. "I need to feel you inside me. Now. Before it's too late."

He protested, saying something about first wanting to make her feel incredible. Knowing things could only get better from here, Marley rebutted in the most effective way she knew. She found his hardness and stroked him. Persuasively.

He groaned. "Since you put it that way . . ."

"I do. Help me. *Love me.*"

"Always," Jake said simply.

Their panted breaths mingled as she struggled with his jeans. The damned things didn't fit right—hadn't been designed to contain the enthusiasm she'd called forth in him—and with a savage sound Jake finally took over. He wrenched open his fly. Eagerly, Marley helped him work the denim lower, easing it downward along with his briefs until he lay fully naked beside her.

She longed to drink in the sight of him. To capture that most masculine part of him in her hands and watch him grow still huger. Even to taste him there, in as intimate a kiss as any designed. But before Marley could so much as drag her fascinated gaze from the sight of his impressive length and girth, Jake prowled his way up her body and ended atop her, drugging her with a long, thorough kiss.

She luxuriated in the heated combination of their bodies, in the solid feel of Jake's weight comfortably against her. This felt right, and so good. All she wanted was to love him, and to be loved in return.

Marley received her wish—and more. With certainty and care, Jake went on touching her. He kissed her, moaning in his throat when she bucked helplessly against him. Desperately, Marley opened herself to him; urgently, he responded . . .

and when finally, *finally* he united them with a slow, seductive thrust, she knew that from here, everything would change.

She clutched at him when he reared back to thrust again, begged when he did so in a maddeningly leisurely fashion. Over and over Jake loved her, and all the while Marley drew ever closer to losing control completely. Her body clenched around him. Her legs shook. Her cries reached a new, more passionate crescendo . . . and Jake never stopped. He cradled her face in his hand, gazed at her sweetly, let her see in his expression all the wonderment and pleasure he felt at their joining.

It was all too much. The corded feel of Jake's straining arms as he balanced above her. The solid glide of him as he entered and retreated. The harsh sound of their breath in the stillness, and the warmth that seemed to surround them. This was the most sensual, the most *connected* lovemaking she'd ever experienced. Marley knew that even if she and Jake were never together again, she would treasure this time forever.

Subtly, Jake shifted. They rocked together, he murmuring words of encouragement, she discovering a new spark engendered by his movement. Tension spiraled inside her. Crying out, Marley held him to her, held him, held him . . . and soon her body shook with a climax so powerful she could only hold on to the strength Jake offered and ride it out.

Gradually, her tremors subsided—only to become different, deeper, more potent as Jake went on loving her. Their bodies fit in the most spectacular of ways. Almost as though her orgasm had freed him somehow, Jake took their union to even more frenzied heights. He thrust harder, faster, gazing into her eyes all the while. Intimacy engulfed them. Then suddenly his body grew utterly taut with tension. His hands convulsed against the quilt beside her head . . . He yelled aloud as his climax shook him.

Marley arched upward, joyfully sharing in his final

thrusts. She stroked his hair, brought his head to rest on her shoulder, felt their hearts pounding together as their bodies relaxed. She was sweaty and disheveled, panting and pulsing—but as she sprawled in graceless satisfaction beneath the man she loved, she didn't care a bit. This was what real love felt like. She knew it, and felt tearfully close to gratitude as she held close the man who'd opened her to it.

"Awww, you're incredible," he said, brushing back her hair with a strong, careful hand. He pressed a tender kiss to her lips, smiled at her fondly, gave her an exceptionally hot hip swivel to punctuate his words. "You, me, together . . ."

"I know!" She flung out her arms, grinning helplessly. "There just aren't words magnificent enough for it."

"Fantastic, mind-blowing, remarkable . . . none of them satisfy."

"You satisfy."

Jake's thoroughly masculine grin warmed her heart. He quirked an eyebrow. "You think so, do you? Because if you want to go again, I'm all for it. Whatever makes you happy."

"This makes me happy. Being with you."

"What a coincidence. I feel the same way."

He rolled her over in his arms. They stretched and snuggled, eventually cuddling up together as though they'd been doing it for years. Marley naturally found the perfect spot near Jake's shoulder to rest her head. Jake curled his arm around her to keep her close. They both sighed and shared a hug.

Afternoon sunlight shafted through the bedroom blinds. Traffic sounds rose from the street below. Cool air teased their overheated skin. Reality intruded—and with it, the memory of what they were supposed to be doing today.

Getting ready for *Dream Date.*

Marley angled her head. She loved Jake's profile, so rugged and appealing. She could have savored the sight of him all afternoon, could have lost herself in the sheer enjoyment of his sculpted features and his perfect ease. But neither of them had all day, and she knew it. Reluctantly, she forced herself a little closer to the duty at hand.

First, she waited for him to put his horn-rims back on. At some point, he'd removed them without her even noticing—a testament to his seductive powers, Marley guessed. He blinked, looking sexily cerebral, then settled back down again. Time for her to embrace practical matters.

"I don't suppose this will be on the quiz?" she asked.

Jake rested his chin on the crown of her head, the gesture comfortable and intimate. "Probably not."

"We'd ace it, if it were."

"Nah. I wouldn't share this with anybody. Not even to win my contract renewal."

Marley stilled. "You wouldn't? You'd sacrifice your job? For my sake?" The implications of it were too great. She couldn't possibly let Jake surrender any more of his dreams—especially for her. "Don't be silly! So what if the world finds out about that goofy face I make when I—"

"And the goofy face I make when *I*—"

They glanced at each other. Laughed.

"Okay, so let's make a pact," Marley suggested. "We keep our orgasmic oddities to ourselves. No matter what."

He guffawed. *You're too much,* said the amused look he gave her.

Marley could only shrug. She'd always been a person who said what was on her mind. That quality had occasionally made her stint as Carly more difficult, and it had gotten her into trouble more than once, too. But given the proper stakes, she figured she could control herself.

"You're on," Jake said, his smile still teasing her. "No orgasmic oddities. No matter what. We have a deal."

We have love, Marley thought, *real love,* and knew it was true. She only hoped that when Jake discovered the truth about her . . . real love would be enough.

*   *   *

By the time Jake made it to his sister Rebecca's place to pick up Noah, he felt on top of the world. He strode with a new spring in his step, laughed with a new easiness, swaggered with a new cockiness. It was all because of Carly.

Carly, the woman he loved.

He'd suspected it before, but making love with her had made him certain. Seeing the affection in her eyes, feeling her body's welcoming embrace as he entered her, letting himself turn completely, crazily vulnerable in her arms . . . all of it had cemented Jake's feelings. He was in love, love, love. All that remained was sharing his revelation with Carly.

He considered it as they lay together atop her unassuming quilt, pondered it as they showered together in her cramped, steamy bathroom. He forgot it, briefly, as he soaped her lithe body, then remembered again as they dressed in the waning afternoon light. A hundred times he deliberated what to say and how to say it—and in the end, remained silent only because the time didn't yet feel right.

Now, walking into his apartment with Noah skipping ahead and Carly trailing behind carrying her purse and her super-Scotch-taped gift, Jake reconsidered. The only possible moment for a loving confession like his was a private one—preferably in bed after a strenuous and fulfilling lovemaking session. Until he could arrange another one of those with Carly, he decided, he would wait.

She came up behind him, Gaffer scampering at her heels. She unleashed the dog, then set down her gift on a table. Just when he expected her to pass by him and enter the living room, instead she cupped Jake's ass and squeezed. He yelped.

"You have a very fine backside," she murmured into his ear.

He watched as she sashayed around him, her demeanor one hundred percent feisty, va-va-voom woman.

"*You* have a very sassy way about you," he replied, secretly pleased at her pronouncement. There was definitely nothing held back with Carly. She was occasionally earthy and always up-front, and that was exactly the way Jake loved her.

That was exactly the way, he was beginning to believe, he wanted to spend the rest of his life with her.

To show it, he drew her close. She lifted her face to his and gave a sexy murmur of pleasure.

Noah had turned in curiosity at the sound of surprise Jake made. His little brows drew downward. Suspiciously, he examined his father and Carly.

They laughed, happily clinging together. There was a new relaxed attitude between them now, an ease born of finally being real with each other. Jake savored it, even as he reached out to give his son's hair a reassuring ruffle.

"It's all right, Noah. Carly and I are just sharing a joke, that's all."

"Oh."

"We'd tell you . . . but it's a grown-up joke."

"Okay." Noah shrugged and called Gaffer. The Yorkie bounded over to him, tongue lolling. The two of them headed for the pile of toys in the corner. Noah switched on the TV with a practiced flick of the remote. Serenaded by the babble of Nick Jr., boy and dog began to play.

Carly gave Jake a look. She *hmmphed.*

"Your cute buns are no joke," she whispered for Jake's ears alone. Surreptitiously, she copped another feel.

"Okay, you're asking for it again," Jake said, then masterfully turned the tables in the only possible way he could. Soon, Carly was running through his apartment, shrieking with glee as Jake chased her. He caught her, flipped her onto the sofa, and tickled her.

"Now who's yelping?" he asked with pretend ferocity.

"Stop, stop!" She gasped the words. "Behave yourself!"

"Behave yourself, Daddy!" Noah mimicked, giggling. "Behave yourself!"

"Hey." Jake shot him a mock-menacing look. "You stay out of this. Do you want to be tickled, too?"

Noah looked uncertain. He bit his lip.

"I didn't think so."

Jake went back to tickling a squirming, laughing Carly. An instant later, thirty-five pounds of little boy landed atop him. Two tiny hands ineffectually dug under Jake's arms, trying to tickle him. Noah's weight unbalanced the whole endeavor. The three of them rolled helplessly from the sofa and collapsed in a heap on the floor, chortling.

Gaffer barked merrily, tail wagging.

Ten minutes later, they couldn't breathe for the laughter. Noah's hair was mussed and his eyes were bright. Jake's heart felt lighter than ever before. And Carly . . . well, Carly was clearly overwhelmed by the amount of macho Jarvis love headed her way. She flopped on the carpet looking dazed, all her energy spent.

Noah crawled over to her. "We really ganged up on Daddy that time!" he crowed, breathing hard.

"That's right." Carly raised her hand for a high five.

Beaming, Noah slapped her palm. Then, after a flash of indecision, he suddenly hurled himself on top of her.

"You're a good tickler," he said, his voice muffled.

He was hugging her, Jake realized. His son was actually hugging Carly, with all the might his two little arms could muster. He squeezed and squeezed, and just when Jake thought Carly might lose the last of her breath . . . she tentatively brought up her arms and hugged the boy back.

Jake could hardly believe it. Noah was an affectionate kid, but ordinarily he reserved his hugs for family. For Noah to share them with Carly, too . . .

She must have become truly special to him.

How had he not seen this coming? Jake wondered. The time Noah and Carly had spent together, the G.I. Joe escapade, their bonding over silly woolly mammoth tales—all of it had led to this. This hug.

Frowning slightly, Jake watched them. As he did, a strange feeling trickled its way inside him. Part surprise, part gladness, part melancholy at seeing some of Noah's affection displaced, it went beyond bittersweet. It put him off guard. It made him uncomfortable.

It made him *think*.

He thought of the future he'd begun to envision with Carly. Thought of his worries that finding a woman to love would divert his attention from Noah. Thought about everything he'd just shared with Carly, and how much he wanted it to continue.

He thought of how happy his son looked, hugging her close.

They could do this, Jake realized. They could all be together, just like this. They could hug and laugh and have tickle fights. They could play terrible touch football, share pizza and wings, refine the funny-body-parts game ("Belly button!" had been Carly's latest entry). For Carly's sake, he and Noah could even learn to love self-improvement theories, award shows, and beef jerky. They'd even have the requisite dog, with Gaffer in the picture. Why not?

Hell, yes, Jake decided in a flash. They'd do it.

Before long, Noah and Carly parted. Noah scrambled to his feet and returned to the TV, his expression happy-go-lucky. Gaffer followed him, settling down to be petted. Carly sat fully upright, looking vaguely bewildered.

She glanced at Jake. A silly smile slipped onto her face. "Where do you suppose that came from?"

"The same place all my mushy feelings for you come from," Jake joked, deadpan. "The men's accessories department at the mall."

Carly waved her hand. "The mall doesn't have a 'men's accessories' department. Macy's does. Nordstrom does. But the mall itself doesn't actually—"

"Are you seriously going to argue with me about this?" He helped her to her feet, letting his hands linger and then twine with hers. "Face it. You're practically part of the family now. There's no turning back from here."

She swallowed, her eyes huge. Probably she was still overwhelmed, Jake told himself. It wasn't every day a woman got to sample sizzling Jake love, insane tickling, and a four-year-old boy's squeeze play, one after another.

She'd better get used to it, Jake decided. Because tonight he meant to take her all the way. Tonight was the night he would finally tell Carly how he felt.

The time had come.

Twenty-One

Tonight was the night she would finally tell Jake the whole story, Marley decided as they settled in after an impromptu dinner of take-out green chile burritos and one kid's taquito. The time had come.

Ultimately, Jake deserved the truth. He was too good a man to be denied it any longer, and Marley owed it to him, besides. She had to reveal her Carly-style alter-ego deception, had to explain the reasons behind it and the necessity for it. She had to make Jake understand. But more importantly, she had to tell him the biggest secret of all.

She'd fallen in love with him.

It was something she'd suspected for a long time now, something she'd tried to fight in her quest to keep her mind on her performance as Carly. After the romantic afternoon they'd spent together, though, Marley knew she couldn't keep her feelings to herself any longer. She loved Jake with all her heart . . . and she believed he might be able to love her, too.

For the first time, Marley believed she'd found a man who liked her for herself, and not for her celebrity status. A man who cared for her because he thought she was really terrific, not because he wanted an introduction to her agent or publicist. A man who laughed with her and talked with her and spent time with her because he wanted to, not because he hoped to score some Tinseltown publicity.

It was almost too good to be true. Finally, she'd found a man who really seemed to see and understand and accept the inner her—not the glossy artifice that made up Marley Madison, TV starlet. "Carly" may have begun as a desperate measure, but she'd led to finding the most important person ever.

Jake.

And Noah, too. Because while the boy still made her feel a little uncertain—and very clueless about kids—he also made her feel happy. Curious. Ridiculously sappy. Hugging him tonight had actually brought joyful tears to her eyes, tears Marley hadn't been able to prevent any more than she'd been able to resist hugging Noah back. Thanks to him and Jake, she'd broadened her horizons—and that had nothing to do with pretending.

Maybe, Marley thought hopefully, she did have more to offer than her celebrity credentials. Maybe she had a lot of love to give, too, and some special people to give it to. Sure, Jake and Noah were occasionally uncouth; they were rough and ready and way too fond of barbecued chicken wings. But they were splendid, besides. They were loving and funny and *fun*. In their presence, the whole world felt open to Marley, and everything in it seemed twice as beautiful.

All because she was in love.

The only way to hold on to those feelings was to come clean. To trust in Jake enough to confide the truth about herself and her alter ego—and pray he understood. If he discovered her charade on the set of *Dream Date* along with the rest of the world, he might never forgive her.

Knowing that, however, wasn't quite enough to nudge Marley over the line into Confessionville. Not yet. Instead, she stayed right there in Denial, lingering as long as she could.

"So," she said as she and Jake sat around the kitchen table, burrito wrappers wadded up beside their super-size drink cups, "how about another round of 'favorite things'?"

"Do you really think they'll ask this kind of stuff on *Dream Date?*"

"Sure. I've seen a few episodes where they did."

"Okay." Making a face of concentration, Jake stared up at the ceiling. Then he snapped his fingers. "I've got one! Ketchup. On your fries, or next to them?"

"Next to them. Why make them soggy?"

Jake agreed. Marley sighed. They were so compatible.

Her turn. "Ummm . . . showering. Facing the shower-head, or with your back to it?"

He gave her a naughty look. "Don't you remember?"

"Oh, yeah." She grinned, then wrote her notes on the notepad she'd propped up against the table's edge.

Jake scribbled, too. Then he glanced up. "Favorite day of the year?"

"My birthday. I think it should be a national holiday."

He raised his eyebrows. "The whole country should celebrate your birthday?"

"Why not? Then everyone could come to a great big party!"

He laughed.

"How about you?"

"You can't guess?"

Marley thought about it. "Noah's birthday? Christmas?"

Jake shook his head. "Super Bowl Sunday. If my team wins, it's Christmas and a few birthdays, all rolled into one."

Rolling her eyes, Marley wrote it down. "I should have guessed. Hmmm . . . how about this? What toy could you not live without as a kid?"

"A baseball glove," Jake said decisively.

"That's not a toy."

"You play with it, don't you?"

"I don't." She made a mock-horrified face. "I run far, far

away from it, and everything like it. Once Meredith was on a neighborhood softball team, and during one of her practices a softball came flying straight toward me in the stands. It was terrifying!"

He patted her hand. "Awww, poor baby. What did you do? Shriek and duck? Enlist your horde of junior admirers to save you? Or did you stun the whole crowd by making a flawless catch?"

"I wish," Marley told him. "I ducked. Unfortunately, I was sitting at the end of the bleachers. The sudden movement unbalanced me. I fell into the grass."

"That's not so bad. Could have happened to anyone."

"I sprained my ankle and chipped a tooth." She winced. "It's like a metaphor for my life. I try to get sporty, I get hurt. I'm telling you, me and sports fields do not get along."

"You seemed to manage okay at the ball game we went to." Jake waggled his eyebrows rakishly, reminding her of the time they'd spent between innings, playing footsie. "I think you're cured."

"It's possible." Marley hoped so. That would make spending time with super-sports-guy Jake much easier.

"I'll bet *your* favorite toy was a Barbie doll," Jake guessed.

She shook her head. "Barbie was a role-playing tool, not a toy. I learned all I know about coordinating a wardrobe from her."

"An Easy-Bake Oven?"

"Could that *be* any more of a gender stereotype?"

"Sorry."

Marley felt bad. "Actually, I did bake my share of tiny cakes and brownies. But my Easy-Bake Oven was not my favorite toy. My favorite was Mr. Wrinkle, a stuffed bear."

She gazed into the distance, fondly remembering the plush stuffed animal's soft fur and understanding glass eyes. She'd been sure Mr. Wrinkle turned real at night and had adventures while she slept.

"He had brown fur and smooth tan feet," she recalled, "and a little pink bow around his neck."

"Poor Mr. Wrinkle." Jake grinned. "Permanently in pink. Did he get his name from the frown lines around his forehead?"

"Har, har." Marley made a face at him, her mushy memories receding. Time to move onward. She consulted the sketchy notes she'd made earlier in the week. "All right, next. What kind of car did you learn to drive in?"

"An eighty-two Bonneville sedan," Jake replied. "Straight from the junkyard. My dad and I rebuilt it, then he taught me to drive it. It was the perfect car for a teenage boy—cheap to repair, loud as hell, and too beat-up to go too fast."

"No speeding tickets?"

"Our police records are not date material," he said evasively.

"You did have tickets!" Marley cried, fascinated. She'd been dating a reckless bad boy type without even knowing it. The closest she'd come to adolescent rebellion had been eating one too many croissants from the craft services table at a photo shoot. "How many? Dozens? Hundreds?"

"If I'd known it was going to help me pick up chicks," Jake said, eyeballing her mischievously, "I would've gotten a few more."

"Come on. Tell me."

Jake shrugged. "About ten. The rest were just warnings."

"You talked your way out of them, huh? Wow. Jake Jarvis, charm-wielder extraordinaire. Does Noah have any idea of his heritage?"

"No, and he's damned well not going to. Not if I can help it. Too much charisma is a dangerous thing. See?"

In demonstration, he leaned forward across the table. He waited until she met his gaze, drew in a breath, and kissed her.

In an instant, Marley forgot their pre-quiz prep work, forgot why it was important and when they needed it finished.

All she was aware of were Jake's lips moving seductively over hers, his hand cradling the back of her head, his knee nudging hers beneath the forgotten take-out napkins still spread over their thighs.

"Is Carly okay?" asked a small voice.

They jerked apart, breaking off the kiss. Noah stood there, his brow furrowed.

"Is she okay?" he asked again. "Because one time, the Muppets learned about CPPPR on *Sesame Street,* and it looked just like that when Grover saved Cookie Monster."

Jake glanced at her. "You wanna be Grover? Or the big blue guy?" he asked in a low voice.

"I don't think I'm equipped for either one."

"Well?" Noah demanded.

"Well, your dad did save me," Marley said truthfully. "In more ways than one. So I guess—"

"I guess it's after *your* bedtime," Jake interrupted. He stood and scooped up his son in one decisive movement, flinging him over his shoulder. The boy hooted, his cheeks flushed and his eyes bright. "Off to tooth brushing for you, buddy."

Noah slumped. "Hey! I've gotta say good night to Carly first!"

"Delaying tactics won't work," Jake grumbled. But he shuffled backward until he stood within Marley's reach again.

"Good night, Noah," she said.

" 'Night." He smiled at her, his boyish grin barely visible between the haphazard strands of his upside-down hair. "See you later."

Noah puckered up. He blew a kiss. Enchanted, Marley blew him an answering kiss, then smiled. She waved to him as Jake began carrying him toward the bathroom down the hall.

"This will take a little while," Jake said as he left, "but when I get back, we're learning all about what kind of car *you* learned to drive in. And your speeding tickets. So be ready!"

His voice faded. The sounds of splashing water and giggling came from the bathroom, followed by what must have been a disagreement about whether or not soap was actually necessary. Barely listening, Marley sat immobile at the table.

She'd learned to drive in a golf cart at the studio where *Days of our Lives* was taped. She'd later had lessons in a BMW sedan from her personal chauffer, who'd gotten permission from her frazzled mother to demonstrate accelerating, braking, and steering (with varied success). Two years after most teenagers got their driver's licenses, she'd been quizzed for her driving test by her co-stars on the soap. How could she reveal all that to Jake?

Quickly, Marley tried to concoct a suitable Carly cover story. Learning to drive in an old clunker, like Jake had? Taking lessons at a driving school? Studying for the test with a bunch of high school girlfriends?

Arrgh. This was hopeless. She didn't want to lie to Jake anymore, Marley realized. And she didn't have to. The time for the truth was at hand.

"Noah's all tucked in," Jake said as he left the hallway. He hooked a thumb toward his son's bedroom, with its faint night-light glow and its cozy warmth. "He'll be out like a light in no time flat. He's got Gaffer with him for company."

He smiled, remembering how the dog had waited obediently outside the bathroom during tooth-brushing time. How he'd padded silently into Noah's room to hear the evening's bedtime story about Rainbow Fish. How he'd curled into a ball beside Noah's bed, plunked his muzzle down, and settled in for a nap next to his new favorite kid.

Okay, so maybe Noah was his only favorite kid, knowing Carly. But that would change once Carly and her Yorkie had spent more time in the Jarvis household. Between sleepovers and birthday parties, there were usually plenty of kids around who—

Hang on a minute. Where was Carly?

Jake scanned the living room. Returned to the kitchen, where their notepads remained—but the food wrappers had been cleaned up. Glanced outside, then scratched his head. No Carly. Nowhere.

Then it hit him. Of course! She'd been waiting for a replay of their afternoon, too. He was sure of it.

With a surge of anticipation, Jake retraced his steps. As he'd expected, he found Carly in his bedroom—staring out the window at the slowly deepening night. He advanced toward her and then hugged her from behind, enveloping her in his arms.

Or at least he tried. Doing so was tricky, given that her arms were crossed over her chest in a gesture both closed off and pensive. He frowned.

"Why so tense?" Jake asked. "What's wrong?"

Carly shrugged. The streetlight outside the window illuminated her profile, but otherwise the room was dim.

"If it's the bedtime routine that's bugging you, you might as well get used to it. It happens every night at this time."

"No, that's not it. I thought it was sweet!" She hesitated, trailing her fingers over the windowsill. "I especially loved the bedtime story."

"You listened?"

A nod.

Embarrassed, Jake rested his chin on the crown of her head. The position was comfortable. It also had the advantage of making it impossible for Carly to look at his face.

"You were wonderful," she went on, her tone taking on more energy. "All those funny voices you did! And the faces you made up . . . wow. I'll bet Noah loved it."

"Noah's asleep," Jake said huskily. "Or on his way there. From here on out, we have the whole night to ourselves. And I know just the way to help you relax."

He loosened his grasp, stroked his palms over her tightly folded arms. Gradually, by the barest degree, Carly's posture eased. Jake nuzzled her neck, blissfully inhaling her unique, feminine scent. First he would show her he loved her. Then he would tell her.

"I can't think when you touch me," Carly confessed weakly.

"Then don't think. Just feel."

"I have to think. I have to . . . ohhh." She turned in his arms, leaning against the windowsill. "I'm telling you, your hands are like a drug. They're dangerous."

"Only if you get addicted." Jake gazed at her in the dimness, possessiveness surging inside him. Carly was his. He wanted to give her everything. "Come closer. I want you to get hooked."

"Too late," she murmured. "I already am."

She raised her mouth for a kiss. Jake was only too happy to deliver it.

Countless minutes later, they'd christened Jake's massive king-sized bed—behind the closed and locked bedroom door, of course. They'd kissed and whispered and loved, tangling the sheets and sharing their hearts. As they'd come together for a second time, Jake had known the course he'd set was the right one. In his bed, in his arms, in his *life,* Carly Christopher was the woman for him.

He propped himself up on a stack of pillows, then pulled her into the crook of his arm. Idly, he let his fingers play over the subtle curve of her naked breast, revealed only slightly above the sheets they'd haphazardly pulled on. Carly's legs twined with his. Her heart beat in rhythm with his. Her breath feathered tenderly over his chest. They were sated, happy, thoroughly relaxed. The moment was perfect.

Jake was ready.

He drew in a lungful of air, preparing to speak. At the same moment, Carly angled her head to gaze up at the ceiling.

"Jake, I have something to tell you."

"What a coincidence. *I* have something to tell *you.*"

"Oh, God." She froze in place. "Are you breaking up with me? Was that a kiss-off encounter? A really sensitive 'see you later'? I've heard of letting a girl down easy, but that's ridiculous."

"It's not that."

A relieved sigh escaped her. Carly glanced at him. In the faint glow from the window, Jake glimpsed in her expression a mixture of gratitude, happiness . . . and fear?

"It's really not that," he told her, hoping to set her mind at ease. "We're just getting started."

"I hope you'll remember that when I tell you what I have to tell you," Carly said. "Because we *are* just getting started, and even though this began by accident between us"—her hand patted his chest, then hers, as though he might not understand which "us" she meant—"I know it could go someplace really special. After *Dream Date*. If we let it."

Her voice had sped up. Jake detected a faint tremor in it, too. He wondered why. Maybe he'd overplayed his hand, he thought suddenly. Maybe making love to her twice in one day had been overkill. Maybe he'd accidentally entered the One-Night-Stand Zone with Carly. Maybe she was trying to tell him she just wanted to be bed buddies with him.

Dismay pinned him to the sheets. He wanted more than that. Much, *much* more.

"I've never done this before," he blurted. "Only with you. You realize that, right?"

She gaze him a quizzical look. "You sure seemed experienced, then," she teased, momentarily lapsing into the camaraderie they shared. "For a virgin, that is. You're like a sexual savant, or something."

At her words, Jake preened. Hell, any man would have. He loved hearing he'd pleased her. Then he remembered Carly was poised to make him her booty-call boy, and realized that continuing in this vein could only lead to trouble. He had to change her mind.

"I've never slept with a woman in this bed," he said. "I've never let anyone stay over. I want you to stay over."

He said this decisively, as decisively as he'd proclaimed the baseball glove his favorite childhood toy earlier. In response, Carly blinked at him.

"You'd better hold off on that invitation," she said softly. "Until you hear what I have to say. Afterward . . . well, if you still want me, I'll be here."

The earnestness in her expression worried him. It was possible, Jake realized, that he'd misread this entire encounter.

"I don't mean 'stay over' just to sleep," he assured her in his most macho voice. Discreetly, he flexed his biceps. "There can be more to it than that. Lots more."

"Shhh." Carly lay her index finger over his lips, then pushed upward. "Just listen. Okay?"

Her eyes begged him for patience. Seriously befuddled now, Jake nodded. "Okay."

"Okay." Carly drew in a deep breath, hauled a portion of the sheet upward to cover her. "Here's the thing. I'm not quite the person you think I am."

Over the next several minutes, she went on to describe the most mind-boggling series of events Jake had ever heard. It began with something called the *Fantasy Family* Fan Club, continued with real-and-raw Talisha, moved past failed auditions and awful meetings with producers, and swept all the way to the morning he and Carly had met at the *Dream Date* offices.

"I begged the receptionist to make sure we weren't paired up on the game show," Carly told him. "I knew I wouldn't be able to remember what I was supposed to be doing while you were there. And I was right."

Gesturing passionately, she went on to explain the creation of her alter ego. She mentioned Archie (responsible for her awesome classic car), her twin sister Meredith (procurer of her fake waitress's job and actual owner of her modest apartment), and a whole cadre of assistants and show biz professionals—including Brian and Sondra, bowling partners extraordinaire.

"Then they're not really beef-jerky lovers from Appalachia?" Jake couldn't help but ask. "Sondra's not really a stripper? Brian's not really a garbage man?"

Miserably, Carly shook her head. "We invented all that. To help make you believe in my *Dream Date* persona."

"But . . . what about the pole dance move Sondra showed me near the snack bar?"

"Well, you've got me there," Carly mused. "Come to think of it, I'd wondered where she'd picked that up myself."

She shrugged and launched onward, chattering a mile a minute now. She explained how her twin sister had tutored her in everyday life, how she'd triumphantly ridden the city bus, how she'd learned to clean and do laundry. She described her acting career, grew teary-eyed at remembering her desperation to prove her dramatic versatility, shuddered at the thought of hawking the ZitKit3000 (whatever the hell that was) in an infomercial.

"So you see? I *had* to do the *Dream Date* thing," she said urgently, squeezing his hand. "An infomercial is like the seventh level of hell for an actor. Even worse, I would have had second billing to that kid who moons everybody in the Farrelly brothers movies!" She waved her hands, illustrating the horror of the notion. "I was at my wit's end. There was no choice but to go through with the alter-ego plan and hope to make a good impression on *Dream Date*."

Woodenly, Jake listened. Everything she'd been telling him began sinking in. A part of him still couldn't believe it.

"What happens next?" he asked slowly. "After you 'make a good impression on *Dream Date*'?"

She bit her lip. "On the final show, I reveal the real me. The Marley Madison, TV starlet, me," she said carefully. "The transformation wows the viewing public, I prove my acting talent and versatility—because after all, who'd have guessed *Allure's* Best Booty 2001 winner could morph into the girl next door?—and my phone starts ringing off the hook with offers. The publicity alone will be tremendous."

Wow. It was quite a plan, Jake thought in a detached way. Crazy, but with a kooky logic. Given the media's mania for transformation stories, given the public's thirst for novelty and surprise . . . well, her scheme might actually work.

"Everything's been going according to plan," she said, still explaining. "Brian and Sondra have seen early cuts of our dates, and they say Carly's been fabulous. They say I'm a new me! A me that's going to hit the big time again. Once the producers and directors and casting agents in this town get a load of what I can do—out of my usual type—they won't be able to get enough of me."

Jake was silent. By now he couldn't think. He could only feel. And what he felt was duped. Betrayed. Played for a fool by a famous Hollywood actress who'd used him as a prop in her outrageous bid for success.

"At least," she said a bit more meekly, "that's what my people say."

Her people? Jesus. She wasn't the same person he'd fallen in love with at *all.* Jake grunted, unable to move for the torrent of feelings inside him. For her, this had all been pretend. For him, it had been . . . so much more.

Until now.

He couldn't speak. Couldn't think. Couldn't even look at her. Instead Jake scanned the room—the room where he'd so stupidly begun showing his love to her—trying to pull himself together. His gaze fell on the stack of *Dream Date* paperwork on the bureau. At the sight, another thought struck him.

This was only a preview. A sample of the colossal disclosure Carly would make during the game show's live finale. A taste of the debacle she'd make of his life, his reputation, his job. Jake would be a laughingstock—the only KKZP "team player" to not only fumble the ball, but to turn it over to the other team for an embarrassing touchdown. His contract would be forfeit. His public image would probably be shot to hell, too. It would be nearly impossible for him to find another anchor job.

All the security and stability he'd wanted for Noah . . . gone.

"Jake?" She touched his arm, her voice worried. "Say something. You're scaring me."

He gave her an anguished look. Carly wasn't the open and honest woman he'd fallen in love with. She was a stranger. A fraud who'd used both him and his son to fulfill her own selfish, Hollywood-style needs.

"I'm still me," she said, tugging on his arm with her stranger's grasp. "I'm a better me! Don't you see? All the important things I told you about me were true. Because of this—because of you—I've learned so much. I've *loved* so much."

"Don't say that." Jake couldn't bear to hear it. More lies from her only meant more wanting from him.

"It's true! I'm me, but I'm Carly, too." Tears filled her eyes and a wobbly smile pushed its way onto her face. "I know it sounds schizophrenic. But both of us love you."

Jake shook off her hand. He had to get away. To think. To plan. To find some way to deal with this disaster. He hurled away the sheets and got to his feet.

"No!" she cried, lurching after him.

The bedding billowed as she flung out her arms. He moved before she could grab him.

"I trusted you, Jake." Her voice sounded hoarse, husky with unshed tears. She beat her fist on the mattress. "I trusted you enough to tell you the truth."

He'd trusted her enough to love her. He was an idiot.

"I know this is a shock," she went on, "but please, don't go. We can handle this. I know we can."

Jake yanked on his jeans. Faced her. "I don't want to."

She flinched. Her mouth opened in shock. "You don't mean that," she whispered. "Nobody who looked at me— who *touched me*—the way you did could mean that."

"I do." He couldn't think about touching her. About looking at her, and loving her. If he did, Jake knew he might waver. In this, he had to be absolutely clear. "I want you to leave."

"Okay." She sighed. "Okay."

Holding up her hands in surrender, Carly rolled over in bed. She scooped clothes from the floor with shaky hands, then put them on in as hunched-over and hidden a fashion as she could. Finally she stood, a rumpled but dignified princess.

A Hollywood princess.

Hell.

Already she looked different to him. Was different.

"I know you probably need time to think this over," she said, sounding reasonable. "That's perfectly understandable."

"I don't need time." Dark, desperate humor rose to his defense. "I need a strategy. Possibly a lawyer. And after your celebrity coming-out party two days from now, I'll probably need a new job. But most of all, I need you to get out."

"What?"

Fury finally won. Jake raked his hands through his hair, barely able to speak for the turmoil inside him. "Carly—Marley—whatever the fuck your name is—get out!"

Her startled eyes widened. Her face crumpled. When she spoke again, the effort it cost her was obvious.

"But Jake, I . . . I love you. I thought"—a gulping sob cut short her words—"I thought you might love me, too. You have to let me explain!"

He turned his back on her. "You've done all the 'explaining' I can stand."

Silence fell between them. In the room where Jake had loved her, where he'd planned to tell her he loved her, he now felt his heart breaking. It was a real physical sensation, a hollow pain behind his breastbone that wouldn't ease. So long as she stood there, so long as he felt her presence . . . he knew it never would.

"Go!" he roared.

She gasped. He heard her shoes clatter together as she hastily grabbed them, heard her feet tread barefoot across the carpet. A faint breeze stirred. Jake fancied it was Carly, returned to herself again and come to hold him in her arms.

He hesitated, feeling the same yearning he always did when she was near.

The door closed softly behind her.

He was alone. Fisting his hands tighter, Jake stared unseeing out the window where he'd stood together with Carly only a few short hours ago. The view would never be the same.

From here on, neither would he.

Twenty-Two

Marley moved through the dimness of Jake's apartment, gathering her things with shaky hands. Around her, everything was quiet. The spicy smell of Mexican food still hung faintly in the air, and the furniture stood with perfect normalcy in the shadows, but she knew things were anything but normal. They would never be normal again.

Jake didn't want her. He didn't love her and he didn't need her. In the moment between living her life as "Carly" and becoming herself in his eyes, everything they'd shared together had vanished. Everything.

Why had she been so stupid as to tell the truth?

Her throat tightened with tears she refused to shed. Somehow Marley made it to the front door. She dropped her shoes and rammed her feet uncaringly into them, then retrieved her purse. All that remained was getting Gaffer, and then . . .

Her gaze fell on the gift bag she'd left on the table. Noah's gift. With a decisive movement, she picked it up.

The boy was sleeping peacefully, Marley saw as she hesitated in his doorway. He'd tangled his little body inside a pile of cartoon-print bedding, arms and legs outflung, and his perfect chubby cheeks were angelic as he dreamed. His hair

stuck up wildly, though—a dead giveaway to his true ener-
getic nature. At his feet in the glow of the night-light, Gaffer
perked up his ears. He regarded Marley curiously.

Aren't we staying here? his canine gaze seemed to ask. *I
thought we were staying here.*

She'd thought so, too. But it turned out that although
everyone else in her life wanted her as a successful actress,
the only man she'd ever truly loved wouldn't have her as that
very thing. The irony of it all was more painful than Marley
could bear.

"Sorry, boy," she whispered to her dog, gesturing for him
to come and be leashed. "I thought this might last, too."

She stifled a sob, burying her fingers in Gaffer's soft fur.
Knowing something was wrong, the Yorkie nuzzled her. He
pushed at her arm with his nose, his eyes kind and worried.

Geez. Doggie pity was the last thing she could handle
right now. She just didn't have the strength. Marley sucked
in a wavering breath and snapped Gaffer's leash to his collar.

As she did, an abrupt sound came from the bedroom
down the hall. *Jake.* She couldn't let him find her here. Still.
Lingering, waiting, reluctant to leave. Marley didn't think
she could endure another harsh command from him tonight.

I need you to get out. Get out!

Remembering the look on Jake's face when he'd finally
understood her deception, Marley choked back another sob.
He'd been shocked, anguished, infuriated. Never had his features looked so stark as they had tonight. Never had he
looked so forbidding.

So final.

Noah shifted in his sleep and Marley knew she had to finish what she'd come here to do. She retrieved the gift bag,
and the sight of it filled her with bittersweet memories of
how excited she'd been to find the surprise inside, how proud
she'd been to have wrapped it herself instead of springing for
her usual perfect-but-impersonal store gift wrap. At the
time, she'd thought doing so had been a reflection of all the
ways she'd changed.

Now she knew she'd only been fooling herself.

Holding her breath, Marley set the incongruously cheerful gift on Noah's bedside. She stood beside him, lingering only long enough to memorize the boy's sleeping features—and to blow an air-kiss for him to remember her by.

She'd have sworn his little hand fisted to catch it.

Another sound came from down the hallway, and Marley knew her time was up. With a silent good-bye for Noah, she picked up Gaffer. Cradling him close, she paused in the hallway to cast a longing glance toward Jake's closed door. She would miss him. In fact, going on without him felt pretty well impossible right now. How would she endure each day without his smile, his voice, his touch? His laugh?

She needed him like she needed gravity—to hold her steady. Without Jake, Marley didn't know how life would ever feel good or true again.

Finally, there was nothing to do but go on. Feeling empty inside, Marley straightened her shoulders. Somehow she found the strength to turn away, to start moving, to walk down the hallway into the living room. There, Marley paused for a final whispered "Good-bye."

Then she let herself out of the apartment . . . and out of Jake's life forever.

Jake didn't know how long he sat propped against his pillow-cushioned headboard, lit sporadically by the flash of the bedroom's TV screen as he mindlessly surfed the channels. He knew that he made it through *Sports Center,* part of the news, a late broadcast of women's bowling. He paused on an infomercial for a knife-sharpening system and blinked thoughtfully at the has-been actor hawking the product.

Was that guy as miserable as Carly—no, Marley, dammit—claimed she'd have been, if forced to do similar acting work?

Scowling, Jake worked the remote again. He found little relief in the constantly changing channels, but neither could he sleep. Memories of Marley's deception whirled in his head, alternating only with remembrances of the moment she'd left him tonight.

Thank God he hadn't actually told her he loved her.

Music videos, talk shows, and *Saturday Night Live* reruns flickered past. Jake paused to rub his gritty eyes with his thumb and forefinger. It was possible he had some kind of freakish emotional hangover, he thought—the result of too much feeling in too little time. He didn't have the faintest idea how to cure the damned thing.

In his one unguarded moment, the theme music from *Dream Date* blasted from the set. A commercial. Jolted, he grabbed the remote and changed channels. Being reminded of the game show was the last thing he wanted.

Okay, second-to-last thing. Because next Jake stumbled upon one of L.A.'s independent stations, currently showing reruns of a particular hit sitcom. The sight of a familiar smile and sassy sashay caught him completely off guard.

Fantasy Family. What were the odds?

Transfixed despite himself, Jake stared at the actors on-screen, recognizing Marley as the ditzy Southern belle she'd portrayed. He'd seen promos for the show, of course. A few years ago, it had been a top-ten Nielsen hit. Jake would've had to have been living under a rock not to have been aware of the publicity juggernaut surrounding the show. All of *Fantasy Family*'s cast members had become stars—but none had shone more brightly than Marley Madison.

Telling himself it was only curiosity that held him there, Jake relaxed his grasp on the remote. He studied the TV screen, frowning. As the episode ended and another began ("A full hour of your favorite *Family!*" the voice-over announced gleefully), he couldn't stop watching. He'd never seen the show from start to finish. His exposure had been limited to snippets on Emmy broadcasts or on KKZP's entertainment news. Probably that was part of the reason he hadn't recognized Marley as herself immediately.

There was more to it than that, though, Jake mused. TV starlet Marley had luxurious pale blonde hair, loads of makeup, a barely-there wardrobe and a self-important attitude. Real-life Marley (or at least Carly) had casual, shoulder-length brown hair, light makeup, feminine clothes . . . and an attitude filled with everything he'd ever wanted. Laughter. Thoughtfulness. Sexy openness.

As the mush-hearted realization struck him, Jake frowned anew. So he could be forgiven for not recognizing her. Big deal. What he couldn't be forgiven for was falling for her. *That* had been beyond idiotic.

He'd never considered himself particularly gullible. Apparently, he was. Marley Madison had dangled her girly-girl bait, hooked him like a prize-winning trout, and reeled him in. Jake would have preferred to skip the part where she gutted him, though. It just hurt too much.

Exhausted and bleary-eyed, he made himself switch channels again. The glare of a bright home shopping channel jerked him partway awake. Jolted by it, Jake switched back to the *Fantasy Family* station.

Ahhh. Carly.

Her face teased him from the TV screen, reminding him of everything they'd shared. The TV Carly/Marley was different, but if he took off his horn-rims and settled for squinting, Jake could almost make himself believe the woman he loved was still there with him.

Next thing he knew, he was waking up to uncomfortably bright sunlight, the drone of the morning news, and the sounds of people talking in the next room. His mom? One of his brothers? It sounded like them, but it couldn't be. Today was Sunday. The only person Jake should have been forced to confront on a weekend morning was Noah, dragging in a blanket to watch Nick Jr. on the floor of Jake's bedroom.

Fiercely, Jake flung off the covers, then went to find out what the hell was going on.

"Wake up, everybody!" Marley cried. She strode into her familiar Hollywood Hills bungalow with her head held high and an uneven smile plastered on her face, clapping her hands to alert the staff to her presence. Gaffer trotted along faithfully at her side. He collapsed on the rug near the foyer, undoubtedly pushed to his doggie limits by the sleepless night they'd passed together. "It's brunch time!"

"Marley?" The cook bustled down the hall, wiping her hands on an apron. "We didn't expect you. Especially for brunch."

"I know. That's why I'm having this one catered. No hard feelings, okay?" Marley turned to the food service workers who'd followed her in and began directing traffic. "You can start setting up in the kitchen. Right down that hallway."

They nodded and passed by her, carrying trays and utensils and platters of prepared food as they followed the bewildered cook to the rear of the house.

"Marley?" Candace emerged from her bedroom, yawning as she pulled on a robe. The personal assistant shoved her hair from her eyes. "I didn't think you'd be back until tomorrow, to get ready for the *Dream Date* taping. Is everything okay?"

Since there was no possible way to answer that question without falling apart completely, Marley didn't attempt to. Instead, she gave Candace a hug.

"You'll come to brunch too, of course, won't you?" she asked, forcing cheerfulness into her voice. Just because her world had fallen apart didn't mean she couldn't still entertain. Did it? "Please call up Heather and Brian and Sondra when you get a chance, too. I'm dying to see everyone. I feel as though I've been trapped in Siberia!"

"Well, Meredith's neighborhood isn't the most posh . . ."

"There you are!" Marley cried, spotting the florist's delivery person hovering outside the opened doorway. She beckoned the girl closer, watching as she maneuvered between the catering staff. "Just put those in the dining room, please. Gerbera daisies! My favorite!"

Briskly, Marley nodded as the flowers were carried away.

Their yellow blossoms nodded cheerfully in the early morning light. With things beginning to bustle all around her, she finally felt the tiniest bit distracted.

Thank God she'd hit upon this plan. She needed something like this. After losing Jake, getting through this day—one minute at a time—had been all she could consider attempting.

"Marley?" Meredith stood at the top of the stairs which overlooked the foyer, gawking at her twin sister. "What are you doing here?"

"Brunch!" Marley cried, flinging out her arms. "Everyone's invited!"

Hastily, Meredith rushed downstairs. Her filmy pink robe—hang on, *Marley's* filmy pink robe—fluttered around her ankles. When she'd reached the bottom, Marley recognized the expensive silk georgette La Perla negligee her sister was wearing, too. It was one Marley had had made especially for herself while visiting Italy. She couldn't believe Meredith—sleep-in-an-old-T-shirt-and-men's-boxer-shorts Meredith—was actually wearing it.

Exactly what, she wondered, had her sister been doing in Marley's place while she'd been gone?

"You're not supposed to be here until tomorrow," Meredith said, sounding breathless. She cast a worried glance toward the upstairs bedroom. "Is everything okay?"

"That's what *I* wanted to know," Candace said.

They both stared at her expectantly, hands on hips.

"What? Stop looking so worried." Marley waved her arm blithely. "I just decided to get an early start on returning to my real life, that's all. I am *so* ready to end this boooring alter-ego business."

She cast aside her handbag and strode to the fireplace. Ahhh. Her Emmy was still there on the mantel, brilliantly gold and beautiful, representing her talent and accomplishments. She might not have true love, but she did have . . . awards.

A sob threatened to shove through her chipper demeanor. Ruthlessly, Marley choked it down. She turned her back on her award and addressed her assistant and sister again.

"Will you two quit looking so bewildered? It's not as though I'm doing something wrong, you know. I'm me again. And I'm throwing a party! A brunch party."

A meaningful look passed between Meredith and Candace.

"I'll go make those calls," Candace said, whirling toward her in-house office. The door shut behind her.

"I'll . . . be right back," Meredith said at the same moment. "Don't move!"

About four minutes later, her sister returned. Her cheeks were flushed, her eyes were bright, her breath was coming faster. Wow, Marley thought distractedly. *Her* wardrobe really agreed with Meredith.

"I think we should go shopping together later," Marley suggested gaily.

Sure. Shopping would provide even more distraction. While shopping, she couldn't come completely undone and she couldn't beg Jake to take her back, either.

She'd definitely have to leave her cell phone at home.

"Wouldn't that be fun?" Marley urged her sister.

To her dismay, her voice cracked, ruining the unaffected casualness she'd been striving so hard for. She'd known her broken heart would make pulling it off pretty tough . . . But hey, she was an actress, wasn't she? Acting was all she'd ever excel at. All she'd ever have. All she'd ever, ever, ever, *ever* have.

Oh, God.

Marley forced herself to go on. "We can get some new things for you—things a lot like the outfit you're wearing—"

Meredith glanced down at herself, as though realizing what she wore for the first time. She blushed.

"—and some new things for me. I'll need something really vivacious for tomorrow's taping. After all, it's not every day I come out as the real me. I'll need a starlet-worthy wardrobe for the job. Then the contrast between me and Carly will be even greater!"

"Right. About that . . ." Meredith gently took her arm.

A half-hour later, Marley found herself seated in her living room, surrounded by friends and family. What had begun as a careful inquiry on her sister's part had morphed into a free-for-all that was making it harder and harder for Marley to maintain her jovial cover.

"We're worried about you," Candace repeated for the second time. "We know something's happened. Is it Jake? Did he—"

"Look, we need to get on with brunch," Marley interrupted.

As it turned out, she was completely unable to hear Jake's name without wanting to curl up and bawl. Thinking of him was just too hard. Knowing she'd never be with him was even worse. Desperately, she cast about for another topic.

"I should really call Andre and make an appointment to have my hair returned to its real color."

"Your 'real color' is the same as mine," Meredith protested, holding out a hank of brown hair in demonstration. "You already have your real color."

Marley pooh-poohed the notion. "Not my natural hair color! My true color. Blond, like Tara." She crossed her legs and assumed a debutante's pose, ready to deliver the catchphrase that had helped make her famous. "Why, I *do* declare! I do declare, indeed!"

Instead of the applause that usually greeted her drawled exclamation, there was silence. Marley slumped a little as everyone exchanged concerned glances.

"Marley, honey." Her mother scooted closer on the sofa, grasping her hand. "You do know you're not *really* Tara, right?"

"Of course I am. I'm Tara from *Fantasy Family.* That's all I'll ever be."

Sondra and Brian looked perplexed. "Until tomorrow, you mean," Brian said. "After you finish the *Dream Date* taping, you'll have lots of new options."

"That's right," Sondra agreed.

"Of course. Now let's eat." Marley stood.

Heather dragged her back down. The publicist leaned forward seriously. "What is it that you're not telling us? Something is obviously bothering you."

Murmurs of agreement were heard.

"What could be bothering me?" Marley protested.

Heather ignored her. "When I got here, you didn't even ask me for the press clips I brought."

"You didn't ask me if I'd had any offers for you," Sondra said. "You didn't even ask about overseas commercials."

"That's right," Brian said, getting in on the act. "You didn't ask me if I had any new career ideas for you."

"You didn't ask me," her mother chimed in, "what I thought of your brunch menu. Eggs Benedict is *so* last year. Everyone who's anyone is going multicultural. In my new Indonesian cooking class, I learned a fabulous recipe you should try."

Meredith raised her head. "You didn't ask me what the hell I'm doing wearing your clothes."

Everyone gasped.

Marley bit her lip. They were on to her. Not even her acting abilities had been enough to save her this time.

"I have to know everything if I'm going to do an effective PR job," Heather said seriously. "Damage control doesn't happen overnight."

Marley wavered. "Damage control" sounded pretty good right now. If Heather could magically transport her back to last night, let her take back the truths she'd revealed to Jake . . .

No. The real truth was, Jake didn't want her. He didn't love her. Not even knowing that Marley had, in many ways, revealed all the most vulnerable parts of herself to him had been enough to change things. She'd tried to be an everyday, ordinary girl next door . . . and she'd failed.

Obviously, she should have stuck with what worked for her. From here on out, that's exactly what she intended to do.

"I don't need damage control." Marley stood and bestowed her best what-do-you-mean-the-other-nominee-won? smile on the group. "I don't need all of you worrying about me, and I don't even need brunch. Truth is, I ought to be dieting again, anyway. What I do need is a fabulous outfit for tomorrow. I'm off to shop!"

Before anyone could disagree, she picked up Gaffer and bolted for the door. Let them hold their inquisition without her, Marley thought. If her staff wouldn't help her carry out this career-saving plan the way she'd originally intended to, then she'd simply have to do it all herself.

She would, too, Marley vowed as she got into her car and gave the necessary address to her driver. Just as soon as she managed to stop the tears that had struck the instant she'd found herself on her own.

Jake stood at the threshold of his apartment's living room. "What the hell is going on here?" he demanded.

"Shhh. Little pitchers have big ears," his mother said, bustling toward him. She held a basket of flowers in both hands and wore a big smile on her perfectly made-up face. "Noah's right over there."

She nodded toward her grandson, who was engrossed in playing near the TV. Jake frowned and gestured pointedly at the people milling about his apartment.

"Mom, why are you here? It's Sunday. I sleep in on Sunday."

"You need to sleep in on Sunday," Stephanie observed, squinting at him. She put down her flowers and stood, hands on hips, examining him. "You look terrible. Why don't you go shave, and we'll talk about this when you're presentable?"

Jake crossed his arms and stared her down.

"Fine!" She pretended to be engrossed in arranging her flowers. "I'll tell you. Your cousin Ronald is coming to town tomorrow, and we thought it would be nice if he stayed with you."

"Ronald? Boogers-and-butt-music Ronald?"

"He's an adult now. He's learned self-control."

"I don't care. He can't stay here."

Stephanie looked crushed. "But we already have Ulrich at our place. Besides, everything's almost ready!"

She gestured toward the rest of the room. His brothers and Bethany were there, too, Jake saw, carrying in groceries, more flowers, and extra pillows for the sofa bed. The activity swirled around him, making his head hurt. Obviously, his mother was on one of her family-first entertaining missions, and everyone was expected to chip in. Including Jake.

"How did you get in here, anyway?" he asked.

"A mother should have a key to her son's apartment," Stephanie said primly.

"I never gave you a key."

"I know. Don't think for a minute that didn't make things more difficult!"

Jake rolled his eyes. This was too much for him. Especially on a day like today. What he really needed was to formulate a strategy for dealing with *Dream Date*. He didn't have time for a houseguest.

Especially one who thought *Fear Factor* was must-see TV.

"Go. Shower." Stephanie gave him a nudge with her elbow. "You'll feel better about this when you're clean."

"Mom, I'm not falling for that. I'm not six years old anymore. I know soap and water isn't magic."

"It's not?" Noah asked from across the room, his little face turning toward them. "But Daddy, you said—"

"Now you've done it," Stephanie muttered, stifling a grin.

Jake smacked his hand on his forehead. What the hell had ever compelled him to recycle the same stupid tactics his parents had used on him?

"Daddy didn't mean that, sport," he said, going to Noah. He crouched beside him, hoping to undo the bath-motivating damage he'd just caused. "Of course soap and water is magic. Why else would bath time be so—hey. What's that you're playing with?"

"A new toy!" his son exclaimed. With a wide smile, he held it up for Jake to see. "I found it wrapped up beside my bed this morning. Do you think Santa brought it?"

Jake looked at the toy Noah grasped. It was a stuffed bear with brown fur, smooth tan feet, kind glass eyes . . . and a little pink bow around its neck. It looked new. It looked cuddly.

It looked exactly like . . . "Mr. Wrinkle," Jake said.

Noah boggled. "How did you know his name? You didn't see the card that came with him."

"Lucky guess," Jake managed to say. Just looking at the stupid bear made his heart clutch, all over again. Creakily, he got to his feet. "A bear like that's probably too babyish for you, though, right?" he asked his son in a too-hearty voice. "You'd probably rather have another G.I. Joe or a Duplo set."

"No!" Noah cried. He clutched the bear to his chest and squeezed. "I love Mr. Wrinkle. I always wanted him."

"You couldn't have always wanted him," Jake argued, pushed beyond the point of reasonableness by this reminder of Carly. Marley. *Arrgh.* "You didn't even know he existed."

"I did too!"

"That's impossible!"

"You can't take him," Noah said, his lower lip jutting out.

"Oh, yeah?" Jake stepped forward.

"Jake." His mother's voice cut off whatever idiotic thing he'd been about to say. "Go take your shower," she urged. "Whatever's bothering you isn't Noah's fault."

"But, Mom—"

"Go." In a no-nonsense way, she pointed toward the distant bathroom. "Right now."

Great. He'd morphed into an eight-year-old again. He cast a defiant glance toward Mr. Wrinkle . . . and his pathetic heart squeezed again.

He missed her. Despite everything, he missed her.

Jake pressed his lips together and headed for the hallway. An instant before he got there, his mother scurried up behind him. She threw her arms around him and gave a gentle hug.

"Hang in there, honey," Stephanie said, patting him on the back. "Whatever's happened, we'll all get through it together."

"Thanks, Mom."

Briefly, Jake hugged her back, ridiculously comforted by her familiar embrace. Her grip was the same, her scent was the same, her murmured words were the same. In his lifetime, his mother had chased away bogeymen and hurt feelings alike with her embrace. She'd celebrated home runs and graduations with it. Wrapped in its power, Jake wanted to believe everything would somehow turn out for the best.

The trouble was, now he knew her curative powers were only as magical as soap and water. In this, he needed so much more.

Twenty-Three

Marley was trying on her third ensemble in the exclusive private rooms of her favorite up-and-coming L.A. designer when they caught up with her.

"We thought we'd find you here!" Candace said from the head of the pack. Sondra, Brian, Imogene, Heather, and Meredith filed in behind her, all wearing jointly accusing looks. "What do you mean by running out on us? We're trying to help you."

"I don't need help." Pivoting, Marley scrutinized the effect of her fuchsia wrap dress, movie-star sunglasses, and high-heeled slingbacks in the mirror. "I'm fine."

Something about the outfit didn't feel right. Like the sequin-spangled tank top and silk pants she'd tried earlier, it seemed . . . off. Almost as though designer duds no longer suited her—ridiculous as that idea was. She beckoned the designer's staff. Three employees surged forward immediately, each bearing a different set of luxurious clothes.

"I'll try that one," she declared, pointing to a gorgeous pale violet skirt and sheer printed blouse. The employee nodded and took the outfit to the fitting area. Pursing her lips, Marley examined her reflection again. "No, this will never do. But I'm glad you're all here. You can help me choose something for tomorrow."

"About tomorrow," Sondra said. "Are you having second thoughts? Because if you are, we can rethink this whole *Dream Date* plan. There *are* other options, you know."

"Other options?" Marley made a dismissive sound and stepped off the platform near the mirror. "Don't be ridiculous. I'm going through with it. I said I would, and I will."

After all, everyone was depending on her. Her staff, her entourage, everyone in this room. *They,* at least, *needed her.*

Determinedly, she strode into the fitting area. A few minutes later, she emerged wearing the pastel skirt and shirt ensemble, new strappy heels, and—again—her sunglasses. They were more than a TV-star affectation. They hid the effects of her crying jag earlier. Her crying jag last night. Her crying jag over coffee, over getting made up, over doing her hair and remembering the touch of Jake's hand as he smoothed a wayward strand over her cheek.

Stop it.

"Now *this* is more like it," Marley said, turning to view herself from all sides in the three-way mirror. Nearby, the designer's staff murmured appreciatively. "The skirt is the perfect length, the sheer top is sexy . . . *This* is something Carly Christopher wouldn't be caught dead in."

"I liked Carly," Sondra said wistfully.

"She was a hoot to bowl with," Brian added.

"She actually went rock climbing with her mother," Imogene put in, folding her arms. "She wasn't so bad."

"As a matter of fact," Sondra said, casting a glance toward Brian, "she was a lot like you, Marley."

Marley dismissed the idea with a roll of her eyes. "Sure. We had the same birthday."

"So do we." Meredith shook her head. "We're not alike at all."

"Carly was a means to an end," Marley told them. "She's not necessary anymore."

"That may be true," Brian said. "But I hope you keep a little of her around."

This was ridiculous. Why were they all so obsessed with her alter ego? Jake had been quick enough to dismiss both of them last night.

"Okay, let's have some focus here," Marley snapped, straightening her posture. She smoothed her skirt, then fussed with her hair in an attempt to brainstorm a starlet style. "Will this outfit knock the socks off the *Dream Date* people? Will it make the audience gasp when they find out that me and Carly are the same person?"

Reluctantly, everyone nodded. With an air of defeat, Heather sat in an antique gilt chair near the mirror. Idly, she pet Gaffer. The Yorkie had been to many designer fittings— he was perfectly well-behaved. Marley was proud of him. All morning, he hadn't so much as yipped.

She turned to the assistants. "I'll need accessories, too. A handbag, these shoes, maybe even some jewelry. Although I can always borrow something—"

"Oh, no," Heather said.

Marley raised her eyebrows. She swiveled to look at her publicist. "What's the matter? You don't think I can get a loan from Harry Winston on such short notice?"

"It's not that. It's Gaffer."

"What's wrong?" Instantly concerned, Marley rushed to her dog's side. She crouched beside the Yorkie, murmuring to him as she examined him for bumps or bruises or any sign of illness. "He's prone to seasonal allergies, but I don't think—"

She stopped. Gasped. With one hand on Gaffer's collar, she stared at what she'd found. "Oh, my God."

They all crowded forward. "What's the matter?"

"It's his collar," Marley said slowly, pointing at the dog's red patent leather accessory. "The decorator stones are *black*. Oh, Gaffer!"

"So? You switched his collar from the one with blue 'gems' to one with black 'gems.' Big deal," her mother said, shrugging. "I prefer the rhinestone collars myself, but I don't see where this is something to get so worked up about."

Sadly, Marley stroked poor Gaffer's fur. "This is the collar with the blue stones. They've turned black because"— her voice wobbled—"because it's a mood collar!"

A shocked silence followed as the importance of this sunk in.

Meredith snorted. "Oh, puh-leeze. A mood collar? Tell me you're not serious."

"She's serious," Candace said, nodding. "Mood collars are the latest thing for pets. Haven't you seen them on TV? In magazines? At a glance, you can see how your dog or cat is feeling."

"Dark blue means perky," Heather explained. Marley knew that her publicist's calico cat had a mood collar, too. "Green means perplexed, red-brown means introspective—"

"And black means depressed!" Marley wailed, now on her knees on the floor, heedless of her designer clothes. She nuzzled Gaffer, finally taking off her sunglasses and casting them aside. "I've depressed my dog! What kind of horrible person am I?"

They all huddled around her, telling her she wasn't a horrible person at all. They made sympathetic sounds. Offered tentative jokes. Her mother hugged her, and even skeptical Meredith managed a few pats for Gaffer.

Marley appreciated their support. But somehow, knowing Gaffer was unhappy too made it impossible for her to hold in her own misery any longer. Tears ran down her face as she dragged the Yorkie onto her lap and cradled him there.

"I'm sorry, Gaffer. I didn't mean for any of this to happen," she babbled. "I thought I was doing the right thing."

A new silence fell as her entourage considered her words. Then Sondra spoke up.

"Doing the right thing?" she asked. "What 'right thing'?"

"Telling Jake the truth about me." Sucking in an unsteady breath, Marley glanced upward. Her heart squeezed in regret as she remembered losing the man she loved. "Last night. I told him everything. About me. About Carly. About inventing my alter ego. He *deserved* to know. I couldn't lie anymore."

Sondra and Brian exchanged a startled glance. Heather looked thoughtful. Candace bit her lip. Only Imogene and Meredith seemed unfazed by the news.

"Good for you, dear," her mother said, patting her reassuringly on the shoulder. "I'm sure you did the right thing."

"Mom's right," Meredith agreed. "You have to tell the truth to the man you're in love with."

Several gasps were heard.

"In love?" Sondra and Brian asked.

"Really?" Heather and Candace said in unison.

"Of course," Meredith replied, giving them all a look to match her *it's obvious* tone. "I knew Marley had fallen for Jake the minute she actually put on that waitress uniform and showed up at the museum diner. The old Marley would have settled for interviewing a few employees to add flavor to her research. But the new Marley really tried to do a good job."

"That accident with the toaster was not my fault." Marley sniffled, then lay her cheek against Gaffer's usually perky ears. She sighed. Poor Gaffer.

"I know." Her sister grinned. She went on. "I knew it was love the minute Marley told me she'd gone to visit Bobby Christopher, and the minute she actually agreed to appear in public with no makeup. In stripes and plaid, no less."

Heather and Candace gawked at this purposeful and un-Marley-like fashion faux pas.

"Only true love could have motivated my sister to go to such extremes," Meredith said. "Only true love could have motivated her to honestly change on the inside. Marley's career might be important to her, but there are limits. I mean, come on. She actually went *bowling.*"

They all nodded, obviously seeing the logic in this.

"Marley set out to learn real life, and she did," Meredith said, giving her sister a brief hug. "Sort of. But what she really learned was real love."

Love. At Meredith's words, Marley let out a new wail. "And then I lost it!" she cried. "Jake doesn't want me. He's right not to want me! I'm a big liar."

"You're an actress," Imogene said soothingly.

"Same thing," Marley grumbled. "It gets worse, too! I realized it last night. There's more at stake here than love. There's Jake's job, too. After I make my big revelation tomorrow, he'll probably lose his sportscasting contract."

"Huh?" Candace asked.

With some effort, Marley explained the whole thing to them. As she talked, the designer's staff disappeared into the other room—ostensibly to find more potential ensembles—leaving her to dole out the painful reality of the situation in privacy.

"So," she finished, "once I reveal myself as Marley, I'll kick-start my career and make the last month of pain and suffering worthwhile, just as I'd planned. But at the same time, I've lost Jake! And I've hurt him, too. He told me how important *Dream Date* was to his news director. I'll probably ruin his chances for his contract renewal forever. He'll look like an idiot for believing in Carly."

"He'll look like he believed your acting ability," Brian said loyally. "The same way everyone else at *Dream Date* did."

"That's right," Sondra agreed. "That's the whole point of this. You're on the brink of achieving everything you've ever wanted for your career! Don't give up now. Remember, you don't know that your surprise will ruin things for Jake."

Marley disagreed. "You didn't see his reaction last night. It was about more than losing me. It was about losing face. About losing his shot at something he really wants for his job. He didn't just do this on a lark, you know. He had to. His boss made him." She sighed, dispirited. "He really loves sportscasting, too."

"I'll bet it was mostly about losing you," Imogene protested, giving her daughter a squeeze. "That would make anyone feel bad."

"Sure," Heather added. "How great can sportscasting really be, anyway?"

"It's great. For Jake." Squaring her shoulders, Marley gave Gaffer another pat. She might have been imagining it, but it almost looked as though his collar's mood stones had begun lightening a bit. "I want him to be happy. The trouble is, I don't have much of a choice here. Either I let myself and all of you down, or I let Jake down."

They stared at her. She imagined them worrying, fearing for their jobs and the way of life they'd become used to. Everything she and her staff took for granted would be gone if Marley didn't revitalize her career somehow.

"Honestly . . . my loyalty has to lie with the people who've loved me my whole life. Not with the man who"—she gulped, reluctant to say the words aloud—"who can't even stand the sight of me."

"Oh, Marley. That's too harsh, isn't it?" Sondra asked.

"No," she sobbed. "It isn't. And I'd better just get over it right now. Because I need to get busy. I need to get over to Andre's for that hair-color appointment."

Resolutely, she stood. She had to go on. Somehow.

"But you found true love!" Candace insisted. "You can't give up on it, just like that!"

With a sniffle, Marley wiped her eyes. She swept them all with a pleading look. "What else can I do? Jake doesn't love me back. That's the truth. Is one-sided true love really worth sacrificing everything I've worked my whole life for?"

They looked down. No one had an answer for that one.

Jake showered and shaved, dressed, and brooded. Then he emerged from his bedroom and apologized to Noah.

"Mr. Wrinkle is from Carly," he told his son as they sat on the living room floor together, the stuffed bear in Noah's arms. "He's a lot like a special bear she had when she was a little girl. Even though we won't be seeing much of Carly anymore"—it seemed sensible to use her alter-ego name, so as not to confuse Noah—"you should feel free to play with Mr. Wrinkle all you want. I think Carly would have liked that."

Noah frowned. "Is Carly mad at us?"

"Not . . . exactly."

"Then why won't we see her very much?"

Jake hesitated. Just thinking of her made his heart ache. He purposely relaxed his fisted hands, then went on. "She'll be very busy. With her job. It's important to her."

"But I want to see her. I made a picture to show her."

Looking at Noah's puzzled face, Jake knew he'd made a mistake in losing his heart to Marley. His heart wasn't his alone to give—it was Noah's, too. His son would suffer from the loss of her. Luckily, he was young. He'd forget her.

Much sooner than Jake would.

"I'll let you know when you can do that," he said. It was the best he could promise. Gruffly, he cleared his throat as he rose again. He ruffled Noah's hair, then went to the kitchen.

Twenty minutes later, over Cocoa Puffs and coffee, Jake revealed to his family everything that had happened. Carly's deception, her true identity, her reasons for appearing with him on *Dream Date*. By the time he'd finished, his mother, Bethany, James, and Nate all sat with shocked expressions.

Predictably, Stephanie recovered first. "Well, son. A part of you must have known the truth all along."

"Yeah," Bethany agreed. "You must have been in denial. Dating a famous TV star without realizing it would be like . . . like buying a flattering bikini on the first try."

"Huh?"

"Theoretically possible. But not likely."

Jake took in their assured expressions and felt even worse. "She looked different!" he protested. "Her hair was different, her clothes were different—"

"Her body was the same, though," James interrupted. "Smokin' hot! Yowsa. Those legs, that smile . . ."

"Yeah. I was so hot for her on *Fantasy Family,*" Nate agreed with a rueful shake of his head. "I swear they iced down her nipples before every episode."

"Nate!" Stephanie and Bethany cried.

He shrugged. "Can I help it if her headlights were on? It was impossible not to notice."

Jake wondered if his brother would notice Jake's fist, headed for Nate's face. He scowled.

"Marley Madison, huh?" James mused. "Yeah. Now that you mention it . . . I would've known her anywhere."

"What? You would not!" Jake said. "You didn't."

"If I'd been sucking face with her over by the front door for half an hour I would have."

"The level of maturity in this room is amazing."

"Hey, at least we're not blind, bro."

Jake buried his head in his hands. His family had a bizarre way of showing their support. The "kick 'em when they're down" method was not what he'd expected.

"Hey, Nate," James said conversationally. "How many Jakes does it take to screw in a lightbulb?"

"I dunno. How many?"

"None. He's too busy screwing an actress without realizing it!"

Fury pushed Jake to his feet. His chair scraped and fell backward. Before it hit the ground, he had James by the throat.

"Take that back, you bastard."

"Whoa! Hey." His brother spread his hands in a gesture of surrender. "Lighten up. I was only kidding."

Jake glared into his brother's startled face. It probably would feel good to beat some sense into him, he thought as he wound his fist more tightly into James's shirt. He could vent some of the anguish that had kept him up most of the night.

"Kid about this," he said, readying a left hook.

"Stop it, boys." His mother's hand closed over his. With a grunt, she yanked his arm downward from its boxer's stance. "This is no way to settle anything."

Maybe not. But it sure as hell felt like one. Rigid with anger, Jake bared his teeth at James. His brother's eyes bugged.

"Jake, let go of your brother right now." Stephanie pried unsuccessfully at Jake's free hand, still at James's throat. "James, if you know what's good for you, apologize this instant."

"Sorry," his brother mumbled.

Reluctantly, Jake released him. He shook off his mother's gentle grasp, then flexed both tension-ridden hands as he stalked across the kitchen. He raked his fingers through his hair, filled with an anguish unlike anything he'd ever experienced. He didn't know what to do with these feelings, but he sure as hell didn't want them.

In the taut stillness, the tinny melody of a cartoon theme song wafted from the living room. *Noah.* Jake groaned. He couldn't attack his brother while Noah was nearby. Another time was another question. But for now . . . for now he'd have to let his idiot brother go on breathing through that nose.

"You two had better settle down," Stephanie warned Nate and James in her most no-nonsense motherly tone. "It's not right to make fun of the woman your brother loves."

Jake whirled to face them, appalled.

"Loves?" James boggled.

"Loves?" Nate echoed gleefully. "Dude, no way!"

"Awww, Jake," Bethany cooed. "That's so sweet."

How the hell had she known? Jake wondered, gawking at his mother's serene expression. *Had it been that obvious?*

Geez, he was doomed.

"It's over," he said tightly, going to the coffeemaker for a fresh jolt of caffeine. He held his cup so tightly it was a wonder it didn't crack. "She's gone."

"Gone? What do you mean, gone?" his mother asked.

"I told Carly—Marley—to leave." Forcing his emotions under control, Jake blew on his coffee. He leaned on the kitchen bar in as nonchalant a pose as he could manage. It made him feel a little less as though he was about to crumble. "Last night."

The four of them sighed. Stephanie shook her head.

"Marley loved you enough to risk telling you the truth about herself," she said. "Don't you think she deserves a little more compassion than that?"

"She used me." He wouldn't entertain the notion that she'd actually loved him. "She used me, and tomorrow she's going to make a fool out of me."

Bethany looked thoughtful. "Actually, Marley could have done that without telling you the truth first. She could have surprised you on the set of *Dream Date* along with the rest of the world."

"That's right," Stephanie agreed.

"Yeah, bro," his brothers chimed in.

Jake glared them into silence. "This wasn't about me. It was about her damned alter ego. About her performance. About her career."

"About you." His mother gave him a plaintive look. "Honey, I understand that you're hurting—"

He deepened his scowl and remained silent.

"—and you're probably justified in being a little angry—"

"This could cost me my job!" Jake yelled. "Damn right, I'm 'a little angry' about it."

"You're resilient," Stephanie insisted. "You could easily find another sportscasting spot, if that's what it came down to. Losing your job is not what's bothering you."

Jake gulped some scalding coffee. Stared across the kitchen as he fought an emotion suspiciously close to grief.

"Losing Marley is," Stephanie finished softly.

"There's no 'losing' to be done. She's already gone."

"You made her leave. Ask her to come back," his sister urged. "Just ask her."

He couldn't. Asking Marley to come back would be like handing her his heart again . . . waiting for her to smash it. Jake knew he was smarter than that.

Still, if only a tenth of what Marley had told him were

true, if only a fraction of what they'd shared had been genuine . . . he couldn't simply forget her. Without her, he felt hollow. Joyless. Like a punter without a ball, like a catcher without a mitt, like a man without his love.

Had he been in denial? Had he known all along, on some level, that Carly was really Marley? Had he loved her anyway? Given his policy of not getting involved with actresses, it was remotely possible that his mind had recognized her— and his heart had insisted on falling for her anyway, using the fiction of "Carly" as an excuse.

No. That was crazy talk, dammit. He didn't believe in mumbo-jumbo psychobabble bullshit. His family had muddled his thinking.

Jake shook his head. "It doesn't matter. With me already in the public eye, the last thing Noah and I need is an actress in our lives. I've always said so. The publicity, the paparazzi, the hassle—"

"Hey, you're always bitching about being misunderstood," James put in. "About how people think a monkey could sit on-set behind your desk and read scores and stats. Who better to understand your job than somebody else who works in TV?"

"Yeah," Nate added cheerfully. "You and Marley probably have more in common than you think."

Actually, he had gotten the sense that Carly understood the demands of his job, Jake realized with a jolt. Maybe his dim-witted brothers were right. Maybe once he and Marley were free from the burden of *Dream Date,* things could work out.

Of course, after the final show was taped, he wouldn't have a job over which to bond with her. Period.

"No. I'm going to go on *Dream Date* tomorrow," he said grimly, "and I'm going to finish what I started. I'm going to do whatever I can to salvage this mess."

"Oh, Jake." His mother eyed his undoubtedly harsh expression and the determined set of his jaw. "Please listen to us. Don't do something you'll regret."

"Yeah, bro," James said. "We didn't know you loved her."

"We didn't," Nate agreed soulfully. "We thought you were just doing the wild thing together."

Bethany shook her head. "You can always find a new job. You can't always find true love."

But that didn't matter, and Jake knew it. True love was an illusion—a make-believe emotion that could vanish overnight. It could be pretended. It could be snatched away, and it had. From here on out, he had nothing else to lose.

Twenty-Four

Even after Jake had arrived at the *Dream Date* taping the following day, he couldn't shake his family's advice from his mind. He strode into the reception area and past the sound-stage early that morning with his mother's, sister's, and brothers' words still ringing in his ears.

Marley loved you enough to risk telling you the truth about herself. She could have surprised you on the set of Dream Date *along with the rest of the world.*

You and Marley probably have more in common than you think.

Ask her to come back. Just ask her.

It was torturous. Pointless, too, given that Marley was already lost to him for good. Now that he knew who she really was, he knew she needed more in her life than a die-hard sportscaster with a four-year-old son and a four-year-old Honda. She needed a man who could look good in a tux, a man who enjoyed having his picture taken for *Entertainment Weekly,* a man who lived for shuttling the famous Marley Madison to award shows and premieres.

She needed, Jake thought, a really good limo driver.

Resolutely, he followed Doug, the *Dream Date* staff member, toward the interview room where his taped debriefing session would be held. There was no point dwelling on what might have been. Not now. Instead, Jake forced his mind to the job at hand.

"All the interviews are being held this morning," Doug said, chattering as they headed backstage. "With all six contestants, in various rooms all around us."

Jake remained silent.

Doug leaned sideways conspiratorially. "This is where we get the real dirt, you know. After four weeks of dream dating, you people usually won't shut up." He chuckled.

Jake ignored him. *He* would shut up. In fact, that was his whole plan. To reveal as little as possible, to grit his teeth and doggedly continue in the hopes of finishing this damned thing. If pure stubborn staying power had the ability to impress his news director's beloved female demographic, then Jake had it made.

"The final Q&A will be taped this afternoon, too, after lunch," Doug continued, oblivious to Jake's chitchat-discouraging responses. "Once we've got all the contestants here, it's just as easy to do the debriefings and the Q&A on the same day."

Jake muttered something noncommittal and followed. He wasn't eager for the live taping. Being revealed as a gullible, lovesick idiot for the entertainment of a studio audience was not on his list of top ten favorite things. If only he'd known what he was getting into with little Miss Cream-and-Sugar all those weeks ago . . .

Hell. He would have done it anyway. Being with Marley had been worth it.

"So, we're right in here," Doug said, gesturing toward an interview room.

The door was open. Inside the stark white space, Jake glimpsed bright lights, video and audio operators, two interview chairs, and a side table bearing a box of donuts, Styrofoam cups, and a coffeemaker.

His gaze lingered for an instant on the coffeemaker. He remembered Marley's cream-and-sugar coffee theories and couldn't help but smile. Even on that first day, he'd known there was something special between them.

Following Doug, he stepped toward the room. At the same instant, a clattering of high-heeled shoes echoed behind him.

"Jake!"

He stopped. Turned. To his surprise, he saw Marley hurrying down the hallway after him, an urgent expression on her face. One of the *Dream Date* staffers bustled along behind her, carrying a clipboard and looking impatient.

"I'd hoped I'd run into you here." Putting her hand to her heart, Marley stopped. She glanced over her shoulder. The staffer was gaining on her. "Listen. I know you're probably still mad at me, but I have to tell you something."

He couldn't speak. He felt Marley's hand on his arm, felt her nearness, and knew he must be dreaming. She looked different to him somehow. Different . . . and very, very necessary. At the sight of her, something inside him eased.

"I'm not doing it, Jake," she said. "I'm not—"

"Hey!" Doug interrupted, poking his head out of the interview room, donut in hand. He frowned. "You two shouldn't be talking."

Marley's assigned interviewer caught up with her. She grabbed Marley's arm. "No fraternizing with the other contestants," she said sternly. "That's not allowed."

She yanked, and Marley's grasp fell away. Jake felt the loss of her touch, leaned forward as the interviewer hustled her away from him. Briefly, Marley struggled. The interviewer admonished her a second time, her words of warning carrying back to Jake.

"You'll both forfeit your chance at the final Q&A round if you keep up like this!"

"Wait," Marley pleaded. She looked over her shoulder at Jake, her dark hair tossed around her face. "I'm going to be Carly!" she cried. "Just Carly. So don't worry! I'm going to fix this."

Stunned, Jake watched as the interviewer jostled her subject away from him. Marley's determined, vulnerable gaze locked with his . . . and in her face, he glimpsed something he'd never expected to want from her again.

The truth.

An instant later, she rounded the corner and disappeared from sight. Jake stood unmoving as the impact of seeing her finally struck him.

I'm not doing it, Jake. I'm going to be Carly.

He knew what she meant. Her plain clothes—and her non-blonde, non-starlet hair—had made her intentions clear. Marley wasn't going through with her publicity-garnering plans to reveal her true celebrity self during the Q&A today. But why?

"Whew! Let's get started," Doug said cheerfully. He dragged his gaze from the corner where Marley and the other *Dream Date* staffer had disappeared, and regarded Jake with a curious look. "I'll bet you've got tons of dirt to dish on that one, huh?"

Jake barely heard him. Marley's hasty announcement, he realized, meant he was off the hook. He could finish out this charade the way his news director and managing editor wanted him to. He could impress the female demographic. He could still have a shot at winning the final round.

He could ensure his contract would be renewed and have everything he wanted.

But Marley would have nothing. If she didn't reveal herself as herself today, she would lose her chance to make the big splash she'd hoped for. She would miss the fanfare and the ready-made E! TV coverage she'd obviously hoped would result from being Carly. All her efforts would be wasted.

I'm going to fix this.

He couldn't let her. It was as simple as that. Jake fisted his hand and stared down the empty hallway one more time, ignoring Doug's babbling in the background. He couldn't let Marley throw away her future. Her luxe life. Her non-participation-in-infomercials policy. Her dreams. Even if it meant sending her away from him forever, he had to do something. Marley's happiness meant too much to him not to try.

Hell, he was no stranger to changing his plans, Jake told himself. He'd changed them when he'd become a sportscaster. He'd changed them when Noah had come along. Was true love any less compelling a reason to shake things up?

Jake didn't think so.

Slowly, he raised his hand. He touched the place on his opposite arm where Marley's warmth had penetrated, and felt a new lightheartedness fill him. As it did, Jake realized exactly what had seemed different to him about Marley during their brief encounter. He hadn't been able to pin it down until just this minute, but now he had.

Today, Marley hadn't looked like an actress to him. Today, she'd looked like herself—like the woman he loved. Somehow Jake knew that from that moment on, she always would.

He turned. Went inside the interview room. "I'm ready," Jake told Doug, then sat down to begin.

In her interview room, Marley grasped the arms of her white leather chair. She blinked beneath the bright lights, gazing intently at the *Dream Date* staffer who'd been debriefing her. Thanks to the half-dozen questions she'd successfully fielded already, she felt as determined and prepared as she had when her driver, Hugh, had dropped her off this morning.

She also felt a little naked. On camera without the ego-bolstering effects of her usual blonde hair, her bodacious wardrobe, and the armor of her celebrity to shield her, everything seemed much riskier. This was scarier than she'd expected. She knew she'd grown and changed as Carly . . . but what if it wasn't enough?

What if *she* wasn't enough?

Seeing Jake hadn't helped matters, either. Why hadn't he reacted? Why hadn't he said something? He'd only looked at

her with an unforgiving expression, tall and strong and remote. He'd stared at her hand on his arm as though hardly
able to believe she dared to touch him. Marley wasn't sure
what she'd expected, but it hadn't been indifference. Just remembering it was nearly enough to break her heart all over
again.

For a moment, she'd thought she'd glimpsed a certain tenderness in Jake's face, a certain flexing of his jaw that revealed he yearned for her, too . . . and was fighting it. But
then her interviewer had dragged Marley away. Her encounter with him had ended.

Stifling a sigh, Marley crossed her legs and refocused her
attention on the debriefing. At least she had the comfort of
knowing she was doing the right thing, she told herself.
Seeing this through as Carly—not revealing herself as
Marley—would ensure that Jake appeared in the best possible light. It would help him get the contract renewal he
needed.

It might even make him happy. He deserved to be happy.
Marley owed him that much. Because when it came right
down to it, she wanted his happiness even more than she
wanted her own.

Besides—there was always that ZitKit3000 infomercial
waiting for her, right? She'd survive. Her friends and family
had helped her to see that.

The interviewer cleared her throat. "Tell me a little more
about your everyday life, Carly."

Back to business. Focusing on her alter ego, Marley
began. "Well, I live in a small apartment. One bedroom. One
bath. A billion dust bunnies."

The interviewer barely cracked a smile.

"It's homey, though," Marley went on, picturing Meredith's
place in her mind's eye. "There are lots of family pictures, a
few plants, potpourri. Books. Outside there's a nice grassy
patch that my dog absolutely loves."

The interviewer brightened. "A dog? What kind?"

"A Yorkie. I got him when he was just a puppy." Marley

went on to describe Gaffer's first few nights at her bungalow (apartment, in the Carly version), when she'd cuddled him in a pashmina (blanket) and let him sleep in her bed. "He still likes to sleep there. Right on top of the pillows. I'm afraid I've spoiled him."

An indulgent smile. "What's his name?"

"Gaffer."

"Hmmm. Unusual name."

"Well, there's a funny story behind that." On the verge of describing why she'd named her dog after the chief lighting technician on a TV or movie set, Marley paused. She had to stay in character. She regrouped. "I'm a huge movie fan! And I always thought 'gaffer' was such a funny word, rolling past in the credits. Ha!"

Her interviewer nodded. Seeming to accept that explanation, she leaned forward. A titillated gleam came into her eyes. "So," she said in girl-to-girl fashion. "Tell me all about Jake."

"Jake?" Marley's voice wobbled. Her heart lurched. She missed him so much. "Well, I hardly know where to start . . ."

You can do this, she told herself. *No matter how much it hurts to remember.*

"Jake is a wonderful man," she said truthfully. Soberly. She folded her hands in her lap and put everything she had into making the interviewer see how truly special Jake was. "He's honest and smart and funny. He's got more integrity than Gary Cooper and Jimmy Stewart put together."

"There's that movie fan coming out in you!" the interviewer chirped.

Marley nodded. This was going well, she realized. More and more, the formerly stern-faced interviewer was on her side. Relaxing a little, she continued. "Jake is like no man I've ever met. He's strong and macho, but he's got a tender side, too. You should see him with his family! They all care about each other so much."

She envied him that a little. She especially envied the bond Jake had with his son. The two of them were a real team, facing the world together—with nothing but the occasional body-parts humor for a buffer. Remembering Noah, Marley smiled.

"Jake probably knows more about sports than any man alive," she said. "He—"

"Isn't he a sportscaster?" the interviewer asked, checking her clipboard. "Yes. So of course he'd know about sports."

"But there's more to it than that. Jake's knowledge of sports goes beyond what he needs for his job." Marley hoped, for Jake's sake, that this part made the cut into the broadcast *Dream Date* episodes. His news director and managing editor would definitely be impressed. "He knows everything there is to know about everything athletic. He's passionate. He's well-informed. He has an encyclopedic knowledge of baseball—"

The interviewer shifted. She was losing interest.

"You know all those numbers on a baseball card?" Marley asked rapidly. "Jake knows what all of them mean. It's not just baseball, either. He knows football, basketball, hockey, soccer. He knows all the players—their statistics, their training, where they went to school, probably what they had for breakfast. It's really amazing. I never used to be much for sports, but being around Jake made me see why people love them."

"You like sports?" The interviewer gave Marley's clothes a pointed look. She settled her gaze on the monogrammed initials painted on Marley's toes (the latest handiwork by Rowena). She raised her eyebrows. "Be serious."

"I am. I'm considering getting season tickets to the Dodgers next year."

"Wow. That's quite a change."

"It is. A change for the better. And all because I took an interest in what Jake liked. I wanted to impress him."

"I'll bet you did." The interviewer nodded. "Football widows everywhere could take a lesson from you."

"It's not about me," Marley said earnestly. "It's about Jake."

"Hmmm. He must be quite a guy."

"He is." Energetically, Marley nodded.

She and the interviewer shared a smile.

"But what about Jake's dark side?" the interviewer asked, leaning forward to fix Marley with a piercing look. "No man's perfect, you know. What don't you like about Jake?"

Gulp. *I don't like that he doesn't love me. I don't like that he doesn't need me the way I need him.*

"Ummm . . ." Marley stared downward. An urge to blubber and blab, Barbara Walters Special–style, swept over her. Swamped in momentary sadness, she struggled for composure.

"Carly? You can tell me," the interviewer urged.

"Well . . ."

Marley focused desperately on her toes, calmed somewhat by thoughts of the woman whose artwork embellished them. Rowena had gone from pampering Marley with an emergency pedicure at the diner to appearing in the latest issue of *Allure*—thanks to a tip Marley had phoned in to the magazine's beauty editor. She was proud of that. Proud of the help she'd given her new friend.

"I like everything about Jake," she said. "Everything."

The interviewer looked skeptical. "Come on. According to my notes"—she shuffled through her clipboarded papers—"you didn't want to be paired up with Jake Jarvis at all."

Marley swallowed hard. That was true. She was trapped. She'd have to deliver something. Some excuse. "Well . . . it's just that he's so good-looking," she tried. "Gorgeous men make me feel self-conscious."

"Carly." The interviewer shook her head, looking disappointed. "I know there's more to it than that."

The pressure built. The lights shone twice as brightly. Marley felt overheated—and under the gun. What now? What now?

Suddenly, the interview room door banged open. Three men strode inside. One carried paperwork, one wore a

Dream Date staff badge (she recognized him as Doug), and one seemed to be in charge. They crossed the room with no regard to the taping going on, and stopped beside Marley's interviewer. The four of them huddled together, whispering.

Whew. Saved in the nick of time, Marley thought.

They clearly had urgent game-show business to attend to. Even the camera operator took a break. By the time her interviewer's attention returned to Marley, she would be able to finesse that last line of questioning right into something that fit her agenda better. Say, Jake's knack for taking charge. Or his remarkable way of making her laugh.

Relieved, she leaned back in her chair and waited for her interview to continue. Despite the "dark side of Jake" glitch she'd just endured, Marley thought things were going well. Sacrificing her career-revitalization opportunity was going to be completely worth it. After this, Jake would be happy and Marley would have a clean slate.

Maybe after a little time had passed, she could call him. Or visit. Encouraged by the thought, Marley felt her spirits lift. She still loved him. Candace and Heather and everyone else had been right. She couldn't just give up on true love.

Then she remembered the way Jake had looked through her in the hallway today. Her new buoyancy deflated as quickly as it had come. He still didn't want her. Probably had never loved her.

Lost in that miserable thought, she almost didn't hear the voice speaking to her.

"Marley?" someone asked. "Marley Madison?"

"Yes?" she replied, automatically looking up.

Four accusatory faces stared back at her. The *Dream Date* staffers folded their arms. Doug shook his head, and Marley's interviewer looked vaguely betrayed.

Whoops. She'd answered to her own name.

"What Mr. Jarvis told us is true, then," the guy who looked like he was in charge said. "You are Marley Madison, and you entered the game show under a false identity. You have some serious explaining to do, Miss Madison."

Twenty-Five

Only one part of what the *Dream Date* people said mattered to Marley.

"Jake? Jake told you about me?" she asked.

Doug nodded, looking disgruntled. "He couldn't quit talking about you. He raved about your acting. Your charm. Your determination and creativity and guts. He even said you had 'remarkable integrity' to come clean to him the way you did about this whole mess."

"I guess you didn't expect him to betray your secret, did you?" the paperwork-toting man asked snidely. "You probably expected him to play along. Poor sap."

Marley was oblivious to his spitefulness. He didn't understand, that was all . . . and she did. Her heart pounded. Her mind spun with thoughts of Jake—Jake, and what he'd just done for her. He'd risked looking like an idiot, risked his contract renewal and his reputation, all to ensure that Marley would get credit for the alter-ego transformation she'd pulled off. He'd known how much her acting career meant to her and he'd tried to help her salvage it.

What Jake hadn't known was that he meant so much more.

"The last laugh's on him, though," Doug said. "I'm afraid you'll both probably be disqualified for this."

"Hold on," the official interrupted, wearing a thoughtful look. "Let's not be hasty."

The four of them huddled together. Words like "ratings," "bombshell," and "publicity" were heard. They broke apart.

"You'll definitely be given a strict talking-to before the final Q&A taping this afternoon," the official admonished gruffly. "This might make for good TV, but we can't let our contestants run amuck."

They all nodded, as though this was reasonable. Ratings ruled, Marley guessed. But she didn't care.

Because Jake did care about her. This proved it. Of course, she couldn't let him throw away his future for her, but still . . . this proved it. Jubilation rushed through her.

Urgently, she stood. She unclipped her mic and rapidly yanked its wire to drag it beneath her clothes and out the hem of her shirt. Marley hurled it onto her interview chair.

"I've got to talk to Jake!" she announced, rushing into the other interview room.

It was empty. Confused, Marley called Jake's name.

When she whirled around, the four *Dream Date* staffers who'd followed her stood in the doorway.

"He's gone," Doug said. "He said what he had to say and then—"

Marley didn't wait to hear the rest. She had a man to track down, a sportscasting snafu to fix, and true love to repair. She had to get busy.

"How about some lunch, sport?" Jake asked Noah. "I think there's still some leftover pizza in the fridge."

"Nah," Noah said. "I'm not hungry."

He slumped on his stool at the bar, dispiritedly cradling Mr. Wrinkle. He'd been like that ever since Jake had picked him up early at Toddler Time today. Quiet. Withdrawn.

Disinterested in his toys and all the things he usually loved. He hadn't even turned on Nick Jr. since they'd arrived at the apartment.

Jake got out the pizza box anyway.

"Come on. Go long!" he said, hefting a slice in the practiced way he and Noah shared. He gestured for his son to go out for the pizza pass. "You'll feel better if you eat."

"Carly says we should eat a salad with our pizza," Noah said, not moving. "She says we need vegetables."

"Vegetables, schmegetables. There's tomato sauce on here." Noah only sighed.

Jake frowned. Then another inspiration struck him. "How about a game of touch football first, to work up an appetite?"

He bundled a pigskin under one arm and his son under the other. Ten minutes later, he and Noah stared at each other across their apartment complex's grassy lawn.

"You're not even trying, Noah!" Jake said as his son flopped onto his back after another miserable throw. "You love football. Try catching this one, okay?"

Reluctantly, Noah got up. The ball bounced off his half-heartedly raised arms. He flopped onto the grass again.

"Forget throwing and catching," Jake announced. "Bet you can't race me to the corner of the building and back!"

He took off at a run. Any minute now, he'd hear Noah whooping and hollering as he raced to catch up. Jake would slow down, pretend to stumble, make a valiant rush for the finish line as Noah scraped past him by a nose. Just like usual. He'd . . . turn around to find his son still lying in the grass?

Seriously worried now, Jake jogged back. His shadow fell over Noah's inert little body. "What's the matter?"

"Touch football is more fun with Carly."

Jake scoffed. "She throws like a girl."

"I want to give her the picture I drew," Noah insisted. His stubborn, give-me-what-I-want Jarvis-style gaze was a perfect imitation of Jake's. "Bring her back, Daddy."

"Awww, we don't need her." Jake's heart ached as he lowered to the grass beside Noah. He picked up the discarded football and rolled it down the underside of his forearm, then flipped it back up again. The trick didn't draw so much as a grin from his son. "We've been doing all right by ourselves, haven't we?"

Noah plucked blades of grass from the tufts beside him. He remained silent.

"We have fun together," Jake said. "And I've got all the love you could ever need, Noah. So it's all good. You have me all to yourself. We have each other."

"You miss her, too," Noah accused. "I saw you with the box Mr. Wrinkle came in. You said you were going to throw it away, but you didn't."

Jake froze. He didn't think Noah had noticed that.

"Hey, you never know when a spare gift box might come in handy," he said with a shrug. "Even Grandma saves those."

But Noah was right. Jake had kept Mr. Wrinkle's box. It sat on his bureau in all its Scotch-taped-and-wrapped glory, faintly fragranced with Marley's perfume and only slightly damaged from Noah's gift-opening frenzy. He'd picked it up while mindlessly tidying and had been unable to throw it away. Somehow, stupidly, discarding the last thing he knew Marley had touched seemed like giving up on her for good.

"Carly was fun," Noah said. He released the fistfuls of grass he'd pulled out, letting the greenery flutter on the breeze. "Make her come back, Daddy. I know you can do it."

Noah's hopeful gaze pinned him. Jake tried to hold fast, but he couldn't stand it. He had to look away. Twirling the football on his arm, he considered his options.

"There's something you need to know," he finally said. "Carly's name isn't really Carly. It's Marley. Marley Madison."

Confused, Noah scrunched up his nose.

Jake did his best to explain. He offered Noah a shorthand version of Marley's acting career, her alter-ego routine, and her famous life outside of *Dream Date.* For a long while afterward, Noah was silent. Then he rolled onto his belly and propped his chin in his hands. He squinted up at Jake.

"Carly—I mean, Marley, was pretending?"

Jake nodded. "In a way. Yes."

"Was she pretending about us?"

The question, so simple and so straightforward, caught Jake off guard. Until today, he'd been too angry to consider it. But now . . .

"No." He was astonished to realize he believed it. "She wasn't pretending about us. She loved being with us."

And they had loved being with her. With Marley around, the laughs were bigger, the hugs more meaningful. Dividing his love between Noah and Marley had never been a problem, Jake understood suddenly, because when they'd been together, they'd all had more love to go around. It had multiplied exponentially, like the price of beers inside a ballpark or the odds against the Cardinals ever making it to the Super Bowl. Freed by the thought, he could hardly believe he hadn't realized it before.

"Then why can't we go get her?" Noah asked.

"Why?" Jake stilled the football in his grasp. For the first time in days, a true grin came to his face. "Because we haven't got that picture of yours yet, that's why."

"Yippee!" Noah yelled. In a shot, he was off to their apartment to get it, with Jake following behind.

Somehow, Jake had vanished.

Marley knew it was true, however unlikely it was. Because she'd been searching for him ever since bolting out of her *Dream Date* interview. So far she'd turned up zilch.

Now she stood inside the KKZP offices, her third stop, having just made an impassioned plea on Jake's behalf to Richard Holloway and Sid Spielman. She'd begged them to renew Jake's contract. She'd discussed female demographics, sports, and show business with them. She'd even mentioned some of the ways Jake had made sports seem (magically) interesting to *her.* To Marley's relief, both men had seemed intrigued. She wound up her impromptu lobbying session with a good feeling—or at least as good as it got while Jake was still on the loose.

"So, you'll be sure to call me if you see Jake, right?" she reminded them, showing them her cell phone. She picked up her purse, preparing to leave, then locked gazes with Rich and Sid. "It's very important that I find him."

The two men nodded. They agreed—very kindly, she thought. Giving them both a final, impulsive hug, Marley continued on her quest.

It wasn't easy. She'd dismissed her driver Hugh after he'd dropped her off at *Dream Date,* and hadn't been able to get ahold of him since. In lieu of her BMW, she drove her beat-up Chanel car, which she'd retrieved after a short taxi ride to her Hollywood Hills bungalow. Marley didn't even take the time to tell anyone where she was going. She was certain she actually peeled rubber from the tires as she roared out of her drive.

Over the next endless hours, Marley drove all over Los Angeles. She fought traffic to the Page Museum at the La Brea Tar Pits, then made her way to Champs Sports Bar, scene of the awful car-door wallop. She dropped by the bowling alley and the ballpark, cruised past Toddler Time and made a third stop at Jake's apartment. Everywhere, memories called out to her. She'd been to those places with Jake. More than anything, she wanted to return to them with him at her side.

The afternoon swept past. Finally, out of options and nearly out of gas, Marley was forced to admit that finding Jake just wasn't in the cards for her today. Clearly, fate had other ideas in store for her—and Jake wasn't included in them. Maybe tomorrow she'd find him. Or the next day.

She wasn't giving up until she did.

Dispiritedly, she drove toward her own neighborhood. The sun hovered low on the horizon as she puttered down the familiar streets, reluctant to admit defeat and even more reluctant to go home. Nothing awaited her there but a mildly depressed Yorkie and a cadre of friends and family who would be disappointed Marley hadn't been able to make this work.

She sighed, still gripping the steering wheel. By now, she and Jake had missed their chance to be part of the *Dream Date* Q&A finale. Marley had intended to find him and bring him back in time to repair some of the damage done to his reputation—live TV could work wonders for something like that. Instead, the game show had gone on without them. Jake's hopes for career salvation rested on Marley's desperate appeals to Rich and Sid.

And on his own talent, of course.

Well, that wasn't so bad, she assured herself as she rounded the bend to her bungalow. Jake was very talented. Things were bound to work out for him sooner or later.

Security gates loomed ahead. Marley's Chanel car chugged inevitably toward them, towing her home against her will. She didn't want to accelerate, didn't want to steer, didn't want to face the emptiness that waited for her. But if there was one thing she'd learned during her time as Carly, it was that just trying mattered. So she punched in her security code, waved to the security camera, and drove inside.

The walk from her garage—where Hugh, curiously, still wasn't in residence—to her front door seemed to take an eternity. Marley trudged along the path in her Carly ensemble of a T-shirt and jeans and sandals, pulling her sunglasses tight to shield her from the sun's setting rays as it headed toward the Pacific. The light was fading from her hopes just as quickly. Before long, she'd be inside. Alone.

"Hey, beautiful," someone said from nearby. "Would you like a cup of coffee?"

At the sound of that familiar voice, Marley jerked her head up. *Jake!* She could hardly believe her eyes, and yet . . . there he was. He sat on her wide front porch steps, right between the begonias and the geraniums, with a Thermos in one hand and a little boy by his side. Noah waved excitedly, bouncing up and down at the sight of her.

Heart pounding, Marley blinked. Jake was still there, looking wonderful and remarkable and like everything she'd ever dreamed of. He smiled as he lofted his Thermos still higher. The gesture wordlessly beckoned her nearer. So did Jake's confident, tender expression.

Marley couldn't help but comply. But she couldn't begin to know what to say. Thoughts and feelings whirled inside her, seeking an outlet and, for once, denied. This man, she thought, had actually done the impossible. He'd rendered her speechless.

"How a person takes their coffee says a lot about them," Jake told her, his voice a deep, loving rumble.

He unscrewed the Thermos lid as though his being there on her front porch was the most normal occurrence in the world. With competent gestures of his incredible hands, he lifted the lid away. A rich, vaguely familiar aroma wafted out.

"Take you, for instance—"

Recognizing her own coffee theories about to be put forth, Marley shook her head. "What are you—how are you—I've been looking all over for you!"

"Later," Jake soothed. "You can tell me all about that later." He accepted the Styrofoam cup a wiggly Noah handed him, then began to pour. "Right now, you need to listen."

She took off her sunglasses with shaky hands, the better to concentrate. The better to see him. The better to savor this moment. Because all at once it felt important. Hugely important.

At the realization, Marley thought she might keel over. After all the drama of today, finding the man she loved at such an unexpected moment was nearly too much. But she had to find out . . .

"Listen to . . . what?" she asked, voice quavering.

"I've decided," Jake told her decisively, "that you're a mocha latte at heart."

He inhaled the aroma of the beverage he'd poured, then handed it to her. Their fingers touched. Their gazes met. At the sizzling affection she saw in his, Marley swooned.

"Hot, but smooth," he said. "Sweet and just strong enough. Beloved by millions—but savored by only one person at a time."

"Or two!" Noah piped up. "There's two of us!"

"Or two," Jake amended. "Noah . . . and me."

His grin was the most dazzling thing she'd ever experienced. His nearness was the most intoxicating. Bowled over by both, Marley felt her knees weaken.

"I have to sit down!" she blurted.

Instantly, Jake offered her his seat. With a grateful, overwhelmed sound, Marley sank onto the porch. Noah patted her shoulder with his little hand. He leaned forward to peer into her face. He smiled.

Her heart melted. How she'd missed them both.

Jake set aside his Thermos and hunkered down in front of her. Still grasping the mocha latte he'd poured her, Marley looked into his face. He met her gaze with one of his own, then wrapped his hands around hers—both of which had tightened on her special coffee.

"So," he said. "Do you suppose a mocha latte like yourself would go well with a decaf, extra-hot Italian roast like me? Real cream and no sugar included?"

Marley couldn't believe it. He'd remembered the coffee theory she'd applied to him all those days ago, at their very first meeting.

At her astonished look, Jake shrugged. "You didn't think I'd forget, did you?"

Mutely, she shook her head. But she hadn't thought it would matter to him so much, either. Although he'd asked the question in a deliberately offhanded way, Marley could tell by the tic in his jaw and the vulnerability in his eyes that Jake really, truly meant it. He wanted to be with her as much as she wanted to be with him.

Before she could say so, he spoke again.

"Marley, I've been falling in love with you ever since that moment," Jake said urgently. "Ever since you sashayed past me, struggled with that coffeemaker, flirted with me over four cups of joe. Ever since you took me into your heart, taught me how to shop, kissed me on a perfectly made bed. I've been falling in love with you ever since then and I couldn't be any more deeply in love with you now."

In love? This was even better than she'd hoped for! In shock, Marley felt her hand go slack on her cup. Luckily, Jake was there to shore up her grasp—to hold her steady and give her strength.

"Well, that's only fair," she said when she could muster words again. A smile came to her lips. She just couldn't hold it back. "Because I've been falling in love with you ever since you looked at me across that crazy petting zoo pen and believed in me enough to let me wrestle with the goats myself. Ever since you danced with me, and bowled with me, and showed me that I could be me without being larger than life."

Jake smiled. Marley knew then that he understood.

"For so long, I thought all I had to offer was this"—her outflung hand indicated the lavish bungalow behind them, then the Hollywood hills beyond—"and I knew it wasn't enough. But because of you, I know there's more. There's more to me if I'm sharing myself with you."

"Sharing has a way of giving back," Jake said with a telling glance at his son. "I just figured that out. If you share enough, you never run out."

Noah nodded solemnly.

Warmth stole into Marley's heart. She had a feeling it would never leave. Not now, not ever. But something still remained to be settled. She wouldn't be able to fully enjoy this moment until she'd tackled it.

"Jake, I know what you did at *Dream Date,*" she confessed. "It was brave and generous—and it was more than I deserved. I'm so, so sorry for everything I've done. For lying to you—"

"You told me the most important truths."

"—for letting you believe I was going through with my plan to become Marley at the Q&A—"

"You didn't, though. That's what matters."

"—for not being able to find you and fix this! I looked everywhere for you today, and—hey. How did you get in here, anyway? The security gate was closed."

She cocked her head, giving him a curious glance.

Jake lifted his shoulder, completely unabashed at his apparent breaking and entering.

"Let's just say your staff is packed with closet romantics," he said. "When I explained what Noah and I were doing here, they couldn't let us in fast enough."

"Hmmm." Marley considered that. "I'll have to give them all raises, then," she announced. "Effective immediately."

"Good idea," Jake said. He shifted, the muscles in his arms and shoulders flexing as he moved. Then he met her gaze again, a certain defiance in his expression. "So, about that coffee-compatibility thing . . ."

"Yes!" Marley cried. "Yes, yes, yes! As impossible as it seems, I'd say we're perfect together." Decisively, she set down her coffee cup and faced him. "One mocha latte, one Italian roast . . . absolute bliss."

"Yay!" Noah shouted. He threw his arms around Marley and squeezed her tight.

She hugged him back. Then Jake leaned nearer, and their hug became a loving huddle. Jake's arms embraced her, his lips grazed her hair, his murmured words assured her. Marley felt at home. At peace. And very much filled with love.

By the time they broke apart, tears blurred her vision. Blinking them away, overcome with emotion, Marley framed Jake's face in her hands. Slowly, reverently, she kissed him.

"I love you," she said, "with all my heart. Forever and ever and ever. Please say you forgive me."

"I forgive you." Another kiss. "Because I love you with all my soul."

Awwww. Jake really was too sweet. How had she gotten this lucky?

"My life can be crazy," Marley felt compelled to warn him, gesturing vaguely toward the bungalow beyond them. "Are you sure that's okay?"

Jake nodded. He grasped both her hands in his and squeezed reassuringly. "Life without you is dull and color-less. It doesn't have any G.I. Joe fashion shows. It doesn't have any Lego Duplo shopping malls. It doesn't even have the sound of high heels tapping on my floors. I've grown to like that sound. If having you means getting craziness . . . hell, sign me up."

"Oh, Jake. You can bet on that. I'm never letting you go."

"Me, either! Me, either!" Noah nudged her. White cray-oned paper fluttered at the edge of her vision as he thrust it toward her. "Look what I made for you, Marley."

Disentangling her hands from Jake's for the moment, Marley accepted the drawing Noah offered. She smiled at the three stick figures depicted there—one tall, one small, and one with shoulder-length hair and tiny high heels.

"It's Daddy and me and you," Noah said. "All of us."

Marley gazed at the paper. "We're all smiling."

"That's because we're together," Jake explained. "Noah told me."

"Very wise." Marley nodded sagely. "Thank you, Noah."

"I intend to make that picture come true," Jake said. "For the rest of our lives. If you'll let me."

Marley glanced down at her stick-figure self. "Does this mean I have to diet?" she joked.

"Nah." Jake stroked her hair and gazed down at the pic-ture, also. "It means you have to love me. That's all."

"I do. I will! No matter what."

"Then the rest will follow." Seeming satisfied—and a little relieved—Jake turned to his son. "Hey, Noah. Where's that football we brought?"

"Right here." The boy handed it to him.

"Good." Jake hefted it, gave it a few practice tosses, then lifted it to shoulder height. He nodded at Noah. "Go long."

Gleefully, Noah scampered down the porch steps. He ran onto the expanse of green so prized by Marley's landscapers and gardeners, jumping up and down.

Still poised, Jake looked over his shoulder at Marley. "Have you ever noticed? This big old yard of yours is exactly the right size for a football game."

He threw. The ball sailed in the air, a graceful spiral against the pink and gold sunset clouds.

"Wow! Noah will be running after that one for quite a while," Marley said. "That's quite a throw."

"That's the idea," Jake explained, coming a little closer. He regarded her with a cocky expression, not even bothering to see how—or if—his toss had been received. "When it comes to me . . . baby, you haven't seen anything yet."

"Oh, yeah?"

"Yeah."

With a wholly masculine grin, Jake captured her head in his hand. He brought his mouth down on hers in a kiss so hot, so pure, so filled with love that it left Marley breathless. She kissed him back with all her might, with all the sweetness and passion she felt for him. Still it wasn't enough. Given a lifetime of practice runs, though, Marley felt sure she could master it.

At the sound of Noah's laughter, they broke apart. Wearing joint grins, they looked to discover him hurling the football straight into the air and catching it. Gaffer had gotten out of the house somehow, too. The Yorkie romped at Noah's heels, tail wagging and mood collar delightfully blue.

"Yeah, we might not be perfect," Jake said thoughtfully, "but I think you're right. We're perfect together."

"Absolutely," Marley agreed.

She jumped to her feet, making a surprised Jake step

back. She kicked off her sandals, then wiggled her toes in the grass. An idea had occurred to her, and she couldn't resist it.

"Bet you can't catch me," she challenged, "you . . . you big old *untweezed eyebrow!*"

Marley took off at a run.

Left behind near the porch, Jake sighed. "You'll never get the funny-body-parts game."

He watched Marley confer with Noah in the distance. She grabbed the football and ran with it, hooting all the way past the expertly landscaped flower beds. She stopped. Taunted him with her hands in the air and her hips swaying side to side.

Grinning, Jake got up. Then he ran. Finally, they were on their way.

Together.

Twenty-Six

Sometime near the end of the first touch football game her bungalow had ever hosted, Marley paused. She'd been dishing out her latest attempt at trash talking ("Those shoes are *so* last season" hadn't fazed Jake a bit) when the sound of a car engine caught her attention.

Moments later, Meredith roared down the drive in Marley's BMW, Hugh at the wheel. She appeared to be wearing something else from her sister's closet. From a distance it was hard to be certain. Meredith did, however, look incredibly comfortable, as far as Marley could tell.

"That's my car!" Marley cried as the sedan zoomed past. "Those are my clothes!"

For the first time, she was stricken with the realization that while she'd been borrowing pieces of Meredith's life, Meredith may have kinda-sorta been doing the same thing with *her* life.

"What is going on here?" she wanted to know. "Exactly *what* has Meredith been doing with my life?"

Jake only shrugged—and managed to score. As for Meredith, nobody knew for sure what she'd been up to, Marley discovered later, although rumors and theories abounded.

Unfortunately—or possibly for the best—she was too busy over the next few weeks to investigate further.

Dream Date invited both her and Jake back for a special encore episode. Thanks to advance publicity by KKZP, it was among the highest rated for the series. Marley and Jake did not win the game show—but as a consolation prize, they were voted "most unlikely couple" in the *Dream Date* hall of fame.

"Hey," Jake said when he learned of the honor, "at least I don't have to wear a banana hammock in the hall of fame picture."

The option on his contract was picked up, lucratively and for many years to come, thanks to shrewd bargaining by Marley's attorney. Jake was never again promoted as TV's studliest sportscaster. It didn't quite seem fitting, everyone agreed, to publicize a happily married man that way.

As for Marley . . . she did not use her *Dream Date* Carly footage in her résumé reel. Instead, strengthened by her newfound confidence in herself and by Jake's love, she pursued a career in independent films, where playing against type was practically a requirement. It was her dream, and then some.

"I don't know how we got so lucky," Marley told Jake a few years later.

They'd rented a cabin near California's Gold Coast for their first wedding anniversary getaway. All was quiet once Noah had been tucked into bed. In that peaceful silence, Marley curled up next to Jake and flung her arm over his chest. Their naked bodies were as comfortable resting as they were engaging in steamy lovemaking. Now they both were sated.

"We had such an unlikely statrt," she went on, smiling up at his profile. "Those dates, that craziness—"

"That love," Jake added, holding her close. "Without you, everything would have been different."

"Sure." Marley wrinkled her nose. "More sports for you and Noah. More junk food. More mess."

"More of the funny-body-parts game," Jake agreed.

"I almost forgot!" Excitedly, Marley rolled onto her stomach, propping herself up on her elbows. "I've got another one. Are you ready?"

"Oh, no." Jake covered his eyes with his hand. "Say it isn't so."

"Hey! I've really got it this time. Really."

"Okay, okay." He uncovered his eyes and raised both hands in a gesture of surrender. He regarded her with a cautious look. "What is it?"

Marley allowed an anticipatory moment to pass. She drew in a deep breath. "Cellulite!"

To her dimay, Jake groaned. "That's not a funny body part. It's a—" He paused. Examined her rapidly fading expression of triumph. Began again. "It's brilliant. Congratulations."

"Really?"

"Yes."

"Oh, Jake." Marley lurched on top of him, covering him with delighted kisses. "I'm so happy. I love you so much!"

"I love you, too," he said. "More than you'll ever know."

"Cellulite, cellulite, cellulite!" she crowed.

"Sweet dreams," Jake said turning out the light.

Marley couldn't be sure, but it definitely sounded as though he were hiding a smile. That was all right, though. After all, perfection only went so far . . . before love took over.

Dear Reader,

Thank you for picking up *Perfect Together!* I hope Jake and Marley's story gave you some smiles, a few laughs, and maybe one or two happy sniffles along the way. With each new book, I try to bring you the biggest, best, most light-hearted story possible—because if you don't deserve a little fun now and then, who does?

Okay. So now the book is finished, and Marley and Jake are deliriously happy. Noah and Gaffer are happy, too. I couldn't be more tickled pink. Seriously. Except . . . by now you're probably wondering—what's up with Meredith?

Me, too! Has she taken over her twin sister's glam life and made it her own? Has she decided to seize a piece of adventure for herself? Stay tuned, because I've just realized that while Marley was busy pretending to be Carly (and falling in love with Jake), so-serious Meredith was taking some chances herself—and getting in way over her head. She doesn't know it yet, but when she meets the fella I've found for her—

Hang on! You've nearly got me spilling the whole story! Well, nope. I'm still cooking up the details, and you'll just have to wait (right along with me) as I find out what Meredith's been up to in *Perfect Switch*, my next Zebra Books contemporary romance. It's due out in 2004. I hope you'll watch for it.

In the meantime, I'd love to hear from you! You can write to me c/o P.O. Box 7105, Chandler, AZ 85246-7105, send e-mail to *lisa@lisaplumley.com*, or visit my Web site at *www.lisaplumley.com* for previews, reviews, my reader newsletter, sneak peeks of upcoming books, and more.

In love and laughter,

Lisa Plumley

Please turn the page for
an exciting sneak peek of
Lisa Plumley's
next contemporary romance
PERFECT SWITCH
coming from Zebra Books
in June 2004!

As far as escorts to a fantasy getaway went, he was perfect. Brawny, well-dressed, quick to smile—and to lend a hand into the evening's limo. At his first touch, Meredith Madison knew she was going to enjoy herself with him.

Mostly because he had no idea who she really was.

That was exactly the way she liked it. The hunk who'd arrived to pick her up just a few minutes earlier had never seen her before. After tonight, he'd never see her again. The realization felt unexpectedly liberating.

She could do this. Swapping places with her glamorous sister, Marley, wouldn't be easy, but she could do it. No one would be the wiser.

Feeling more sure of herself, Meredith smiled. In the sleek black stretch of leather, steel, and chrome she and the hunk shared, she watched him lower his broad frame onto the seat across from her.

The natural athletic grace of his movements intrigued her. So did his hands—big, square-fingered, and wholly masculine, they were made for fixing things. For laying out maps of conquest. For caressing the small of a woman's back while escorting her into a room, or cradling her cheek while kissing her.

Not that *she* needed to be fixed. Or conquered, Meredith told herself as she swung her feet onto the limo's cushy up-holstery in her favorite casual pose. She'd never allow any-one to tell her what to do. But this adventure included an escort. If he wanted to kiss her later, who was she to argue? After all, the invitation had promised her "the fantasy of a lifetime." That's what she was here to claim.

The limo driver closed the door with an expensively sub-dued *thunk*, then stowed her borrowed overnight case in the trunk. In the interest of being prepared, Meredith had brought a change of clothes and some toiletries. The fact that the driver hadn't even blinked when she'd handed over the case had only confirmed her suspicions.

The invitation she'd co-opted from Marley must have been for a comped stay at a new luxury resort, just as she'd thought. Her twin sister had enjoyed countless such perks from various places, all hoping she'd lend her famous starlet charisma to their let-us-pamper-you atmospheres.

If she didn't like it, Meredith reasoned, she'd simply cut her stay short. If the place turned out to be as showy and pre-tentious as the luxe Hollywood bungalow she'd been house-sitting for Marley for the past few days, she'd bail out and spend the weekend fighting for a place to stow her ratty old sneakers in Marley's sequin-spangled closet.

The overall gorgeousness of the man who'd arrived to take her to the resort boded well, though. Dark-haired, dark-eyed, and possessed of a manner undoubtedly meant to put skittish guests at ease, he gave Meredith a distinct sense of being in capable hands. Warmed by his influence, she re-laxed.

So what if she wasn't a star actress like her sister? Meredith thought defiantly, hugging her knees. She deserved a little downtime, too. She'd spent the whole day at the museum, cataloguing pop culture reference materials—the dustiest, most thankless part of her job as an advertising historian. Now it was time to cut loose.

As if in accord with her thoughts, the limousine accelerated along the drive and left the house behind. It began the winding descent through the Hollywood Hills toward the L.A. basin, bearing her toward her mysterious destination like a modern-day Cinderella's pumpkin-turned-limo. Sure, she didn't have a fairy godmother, and Meredith was more likely to wear Tevas than glass slippers. But the analogy felt apt, all the same.

Through the tinted windows, flashes of vibrant summer sunset came and went. So did Meredith's bravado. She couldn't help it. Kidnapping someone else's identity—even temporarily, and just for the fun of it—wasn't an everyday occurrence for her.

Her escort turned his attention to her again. "Sure you're ready for this?"

"Of course. I was born ready."

"Good. I'm glad to hear it." He clasped his hands loosely between his spread knees, the gesture both confident and re-laxed. He nodded toward her arms-locked-on-knees pose. "Because you look a little uneasy. For a minute there, I thought you'd changed your mind."

Great. He was handsome *and* observant. If he guessed somehow that she wasn't really who she'd claimed to be . . .

"Me? No!" She unclasped her knees, realizing for the first time exactly how tightly she'd been hugging them. Maybe she *was* more nervous than she wanted to admit. Deliberately, she sprawled sideways on the limo seat and gave him a provoca-tive look. "I'm yours for the night, Prince Charming."

"Tony," he reminded her. "Tony Valentine."

Tony Valentine. That's right. He'd told her that when he'd arrived.

Disappointment stole over her. She didn't want to be re-minded of who he really was—a man with an identity, a past, and a job to do. In her mind, "Prince Charming" worked per-fectly well as a nickname. It synced up nicely with her Cin-derella fantasy. So did the even more appropriate "Hottie." Both monikers kept her macho escort at arm's length, a dis-tance Meredith needed. For tonight, she truly wanted to feel

like Cinderella—a naughty, punk-historian Cinderella, removed from her ordinary life for as long as the fun lasted.

But apparently, Tony wasn't the kind of man who would
let himself be generalized. Probably, he saw himself as a
unique version of super-stud escort, and liked to be treated
as such. She wondered how he saw her. Unlike her absentee
twin sister, she wasn't exactly—

No. Making comparisons was *not* what she needed.

"Okay. Tony it is. We might as well get started," Meredith
announced instead. She swung her feet from the seat and
faced him. In the confined, vaguely rocking limousine space,
their knees nearly touched. "What happens next, exactly?
I'm new at this."

For a moment, he only continued to watch her. Thoughtfully.
His gaze hadn't left her since he'd sat down, she realized
then. The whole time she'd been classifying his attributes
like the trained academic she was, he'd undoubtedly been
studying her, as well. The man was *good*. Not to mention uncomfortably observant.

"You thought this was for just one night?" he asked.

"Okay. I'm yours for . . . as long as it takes!" Meredith
returned gamely. Never let it be said she wasn't up for adventure. "Now that I've met you, I feel much better about
this whole idea."

That seemed to please him. He delivered her a devastating smile, one that actually made her heart pound a little
faster. Placing her hand automatically over her chest, Meredith
smiled back. This man was even more charming than she'd
thought. His interest in her felt remarkably genuine.

Wherever this resort was, she *had* to recommend it to her
friends. So far, just riding in the limo with this guy offered
more excitement than her Friday nights usually delivered.

"That's good," he said, nodding. "I do want you to be
comfortable. You're our star attraction, after all."

"I *feel* like a star attraction."

"And you look—"

He broke off, his dark-eyed gaze darting to her feet. It

skimmed over her flip-flops, traveled along the comfy, utilitarian-pocketed length of her khaki cargo pants, snagged on her T-shirt and the L.A. museum sweatshirt tied around her hips. Finally, it wound up on her Dodgers baseball cap. A smile quirked his lips.

Inwardly, Meredith cringed, half-expecting the inevitable comparison.

"Great," he finished, seeming to mean it. "Really comfortable."

She shrugged. "All of my ball gowns chafe."

"Ahhh. I see." His smile widened. "I have the same problem with my tuxedos. They rub my sense of machismo raw."

"Hmmm." She pretended to consider it, letting her attention roam upward from his large, leather-clad feet to his L.A.-casual pants and knit shirt. Both were dark and well-fitted. "Your machismo seems to be limping along okay to me."

"Maybe." He offered her a good-natured grin, leaning closer as though confiding in her. "But you haven't seen the Victoria's Secret number I've got on underneath this."

Meredith froze. Was he . . . serious? She'd been on dates with some unlikely candidates before, but this—she'd thought—was different. Oh, God.

"Kidding." Tony grabbed a fistful of knit and lifted his shirt neck-high. The motion revealed a tantalizing flash of taut abs, muscular chest, and a smattering of dark hair. Too quickly, he covered himself again. "Sheesh, you're easy."

"Easy? You haven't proved a thing," she shot back, raising an eyebrow. "For all I know, you're wearing a thong."

"For all I know, *you* are."

"Maybe you'll find out," Meredith purred. "Later."

"That sounds like a challenge." He paused, regarding her with blatant masculine interest. "I enjoy a challenge."

"Most men do."

He shook his head. "Not like I do. Otherwise, I'd never have taken on this job in the first place."

Something rueful flashed in his eyes. Meredith wondered at it. Ordinarily, she loved her job. But she couldn't imagine having one like his. Being an escort to spoiled actresses and other Hollywood types couldn't be easy.

"It's not so bad, though." Releasing a pent-up breath, he finger-combed the wavy brown hair away from his forehead. He scanned the bulging manila file folders, cell phone, pager, and sunglasses arrayed haphazardly on the limo seat next to him, then brightened. "I'd been warned you might not even show up."

"I'm glad I did."

"Me, too. The night's looking up."

"I'll say."

Something about him appealed to her—something beyond his remarkable good looks. His cockeyed point of view? His easy laughter? His teasing ways? Meredith wasn't sure what it was . . . but she *was* sure she wanted to make the most of her time with him. Now that Tony had accepted her as Marley, the liberating effects of being incognito were kicking in. He thought she was someone else—which left Meredith free to be as wild as she dared.

After all, nobody would ever know what she did tonight. Nobody . . . except her and the hard-bodied hunk seated across from her.

He took out a clipboard. Poised a pen over the sheet of paper fastened to it. Fixed her with a businesslike look.

"Humor me with some preliminary feedback," Tony said, rubbing his thumb up and down his pen. "What do you think of the experience so far?"

Reluctantly, Meredith lifted her gaze. She'd never before longed to morph into six inches of plastic and ink. But watching Tony stroke his pen, so slowly, so provocatively . . . *Criminy!* What was she, some kind of ballpoint fetishist?

"It's very . . . stimulating," she said.

He didn't so much as quirk an eyebrow. He scrawled *stimulating* on the paper. "The limo pickup is meant to set the correct mood for the experience to come. Do you like it?"

"The mood?" *Sexy, flirty . . .* "Absolutely."

Tony scratched a check mark into the designated box. Meredith leaned over, squinting at the remaining questions. A dispiriting number of them filled the page.

"Aren't opinion surveys usually reserved for after a guest's stay?" she asked.

"Ordinarily. But you're not just any guest." He checked his watch. "I'll want your opinion on the arrival process, too. We ought to be there in fifteen minutes."

So soon? Impatiently, Meredith frowned at the clipboard. Her whole life was ruled by clipboarded lists, museum pieces to be archived, and the other demands of her job. Tonight, she intended to break free.

Still concentrating on his list, Tony glanced up. "Our guests are meant to experience 'the fantasy of a lifetime,'" he said. "Are we off to a good start on that?"

The fantasy of a lifetime. His words echoed the invitation she'd snagged. They also served as the best opening she'd had since stepping into the limo with him. Meredith seized it.

"No."

Tony frowned. "No?"

"No." In as fluid a movement as her cargo pants and hip-tied sweatshirt allowed, she slid onto the limo seat beside him, into the space unoccupied by papers and gadgets. His body heat touched her. His presence enveloped her, even more strongly than it had before. She drew in a deep breath. "So far, there's too much talking. Not enough touching."

His eyes widened.

Thrilled with her own audacity, Meredith put her hand on his knee. "You know . . . touching. Like this."

His leg tensed, muscular and strong beneath her palm. She would enjoy that strength if things went well between them, Meredith mused. Maybe she'd invite Tony to dinner at the resort. See what developed. Canoodling with a hottie like him would sure as heck beat lounging poolside.

He nodded, staring transfixed at her hand on his knee. "I know touching," he agreed.

His voice sounded deep. Undeniably sexy. As sexy as Meredith felt while undercover as her glamorous twin. She'd never been timid. In fact, she prided herself on being upfront. Unconventional. Occasionally rebellious. But this . . . only giddy momentum could have carried her through it.

"Touching, touching . . ." Tony pretended to scan his clipboard, then raised it with a manly shrug and a teasing grin. "Nope. That's not covered on the opinion survey."

"To hell with the opinion survey." Meredith seized it. She tossed it onto her just-vacated limo seat. "I don't need prompting. I'm perfectly capable of telling you what I think."

His look of interest returned. "I like a woman who speaks her mind."

"I like a man who recognizes a come-on when he sees one."

"Are you suggesting I don't?"

She squeezed his knee. "Let's put it this way . . . I'm not evaluating the flexibility of your anterior cruciate ligament here."

Tony raised his eyebrows.

"My favorite tight end nearly missed the playoffs last year because of a torn ACL."

That stopped him. "*You're* a football fan?"

Whoops. Her sister Marley didn't know a quarterback from a Quarter Pounder. Scrambling to cover, Meredith shrugged. "I learn all kinds of things researching roles. Acting is my life's work, you know. I take it seriously."

Tony stilled. One moment, he was right there with her, enjoying the banter between them. The next . . . whoosh. He was gone. What had she said?

"I take my work seriously, too." He eyed the clipboard, preparing to reach for it. "There's a lot at stake here."

Damn. She'd gone and reminded him of work. There went her first opportunity to be TV-starlet wild. Unwilling to quit so easily, Meredith lunged sideways, intercepting his grab for the survey.

Tony's chest met her shoulder; his arm brushed hers, almost cradling her from behind as they both reached across the limo. They were as close to indulging in vertical "spooning" as possible while still sitting side by side, Meredith realized. But his arm was much longer than hers. He could still reach the clipboard, even though she couldn't.

He didn't, though. Instead, Tony paused. He looked at her, then smiled. The space between them grew taut with expectation.

She canted her head toward the clipboard. "Write down an A-plus for everything," she suggested, giving him a saucy look. "I'm wildly optimistic."

His gaze dropped to her lips. Poised with his arm still outstretched, Tony slowly brought his hand up to her face. He skimmed his fingertips along her cheek. His touch felt every bit as sure and pleasurable as she'd imagined it would. Purposefully, he lowered his head.

"You have reason to be optimistic," he assured her.

A kiss felt inevitable. Waiting, Meredith held her breath. Crazy as it was, she wanted this. Wanted *him*. Yes, *yes* . . .

Into the silence, intercom static crackled. "Five minutes, Mr. V.," the driver announced.

Meredith started. Tony blinked. The spell between them scattered. He grabbed his clipboard in one swift motion, then shoved it amid the rest of his belongings. "That warning's for you. I thought you might want to get ready for your entrance."

Puzzled—and yes, okay, disappointed—Meredith stared down at herself. She gestured toward her casual clothes. "Do I look like I'm into making an entrance?"

His perplexed expression matched hers. "You did last month at the premiere of that new Jennifer Lopez movie."

Arrgh. Another forehead-smacking moment. She was supposed to be Marley. She had to remember that.

"I decided to go for the celebrity-caught-by-surprise look," she ad-libbed. "You know, like in paparazzi shots."

"How appropriate." Wearing the expression of a man with a private secret, Tony tugged the brim of her baseball cap.

Then he gestured toward her cargo pants, T-shirt, sweatshirt, and flip-flops. "Just so long as all this is gone by tomorrow."

"Tomorrow?"

"Right. Just like me, you have a job to do here. Remember?"

Openmouthed, Meredith stared at him. "A *job*?"

Tony grinned. He rolled his eyes, as though she really *were* her famously flighty twin sister. "Never heard the term, princess? J-O-B. It's the thing Valentine Studios hired you to do at this shindig. I've got the contract right here."

He reached for the manila folder beside him, leaving Meredith gawking. What did he mean, a job? Why hadn't Marley warned her about this?

Oh, yeah. Because Marley didn't know she was here. She didn't even know Meredith had accepted the invitation on her behalf. Because she *couldn't* know, ever, or Meredith would never live it down.

She summoned her wits—and the original invitation from one of her cargo pant pockets. She waved it toward Tony. "What about this? This isn't a contract. It doesn't say anything about a job."

"That's a courtesy invitation." He didn't even glance up at the heavy cream cardstock, engraved in sensual, bold-faced script, which had enticed her into this whole mess. He rifled through his file folder. "Similar to the ones sent to the registered guests you'll be responsible for teaching at Valentine Studios' actor fantasy camp."

Teaching? "Actor fantasy camp?"

"Yes. Didn't your people brief you?"

Mutely, she shook her head.

"Figures." He made a face, his impatience with her supposed entourage plain. "The short version is, actor fantasy camp is like a live-in studio tour. The idea originated with baseball fantasy camp. Only ours is done Hollywood style."

Okay. Baseball fantasy camp she was familiar with. That, she understood. She'd spent much of her teenage years watching televised MLB games with her dad while her mom ferried Marley to one audition after another. But the rest . . .

Efficiently, Tony plucked a glossy tri-fold brochure from the file. He pressed it into Meredith's grasp. "The Valentine Studios camp is debuting this weekend, featuring our inaugural celebrity attraction: Marley Madison. AKA, *you.*"

Her? This just got worse and worse. Holding the brochure, Meredith blinked at her sister's glamorous likeness on the front cover. Set against a background of the usual images— the Hollywood sign, a director's chair, glittering stars, and a movie clapboard—the photograph showed Marley at her starlet best: decked out in designer duds, expertly colored blonde hair, and artfully enhanced breasts.

"We have guests booked from all around the country," Tony continued. "Classes ranging from Diva Dramatics to Tabloid Tattling to Star Schmoozing 101—ahhh, here it is."

He brandished a contract. Meredith snatched it. After scanning several pages of legalese, she recognized Marley's loopy signature on the final page.

Apparently, her sister had agreed to a two-week "actor fantasy camp" appearance—and then conveniently forgotten it. Meredith had unknowingly stepped smack into the middle of the whole mess.

She shoved the contract and brochure back. "I can't do it."

"Nerves? I expected that." Tony grabbed something else from his pile of things. He offered it to her. "Here. Breathe into this."

She stared. "A paper bag?"

"Best thing to cure hyperventilating."

"Trust me. I am *not* the type of woman who hyperventilates."

"You might be." Grinning, he gave her an exaggeratedly lascivious eyebrow waggle. "Given the right stimulus."

"Oh, puh-leeze." She was in enough trouble already.

"So distraction doesn't work for you, then. Fine. Try the bag."

"No." She thrust the brown lunch sack into his hands. "This is ridiculous."

"It's effective." Stuffing away the bag, Tony scrutinized her. "Would it ease your mind if I told you the real reporters and potential investors aren't arriving until later?"

He looked at her hopefully.

She hated to disappoint him, but . . . there would be reporters there? Yikes! Marley was going to kill her! Sure, they were twins. But where their lives were concerned, Meredith and Marley couldn't have been more different. She was not cut out to take her sister's place—not for an event like *this*.

"Reporters?" She swallowed hard.

"At least one. From *Inside Hollywood* magazine. He—or she—will be posing as a guest in order to write one of their 'Insider' profiles." Tony glanced out the window as something flashed overhead—the Valentine Studios gates. "Hell, I'm running this thing, and even I don't know which journalist has been assigned. It's a gamble, all right."

He chuckled, apparently unconcerned. The big galoot.

Trying not to panic, Meredith analyzed the situation. She'd gotten into this. But there was still time to get out. Once Tony knew who she really was, he'd realize he had to change his actor fantasy camp plans.

"Tell the driver to circle the block." She slapped her hand over the limo's control panel, looking for the intercom button. "Driver! Go around the block, please."

Tony removed her finger from the button she'd chosen. He looked amused. "That's the cigarette lighter."

"Well, we can't go any farther." Meredith twisted. She rapped on the partition. It summarily slid down. "Driver, please stop the car."

"Harry, stop this car and you're fired."

The partition noiselessly rose again. The limo prowled through a shadowed pathway between two enormous soundstages, just as though she'd never spoken.

"Arrgh!"

Tony cupped her face in his hands. Kindly, he studied her.

His air of calm reached out to her. It nearly succeeded in lulling Meredith into forgetting the snafu she'd gotten into.

"Relax," he said. "I know you're nervous. Once you make your entrance, you'll feel fine. All actors are that way."

She nearly sighed. He really was being sweet—for an unreasonable, misguided, know-it-all actor fantasy camp executive.

She'd liked him better as a fantasy escort.

Still, too beguiled to resist, Meredith curled her fingers around his. Their warmth mingled reassuringly.

She had to play it straight with him. "Look, Tony. I'm not who you think I am. I'm—"

"Your red carpet awaits," he interrupted, preoccupied with something outside the window. The limo stopped. He twined their hands together, his grasp steady and encouraging, then gave her a squeeze. "Ready or not, here you go."

An instant later, their uniformed driver whisked open the door. The screams of—were they fans?—hurtled toward Meredith, followed closely by a brilliant flare of flashbulbs. Blinded by them, she clung to Tony as he hustled her out of the car.

In a moment, they stood together on the red carpet. A hush fell over the spectators.

It only lasted a second or two. By the time Meredith regained her wits, the uproar had begun again.

"You've got the wrong woman," she said to Tony through clenched teeth, desperate to make him see reason. "I'm an academic, not an actress!"

He cupped his ear. He shook his head, indicating he couldn't hear her in the din. Then, with a cheery smile, Tony held up their joined hands in greeting.

The crowd loved it. The shouts grew louder. The flashes increased.

This was insane. Squinting, Meredith could just make out the scene. Reporters and paparazzi lined the area behind the velvet ropes, which separated the rest of the Valentine Studios back lot from the red carpet. Along the length of that red carpet more people waited in the post-sunset afterglow, screaming crazily as they waved eight-by-ten glossies of Marley. Fans, Meredith assumed in a daze. There were reporters *and* fans there.

She had to get out of this. Now, before it was too late.

"Marley! Marley! Over here!" someone yelled.

"Say it, Marley! Give us your catchphrase from *Fantasy Family*!"

"Marley! Can I have your autograph?"

It was all too much. Tugging her baseball cap lower with her free hand, Meredith tightened her grasp on Tony. He offered her another reassuring squeeze, but didn't look her way. Frustrated, she yanked as hard as she could.

That did it. Quizzically, he faced her. "Hey, what the—"

She cupped her hands around her mouth. "I've got to talk to you!"

He probably still couldn't hear her. But whatever he saw on her face convinced him she meant what she was saying—and it was important. Tony took one look and blessedly hustled her into motion.

Sheltered against his chest, held there by his burly arm as they maneuvered the rest of the way down the red carpet, Meredith felt protected. Safe. Indulged. But when they reached Tony's private office and he shut the door behind them . . . well, clearly the jig was up.

"Okay." Looking aggravated, he shoved a hand through his hair, then turned to face her in the sudden silence. "Exactly what the hell is going on?"